GIRL IN THE SHADOWS

ALSO BY GWENDA BOND

Cirque American Series

Girl on a Wire

Lois Lane Series

Fallout
Double Down

Other Books

Blackwood
The Woken Gods

Praise for Gwenda Bond

For *Girl on a Wire*

"The mystery is tense and nerve-wracking, and the acrobatics are gorgeously hair-raising."

—*Kirkus Reviews*

"A fascinating and enjoyable foray into circus life as seen through the eyes of an ambitious and talented performer."

—*Publishers Weekly*

"A skillful blend of modern-day circus tales, classically ill-fated love, and mystery."

—*Booklist*

"With a thrilling mystery, a hint of magic, and a touch of romance, *Girl on a Wire* takes readers into the fascinating world of circus performers."

—*School Library Journal*

For *Fallout*

"This lighthearted and playful tone permeates the novel, making for a nifty investigative mystery akin to *Veronica Mars* or *Buffy the Vampire Slayer*. Readers are in for a treat. A spectacular prose start for DC Comics' spectacular lady."

—*Kirkus Reviews,* starred review

"A spirited, engrossing story that kept me flipping pages and rooting for stubborn, clever, fearless Lois Lane."

—Shannon Hale, *New York Times* bestselling author of *Dangerous*

"So it's basically Lois Lane in a *Veronica Mars*-esque plot, which sounds like all kinds of awesome."

—*Entertainment Weekly*

"It's not a bird, it's not a plane, it's Lois Lane, boldly following clues wherever they lead, taking readers along for a thrilling ride."

—*Chicago Tribune*

GIRL IN THE SHADOWS

GWENDA BOND

SKYSCAPE

SKYSCAPE

Published by Skyscape, New York

www.apub.com

Amazon, the Amazon logo, and Skyscape are trademarks of Amazon.com, Inc., or its affiliates.

ISBN-13: 9781503953932
ISBN-10: 1503953939

Cover design by M. S. Corley

Printed in the United States of America

To all the magical ladies,
may you get the spotlight you deserve.

prologue

I was waiting in the wings backstage at the Menagerie Hotel and Casino, preparing the equipment for my first stage illusion. Straitjacket, check. Oversized timer and mood-music speakers, check. And, most important, transparent coffin, check. As I lay bound inside it, I'd press a button that would expel all the air in the coffin with a dramatic puff, for my audience's benefit, and then I'd pull off a daring escape.

The coffin might sound morbid, but I wasn't planning to die in it. I was planning to live.

Forget college or a normal future. I wanted to be a magician: the Miraculous Moira.

I'd just never quite managed to tell my dad that.

Dad, a.k.a. the Mysterious Mitchell, Master Magician, was the person I'd be performing for today, though he didn't know it yet. I had no choice but to wow him, the toughest one-person audience in town. He was currently in the midst of his show's grand finale.

Out in the theater, his audience began to murmur right on cue. They'd seen Dad draped in chains, then locked inside a scary-looking safe that was lowered into a giant tank of water. Black screens were raised on all sides while they waited for him to get free. He always stayed in long enough to let the more bloodthirsty audience members squirm in anticipation of witnessing a failure, a dramatic death on the stage, a legend in the making, an anecdote they could trot out at every future cocktail party.

The music swelled. I stepped forward to watch as the showgirls-turned-lovely-assistants pulled aside the screens around the tank, revealing the safe open inside it. The audience gasped, signaling Dad's triumphant reappearance high in the rigging above the stage. His overly styled hair was deflated, his puffy shirt and leather pants dripping wet; a crew member had doused him with a bucket of water after the safes were switched out, though the audience would assume it was from the tank. He waved, shaking one last chain off his arm. Then he grabbed a line of black nylon rope and swung down to center stage.

He bowed to wild applause. Closing my eyes, I imagined it was for me.

This two-thousand-seat theater, home to the biggest magic show in Las Vegas, felt like *my* home. I lived here in the shadows, in *his* shadow.

But I wanted to step into the spotlight.

While Dad was out in the lobby chatting with fans, taking pictures, and signing programs and headshots, I wheeled my gear onto the stage and set up my props and the coffin. I breathed freely while I could, but nervously. Oh so nervously.

It wasn't entirely my fault that I hadn't told him yet.

Dad had raised me with a fairy-tale-ish story about my absent mother. She'd been the loveliest of the lovely assistants, talented enough that she could have been a magician herself. But they weren't together long before she pulled the ultimate disappearing act. Gone. Poof. Dad couldn't even thank her for depositing me with him when I was barely a year old. She'd left no method to contact her.

Six years ago, at the tender age of twelve, I decided to learn a card trick and surprise him. I figured if my mother and father were both good at magic, I could be too. I started with a basic find-a-card and was practicing it in the dressing room for the lovely assistants. Someone had run to get him. The girls were clapping and laughing, humoring me . . .

When Dad came in, he exploded. "My daughter is *never* going to do magic!" he said.

After a moment of shocked silence, I couldn't stop the tears from coming. "But you and my mother," I'd managed. "I can do it."

"You can't be a magician," he told me. "No. The magic business will never fully embrace a woman. It isn't what the audience wants. You can never be a magician, Moira."

Dad was usually the definition of a supportive father, and his outburst scared me enough that I shelved my interest in magic . . . for an entire month. But I kept coming back to the cards. There was a feeling building inside me that this was what I was meant to do. I could only ignore it for so long.

After that, I learned magic in secret. I became fascinated with escapes, and with finding stories about the women in magic history who were proof that what Dad had said wasn't exactly right.

The first time I held my breath for three minutes successfully, I wanted to tell him. The first time I held it for four. The first time I got out of handcuffs. Unable to use him as a test audience—as much as I wanted to—I started to sneak out and perform for tourists at sixteen. Quick sets with no name given, not even a fake one.

The first time I slipped a straitjacket was on the street.

I had never told Dad anything. Never said a word, never shown him what I could do. Not until now, tonight. Would he be angry? Proud? A mix of the two?

I'd worked hard to create a stage illusion that was his favorite combination of a nod to one of the greats with a fresh spin. Except the great

I'd chosen to honor was Adelaide Herrmann, who toured as the Queen of Magic in the late 1800s and early 1900s, following the sudden death of her husband, the celebrated magician Herrmann the Great, in the middle of a tour.

The moment the back theater door swung open and Dad came in, trailed by an entourage, I came to attention. I bowed in the spotlight I'd ensured was left on—the spotlight that kept me from getting a good look at the rest of the group as they approached.

"What's this?" Dad said. He was in dry clothes, a replacement puffy shirt and black jeans.

"I want to perform a new illusion for you. An escape."

He was silent for a moment. "A new illusion for me? But why would you be the one—"

"No, an illusion for *me*." And then I said it: "I want to be a magician."

His eyes raked across the stage. They settled on the straitjacket draped over my arm, then moved hard back to my face. "I don't know what nonsense this is, but I won't tolerate it."

My cheeks went hot. "I've been working on this for a long time."

"No, you have not."

"I have!" I held up the straitjacket, ready to put it on. "If you just watch, you'll see."

He climbed onto the stage and took long strides over to me.

"Moira," Dad said. He reached out and lowered my arm. "Look, Raleigh's here."

"Hey, Pixie," Raleigh said. He leapt up to join us, then reached down to ruffle my black curls. He'd always used the nickname for me, and treated me like a kid sister.

Raleigh was Dad's former apprentice, only four years older than me. He had deep-black skin, the sleek lines of a race car, and a drawl and smile that made women dizzy and sometimes ditzy. He'd turned down Dad's offer of a permanent job to make his own way, traveling around as the Southern Sorcerer.

He did an appreciative double take and leaned back. "You're all grown up . . . and dressed like a waitress. And you're going to do some magic for us?"

"Yes. And once he sees it, Dad's going to admit that I have what it takes to be a magician."

"Really?" Raleigh said, eyes widening in surprise.

"No," Dad said. "Not really. Tell her how ridiculous this is. She's going to college this fall."

"Dad, won't you even give me a chance?"

"Maybe the old man's feeling threatened," Raleigh said, an attempt to defuse the tension. I forced a laugh. "Let's see what she's got, Mitchell."

Dad was frowning. "I haven't seen you in ages. I don't have time for this . . . exhibition."

He had scared me those years ago when he'd yelled. But now I was just frustrated.

"Dad." I fought to keep my voice even. "I'm your daughter. Please."

"I can only indulge so much," he said, like I was the one in the wrong.

And then I understood. Nothing I did would matter. He was never going to agree. Once he'd made up his mind, he rarely changed it.

Dad turned to Raleigh. "Poker?"

Raleigh nodded, but when Dad started walking and the rest of the guys went along, he lingered and came in close. "Parents don't always know what's best, Pixie," he said.

Before I could respond, he followed my father, saying, "I have news from that crazy billionaire's circus that might interest you. He called me . . ."

Something dropped out of Raleigh's jacket and onto the floor behind him. I thought it was by accident, but I didn't stop him. Instead, I walked across the stage and picked it up: a black envelope made of thick stock. As I tried to open it, I realized the envelope was the letter itself, cleverly folded. Or, rather, not a letter. An invitation:

CONGRATULATIONS!

YOU HAVE BEEN HAND-SELECTED

FOR AN EXCLUSIVE AUDITION

TO JOIN THE CIRQUE AMERICAN AS A PERFORMER

ON OUR ALL-NEW MIDWAY THIS SUMMER SEASON.

BECOME ONE OF THE CIRQUE'S

WORLD-FAMOUS REAL-LIFE MARVELS

AND DEATH-DEFYING ACTS.

ONLY THE BEST OF THE BEST WILL MAKE THE CUT.

There was an address in Sarasota, Florida, followed by the date. It was only a few days away.

Maybe Raleigh hadn't dropped it by accident after all.

part one

before your very eyes

one

Four days later, I turned the triple-cherry-red convertible that I'd inherited from Dad when I got my license onto the bumpy, unpaved road to the Cirque American's winter quarters. The intensity of the everglade-green foliage hurt my eyes. Not surprising, since they were gritty from a thirty-six-hour drive with as few stops to rest as possible. I had pulled over at a gas station to do a quick primp and put on my simple costume, and now was so full of nerves I thought I might vibrate right out of my skin.

Could I do this? Dad didn't think so. I almost understood his objection—it was true that no female magician had ever become as famous as the top male ones. Magic was still a man's world, a boys' club. But that only made me more determined to be the first: the first woman as well-known for her magic as Houdini or David Blaine or, well, Dad.

It hadn't felt good to abandon him to come here. But he'd forced me into this.

I had trundled contritely into his office the day after our fight with a made-up story about how I'd seen the light and would be practical from that moment on—starting with a precollege program across the country at Cornell over the summer. I handed him a forged letter about it and told him I'd neglected to mention it because I thought he'd make me go. He hadn't been happy about my imminent departure, but what could he say? *Stay here with me and learn magic?* Nope.

So here I was.

The Cirque grounds came into view ahead, swarming with people. The uneven rows of RVs and trailers, many having seen better days despite being painted with murals or the Cirque's swirling logo, didn't match up with what I'd conjured in my head.

You expected Las Vegas hotels and neon and flashing lights and the sound of the next jackpot always nearby.

I found a dusty parking spot beside a few other cars and trucks, some with campers hitched to the back. Red buildings were clustered in the distance like bright gemstones around a crown jewel—in this case, the enormous red-and-white-striped tent at the top of the slope.

After I got out of the car, I stood looking at it for a long moment. My destination and, I hoped, my destiny.

I tugged a short tailored tuxedo jacket over my simple black pants and fitted white shirt, and felt face powder begin to settle into my pores with a sting as the Florida humidity summoned forth sweat. In the jacket pockets, I stashed two custom decks of the slightly smaller, bridge-sized cards many magicians preferred, and a pair of handcuffs, just in case. I'd brought the equipment for my daring coffin escape, broken down into component pieces in the trunk. But I wanted to survey the scene first.

A spaghetti-thin blond boy with a duffel bag draped over one knobby elbow breezed past me and asked, "You run off from a gay wedding?" He laughed at my feminine tux.

His laugh wasn't mean per se, but my eyes narrowed. Several of the women who worked at Dad's show were lesbians or bi, and I'd been in one couple's wedding.

"What if I was?" I asked. "And it would just be a wedding, period."

Another boy drew up beside the first and punched him in the shoulder—hard enough that he took a step back. Then the new boy turned to me. He must not have noticed me before his friend spoke, because his once-over went on way too long. Long enough to turn into staring.

I ordered my makeup to stay put, sweat or no sweat, and tried to hide any reaction to the exam. Distressingly, I found it difficult to be offended.

The boy was tall, wearing a black tank top that showed off a tan and a strong build. Long brown hair brushed his chin, and his eyes flashed like pennies tossed into the air. I had a trick where I threw a handful of pennies and caught them on the return trip only to reveal an empty palm. He should have been as easy to dismiss as those coins were to make vanish, given that being cute didn't make up for having bad taste in friends. But he wasn't. There was something about the cut of his jawline as he angled it when he saw me neutrally returning his examination that made me wonder what his story was.

"Ignore him. He's an idiot," he said, finally.

"I can believe he's an idiot. What's your excuse?" When he looked amused but didn't say anything, I added, "For staring."

"Sorry. There's something . . . about you," he said. "Your eyes. It was almost like I recognized you. But I don't think we've met."

My eyes were a perfectly ordinary green. I rolled them. "We haven't."

No way I'd have forgotten.

"What are you?" he asked. There was a vague lilt to his voice, not quite an accent. "Here for, I mean."

In answer, I slipped my hand into my pocket and whipped out a deck of cards. This was no time to be flashy and put on the cuffs for a trick of my own design, so I executed a perfect circle fan with the cards instead, thrusting them to one side and forming them into a complete circle. The backs were red and black and white, patterned to make a round roulette wheel.

The circle fan looked easy, done right. This was.

The other boy cackled in response and nudged the brown-haired boy's shoulder. To his credit, he stepped away from his howler monkey of a friend.

"Name's Desmond, but you can call me Dez," he said, tipping his chin down to me before starting to walk away. "And *that's* not magic," he added, pointing at my cards.

Yes, it was. It wasn't what I was most proud of, but the hours of practice that single technique had required to master scrolled through my brain, the endless time spent training my fingers to find the right position automatically. I could count on one hand the number of magicians who could do it as well as me.

"It's impressive anyway," he tossed over his shoulder.

I stood in offended silence. He stopped and called back, "Auditions are this way, Girl Who Hasn't Told Me Her Name Yet."

I could have introduced myself then, but I decided it was smarter to keep something up my sleeve. Still, I trailed them through the grass and vehicles, arrogant Dez and his cackling sidekick. Dez had one of the black envelopes in his left hand. I was curious what *his* act was.

We reached a table set up outside the giant tent, where a few business-suited women were collecting invites and checking names off a list.

I waited until Dez was done signing in before I approached. The petite woman taking names and dispensing numbers barely even glanced at the much-labored-over fake ID that provided me with a different last name. I hadn't been able to resist giving it a showy flair, so my new handle was Moira Miracle.

Mostly I didn't want Dad to know I was here, which would be inevitable if people found out I was his daughter. I also worried my real identity would set expectations I couldn't live up to.

I handed her the black invitation.

She squinted at it, then at her list, before frowning up at me. "This wasn't yours," she said. "We've already given this spot to its rightful owner."

Crap. This was something I hadn't prepared for.

"But it, um, found its way to me. So you might as well give me a chance?" I hated that it sounded like a question. That it *was* a question.

The woman cleared her throat.

And Raleigh stepped into view, dressed in his full stage suit and a top hat embroidered with a spooky skeletal head. "There was a lot of confusion when I showed up without my invite, Pixie. But now everything is clear to me," he said, drawl more pronounced than usual. Raleigh never showed annoyance in an out-of-control way. "You picked my pocket."

I couldn't believe this. "I thought you dropped it on purpose."

"I didn't drop it."

"I'm not lying. I—"

"Regardless," the suited woman said, "you can only audition with an invite. There were a limited number distributed, and this one's taken. He's already been seen and hired. Sorry."

I felt like I'd been sucker punched. "Raleigh?" I had to stoop to pleading with him to help me.

"Does he even know you're here?" he asked.

He meant Dad, of course.

Dez appeared beside us. "Problem?" he asked, giving the woman at the table a smile I would've had to admit, if pressed by some instrument of medieval torture, was charming. And practically irresistible based on her eye-batting reaction to it. "I can vouch that she's an incredible magician," he said.

Raleigh was giving Dez a *who's this guy?* look.

"He's right," I said. "And I'm guessing if Raleigh's hired, then your main magic act is covered, though he might let me open?"

Raleigh shook his head, and I rushed on. "But even if I can't do that, I'd still like to audition to work the midway crowd. You'll need people to keep them lingering instead of going to the main tent before it's time. Close-up is what I'm most experienced at." While I had my bigger illusion ready to go, I'd never performed it for a crowd. Getting a spot was my main goal, and I was sure I could convince Raleigh, given time.

The woman glanced between Raleigh and me, and then at Dez, still smiling and charming her pants off for some reason.

Please, please give me a chance. I considered holding my breath. Maybe if I went for four minutes, she'd be impressed enough to cave.

"I'll have to make a note," the woman finally said. "But I'll allow you inside, Miss Miracle. Without an invitation, you'd *better* be a miracle."

two

I resisted the urge to leap into the air. A magician needs to cultivate a certain mystery.

"I will be entirely miraculous," I said, smiling. "And thank you." I wanted to thank Dez, but he grinned at me and disappeared back inside the tent. Leaving me to face Raleigh, who took my elbow after I accepted my audition number.

"You'll be last," the woman said.

I awkwardly pinned it on my lapel one-handed as Raleigh steered me through the people gathered outside the tent: a tattoo-covered contortionist bent backward in wheel pose, one leg pawing the air; a man with bulging muscles twirling a thin woman over his head; a guy playing music on a theremin for what could only be some kind of modern freak show. Most of them would have been right at home at an audition for Cirque du Soleil.

"Moira," Raleigh said, releasing me, "what are you doing here?"

"Auditioning. Dad's going to force me into college this fall. I can't convince him—you saw that—so I have to *prove* he's wrong. I have to go after this another way."

"Moira," he said again, "you shouldn't be here. I have to call him."

"Please. Don't do this to me."

"I never had family who wanted to protect me, Pixie," Raleigh said, giving the impression of lightening up, even though I was sure he hadn't.

"Or to hold you back. You risked everything. You know my mom's never been in the picture and so Dad is overprotective. He's going to overprotect me right out of what I want to do." I put a hand on Raleigh's arm. "I won't be any trouble, I promise. Besides, I'm eighteen now. Technically I can do whatever I want."

"Playing the motherless-child card is low." Raleigh sighed. "You still have to audition, and it's a tough crowd. And if you do make it, the minute you're in trouble, I'm calling him."

I gave a little leap in the air. So much for my air of mystery. "You won't regret this. There won't be any trouble."

"Wrong, but I seem to be doing it anyway," he said. "Let's go in."

The stands inside the tent were half-full, and a panel of four judges occupied a table between the audience and the center ring. One of them was the Cirque's owner, the famously wealthy Thurston Meyer. I recognized another as Jules Maroni, the wire walker who'd become a huge star almost overnight, but then botched the last show of the season. I'd seen playbills for a competition featuring her when I was in Paris with Dad over the summer. And here she was back for the new season, which I respected. The other judges were an older woman with a polka-dot scarf knotted at her neck and a girl with short hair wearing a man's suit and bow tie.

I scanned the stands to find a place to sit and pretended not to see Dez wave from where he sat near the middle. He patted the bleacher beside him.

Raleigh nudged me toward the end of the second row, then ticked his chin up in Dez's direction. "You know that guy?" he asked.

"No, but I owe him one."

"Be careful how he collects," Raleigh said.

"Ew," I said. "But thanks for the Cro-Magnon response and the fake-big-brother act."

"Don't forget you owe me too," he grumbled.

What I hadn't thought about was that venturing inside meant watching the rest of the auditions before mine. They hadn't been lying. It was a tough scene. Everyone was *so good*, and some of them still didn't make it. The judges deliberated after each performance and made their decision on the spot. The tent slowly cleared out of people there to audition and filled with circus performers hanging out and watching. I tapped my fingers on the stands, getting more and more nervous. By the time the older woman turned and nodded to me, I was sprung as tight as a gun cocked to fire for a bullet catch.

I stood up, taking a few deep breaths on my way over.

Thurston Meyer smoothed back a swoop of brown hair. "It's a good thing we're not the same size or we'd always be wearing the same outfit," he said.

It took me a few pounding heartbeats to understand what he meant: he was wearing a T-shirt now, but in the promo photos his ringmaster's costume was similar to my modified tux. "Right," I said, trying to sound like I was in on the joke. "That would be awkward."

Not as awkward as this moment, but . . .

The older woman shook her head the tiniest fraction, her hand coming up to the scarf at her throat, and consulted a list in front of her. There was handwriting beside one of the names on it. She leaned over to exchange a whisper with the girls next to her. Jules Maroni looked me up and down, almost like she was trying to place me. The girl in the suit did a survey too, though she smiled apologetically at me. Jules said something back to the older woman. The woman handed Thurston the sheet of paper.

"Aha, the invitation thief," he said. "I don't think your behavior should be rewarded. We sent scouts all over the country to make that list. Those spots were earned."

I swallowed. "Give me a chance to earn one now."

"We should," Jules chimed in.

The owner didn't react to that, other than to give me a hard assessing gaze, not unlike one of Dad's when he was sizing up a girl new to his show. "Act name?" he asked.

"The Miraculous Moira. I want to do close-up magic for your crowds, with an escape twist."

He crooked his head to where Raleigh sat. Raleigh, who didn't bother to speak up in support. But it must not have mattered. "Since you seem to know the magician we've already hired, let's see what you can do," Thurston said.

The tent had grown silent, more than it had for the other auditions so far, and I scanned the stands. Dez grinned at me and leaned forward, elbows on his knees. It occurred to me that I hadn't seen him audition yet, even though I was supposed to be last.

You came all this way. You can do this.

"Miss Miraculous?" Thurston prompted.

I took the handcuffs out of my pocket and held them up, dangling. I removed a deck from my pocket with my other hand. My fingers trembled, which they never did.

I gave a stiff smile to the panel of judges. Thurston and the older woman already seemed bored, but the girl in the suit continued to smile and Jules seemed interested. I closed the cuffs around my wrists with an audible *click*, and that perked them up.

"Playing cards have existed since at least the ninth century, which we know from a record set down by the writer Su E, telling of Princess Tongchang using them in imperial China. And yet the mysteries any ordinary deck of cards can present are still vast. The ability of simple cards to amaze is undimmed." I walked toward them, shuffling the cards, handcuffs and shaky hands notwithstanding. It had taken an age to find cuffs that allowed enough movement for me to do this, and another age to learn how to work with the cards while wearing them.

"Pick a card," I said, holding them out. "Each of you."

Each of them did. I motioned for them to reinsert their cards back into the deck, looking away so I didn't see where. Something was . . . off. The feeling could just be nerves, but I had the sensation that I was hovering outside my own body. And not only that, specifically hovering way up high in the top of the tent spire above us. Like some force was pulling me there. Was it stage fright? I could have all the skill in the world, but it wouldn't matter if I sucked at performing.

"Good," I said as I backed away, trying to ground myself. "Keep the card at the forefront of your mind. Let it be the only image there."

I shuffled several times, cutting the deck again for good measure, but it was like a puppet was doing it for me. I controlled the movements, but I wasn't *in* control of them. I almost dropped the cards when a shuffle went wide, and I had to pull against the cuffs.

Time to wrap this up.

I advanced a few steps closer, holding the deck flat on one palm, waving the shaky fingers of my other hand over it like a diviner. Someone in the stands laughed, but I refused to look in that direction. I picked up the card on top of the deck. "Is this your card?"

I flipped the card to show its face and held it up at Thurston, and without waiting, flipped the next, showing it to the older lady. "And yours?" Then the third to the nice girl. "And yours?" And then to Jules.

There was dead silence.

Thurston exchanged a look with his fellow judges. "I'm afraid not. Thank you for your—"

It was like I'd plunged from above back into my body. I gave a flourish and was out of the handcuffs, had them stashed back in my pocket.

"Not yet!" I raised my hands.

I'd come so far. Failing would mean Dad was right and I couldn't be a magician.

I steeled myself, pretending it was only these four judges and me. But I didn't *believe* it. I refused to look over and see Raleigh's no-doubt-disappointed face. What if he told my dad about this? He'd think I was an amateur, overpromising; no one did card tricks in handcuffs.

"One more chance?" I asked.

"Wow us," Thurston said. "The cuff trick was good. The card trick was amateur hour. We're here to be wowed, just like the patrons of our shows."

I launched into some patter, feeling more on solid ground. I'd go simple and do the circle fan again, but double it for difficulty. "The circle is a familiar and comforting shape to us. It can represent a planet, a life. The circle is a whole, not unlike the ring I stand in." I swapped my smaller deck for two slightly larger ones, which felt more substantial in my hands. Both had roulette-wheel backs.

I made an infinity symbol, a figure eight, swooping my arms through the air and ending with them straight out to each side. The fans began to form, my hands arranging the cards into their red, white, and black wheel pattern. I willed the judges to be impressed.

"A circle leaves nothing to chance," I said.

Except . . . I couldn't quite complete the circle on one side for some reason. My hands started to tremble again. And I started babbling. "A circle's like, uh, a rainbow joined with another one, surrounded by gold . . . on all sides."

A flood of heat burst through me like I was at the center of a fire, standing inside a flame so large it filled the entire tent. When it was gone, my hands could have been burning. I glanced over at my right hand and dropped the cards in both. They flew everywhere.

But not before I saw that the backs of the ones on the left side had changed. They were a rainbow of colors as they landed on the ground around me, a rainbow of colors edged in a thick band of gold. The others were the same as they'd been at the beginning, roulette pattern in place.

I stood there, gaping down at the transformed cards until Thurston said, not unkindly, "Thank you. That's a wrap on—Oh, wait, somehow we have one more act to see."

I didn't move. My fingertips were still hot. I'd freaked out and failed miserably.

I was also either hallucinating or I'd just done actual magic.

three

Fighting to breathe, I bent to gather the cards I'd dropped with such epic clumsiness. I ran my fingers across the smooth surface of the transformed back of the first one I picked up. A check of my fingertips—which felt normal again, not overheated—revealed nothing unusual. No paint came off the cards. But the backs were definitely a rainbow bordered in shiny gold. *How?*

My hands were shaking again, but I finally assembled the cards into a stack and shoved it inside my coat pocket. I took another deep breath and started to walk out of the tent. Outside in the sunshine, I could try to figure out what in the world had just happened.

Magic wasn't real.

"Approach the table," the older woman judge said, her words stopping me. She beckoned with red nails.

I scanned the tent. Everyone was looking at me, most with pity. Raleigh stood behind the judges, with the grace to seem confused by my floundering. The girl in the suit at the table wore an expression like I'd told her I was dying.

It's okay. I'm not. I already died during my act.

"Come to the table," the older lady prompted again, waving me over.

"Of . . . of course." The words barely made it out. I bit my lip against a panicked smile and walked toward her. *This whole thing really might be a hallucination or nightmare.* As I walked, I pinched the skin on my arm inside my jacket sleeve, hard, since that's what people always did in these situations in movies.

Ow. So much for being asleep. Then again, I hadn't slept that much for the last few days, so *that* could explain it . . .

I stopped in front of the judges and shrugged off my coat. The air was a welcome hit of cool on my sweat-soaked shirt.

"I'm sorry I wasted your time," I said.

Dez joined us at the table, stopping in front of Thurston. *Great.*

At least I'd given a fake name. If Raleigh stayed quiet, it could be like none of this ever happened. I could slink back home and tell Dad I'd decided against summer at Cornell. He'd be so happy to have me back home for a few more months that he wouldn't question it much. Hopefully, I wouldn't start hallucinating like this all the time.

But the elegant older woman wasn't ready to let me go yet. Her eyes narrowed, considering. "Let me see one of those cards," she said.

I blinked at her.

Dez leaned a hip against the table, and his leg made a dull bang when he did. Silver knives were held in place by sleek leather straps on his forearms, along his torso, and down the thighs of his pants.

"Nan?" Jules Maroni frowned at the older woman. They did resemble each other.

The older woman ignored her. "I would like to examine one of your cards. Now."

I was afraid to show her a changed card. I was afraid to even look at them—that they'd be back to normal and I was definitely going crazy. Not that the alternative—believing I might have done *real* magic— was better. Already part of me was spinning theories about how these weren't like my usual decks, that I'd ordered some new kind of trick by mistake.

But there was no trick that made the pattern on the backs of cards change *for real.* Just like there was no such thing as *actual magic.* As far as I was concerned, the few magicians who pretended they had supernatural abilities were the lowest of the low, trading on a kind of superstition that should no longer even exist. Magic was a blend of artful tricks and impressive feats. Magic was about illusion, perception. Deception, not reality. Magic was well-crafted lies woven into stories no one believed were true, even though they delighted in seeing the convincing falsehood with their own eyes. It was not, well, *magic*.

I reached inside the opposite coat pocket from where I'd stashed the disaster deck and removed the second-to-the-bottom card. Then I handed her the same one I'd wrongly claimed she chose earlier.

She sniffed and passed it back. "No," she said, "one of the *other* cards."

What was she after? My pulse was racing. I had to get out of there.

Jules nudged the girl in the suit. "You try," she said. So that girl whispered, loud enough for me to hear, "What's going on?"

"Jules and Dita, mind your own business," the older lady said. Her gaze was steady on me, and I recognized in it the times when Dad wouldn't give me my way. She intended to examine one of the cards.

"I'm ready to perform anytime," Dez said. "I waited until last so no one would have to follow me."

"Shh," Thurston told him, indulging the older woman's whim. "This is Nancy Maroni," he said. All it meant to me was confirmation that she was related to the wire walker at the end of the table. "We do as she asks."

Dez's face split into a grin that was so far past charming it could only be described by a word I'd never used before in my life. I'd only ever seen it in the romance novels I borrowed from the girls at the theater, but it fit. He was rakish. "*The* Nancy Maroni?" he said. "The famous trapeze flyer? I'd wait all day to perform for you."

"I go by Nan," she said.

I'd have sworn she thought the same thing I did: *rakish*. "And that won't be necessary. You're on as soon as Moira here lets me inspect the cards she used in her final . . . trick." Her palm extended to me.

I didn't see any other way, so I passed her one of the rainbow cards.

Nan put it between both of her wrinkled palms. "You come from a performing family? Magic? Your father or mother? What brought you here?"

Obviously, I couldn't say yes. And had she put a slight emphasis on "mother," or did I imagine it?

"No, just me, on my own," I said, careful not to look at Raleigh. "I came to do magic."

She raised the card to conceal a whispered conversation with Thurston. After they finished talking, she returned the card to me, and Thurston sat back. She watched the owner with expectation.

"We each get one override," he said, sounding agreeable.

She returned her attention to me. "You're hired, Moira. For now. I'll want to talk to you."

"What?" I said it at the same time Dez and Raleigh did.

But while we were all in disbelief, I decided to embrace my good fortune, even if I was worried by how she'd zeroed in on the cards. "Thank you," I said, and made to leave before she could change her mind.

Disastrous audition or not, I still wanted this chance at my dream. I'd figure out what this Nan Maroni knew about the freaky accident with the cards later when I talked to her. I was hired . . . for now.

"Not so fast, Moira," Dez said, lingering over my name. "I need an assistant."

What *I* needed was to leave this tent.

"No thanks," I said. "I'm no one's lovely assistant."

The rakish act must have been getting old to Thurston too, because he said, "You were told to bring everything you need for your act. If you need an assistant and don't have one, we can't help you."

Dez grinned at him recklessly. "I recruit from the crowd. And right now I'm recruiting the Miraculous Moira. Who owes me a favor."

"Why are you doing this?" I asked, honestly curious.

"I helped you out," Dez said, "and you just had a stroke of luck. Why not pass it on?"

He lifted his palms and pressed them together in a plea, still grinning.

Raleigh opened his mouth, probably to say no on my behalf, and that made me want to plant my own flag. "Fine," I said. "I'll do it."

The short-haired girl, Dita, glanced between me and Nan—who I discovered was still coolly watching me—then reached across the table and lifted my jacket from my arms.

"This is the weirdest day," Thurston mumbled. Raleigh grunted agreement.

"Follow me," Dez said, sweeping toward the center of the ring.

While we'd been conferring, it appeared Dez's other assistant—the annoying friend from before—had been waiting to set up a large wooden board with various target circles marked out on it between dangling straps. Dez led me to it and positioned me against the wood. His hands touched my arms, shifting me this way and that.

I can't believe I let him talk me into this. "What are you doing? You're just moving me back and forth."

"Fun, right?" He took my wrists before I could protest and lifted them to either side of my head. His face was near mine.

"What—"

"It's a shame we can't use your cuffs. But you can get out of these if you need to," he said, putting one loose strap across my right wrist and another across the left. "Which you won't."

Then he strode across the sawdust of the ring and stopped more than a dozen feet away. There, he unsheathed a knife from his forearm.

That had to be way too far for an accurate throw. He lifted his voice when he spoke. "I'll spare you my usual warm-up, though it is very clever. Instead, I will deliver to you a death-defying act." His hands were as quick as any magician's, and he had three knives swiping through the air high over his head before I even saw him remove them. He added a fourth, the blades flashing in a lazy rhythm as he juggled them, and continued speaking casually. "Didn't we all just see this lovely lady here avoid death on the stage and get herself hired? I think she can do it again. She's won me to her side."

I moved, about to slip my wrists from the cuffs. Dez raised his voice as he said, "Stay where you are."

You mean where you put me. Though how he could possibly have seen my fraction of movement and continued juggling was beyond me. Like so many things that had happened in this tent. Before I could tell him I *was* going to move and then leave, one of the knives was flying from his hand toward me with such speed I could never have dodged it.

I didn't even have time to try.

It sank with a *thunk* into the wood beside my head.

I strained against the straps. I'd had enough of this. My heart was racing again, and a hint of that heat from before spread through my chest.

"Don't move," Dez said lazily.

I went still. The sensation of heat faded, and I vowed to not even breathe.

Another knife sliced through the air. The blade sank into the board beside my leg, but I remained completely still. Growing up at the Menagerie and learning about the art of escape had taught me that dangerous things are more likely to occur when people screw up their roles, miss their marks. Accidents happen when you let fear get to you badly enough to make you flinch. And I didn't know what would happen if that heat like a flame inside flared back to life . . . I didn't understand what had happened the first time.

I closed my eyes and pictured myself walking away from this board and outside, in one piece. Dez's next throws came one after the other, as smooth as a hail of bullets.

Thunk thunk thunk thunk . . . The blades sank into the board around me. Only when they stopped did I open my eyes again.

Dez sauntered toward me, as cocky as before. I was done. I wrestled one of my wrists free and used that hand to undo the other side. I stepped away from the wooden board. Dez showed no concern at this.

He stopped about six feet away and smiled at me rather than focusing on the target as he tossed the three final blades.

Thunk. Thunk. Thunk. They sank into the wood.

Dez walked closer, placing his hand over his chest as he neared me. And he said loud enough for everyone to hear, "See what you inspired?"

I looked back to the target where I'd been standing moments before and saw he'd created a perfect heart shape made of knives. But when I turned to Dez, convinced this was some kind of joke, he was too busy waiting for the judges' verdict to give me a second glance.

The audience in the stands began clapping and catcalling. All but Raleigh, who was frowning at the heart of blades.

The judging panel wasn't such a tough sell after all. Thurston's face split into a broad grin, and he lifted his hands to clap. Dita and Jules were both beaming, impressed. Nan remained serious for a long moment, until a smaller, more controlled smile crossed her lips. Then, and only then, did Dez take his bow.

While they were distracted, I made my escape.

four

I didn't quite manage my disappearing act without anyone noticing. Dita must have been paying some attention to me, because as I passed behind the judging table she got up and slipped my jacket into my hands.

Air. Now. And a minute alone to think.

Outside was the same strange tangle of people as before. If anything, the crowd had grown. I kept my head down. When I reached my convertible, I jammed the key into the lock and let myself inside, then leaned my forehead on the steering column. The top was up, so I had that layer of protection.

My cards had transformed. I'd been a disaster and gotten hired anyway. And the apparently legendary Nan Maroni suspected . . . something. What the hell was going on?

I took out my phone and stared at it. There was a text from Dad, who never abbreviated anything in his messages and expected the same in return: Did you get there all right? Send me an address for a care package. And call me later. I miss you already.

An address? Sure, send it to my car. I went to my contacts and stared at the word *Dad* for a good half a minute, deciding whether to call him. But, no, he couldn't help me. Not with this. What would I do? Blurt out that I wasn't anywhere near Ithaca, New York, and add, *Hey, have you ever heard of anyone transforming cards? Or being filled with heat and then, hocus-pocus, magic suddenly changing reality?*

There was no one I could tell about this—especially not Dad.

A text popped up from Raleigh: You OK?

I texted back: Just need a few.

I tossed the phone into the passenger seat and rested my head on the steering column again. I had no idea what I was going to do.

Rap, rap.

I forced my eyes open. It felt like sand was clogging them, and the right corner of my mouth was damp with drool. I'd fallen asleep.

Not catching more than a catnap for three days and then bombing miserably and having some sort of bizarre physical spell come over you in which you cast an *actual* spell would do that to you, clearly. If my forehead hadn't been resting on the steering wheel, the likeliest explanation would have been that the entire day was a vivid dream.

Rap, rap, rap.

Right. Someone was knocking on my car window. That was what had woken me.

With a fortifying breath, I turned my head.

Dez grinned down at me, cocky and, yes, still rakish. He said something that I couldn't make out through the glass, then reached out and tried to open the door.

I held up a hand. *Wait.*

Not that I wanted to let him play voyeur as I primped, but I did take a second to run my hands through my hair and discreetly wipe away the drool.

I unlocked the car door, and Dez reached down and opened it. "Welcome back to the land of the not-sleeping," he said. "There's a minor search party looking for you."

When I climbed out, I tried to keep my distance. Even so, Dez was mere inches away. I remembered the heart he'd made with the knives. I couldn't even look at him, and he made no move to give me more space. Today had been full of a lifetime's worth of mortifying, confusing incidents. And it wasn't over.

"I would have told them I thought you'd be here, but I was being selfish," he rattled on, oblivious to my discomfort. "I was afraid I'd never see you again. It was a relief to find you drooling on your steering wheel."

I blinked at him. He couldn't have seen that, could he? "A nice guy would never mention that."

"True." He grinned wider.

"Are you ever serious?" I grumbled.

"Only when forced to be."

But his grin slipped away, and I wondered how much of his bravado was, well, bravado. The pretense of being cool under pressure. A highly successful imitation of confidence.

"You didn't compliment me on my death-defying act, for one," he said. "It's rude to bolt after someone has made a heart around you with knives. It's like you didn't think the gesture had meaning. I've never done that before. You inspired me."

My own heart beat rapidly, like it wanted to listen. I told it to wise up.

"You said people are looking for me—who?"

"Your spooky magician friend who doesn't like me," he said, shoulders shaking in a mock shudder. "And Nan Maroni, circus royalty. She wants to talk to you. Did you know her before? Did she think you were from a family she worked with way back when or something? She seems pretty in your corner for a stranger."

He was watching me with that half-serious expression again.

"No," I said. "I guess she's just nice."

I was as suspicious of her motives as anyone. But I didn't see any way to avoid talking to her.

"Fate has its plans, and it doesn't consult us," he said. Pretty words, but he looked almost embarrassed by them, his hand gravitating to the back of his neck. "Somebody I know says that all the time. I'd better take you to Nan."

I pretended to be unconcerned. "Lead on."

To my surprise, Dez stayed quiet as he led us across the expansive grounds. There weren't nearly so many people milling around as before. We threaded through a maze of caravans and trailers. I hadn't given much thought to the travel arrangements when the Cirque was on the road, and the fact that people seemed to have brought their own accommodations was worrying. My neck already hurt from sleeping in the car.

But I had much bigger problems than a potential lack of a place to stay.

"Here we are," Dez said, as we neared an older RV that had the Cirque's logo and the words *The Amazing Maronis* painted on its side.

The girl with the short hair and bow tie, Dita, who I'd instinctively liked, stood near it. "You found her," she said. "Maybe everyone will stop flipping out now."

"Everyone?" I asked.

"Well, Nan," she said, ticking her head toward the RV. "She wouldn't say why, though."

I couldn't tell if she was curious or suspicious or some mix of the two. I also hadn't noticed before, but there were faint circles under Dita's eyes, the telltale signs of bad sleep.

Raleigh strolled up to us from the opposite direction. He shook his head at me. "You're lucky I didn't rat you out already, kid," he said.

The fact that he called me "kid" was annoying. "Raleigh, not now." I barely got the words out. If he told them about my dad, what were the odds I'd get to stay on? Slim. Even if Thurston Meyer didn't care, someone would hear and get word to Dad. He'd come.

"Your boyfriend has a temper," Dez observed.

I was way too smart to develop a thing for a heartbreaker like Raleigh. "Ha. He's so not my boyfriend."

Dez's grin was back. "I wasn't going to ask, but good."

"Where'd you disappear to?" Raleigh asked. I was distracted by Dez knocking on the front door of the RV.

It opened, and Nan appeared. A swirly black-and-white skirt matched the scarf at her throat. She might be a grandmother, but she didn't dress the usual part. She looked like she'd stepped out of a fancy event.

"I thought you'd pulled a vanishing act on us," she said.

"I needed some air."

She waited with sharp eyes, like she knew I had more to say. I found myself wishing I'd taken advantage of Dez's knowledge and quizzed him about her on the way over.

"I don't usually . . . mess up like that. I'm a talented magician, and I'll prove it. But I—" I stopped, not wanting to blurt out a question about magic in front of everyone else.

"I recognize talent when I see it," she said neutrally. "Come in."

I hesitated but finally took a step toward her. Raleigh made to follow, and she said, "I'd like to speak to her privately."

"We'll wait here," Dita said.

Dez waved and took off, apparently not interested in hanging around.

Hoping Raleigh didn't give me away while chatting with the girl, I crossed the threshold, climbing shallow steps into the cabin. Nan stepped back down to close the door behind me.

The interior was shabby chic, framed photographs and colorful vintage and new circus posters dominating what little wall space existed.

There was a small kitchen and living room visible, and a hallway that presumably led to the sleeping areas.

Nan breezed past me and sat down on the far side of a built-in bar-style table near the kitchen counter. She gestured, and I settled into the small wooden chair opposite her. There was no point in dancing around why I was here. "Why did you ask to see my cards?"

"I think you know the answer." She gave a slight shake of her head. "What I want to know is what you're doing here. I couldn't risk you leaving without finding that out."

What is she talking about? "I'm here to do magic. It's all I want to do."

"Yes," she said, "magic of the kind that I've only heard legends and stories about. In fact, the only people I've ever heard of who can transform objects like you did—that card felt new, and it had your magic all over it—are the Praestigae."

I was officially lost. *My* magic? "The presti-what?"

"Those same stories say not to trust you, that you only look out for your own. So I'll ask again: Why are you here? And are you the only one?"

So she thought I was part of some secret criminal society or something? She pronounced it "press-'tee-jie."

"I don't know what you're talking about," I said.

"Stop. I don't know much about the Praestigae, which is how you like it . . . You take what you want and move on. The consummate con artists, using magic for gain." She shook her head. "I probably shouldn't even be confronting you. But I recently lost someone dear to me, dear to my family, because of magic secrets and games. Because of the good luck coin from the Garcia family—you've probably heard that legend too."

"What?"

"Wait . . . is that why you're here? Roman's coin is gone. No magic object is worth the pain that thing caused."

I struggled to catch up. "Are you saying that there is *real* magic?"

Her eyes narrowed again, and she considered me. "You, my dear, are very skilled at playing dumb."

I didn't understand anything she'd said to me, except that she knew something about magic. And that she held the fate of my job in her hands. "I'm not playing anything. Not about this." I sucked in a breath and let it out. It felt crazy to talk about this, but I did it anyway. "Nothing like what happened in the tent has ever happened to me before. I swear to you that I'm not lying."

"How could that possibly be true? Magic presents early for those who have it."

"What you're saying isn't easy to believe either. If magic is real, why doesn't the entire world know?"

Silence stretched out between us. I felt confused and frightened and shocked all at once.

At last, she spoke. "The world doesn't want to know. Not most of it. And there isn't much left to know about. Is your mother's power the same as yours?"

"My mother left when I was too young to remember. I've never heard from her." I had to make her understand. "Back there, today . . . I felt this tug, like something pulling me outside myself, and then a surge of heat, and then the cards were different. I wasn't in control of anything. I don't know how they changed. It's *impossible*."

"It's true you didn't seem in control. But if you're telling the truth, this is even more complicated." She sighed. "Will you let me give you a reading? That might convince me you're not just worried I caught you."

Her attention dropped to the center of the table. An oversized deck of cards lay packless across the laminated surface. They were obviously old, with swirling designs hand-painted on the back in red and black and white. I hadn't even noticed anything was there and half suspected she'd sleighted them out.

She reached out and lifted the top card to show it to me. A man dangled from his feet off a trapeze. The words *The Hanged Man* were painted at the bottom of the image. They were tarot cards. She meant *that* kind of reading.

"My mother made these cards and imbued them with magic. Which means I am uniquely suited to read what they say. Magic manifests in a specific way within family lines, and it always comes from the mother. Our magic is small next to yours. It allows only a simple effect, to bring out the essence of an object and amplify it."

What she was saying would mean that my mother, the fairy-tale assistant who could have been a magician herself, had magic too, and it was probably the same as mine. The entire concept was absurd. I wanted to laugh or cry or scream or run. To not believe it and to believe it all. This woman thought I had magic. *Real* magic.

"Fortune-telling is, um, bogus," I said. "You just pick up on cues, ask questions, and then make statements so general there's no way they can be disproven." Similar to a mentalist act or the spiritualist hoaxers Houdini had hated so much.

"I speak for the cards, and *these* cards tell the truth. That is what my mother brought out within them. Are you saying no? If you are, that means you have something to hide. It tells me I was right about you." She held up the hand-painted tarot deck and fanned the cards out with their backs facing up. Whatever she was, she was no cardsharp. Her technique was passable at best.

But I wasn't lying, so fine. "What do I do?"

"Pick a card, and concentrate on allowing it to show your true essence. If you are here under false pretenses, I will know. The cards will tell me."

I reached out, happy to do anything to prove I was telling the truth and get clear answers. I ran a fingertip along the entire span of cards she'd fanned out and gently removed the seventh from the left. Noting the card's position was as natural as breathing.

"Lay it flat so I can see it," she said.

I looked at it first. A figure wearing a robe with suns and moons, woman or man I couldn't say, stood on an outside stage, holding a snake in one hand and a wand in the other. The moon above was red in a black sky. As I studied the card, my fingertips heated, or maybe the card heated in them. I felt that warmth surge through me again, and the painted magician on the card began to move, limbs stretching, face turning away and then back. Around him shapes of animals and humans emerged from the night. One of them was a girl—

Nan's fingers plucked the card away. "You were changing it," she said, her voice shaking.

She was right.

The face of the magician on the card wasn't the same anymore. It was my father's.

And the girl at the edge of the stage had short black curls, her hands held out in front of her, handcuffed at the wrists. To be precise, she was now me.

I blinked at the card, stunned, then looked back to Nan. Her mouth was open in shock.

I felt cold all over, a contrast to the heat that had surged through my fingers moments before. "I'm so sorry," I said. "You told me your mother made these."

I didn't have anything from my mother—except, it seemed, this unwieldy magic—but I could guess that Nan would consider these cards from her mother to be precious.

She took a slow breath, and when she let it out, she'd regained her composure. "When your magic came into contact with the card's, you transformed it . . . It shows your essence now. This is your story. You are what you say."

She set the card down between us sideways, so we both could see the image better. Together, we peered into it.

In the background behind my father and me were two shadowy, unrecognizable forms, stopped midtransformation. One was a woman with long red hair, who wore a black dress; some shape seemed to wind around the top of her head, but it was impossible to tell what it was. She was otherwise indistinct. The other form was blurrier, possibly male but not clear enough to swear to it. They both gazed up, where two small shiny objects fell toward them from above. The previously black background now featured the red and white stripes of the tent. Some white and red and yellow spots beside it, like bright lightbulbs, hung on a string in the sky.

"Who are they?" My finger hovered over the background. I pulled it back when I realized what I was doing and that she might not want my hands to touch the card again.

"I have no idea," she said. "You definitely transform things. I don't know why your mother would have left you . . . She must be one of the Praestigae, given your power. The only reason your magic wouldn't have expressed itself is if it were purposely hidden. Something here woke it. But I will tell you the most important thing your mother should have: your magic is dangerous."

The words brought a chill. *Your magic is dangerous.*

"How?"

"Think of magic like you are a cup and you hold magic inside you. You drink a little, or pour a little out, and it can be refilled. Use too much, and that process becomes harder. And should the cup ever be emptied completely, then it will break. Magic has consequences."

"Like what?"

She frowned, as if she didn't want to answer. But she did. "The kind of magic you can do, it's strong. It's extremely powerful. If you use too much all at once, it could kill you."

"Oh, well, that's no big deal, then." A bad joke, but the truth in her words somehow sang to me. My bones vibrated with it. "I only want to be a magician."

"You will have to learn to control your powers. To conserve them."
I didn't want to use real magic at all. "But I can stay? What did you tell Mr. Meyer?"

"I told him I saw something in you, and that I wanted to talk to you before we dismissed you." She paused. "You *can* stay, though it might be better for you to go home. Ask your father to find your mother. Or not. She may have her reasons for abandoning you."

No. "I can't go home."

"I figured as much. You remind me of my Jules. Stubborn. Driven. You'll have to take care. People who can do magic . . . other people will want to profit from it, be threatened by it, or both. Be careful who you trust with this secret. And be careful how you try to use your magic. The cup cannot be emptied."

"No dying. Got it."

It was another bad joke, and neither of us laughed. I had enough to think about. I couldn't take anything more. So I got up to leave.

"They'll be wondering why I'm still in here," I said.

She nodded and then escorted me the short way to the door. Raleigh and Dita came forward to meet us when it opened, and I stepped down to the grass. Nan lingered.

"You're staying?" Dita asked.

I nodded. Which meant living arrangements were a problem I had to deal with now. "About that, where does everyone sleep?"

"We're a tent circus," Dita said, gesturing at the RVs and trailers around us. "And we don't do the same route as the Greatest, so we drive caravan-style to our dates."

I assumed she meant the Greatest Show on Earth, but I didn't question it. That part didn't matter to me. "Could I rent something? When do we leave?"

Dad might protest transferring me such a big chunk of money, but I didn't have many options.

"We leave tomorrow," Dita said.

"So soon?" I blurted. "We don't even get to rehearse the midway?"

Dita shrugged. "Thurston has a 'go big or go home' thing. He says the energy will be better if the midway debuts on the road. He's not even giving us the full schedule until we get to Jacksonville."

Nan cut in. "Every place in town with rentals has been cleaned out by now. I'm guessing this means you don't have anywhere to stay?"

That I didn't know the rules of circus life—especially Cirque American life—was becoming as clear as glass so invisible the audience never so much as glimpsed it. Not to mention I didn't even know the rules of my own life. *I can do magic. Magic that could kill me.*

"You drove here, didn't you?" Raleigh said. "In that ridiculously small car. I guess you can stay with me. I managed to rent an old trailer from a friend."

"If you want, you can stay with me and Remy," Dita said. "We just got our own place."

There was no doubt I'd rather stay with her than Raleigh. He knew me well enough that he'd see I was hiding something.

"That would be great," I said to Dita. "I can pay rent."

Nan gave us a satisfied nod and closed the door. Raleigh said, "You're all right?"

I nodded. I didn't want to run the risk of lying out loud and being obvious about it.

"We can grab an air mattress from supplies," Dita said, starting across the grass. "I'm curious about Nan's interest in you."

"Me too," Raleigh said.

"Are you guys related?" I asked her, to deflect.

"Me and Nan? Ha," she snorted. "No. Our families hated each other until last summer. No one can believe the Garcias and Maronis are now friends, mostly."

The Garcias. Nan had mentioned them and some kind of coin when she'd been accusing me of being in that secret society. The one my mom belonged to. In theory.

There didn't seem to be much of anything neutral to say back to Dita or Raleigh about why Nan had taken an interest in me. *Your magic is dangerous. The cup cannot be emptied.*

For once, I was the one not holding any cards.

part two

pay no attention

five

When I woke the next morning on my air mattress in the tiny, cute room I was sharing with Dita in her and her brother Remy's tiny, cute silver Airstream, I discovered Dita already up. Wrapped in a gray robe that seemed to be a man's, she held a slender mystery novel with a creased spine in front of her and leaned against the wall behind her bed. But she was staring over the book at me.

"Good morning," I said, which seemed safe.

"So," she said, lowering the book, "don't you want to know why I invited you to stay here?"

I'd wondered, but I was too wiped out the night before to ask. I went straight to sleep. "For the rent money, I assume. How much do you want?"

"No, not for the rent money."

"What then?" I glanced over at the narrow closet simply to avoid looking at her.

I'd noticed when I hung up some of my clothes the night before that most of her things were of the same variety—crisp men's shirts and pants, a few suit jackets, and a lot more bow ties. The room itself was bare-bones, but there was a pleasant hint of spicy cologne in the air.

"Oh God," she said, and I looked back to find her shaking her head. "I didn't mean to make this awkward. It's not—I'm not interested in you. I mean, I am, but not like *that*."

"That didn't even occur to me," I said. "So, why am I here? There's obviously a reason."

"There is. Last season . . . I lost someone. It was over this . . . thing, over the Maronis and Garcias' ancient history."

Wait, I thought. Nan Maroni had mentioned this too. The loss and the magic coin. "Some coin?"

"What do you know about it?" Dita demanded.

"Nothing. Nan mentioned it in passing. She wanted to, um, make sure I wasn't here because of it." I paused. "I'm not. I had no idea what she was talking about. You want to explain it?"

She swallowed, not so skilled as an interrogator. "No. I just don't want to get left out again. I had no idea what was going on, not until it was too late. Why would she ask you about that?"

Oh no. I hadn't thought this far ahead. "Because I'm a magician and sometimes we work with coins? Anyway, it was all a misunderstanding. I'm just here to do magic." I added, "The stage and close-up kind."

She gave me a long, hard look. "People tell stories about Nan Maroni, you know. There's truth to them."

I didn't know, but I could guess they had to do with magic. The real variety. Which she'd told me explicitly to keep hidden from anyone else. And anyone included Dita, no matter how much I liked her or how much she was helping me out by letting me bunk here.

"What kind of stories do you mean?" I asked.

She sighed. "Never mind. But if there's anything to know, anything weird, you'll tell me?"

I shrugged one shoulder. "Sure. Why wouldn't I?"

Because I can do magic and so could my absent mother . . . who maybe I should track down. Except I'd prided myself on never pining for her, on never wanting to find someone who plainly didn't want to be found. Not to mention that she was apparently wrapped up with some dangerous people. I'd have to Google that name—the Pressteejie?

Oh God. This was too much thinking before breakfast.

Dita still didn't look entirely convinced, so I decided to distract her with directness. "Okay, new topic—I know we just met and this is truly none of my business, but if you're gay or bi or straight as an arrow or whatever variety or combination thereof, I'm cool with it. I'm straight, but I have zero problem with anyone being otherwise. Also, where do we get the delicious breakfast foods?"

Dita's eyes went round. I'd thrown her off the trail of my secret, at least. "I . . . I'm pretty sure I'm bi . . . Not that it matters right now. But I just feel more like myself when I dress in men's clothes."

"The look suits you. But I still can't believe you're not into me." I shook my head sadly. "How will I get over this?"

Her expression turned slightly wounded. Then I smiled. She chucked the paperback at me.

"Oh," she said. "You're one of those. Onstage, always performing."

I climbed to my feet. "That's where you're wrong. I've never been onstage performing. I've always been the one behind the scenes. Or in a small crowd, slipping away right after."

"Huh," she said. "You fooled me."

"I've *wanted* to be onstage for a few years. Just never had the chance."

"Why not?" she asked, sounding legitimately curious.

Note to self: stop being interesting. I ducked the question. "I'm here now, and that's what matters. You said who you like doesn't matter right now for you. Why?"

Her face subtly shut, like a window being pressed down to the sill. "I can't imagine being with anyone right now."

There was a story there, one she didn't want to talk about. "Got it. Do you mind if I take the first shower?"

"Go ahead," Dita said. "We'll hit the mess for your 'delicious breakfast foods' and then the road. Everyone packed up their gear last night or this morning. You'll drive behind us in your car?"

"Sounds plan-ish."

When I slipped a clean pair of jeans and a T-shirt out of my bag, I also grabbed a deck of new cards. I concealed them under the shirt as I made my way up the small hall and into an even smaller bathroom. My fingers itched with the tug, the pull, the desire to be in motion. I needed to prove to myself that I could still do the kind of magic I wanted to.

But I also wanted to test my newfound ability. Part of me didn't believe in it. I didn't plan to empty the cup, just experiment by taking a slow sip from it.

Cramped for space, I climbed into the shower and dumped the cards into my hand. Then I began to shuffle them. I created a mental image of each card in my mind, learning the deck automatically while I did. My fingers moving nimbly, each motion perfect, controlling the cards. I made them fall like rapids of a river, one into the next into the next, and scooped them up and made them into an accordion flowing back and forth between my palms. I riffled them, living for the satisfying familiar *snick snick snick* as they returned to the exact positions I wanted them to. I held my arms tight in front of me, completing two circle fans. No problem this time.

I set down all the cards except one. Slowly, I laid that card flat on my hand. I added my other hand on top, pressing the card between my palms. *Change,* I thought, as hard as I could.

But I didn't feel that warmth this time. The card was a card, the jack of hearts before I touched it and after. My fingertips were just stupid fingertips. My palms declined even to sweat. Nothing happened.

When the magic had struck before, both times, I'd been completely powerless to guide it. All those hours of practice to learn my magic skills had been aimed at ensuring that control of my body and focus during a trick or an escape was effortless, total, and ever-present. I didn't want to feel the way I had yesterday again, and especially not while performing.

But apparently this supposed magic I had wasn't going to come out for practice today.

"Moira, everything okay?" Dita called softly.

"Fine," I lied, then put the cards on the sink ledge before I twisted the shower on.

Being part of the caravan to Jacksonville was another weird new experience to add to my list. Even for a Vegas girl, the sheer scale of this enterprise and all the people involved was impressive.

I stayed behind the Airstream, which Dita's brother Remy was piloting while she played passenger. I was glad I'd seen the mural on the side of their home before I'd met Remy—it interrupted the silver side of the trailer and pictured Dita perched on a platform holding a trapeze and Remy swinging out on another. A third figure's face was concealed but muscular arms reached out to catch the boy's hands. Fancy script said *The Flying Garcias, with the Love Brothers and the Goddesses of Beauty*.

The image had given me some warning of how much black-haired and brown-eyed Remy looked like a movie star, down to the muscles. Swinging from a trapeze would do that to you, I guessed. Remy and Jules, the famed wire walker, were a solid item, according to Dita, and I could look forward to them ignoring everyone else when they were with each other.

Some of the staging crew was already on-site at our destination, but we were still nestled in a miles-long line that included performer families' RVs with murals and logos, semis with the tents and sets and more of the work crew, and a massive assortment of other vehicles, including a couple of horse trailers. The horses belonged to the only animal act in the show besides a routine of very well-cared-for dogs, again according to Dita. Though she'd had that sad look again when she said it.

While I was alone, I had another item of business to arrange. I took out my phone and scrolled through my contacts, selected the name Amber, and put the call on speaker. She was one of Dad's former assistants, a bubbly brunette who'd left Vegas a few years earlier to move to Ithaca, and we'd kept in touch occasionally. Many of the lovely assistants, current and former, liked to play at being a maternal influence. Or some sort of positive influence anyway.

"Hey, Moira," she said, answering on the second ring. "Good to hear from you. What's up?"

"I need a favor," I said, and proceeded to ask if I could tell my dad I was staying with her for the summer. It took a little convincing and a lot of assuring her that I was completely safe, but eventually I hung up with an address to give Dad for his care package and any that might follow.

I waited until we were waved into a giant flat lot on the outskirts of Jacksonville, directed into parking rows, but as soon as I was stopped, I sent him a text: Here's my address. Hope the show went well! Miss you!

He texted back almost immediately: I should never have let you leave. I'm surrounded by incompetents, and there's no one to complain to.

I snorted. Be nice, you hired them. ☺

It felt strange to be texting with Dad instead of just talking to him, and to be so far away. And to be lying to him. I was doing too much of that.

I got out of the car, joining a throng of other people getting out of their vehicles. Dita and Remy stood outside the Airstream, gaping at an enormous Ferris wheel set up next to an empty stretch of field. The metal wheel rose high up in the air, the spokes covered in lights and ending in open-topped cars. Their doors were painted with the Cirque's logo.

"I take it this is new?" I asked.

"Um, yes," Dita said. "Very."

"It's so . . . big," Remy said. "Let's go over there."

The rest of the Cirque had the same idea, and we were gathered around the base of the wheel, stretching up and up and up, a circle that seemed to hit the sky, when Thurston appeared.

"Hello, everyone!" He was in casual clothes, but he instantly put on his air of command. I could picture him in the center ring. "Surprise number one! We can't just repeat our triumphs, or our tragedies—we must move forward and grow. But we also can't forget. You may not know that the first Ferris wheel in the world was built in Chicago, for the 1893 World's Fair. It was the showpiece of the very first midway. Those of you who have been with the Cirque know that we will never return to Chicago, but we will always carry it with us—figuratively and now literally."

He paused here, and his eyes found us near the front. Remy had his hand on Dita's arm. Her face was carefully blank. Jules had joined us at some point, on Remy's other side, and she had tears in her eyes.

Thurston continued.

"This wheel is the largest transportable one in the world, and it will come with us. Which means that we will hit bigger cities for several days, leaving enough time between dates for the seventy-two hours it takes to reconstruct. Luckily, I'm good at math, so it doesn't take that long to break apart. I want this year to be better than the last. So pick up the season's schedule, and get ready for a parade tomorrow that will bring all of Jacksonville to the greatest show they've ever seen. Midway people, look at the solemn faces around you. I expect you to knock it out of the park, make the Cirque even better. It all starts tomorrow!"

The petite woman who'd checked me in the day before and several of her army were distributing sheets of paper. I grabbed one, aware that I didn't understand the full story of Chicago—and knowing from the faces of Dita, Remy, and Jules that I wasn't about to ask them for it now. I did remember that was where I'd first seen Jules on TV, daringly dancing above the downtown. I wondered if it had something to do with that.

A list of cities and dates ran down the page in my hand: Jacksonville, Atlanta, Memphis, Saint Louis, Kansas City, Dallas, El Paso, Albuquerque, Phoenix, San Diego, Los Angeles, and—last but looming largest for me—Las Vegas. Our final city, over Labor Day weekend.

I counted twelve weeks from today until we'd be there. That was how much time I had to figure out how to put together an act that would leave zero doubt of my abilities in Dad's mind.

six

Opening day dawned thick with a tension that had begun to build the night before. The mess tent was swimming with it at breakfast—the excitement of the season kicking off and whatever Thurston and Jules's rumored surprise was.

At our long breakfast table in the catered tent, I'd wolfed down banana-blueberry pancakes beside Dita, who inhaled a stack of bacon and toast. The back wall featured a projection of Jules walking above a bridge high over the river here last year. I admired the daring of it. But that was apparently not the plan for this season—Jules would be doing something else, and we wouldn't know until it happened.

For me, the excitement was coupled with the anxiety that my magical powers continued to refuse to show up whenever I snuck off into a corner to attempt to test them out. I was increasingly afraid they would come without warning, making it impossible for me to ever practice controlling them.

Less than two hours after breakfast, the season was officially about to get its start.

"Step right up," Thurston called out over a bullhorn. He was wearing his full ringmaster tux and tails. He waved the midway and Cirque performers—we'd neatly segregated ourselves—toward a trio of large buses to head into town.

From chattered explanations, I'd learned we were doing the reverse of what the Cirque had done last year. Instead of parading from here into town over the bridge, we'd be traveling to the city on these buses, then leading a parade back over the bridge to where we were staged. The hope was that excited fans and city people would follow us, showing up for whatever was the cap-off surprise at the tent, then stick around the midway and stay for the first show. Buses would take people back to town later, and then after a quick meal break we'd be on again for the evening performances.

Everyone was decked out in their costumes. Which meant it was like a massive chorus line of showgirls on the loose, except with fewer feathers and not so scantily clad. My outfit was pretty tame as these things went, of course—black jacket and pants with the supplies I needed stashed in the pockets. I made a mental note to ask Raleigh for some costuming help.

I boarded the third bus after most of the people were already on, not wanting to get trapped at the back surrounded by strangers. That enabled me to slip into a seat near the front. Dita was the only one I could describe as a semi-friend here at this point, and so it was fine that no one took the spot beside me.

Well, until Dez peeked onto the bus. He grinned when he caught sight of me. His grin felt . . . honest. Like legitimate happiness at seeing me.

That amplified when he said, "Finally. I checked the others for you first."

His friend appeared behind him. "He did. It was cray annoying."

"You know who else is cray annoying?" Dez asked. "You, Brandon. You are cray annoying."

Brandon laughed, highly amused. I would never understand why so many boys related to each other through mockery.

The two of them boarded, and Dez—unshockingly—swung into the seat next to me. He wore an outfit not dissimilar from my own, though his shirt was black instead of white and unbuttoned to a degree that should have been tacky but managed to look reckless and hot. He had a few knives strapped onto his legs and arms for appearances.

I tried to come up with a flippant response to his having searched me out, but a good comeback eluded me. There was an unwelcome fluttering instead. Particularly when Raleigh climbed on last, carrying his top hat in his hand, an opera cape over his suit for effect. He looked over at me and took in Dez, then swung into the row in front of and across the aisle from us. We were dressed like barbarians next to his elegant Phantom of the Opera.

Dez tilted his head closer to me, his face so near mine I worried I'd feel his breath if he spoke. Or vice versa.

"I don't think he likes me," he said.

And I was right. He'd pitched it for my ears only, which meant I felt the words against my neck. It was practically like he'd touched me.

I resisted the urge to shift nervously. The problem was, the breathy not-quite-touch had felt nice. "I can't imagine why," I said, at normal volume.

Dez threw his head back against the headrest of his seat and put a hand over his heart. "Once you get to know me, really know me, you'll feel different, Moira. I know I seem cocky, but I'm a puppy at heart." He turned those brown-penny puppy eyes toward me.

I sighed. "Let's not talk about you. Let's talk about—"

"You?" Dez grinned again, wolfish instead of rakish.

"No," I said, and I saw the corner of Raleigh's lips quirk. He was eavesdropping. "Let's talk about your act. Where'd you learn how to juggle knives?"

"Where'd you learn magic?"

"I asked first."

The bus driver got on and levered the lumbering vehicle into gear. I wondered why Raleigh's lovely assistants weren't riding next to him. A headlining magician couldn't get by without at least one.

Dez leaned forward to block my view of Raleigh. "I taught myself."

To juggle *knives*? Holy crap.

I'd taught myself too, obviously. Setting timers, reading tutorials, sneaking obscure books from Dad's library. I was careful to always do the dangerous exercises, like submerging myself bound or in a mask, when someone was around and would hear if my safety alarm went off. But knife-throwing? How could that be safe to learn solo?

"So you started with regular objects?" I asked. "Apples? Balls?"

"Balls!" Across the aisle, Brandon brayed a laugh, and my cheeks went up in flames. We were surrounded by eavesdroppers. "He started on a bet. With butcher knives!"

"Shut up, moron," Dez said, smooth as glass and with as sharp an edge.

Chastised, the other boy shrugged, but then gazed out the window. He must have only been Dez's helper, because he had on casual jeans and a tank. A duffel rested at his feet.

"Yes," Dez said. "I was dared to. It wasn't a situation where I could say no." He shrugged. "But I'd never have known I was capable of doing it if I hadn't."

I felt that way sometimes about having to be my own teacher. Dad would never have pushed me as hard as I pushed myself—he'd never have let me take so many risks.

"I wasn't all that good," he said. "I did cut myself."

He pushed back the sleeve of his shirt, and I saw the raised line of a scar slashed across his forearm, still red, like it was angry. I touched it before I could stop myself.

He was smiling at me again when I looked up, and I yanked my hand away. "Ouch," I said. "Sounds kind of stupid, if you ask me."

"Oh, it was," he said. "I'm full of bad decisions. And worse luck."

"That's the truth," Brandon said.

"I'm having a private conversation with the lady," Dez informed him.

"No, you're not," Raleigh said lazily.

Dez didn't look mad. He shrugged again. "Another time, then. I'll just have to be content to bask in your presence, beautiful Moira, sharing it with the undeserving who don't appreciate you like I do."

"Bask away," I said with bone-dry irony. But I hadn't liked thinking of Dez being so cavalier about tossing knives into the air and one coming down and slicing his arm deep enough to leave that scar. I also couldn't conjure a mental image of anyone who would be callous enough to seriously dare someone to do that.

So Dez was a mystery too. Maybe we all were. Maybe being a mystery was what brought people to the Cirque in the first place.

"Why'd you make me do your act with you?" I asked when the silence stretched too long.

"I wanted to make you a heart," Dez said.

"Uh-huh. How many of those have you made? Hundreds?"

"I told you—you inspired me."

I looked away, out the window. *Don't believe him. Pretty words.*

"A penny for your secrets," Dez said, nearly whisper-soft. His hand touched mine, and I turned back to him as he flipped my hand over. He pressed a penny into my palm.

I closed my fingers around it.

"It's *thoughts*," I said. "A penny for your thoughts."

"I'd take those too, but I think they're worth more."

"More than secrets?" I asked.

"You do have some, then. Interesting . . . Care to share?"

He stared at me, waiting, and I forced myself to stillness. As long I didn't move or react, I wouldn't give away anything else.

The bus ground to a halt.

Dez smiled at me. "Another time."

The driver opened the doors, and he stood up in the aisle, waiting for me to go out first and blocking Brandon from cutting in front of me. I walked off the bus behind Raleigh, and only when I stepped onto the pavement beside the same brilliant-blue giant of a bridge that

Jules had been crossing in the video did I realize I still had the penny in my palm.

"That guy's trouble," Raleigh said, swooping around to face me, as much superhero as Phantom with his long cape.

"So are you," I said, thinking of his endless slew of beautiful temporary girlfriends.

"True. But be careful."

"Please. I'm not even tempted." Hooking up with boys wasn't why I was here. Besides, Dez's show of interest probably didn't mean anything. None of that explained why I put the penny in my pocket, like it was part of my precious sleight kit.

"Places, everyone!" Thurston again.

The herd continued to divide by hierarchy for the parade, though it wasn't quite as pronounced from high to low as for the bus ride. Thurston in his ringmaster tux was up front with the band and its shiny brass instruments and red, white, and blue marching band uniforms. We miscreant midway performers followed them, saving the Cirque performers, the best, for last.

A massive crowd was waiting for us, overfilling the blocked-off streets that led into downtown Jacksonville and up to the edge of the bridge we would now cross. The bridge itself was all the more enormous when you pictured Jules walking above it. Speaking of which, I hadn't seen her around all morning. Hmm . . .

As we were lining up, I tried not to gape. I failed.

"You act like you've never seen a show before," Raleigh said.

Dez was talking away to a group of tattooed contortionists and aerial silks flyers a few feet from us, occasionally catching my eye.

"I've never seen anything like this," I said.

It was true. There were clowns in white face makeup painted with distinctive black or red triangles and classic harlequin patterns, their baggy white outfits billowing around tall stilts. The Garcias were in their tight, glimmery black trapeze outfits with red accents—Dita hardly looked like herself, though she'd pulled on a suit jacket over the tiny scraps of fabric that made up her costume, a touch of her own style. With her was a bulkier version of Remy, who I assumed was the brother I hadn't met yet, Novio.

Yapping dogs in costume orbited around an older woman dressed in a sergeant uniform. A beautiful blonde woman on a tall stomping horse with a tricked-out saddle must've been Jules's mom. Her father—a wire walker too, I'd gathered—wore plain black like me.

"You're gawking again," Raleigh said. "I think they want us over here."

He steered me that way, and we were joined by a lovely assistant—I knew there would be one around here somewhere—in a black satin evening dress and white gloves that came to her elbows. She and Raleigh made a striking couple when he offered her his elbow and she hooked hers through his.

"Where's your bird?" the assistant asked him.

"Bird?" I said.

"Shh," Raleigh said to her, looking sheepish.

Okay, I didn't need to know what that was about.

"Welcome, Jacksonville, to the second season of the great, the astounding, the amazing and best circus still going . . . the Cirque American!" Thurston boomed.

The pronouncement was met by cheers from the audience behind us, and from the performers at the back. Then Thurston gestured, and in front of us the band struck up its music, like something out a 1950s nightclub. Peppy, loud, with lots of horn and drums.

And we were moving.

The walk was on the long side, but it sped by. Various Cirque performers took the spotlight as we crossed the bridge, the procession pausing and making a small circle at the back so the followers behind could see. At least some of them could.

Jules's mom's tall horse bowed low and then reared high and danced in a circle. The tattooed contortionists contorted, twisting themselves into human pretzels, only to then be shown up by the Cirque's actual acrobats in their silk costumes, building a tower of bodies that stretched high above the roadway.

The mood continued to build, tension turning to anticipation. I wanted one of those performing spots badly, and it must have showed. "This isn't our scene," Raleigh said. Then, correcting himself, "Not mine, anyway. In any case, there may be photos. You'd best stay out of the limelight today so your dad doesn't see."

The photo thing had never occurred to me, and put a slight chill on the rest of the parade. I considered getting a mask—it would help with my boring costume issue.

At the grounds, the band marched us all the way to the tent, then past it to the Ferris wheel. Thurston waited patiently beside it for the entire mass of people to arrive, conferring with a workman there. Jules's father had joined them, I noticed.

Once the crowd was assembled—midway, Cirque performers, and actual audience—Thurston spoke again. "I'm excited to show you a new marvel we've brought along this year, a Ferris wheel inspired by the original." He stepped into a small operating control center at the base of the wheel and pulled a large lever.

We gasped.

Lights flared to life along each of its arms, stretching high into the sky above us. White, red, and gold. The paint on the cars themselves was blue, and the rest of the frame painted white. Like a visual hat tip to the Cirque.

"And I'm happy to introduce one of our favorite marvels, to open the season with all due grandeur." Thurston pointed up, and we strained to look where he indicated. The top of the wheel was higher than the tent—two hundred feet up, at a guess.

A girl in a short blue dress stepped free of the very top spire of the big top, balancing a long pole across her arms. Only then did we see the wire that ran from the tent to the Ferris wheel, angled up because of the massive machine's height.

Jules didn't waver as she moved out onto the wire toward the wheel. She didn't pause or slow. She took one step and then another. And another.

I felt someone jostle me, and I looked over, expecting to see Dez. But it was Dita and Remy. Remy gazed up, starry-eyed. Dita punched his arm. "You knew and you didn't say anything!" she said.

Remy didn't look away from his girlfriend.

Who could blame him? It was hard to look away from her, riveting-high above us. She placed each foot so surely, continuing to walk upward at a slight angle. The crowd around us cheered in delight at the spectacle.

It wasn't her bridge walk, but it was just as grand. In fact, I liked this more. It made her more a *part* of the circus. I couldn't have spoken for the rest of the company, but I got more excited with each step she took.

Soon it would be our turn.

Soon we would take custody of this audience.

She'd done us all the best favor in the world—as long as we were up to the challenge of not being a letdown after this.

There was a lesson for me here: Jules had come out of nowhere and made herself a name by being bold. What she was doing up there was dangerous, and she did it anyway. Watching her, I felt like I could do the same.

seven

The midway was set to stun.

A modern sideshow act had its fire-eaters onstage as I passed, all six swallowing flames they'd designed to burn a variety of colors while wearing elaborate, fantastical makeup and costumes that made them as much creatures as people. It was far cleverer than the goth Renaissance Faire twists I'd seen on these things at showcases back home.

I was nervous, given my catastrophic audition. But I didn't have a choice. My job required me to attempt a trick, pray I got it right, rinse, repeat. After seeing what Jules had done, I'd run back to the Airstream to grab my straitjacket. Before using it, I wanted to try something simple, find my performing legs again.

I picked a spot between stages, set the straitjacket down on the ground behind me, and removed a fresh deck. Then I waved to a family walking by. "Would you like to help me with a quick trick?"

A little boy grabbed the arm of a bearded man beside him and said, "You have to, Dad!"

The guy shrugged. "Sure." As they came closer, he added, "I've never seen a girl magician before."

No kidding. "Prepare to be extra-amazed, then," I said, forcing a smile.

I gave a showy shuffle of the cards, then removed my handcuffs from my pockets and secured my left wrist, clicking the cuffs shut.

"Test these, please. And close the right side." The man completed the task.

We'd attracted more of a crowd, which made me part relieved, part extra-nervous. The people spread in a semi-circle around me and my volunteer. I fanned the cards, hoping they were impressed by my wearing handcuffs while I did it.

My plan was to execute the same trick that had eluded me at my audition. It was simple enough aside from the cuffs, and I needed to prove to myself that I could do it when it counted. "Pick a card," I said, "but don't let me see it."

The man dithered over which one to choose, moving his hand back and forth. Finally, he plucked a card free, cupping it close to him.

"Look at it. Remember it," I said.

He did, peeking carefully—as if that would prevent me from figuring it out. The little boy tugged on his arm, and he bent to show it to him too.

"Now put it back into the deck."

He straightened and slid it carefully back among the other cards.

I showboated with my shuffling, earning gratifying applause at one point. I made the cards dance to the extent possible with the cuffs, a controlled waltz from side to side in front of me, up and down, arranged and rearranged. "You've seen me thoroughly shuffle, correct?"

The bearded man nodded, and the crowd did too. My worry remained, but I saw the thread of something else, the thread of what I wanted. Amazement.

I pulled on the card I was certain would be the man's. I let the rest of the cards fall dramatically around my feet. And I held up that single card.

"Was your card the two of clubs?" I asked.

The man smiled. "It was. It was!"

The rest of the crowd applauded.

Whew. I could still do magic, in front of people even.

I gathered up the fallen cards and worked my way from the midway's far end toward the big top slowly and steadily, doing card and coin tricks, usually in handcuffs. The tangle of performers who'd been outside the big top during auditions had grown and morphed into an alternately roving and stationary arrangement of wonders.

This new world would require navigation. I'd have to map it each time I worked the crowd. Smaller tents and open-air stages dotted the sides in some sort of genius irregular pattern that must have been deliberate, if only you were Thurston, its architect. The Ferris wheel sat in the inexact center. The entire setup was designed to give an intriguing, memorable journey to the circus tent.

Dez's stage was just past the Ferris wheel, prime real estate he'd probably charmed his way into. The wheel was an instant megahit, in constant operation with a long line of people waiting. I spotted a TV camera. It was currently filming the over-the-top, charismatic Dez.

After a moment's hesitation, I walked to the back of the crowd and lingered to see his act. I should have known better.

He was in full charm mode, escorting a woman with her hair dyed a bright turquoise from the large gathered crowd—mostly female, I noted—up onto the stage. She was blushing at whatever he'd said. He motioned for her to lift her arms and placed the straps over her wrists, the exact same way he'd done for me the other day. Grinning Brandon was at the edge of the stage.

Dez spoke up, so the crowd could hear. "It takes real bravery to stand motionless while knives are being flung at you. Which is why I help out with a little light bondage. But Kristy assures me she's ready and not at all afraid."

Good for her. If that was true, she needed to be more suspicious of charming boys. So did I. The penny Dez had pressed into my palm earlier was tucked away in my pocket. Which made me feel increasingly dumb. Though maybe it was an okay kind of dumb to be?

I could deny it all I wanted, but I liked Dez's attention. The assistants back in Vegas would have had lots of advice to give me backstage. *Moira*, they'd say, *don't fall for his lines. They're just lines.*

In this imaginary conversation, I replied, *But what if they aren't?*

Dez swept a gaze out at the audience and . . . caught me watching. Maybe. A slight frown flitted over his face. Again, maybe. He was back in stage mode too quickly to be sure.

He lazily juggled a trio of knives, adding a fourth. They flashed like the sharp threats they were as the lights caught them at the highest part of the arc.

Then he began to throw.

The jaw-dropping effect was as strong from the audience point of view as from the target board. Though not as heart-pounding.

Kristy, the audience girl, flinched only once, and Dez clucked at her not to move. I knew I shouldn't be standing here. I should leave. I fully expected him to make a heart shape around her, like he had around me. The thing he'd *claimed* I inspired.

It would only underline the fact that I wasn't anything special to him. But a perverse need to see whether I was right made me stay rooted where I was.

And, yes, when she stepped away from the board, he had done just that. The knives formed a pretty yet sinister heart shape. He took her hand, and she bowed, blushing.

I bolted for the space in front of the next tent, my cheeks red too. This was another excellent reminder that I wasn't here for distractions like Dez. I was here to work. Dumb was dumb.

The Cirque's performance would start soon enough, the midway wrapping up. Thurston didn't want us in direct competition. The crowd would be ushered out from a side exit at the end of the show, so that they didn't end up on the dark and deserted midway.

People were beginning to flock toward the tent, tickets in hand. I held the straitjacket in front of me, making it clear I was about to do something with it, and marched to the very entrance of the circus tent.

When I got there, I took a deep breath, and then turned to face a not-small audience who'd gathered around.

"We think of Harry Houdini when we talk of the art of escape," I said.

I dropped the straitjacket and removed my coat—taking the handcuffs out and handing them to a little girl in a *Frozen* T-shirt at the front of the pack. "Can you hang on to these for me?" I asked her.

She nodded solemnly and took them.

"But many women have also completed escapes just as great as Houdini's," I said, projecting my voice. "From a woman named Minerva in the 1900s, who Houdini had shut down because she was competition, to Dorothy Dietrich, one of the greatest escape artists of all time, still alive today. And what's a favorite to escape from? The straitjacket." I picked it up so they could see it. "You can see why. The sleeves are sewn shut at the ends to prevent use of the hands, and are then pulled tight across the front of the chest and fastened in the back. Additional straps at the back and through the legs make it impossible even for someone with adrenaline surging through their body, increasing their strength tenfold, to get free. The inescapability of a straitjacket is the whole point."

I held out my hands to the little girl and waved her forward. A face-painter had left an elephant on her cheek, the only place you'd find one of those noble giants at the Cirque. "Do the handcuffs feel real?" I asked her. "Are they strong?"

She nodded, blue eyes giant. Her willowy mother had one hand on her shoulder but didn't protest.

"And would you take a look at this straitjacket and confirm that it feels real too? If it's okay with your mom."

The little girl eagerly stepped forward, and the woman removed her hand to let her.

As if I'd assigned her the world's most important task, she did as I asked. She pulled at the canvas with her small hands, tested the straps. She still held my cuffs, the small key protruding from the lock.

Randomly, I found myself thinking again of the penny Dez had given me, still in my pants pocket. *I was a fool for keeping it in the first place. I should give it to the little girl. Get rid of it.*

I didn't.

"Are you satisfied there's no trick to this garment?" I asked her.

"Yes," she said, her voice as small as she was but steady and confident.

"Now," I said, and swallowed for effect, faking nervousness about what was to come. "I'll need two volunteers to help me get into the straitjacket."

The little girl tugged at her mother's sleeve, and the woman stepped forward. A frat-type boy in cargo shorts was the other volunteer. They picked up the straitjacket. "Just pull it onto my arms and into place," I instructed.

Who knew what might happen with me trapped inside the strait-jacket?

But my magic had been MIA all day, so it was a chance I decided to take. I raised my arms to fit into the long sleeves. The angle was important; I kept my shoulders wide, pulling as much air as I covertly could into my lungs. A small amount of wiggle room could make all the difference in an escape, no matter what the restraint.

There was an awkward moment as they negotiated holding on to each side, and then the rough canvas slipped across my skin. The woman stepped in front of me, blocking my view of the crowd until they'd pulled the jacket all the way on.

"Great job," I said. "Now I need you to tighten all the straps. Don't make it easy for me to do this—really make them tight."

I subtly refilled my lungs as soon as I was done talking, before they started their new assignment.

"I don't see how it could be too easy, but okay," the frat boy said. He got a little too much enjoyment out of vigorously testing each one to make sure it was tight enough, yanking hard. I paid careful attention to the position of my elbows as they secured the arm straps, faking resistance a fraction earlier than it would've naturally occurred.

Once they were finished, I released my breath.

"You're both satisfied there's no way for me to get out of this without practicing the art of escape?" I asked.

The woman and the guy both nodded, and so did most of the crowd. I had them invested.

One of the things that makes a straitjacket escape in plain view so effective is the crowd's certainty it's not a trick. And it's not, not really. It's a true escape.

The people in the audience invest because they can't imagine any possible way they'd get out of the restraints the escape artist is in. They expect the person to get free but have no idea how it will be accomplished. That's what makes it magic, and not a simple physical feat.

"Does someone mind starting a stopwatch on their phone?" I asked.

The willowy lady held hers up. "Ready?" she asked.

"Go," I told her.

I began to work. Sweat streaked down my face. The straitjacket was like a pressure cooker in the humidity.

This wasn't an escape for the weak.

The crowd around me had hushed entirely, and I strained to keep my focus. Any escape could be flubbed if you allowed yourself to be distracted. Any escape involving real restraints—like the ones I was currently in, fraction of wiggle room or not—could cause serious injury without the right level of care.

A bright flash in the crowd caught my eye, and I realized the news crew had migrated down here to film me.

I swallowed back an admonition for them to stop. The odds Dad would see some local affiliate's coverage were slim. And I could take pleasure in bumping any footage of Dez. Assuming I managed to.

Assuming I nailed this escape.

I wiggled my upper arm, constrained to the front of my body, using that slight amount of play I'd arranged to have. I pressed my elbow up with sheer will, and a little more, and a little more, grinding it inch by inch toward my head, the second arm following because it had no choice, with the hand of the arm I was moving beneath it.

There were uncomfortable groans and noises of worry as I began to twist and writhe and work to get free.

I pushed up and slipped my head under my arms, bringing them both above my head and then around to my front. A familiar blaze of pain flared. Contrary to popular belief, dislocating a shoulder isn't necessary for this escape, but that doesn't mean it feels like a nice day in the sunshine.

The crowd clapped.

Scanning them, I let the discomfort pass. The hardest part was over. Now it was down to undoing the buckles and straps. Still complicated, but the home stretch.

Until I glanced into the crowd and recognized a few of the faces looking on. Thurston and Raleigh, side by side. Thurston was already in his ringmaster tux and tails while Raleigh was in civilian clothes, done performing. They observed with interest.

Then there was Dez, just to the right behind Thurston. Dez looked like he might rush forward.

Like he cared if I was in trouble.

I closed my eyes and ignored his presence.

Or tried to.

That heat flared within me. Not the bright hot pain I was used to at certain moments during an escape like this. It was my magic.

No, no, no. Don't ruin this for me. Thurston's watching. Everyone is watching.

I would not be humiliated in front of Dez—not again—and not after he'd made that stupid heart around someone else while I looked on. I'd have to get out of this quicker.

I wriggled as hard as I could, forcing one hand down to undo the bottom strap that looped around my legs. When my fingers slid flat, open-palmed, over my pants pocket, I detected the shape of the coin within it. Dez's penny, not one of my prop coins.

Seconds from panic, my hands on fire, I sucked in another breath and fumbled the bottom buckle free.

"Is he okay?"

"Call a doctor!"

There were gasps in the crowd, and the heat coursed through me so much I was almost afraid to look. But they weren't talking about me. Raleigh and Thurston were crouching over Dez's prone body.

Dez had his hands over his chest, and he was shaking. Other people in the crowd moved, and it blocked me from being able to see him.

But my hands had greater play now, and it was about forcing them around with the intent and strength to undo the buckles on the back. The straitjacket loosened finally as I did so. *I can do this.* Escape the danger of myself. Find out what was happening to Dez.

I prayed.

The last buckle resisted for a second, my hand heating it. I forced it loose, and then whipped the straitjacket off, tossing it aside. The roaring in my ears became the roaring of the crowd. The fire of my pounding heart was like the fire in my hands.

But then that receded, and I was . . . back to myself again. I didn't feel that distance, that sense of careening out of control toward something I didn't want to happen, of flame flaring deep inside and devouring me whole. I could think and act without panic, and though I wanted to collapse in exhaustion, I didn't.

The surge of magic seemed to have passed. I fought through the crowd, a few people applauding despite the fact that someone was obviously down among those gathered. When I reached Raleigh and Thurston, Dez was sitting up, waving them away. He looked scared, his face pale and covered in a light sheen of sweat.

"What happened?" I asked.

"We need to get you to a medic," Thurston said to Dez.

"I'll be all right," Dez choked out. "Moira here almost gave me a heart attack."

Had I? I started to shake my head, and he added, "With her beauty."

He gave a smile that was hardly convincing, but if he could say something like that, maybe he would be okay. The petite drill sergeant who seemed to run things around here showed up then and pushed us aside. "The doctor's waiting," she said.

Dez didn't protest as she assisted him up and led him away.

"Good job, Miss Miracle," Thurston said. "Nan was right about you." But he cast a worried glance after Dez and the woman.

"Nice work, Pixie," Raleigh said. "Next time you'll get your applause."

The crowd dispersed into the tent, because showtime had arrived. Thurston and Raleigh left too. I checked my pocket and took out the coin to see if I'd transformed Dez's penny like I suspected I had.

Yes, it was different.

But not in any way I could have expected.

The misshapen copper now held the shape of an anatomically correct heart. No longer a smooth circle, it had rounded metallic muscles, and veins and arteries poking out.

What had hurt Dez was no mystery. Not to me. It was my out-of-control magic.

I sank to the ground, not caring if anyone saw. Dez could have been seriously injured—maybe even killed—and it would have been a complete accident.

My palm curled gently around the metal heart.

eight

I flipped onto my other side again in the darkened bedroom. With every move, the air mattress rustled beneath me.

No way I was getting any sleep tonight. Instead, I'd spent the last however-long tossing and turning, thinking about my magic. More than that, thinking about Dez. Word after the last show had been that the doctors hadn't found anything wrong with him, but I hadn't seen him again yet. My phone was beside the mattress, and I reached over and swiped to see what time it was. If it was after two, I'd stay put.

Only midnight.

I eased out of bed, grabbing my jeans and shoes from the floor. But I wasn't quiet enough, because Dita sleepily said, "Moira?"

"Can't sleep. I'm going to take a walk."

There was enough light through the bedroom curtain from a security pole outside to let me see her shift onto her elbow. "You need company?"

"No, you stay here. I'll be quiet when I come back in." I paused. "Where am I likely to find anyone who's up?"

"There's usually poker or a fire pit at the edge of camp. Dad plays sometimes. But it'll be mostly crew."

Something told me that any hope I had of locating Dez was there. He didn't seem the type to go to bed early *or* make a fussy distinction between performer and crew. I pulled the jeans on and tucked in the oversized T-shirt I'd been attempting to sleep in. At the last second, I went back to grab my jacket, in case it was chilly out.

The night was cooler than the day had been but still sticky with humidity. I kept the jacket on anyway, like it was armor.

I'd hurt Dez—without even the slightest intention. I'd been completely out of control again.

I crossed the moonlit grounds, winding between RVs and campers, toward what I thought was the camp's back edge.

So far, my magic gave me no warning. The first time had been during my audition, so while performing, and Nan Maroni had said it was woken up by something. The second time had been when I touched her supposedly magic tarot cards, when she'd been explaining to me how magic was real. The third, obviously, when I caused Dez to fall to the ground, creating a heart I suspected might be an exact replica of his—I had no idea how that was possible, but right now *anything* seemed possible—out of the penny he'd given me. So while performing again.

Not a good sign that two out of three had been while doing my preferred kind of magic.

What was I capable of now? Anything except making the magic come when called. And learning how to control it, like Nan said I had to for safety.

Passing into a shabbier part of camp, I detected voices in the distance, and some laughter. I followed the noise and came to a portable fire pit, just as Dita had predicted. A scattering of people stood drinking from cans or bottles on one side, and on the other a small folding card table had been set up. Several guys sat around it on flipped-over waste cans.

Dez was one of them.

Breathing. Alive. Appearing to be well.

I approached the table. Brandon was the only other person I recognized. A man with a short devilish beard was shuffling, in a dark suit jacket that struck me as overly formal. Particularly given that one of the other players wore a wifebeater with nothing underneath. Dez's attention was glued to the shuffler.

I needed to hear from Dez that he was okay. And . . . to know what he'd felt. I walked around the table and crouched beside him. "Can we talk?"

He did a double take in surprise. "Not a good time," he said, low.

A spike of irritation shot through me, but I had no right to that.

The man with the beard said, "Desmond, give her your seat. I'll deal her in."

"Um." I hesitated. "I'm not staying."

"Have a seat," the man said.

"She can take mine," Brandon said, hopping up from his perch on Dez's other side.

Dez shrugged at the man, but his voice was tight when he spoke again. "Do you know the rules?" he asked me.

Please, I wanted to say. *I'm from Vegas.*

The man said, "She can pick it up. I said I'd deal her in."

Dez's shoulders set, but he said nothing. No quip. That was a first.

I went to Brandon's overturned can. "I'm a quick study." I figured a single hand of poker couldn't take that long.

The man in the suit coat began to deal us out hands for five-card stud. A basic variation of poker at best. The only problem was, he was using a mechanic's grip on the cards, holding them just so, his finger curled around the side. Also a basic variation—a cheat.

And an easy one to spot for anyone who knew cards like I did.

"You have a lot of practice dealing?" I asked.

The man smiled at me, teeth glinting, and didn't answer.

Dez couldn't get too close, so he leaned over a little. "Just play. What are you doing here?"

"I wanted to see how you were."

"Cute girl," the man said. "But remember, Desmond, you're here for a job."

There was something about him that made my skin want to peel off and crawl far, far away, and the cheating wasn't even it.

"Oh, I won't forget, Rex," Dez said. But with no hint of his usual grinning good humor.

The other players picked up their cards, so I did too. He'd dealt me two pairs. A glance around the table told me no one else was very happy with their cards, though of course they all tried to hide it. But part of a magician's job is to read people. A carefully neutral expression can tell you as much as a grin or a grimace, in the right circumstances.

All I wanted to do was talk to Dez, but now this Rex guy was making me angry. Somehow I could sense that I had the only competitive hand. He was trying to lure me into betting big, at which point he'd let me win, lure me in for another hand, then take my money. I probably read "rich girl" to him, just as he read "weird creep" to me.

Not so fast, weird creep.

I watched him as the others began to throw their money into the kitty. No way I was going along with this, and I just happened to have a regulation deck in my pocket. I always did. It wasn't hard at all to quickly palm one each from the pairs and replace them, no one the wiser.

The man leaned forward slightly when the betting came around to me.

"What'll it be, girl?" he asked.

"I got nothing," I said. "I fold, I guess."

And I tossed my cards on the table, faceup—against the rules, but I wanted him to wonder where his scheme went wrong. No pairs in sight.

"Funny," he said. He alone had a chair with a back, I realized, when he leaned into it. He rested his hand on the table, the deck still in it.

"I thought you'd put in something good. I've heard of some monster gambles at the circus. I was just telling these boys earlier . . . I know stories about things won and lost that would make you curl your toenails or claw out your eyes. Things that a man would kill for."

Holy shit.

"Huh," was all I managed.

"You're not supposed to show your cards," Dez said. "Not until the end of the game." He made a scoffing noise. "Sorry she ruined this hand, guys. I better walk her home."

He didn't move, though, despite my jumping to my feet, more than ready to go. The man inclined his chin. "Probably best. But come on back, Desmond. Throw your hands back in, boys, and I'll redeal. Night, princess."

I resisted the urge to make a face, mostly due to the way he made every hair on my arms stand up with that eye-clawing, man-killing remark. Brandon and Dez could be called boys, but the others in the game were grown men. I wondered why they didn't protest being called otherwise.

Dez got up quickly and took my hand. He practically pulled me away from the game and away into the night.

"Who is that guy?" I asked. "Does he work here?"

Dez stopped and whirled to face me. "No . . . He's visiting. A family friend," he said. The RVs were a maze in front of us. We hadn't quite reached them yet, and we were far enough from the fire pit for privacy. "Do you know how stupid it was for you to try to cheat him?"

"I wasn't trying to cheat. He was."

"Moira," he said, reaching for my hand again. I let him take it, though I didn't understand why.

"I don't want to talk about that," I said. "How are you? What happened before? In front of the tent?"

"Oh, that. Nothing. Doctor called it an 'unexplained cardiac event.' I signed something and refused the rest of their tests. I feel fine."

I wished I had a better view of his face. "What did it feel like?"

"This is going to sound wussy," he said.

"There are worse things."

"Like somebody set my heart on fire," he said. His thumb stroked across my hand. "Maybe it was you."

A strangled noise escaped me, and he went on. "It hurt a lot. But I'm fine now. Over as quick as it started."

He sounded certain, but . . . "You're sure? Maybe they should run the tests."

"Fate has its plans, and it doesn't consult us. Why bother?" he said. Then he tilted his head to one side. "And here I thought you were mad at me." He was getting closer. "I thought you wanted to talk about what happened before that."

He released my hand and put his over his heart, something I was beginning to recognize as a go-to move. It reminded me about the now-heart-shaped coin, and that he was probably right about not needing any tests. The coin was still in my pocket.

My heart beat harder. "I don't know what you mean."

"You wound me, my lady."

"We're doing Shakespeare now? You're only mad north-north-west?"

"You're the one who's mad." He said it like simple fact, indisputable.

"Why would I be mad?" Was that why I'd transformed the penny? Why my magic had reached out for Dez?

That surge of magic seemed to come when I was upset, and this boy could definitely upset me. I knew I should get out of there. Get as far from him as possible and stay that way. It couldn't happen again.

"You're mad because I lied to you," he said. "I don't blame you. But I wanted to explain. I was coming to find you when . . . unexplained cardiac event."

Okay, so it stung that he'd figured out seeing him make the other heart had hurt me. Stung like a cut from a sharp little knife. He had no right to figure that out. We didn't even know each other.

You could've killed him.

But my regret didn't speak. My pride did. "You think I didn't know it was a lie? That you don't make a pretty knife-heart for every girl you meet?"

The girls at the theater had warned me more than once about the danger of charm. Beware the smooth-tongued boys, the ones flattery comes easy to. There's nothing wrong with *wanting* to believe it, even with believing what they say is true—you are beautiful, you are smart, you are unique—but it's foolish to assume it *means* anything. *Sweet nothings* was an apt phrase. Taken seriously, sweet nothings became bitter regrets. The girls were certain of it.

Dez sighed. "I wanted it to be true when I told it to you."

"That's not how the truth works. Something either is or it isn't."

"You'd know more about that than me. The truth doesn't come easy to me," he said. "It's not like throwing knives. It isn't part of the world I come from. Lying is always easier there, how you get what you want."

Just like the girls at the theater had said. I was intrigued, despite myself. "That's an awful way to get what you want."

"Probably," he said.

His hand cupped the side of my face and he leaned in for a kiss. And for whatever stupid reason, me and my beating heart kissed him back. His lips moved softly against mine, and blood roared in my ears.

What was I doing?

A warmth spread through me, and I worried it was the beginning of a flare of my magic. I couldn't risk it.

I pushed him away.

"Moira?" he asked, his breathing unsteady.

"I'm glad you're okay," I said.

I fled into the night, fully aware that it was silly to be disappointed that he let me go without a protest. The weird creep had ordered him to come back, after all.

nine

I overslept the next morning, and the time until lunch passed in a haze of distraction.

I knew what I had to do now. I had to find my mother—and fast. She was the only one who could tell me how to control this cursed magic. I also relived that kiss over and again. No matter how much I tried to stop thinking about it.

"You're quiet," Dita said at lunch in the mess tent. "Where'd you go last night?" We sat at the end of the second table, in what was quickly becoming our spot.

"Just walked."

I must've looked shifty, because she said, "Run into anyone?"

"Um."

She nodded to a point over my shoulder. I looked, and my eyes locked with a penny-colored stare. Dez smiled and waved.

I turned back around. "I might have run into Dez."

"You don't say," she said, thick with sarcasm.

"I'm changing the subject," I said. "Is there anyone with a computer I could borrow? I need to fill out a form my phone doesn't like."

It was true. The Nevada vital statistics office was far from mobile-friendly.

"Thurston has one in his office," she said, picking up her tray. "I'll show you."

We got rid of our lunch remains, and she led me through the Florida sunshine right to the door of his giant office trailer. There was an American flag in the window. Dita tapped on the door.

Thurston opened it. "Hey, boss," she said. "Can Moira borrow your computer?"

After a few moments passed, he waved for me to come in. "Of course. Help yourself," he said. "Dita, about yesterday's shows—"

"I'll see you later," she said. "Gotta get changed for the parade, and Mom scheduled a rehearsal first." She didn't look thrilled, and I couldn't tell if it was about the rehearsal or whatever Thurston had been about to say.

I slipped into the door past him. He frowned after Dita.

The interior was luxurious for an RV, accented by faux wood paneling and outfitted to the maximum of deluxe. There was a living room, a full kitchen, and a desk with a flat-screen monitor on it.

I headed to the big desk. Thurston Meyer was the kind of famous that made the cover of *Time*. He'd revolutionized the tech world, and then decided to appoint a new CEO and pour his billions into his enthusiasm for the circus.

"You don't miss tech?" I asked, tapping the computer to life.

"I was good at it," he said. "But I don't think I ever loved it. I love this, though—and I'm probably not nearly as good at it as I was at that. Some of us like a challenge more than what comes easy."

"Tell me about it," I said.

Which reminded me I should e-mail Dad, and I would. But first I Googled "Nevada birth records." I couldn't be sure that was my original place of birth, but Dad had been in the early days of the Menagerie gig back then. He wouldn't have been on the road much. It was likely enough I'd been born there.

"You're not intending to rummage through my desk for priceless artifacts or money or anything, are you?" Thurston asked, from where he lingered near the door.

I was startled enough to look away from the Office of Vital Records website I'd pulled up. "I wasn't planning on it. Do you keep a lot of those around?"

"I'd never leave things like that in here," he said mildly. "Lock the door on your way out."

I read the requirements and then filled out the application to order a copy of my birth certificate. I could hardly believe how simple it might be to find my mom. Put in an application, wait for it to show up in my e-mail, then search for her name online. With a name, you could find anyone, even if they were part of a secret criminal society, right? Could it be this easy?

A girl could hope . . .

And pray that she didn't give anyone else an unexplained cardiac event—including herself—first.

I put in my credit card details, checked the box to pay extra for digital rush delivery within twenty-four to forty-eight hours, and then let the little arrow hover over the Submit Request button.

I closed my eyes and clicked.

Later that night, I made my way to Raleigh's tent. I'd been working nonstop on the midway for almost an hour and needed a break. Plus, I couldn't resist the allure of seeing a magic act, and I knew his last show of the day was taking place now.

And I was a little homesick. This was the closest I could get to normal.

The tent was plain black, but the flaps that formed the entrance were painted to resemble skeletal jaws. Raleigh had grown up in New

Orleans, and he'd decided to enthusiastically embrace the role of voo-doo conjurer as his stage persona. Which made his acts more forgiv-able than the traditional cultural appropriation by magicians. Like the famous Chung Ling Soo, who was actually an American of Scottish ancestry named William Ellsworth Robinson.

I made my way in. Rows of chairs were set up inside, but all of them were occupied, so I stood in the back. Raleigh's stage was flashy and even more familiar than I'd counted on. It was a smaller set of Dad's, one he'd used on the road for a short stint on Broadway. No wonder Raleigh had come to call on him.

On the stage, Raleigh completed a slight bow, handsome in his tails and top hat, in command of this space. "No one enters the dark of the sorcerer's tent unless they want to see the marvels that only darkness can create."

He moved from where he'd been standing to block a cabinet, taller than him, painted with bones that hadn't been there when it belonged to Dad. I recognized the gold on the edges, though, replicated on the sides to further distract the eye.

"Down in New Orleans, where I grew up, and out on the bayou, visiting a grandmother full of stories, darkness and its marvels were all the rage," Raleigh said.

This was half truth, half lie, so far as I knew—he had grown up down there, but my impression was that it had been him and his mom and a rotating series of husband prospects. Raleigh had been dirt poor and dead set on becoming a magician when he'd turned up in Las Vegas.

"And a figure who frequently featured in those stories was Marie Laveau, the most famous voodoo queen of all time. No simple hedge witch." He began to undo the three latches on the cabinet door as he spun a tale of the powerful Laveau, the terror of New Orleans in the 1820s, leading sacred dances in the public square and selling gris-gris and offerings to the spirits in exchange for the tawdry secrets of prominent men. "The most feared and respected woman who ever stepped foot in New Orleans." He flung open the door, finally, and out stepped a facsimile of the queen herself.

His latest assistant's dark skin was accentuated with glittery touches of makeup, and she wore a headdress and a gown. She played the part of voodoo queen well.

"This is Marie here."

The audience laughed, a little.

Raleigh narrowed his gaze on us, still smiling in the audience.

"Oh, but I wasn't joking," he said, lifting her hand to his lips and kissing it. She smiled, permissively, as if it were her queenly due. He released her hand and ranged across the stage. "You see, among the many stories about Marie Laveau was that she remained ageless and beautiful for a hundred and twenty-five years or more. That she was seen even after her death."

While he'd been talking, "Marie" climbed back inside the cabinet, and now Raleigh came back to it and refastened the door. He gave each latch a deft turn, and said, "But in truth, it was only partly Marie who was so beautiful and long-lived and fearsome. She had a daughter."

He opened the cabinet door, and Marie stepped out once more—followed by a second Marie, the spitting image of her.

"Marie the second!"

I knew it wasn't truly another person, but some clever trick of light and smoke and mirrors—maybe even a twist on an old-school magic lantern—that made it appear there were two voodoo queens onstage now. They stood side by side, identical, unmoving. I couldn't help wondering if my mother and I would look alike when I found her, and if our magic really *was* the same.

Raleigh flourished and waved his hands behind the door as if to check for anything else inside. Distracting us. Then he redid the latches as the two women stood still, before opening the cabinet again. "And a granddaughter, also filled with power."

And out stepped a third voodoo queen to join the first two—my guess was that the original Marie had just stepped out of the cabinet, having reentered when Raleigh flourished, and the others were projections or reflections. An impressive illusion. The crowd applauded.

Raleigh silenced us with a look. "But we in this room know that voodoo queens, no matter how beautiful"—the women preened on cue, regally mirroring each other, with motions as identical as they were, which they would be, since only one was real—"no matter how powerful someone might be, they do not live forever. At least, not in their mortal flesh." He opened the cabinet door and gestured, and as he talked, they appeared to reenter it, disappearing inside, one by one.

This was a clever illusion in itself, but he was building to something. "So the story goes, Marie Laveau shared one spirit across three bodies, and when the last finally perished, it did not die, but transformed. And what form did she take? One that would allow her to watch over their city, of course. Her city. Would you like to know what form this transformation took?"

I was leaning forward, unsettled by the word *transformation*.

He spun the cabinet once, so we could get a look at how slender it was. The three women were inside so far as the audience knew, but only the one would really be pressed inside, probably behind a back compartment. Suspecting his methods didn't take away from the wonder of it, though. He'd gotten better since the last time I saw his act.

This time Raleigh flung open the cabinet door, and even I gasped when a span of wings emerged and spread out in the air. A large black bird with a necklace of white feathers on its throat flew toward us. "She transformed into a crow, the messenger between this world and the next," Raleigh said.

The crow swooped overhead with an almost balletic quality in its timing, and then back to Raleigh to perch on his extended forearm.

Raleigh bowed, and the bird stayed put.

The crowd was on its feet. Raleigh basked in the applause, as his due.

I couldn't blame him. *That.* Now *that* was magic. For a second, I let myself envision my daring coffin escape taking place on this small spooky stage, and that the enthusiastic applause was for me.

Not that I coveted Raleigh's success. One of the girls at the theater had told me a long time ago never to confuse jealousy and envy. Jealousy was for the mean-spirited, those who didn't believe they would achieve something, and so didn't want anyone else to have it either. Envy, on the other hand, could be useful, unless overindulged. Envy could make you stop for a moment and consider whether what you envied was something you truly wanted. Being honest about what you truly wanted was the beginning of achieving it.

I waited until Raleigh had taken one last bow, joined by his Marie. The bird hopped off his arm and took up residence at the top of the box. The audience began to file out. I should have gotten back to work, but I made my way over to him.

"Congratulations," I said. "That was a truly great illusion."

He glanced right and left, still glowing with the adrenaline of a good performance. "Don't use the 'i' word in public."

"I hardly qualify," his assistant said, shrugging at us. She rolled the cabinet off the stage.

"What's up, Pixie?" Raleigh said, and I realized we were alone now. Though "Marie" could have been eavesdropping. I waved him to the edge of the small stage.

The crow fluttered up to Raleigh's shoulder. Dad had done a few things with doves, smallish and pale, easily trained. "Where'd you get the crow?"

The bird let out a *croooooak.*

"Oh, Caliban," Raleigh said, eyes flicking affectionately in its direction. "I have a friend who's into wildlife rescue and, um, Caliban was a pet, but he got turned out and she found him—he wasn't really up to hanging out with regular crows, since he's an African pied, and he, uh, he likes me."

"Raleigh, are you embarrassed that you have a pet? Pets are *supposed* to like you."

He didn't answer.

Caliban was just as striking up close as when he was performing, like a small raven with a necklace of white feathers. I wanted to touch him, but Raleigh didn't invite me to.

"Spit it out," Raleigh said. "What do you want?"

I'd planned to ask him one thing, but something else spilled out first.

"If I do well for the next week or two and if I can get this illusion I've been working on perfect—the one I was planning to do for Dad back in Vegas—what are the odds you'd let me open for you? I need some stage time," I said. "If this is my shot, I have to know I can do it."

"Not until your performance is flawless."

Flawless was a hard target. But . . . "Understood."

He held out his arm, and Caliban fluttered down to it. I could tell he was about to leave.

"Wait," I said. "Did Dad ever talk about my mom to you?"

He frowned. "No, never," he said. But he paused.

"What?"

"Why are you asking? Shouldn't you talk about this with him?"

Honesty was the best policy here. "I don't want to hurt him."

He scrubbed his left hand against the back of his neck. "He told me she was the only woman he'd ever loved, and—" He must have seen some glimmer of hope reflected on my face, because he rushed on. "And the only one he'd ever hated."

"Hated?" I blurted it out. His story about her had always been told in affectionate tones. "Why?"

"I don't know," Raleigh said. "Maybe he had every reason, maybe he had none."

Which left me plenty of worst-case scenarios to imagine until I found her.

ten

After the midway went dark, my sleights over for the evening, I lingered to watch the Cirque's last show of the day from the back of the big top in a section marked "Standing Room Only." The show was sold out, something that seemed to have the admin staff already high-fiving each other. Several other midway performers were here too, all flush with the success of our hours of performing.

The finale was nearing when Dez turned up. I was trying to pretend I hadn't been waiting for him. Hoping too. I shouldn't have been doing either.

"Hey," he said. He'd changed into an old black T-shirt gone gray and beat-up jeans, and it was like some sort of curse on me that he managed to look even better than he had earlier.

I gave him a small smile and focused on the performance in progress.

"These two legendary high-wire walkers insist on doing part of their act together these days, and I think we can all bask in our luck that this is the case," Thurston announced. "My favorite father-and-daughter team."

Jules and her father, of course. He'd begun with a still and solemn walk across the wire with no aid, simple but riveting. Then he turned back, breezing across the wire, and now Jules stalked out, idly twirling a parasol. They met at the middle of the wire to thunderous applause. There were a dozen or so girls dressed in Jules-esque red tutus in the tent, all cheering.

"You like this circus stuff?" Dez asked.

"Yeah, I do. It's amazing," I said.

The entire show had been great. The performers were top-caliber, and Thurston's costume and styling department kept everything on the classic side. I approved, in the same way I vaguely disapproved of Dad and most magicians' costuming. Far too many mullets and too much tacky leather; the girls at the theater frequently cackled about starting a makeover service for magicians. No one would ever argue that they didn't need it.

"You're right. It is amazing. Like you."

I ignored the way the words shimmied up my spine and made me want to stretch into them like a cat. There was a slight hint of booze to his scent. He must have had a drink after his last performance.

"Magicians are supposed to be amazing."

Jules and her father took another bow midwire and then, in a comic bit, bumbled around each other—and took another bow to show the bumbling was for effect only. The audience laughed.

"Who taught you how to get out of a straitjacket?"

I managed not to be too offended that he was asking again how I'd learned magic, like it would have been impossible that I'd taught myself. "No one. Everyone. I learned. Straitjackets were hard, but I managed."

Dez nudged me with his shoulder. "You learned by yourself how to get out of a straitjacket."

I shrugged, like it was no big deal, though it had been. "Obviously I had to wait until I was in front of people to do it with the straitjacket really on."

That had been my most nerve-wracking day, not knowing if my prep would pay off or not.

"Did your family friend leave?" I asked.

"Did I say family friend? More of a family curse," Dez said. "But yeah, he's gone. Took all our money with him too."

"Good." Thinking about him made me want to shiver. "Not about the money, but the gone part."

Jules's father walked to the other end of the wire and stepped off onto the platform. Left in the spotlight, Jules twirled and danced across the wire to conclude the act, as wonderful as she had been earlier. And—also a humorous touch—the crewmen brought out a net and put it below when she finished. She closed her parasol, smiled, and jumped off, spinning down into it with a move she must've learned from Remy.

The crowd loved it. They loved that Remy was waiting there to give her a kiss on the cheek too.

The rest of the Garcias ran out, then, as Jules exited, the lights signaling that it was time to shift our attention to them. They gripped ladders that rose to their aerial platforms and swings. The trapeze act would close the show.

This was what I'd really been hanging around for. I wanted to see Dita's performance. The way she'd seemed to dread rehearsal had me curious.

I couldn't help feel a twinge, thinking about how tight these families were. Their situations seemed so simple compared to my own. My missing magic mother and non-abandoning but disapproving father. Then again, all family dynamics probably looked simpler than they were when viewed from afar.

I turned back to watch the Garcias.

Thurston pattered on about the Love Brothers and the Goddesses of Beauty. The older brother, Casanova, a.k.a. Novio, dominated one side. Romeo, a.k.a. Remy, dominated the other. In addition to the two Garcia boys and Aphrodite, a.k.a. Dita, there were two blonde performers, identical twin girls. They launched themselves out into tight spins first, Novio catching each of them on an arm, much to the audience's delight. The act proceeded with more variations on this. I kept waiting for Dita to leave the platform.

And waiting.

There was a smile visible on her face from down here, but when it stayed and stayed, I suspected she was forcing it. Finally, once the blondes had careened—with grace—down into the net below, Dita grabbed the swing.

She looked like she was born to be there, moving with power through the air. She kept building and building her momentum. I could see Remy shouting some encouragement from the platform, but I couldn't hear him. And then she released the swing and she hung there for a second, like she was in slow motion, before she tucked into a ball for her somersaults.

Watching the blondes and Remy do this move had taught me enough to know that she was off on her timing.

"Oh no," I said softly.

"Not good," Dez murmured in agreement.

She managed one rotation before, rather than grabbing her brother's hands, she fell awkwardly into the net. The crowd gasped.

Thurston had been an involved announcer for the entire show, but he said nothing about what had just happened. "And now, what you've all been waiting for, Remy Garcia will attempt the quadruple somersault, one of the most difficult feats in the world." Remy waved and bowed from above, taking the swing and drawing all eyes away from the ground and onto him. "During a live performance last season, Remy became the youngest person to achieve the quad. He's hoping to do one every day this season. And if he does, he'll set a world record that's unlikely to ever be broken. So hold your breath . . . Here he goes!"

The audience might have been as disquieted as I was by Dita's flub, but they moved on fast. Everyone was on their feet, obeying Thurston's command.

Remy swung through the air with an ease that seemed natural-born but must have taken years of practice. The same ease Dita had, but with a greater power behind it. He sliced through the air, his brother prepared to catch him, and when Remy launched out into his somersaults, the crowd started to count, but he was too fast for them. "One, two—"

Wild applause erupted as he completed the fourth and grabbed Novio's hands. It was so fast, like a magic trick in plain sight.

I applauded too. At least until I saw Dita, on the floor beside the net. She looked downcast. Jules had her hand on Dita's arm.

"Can I see your phone?" Dez asked.

I passed it to him. "What for?"

He held up a finger for me to wait and pressed in a number, then held the phone to his ear. "Brandon? Save this as Moira's number."

He listened for a second, then, "You're disgusting."

He grinned at me and passed it back. "Don't text me anything you don't want Brandon to see. We share a phone."

I practically sputtered. "Why would I . . . What . . . You're assuming . . ."

"Yes," he said, leaning closer. I thought he might kiss me again, and I knew how I felt about the possibility when I didn't move a muscle to shy away. Even though I should have.

But all he did was say, "It was a good kiss. See you later."

Still vibrating from my encounter with Dez, I wound my way around the big top to the backstage tent the Cirque performers used. I paused only to buy one of the few remaining sticks of cotton candy. Sweet, pink, and sticky. I wasn't a doctor, but I suspected it might have curative powers.

The space was a jumble of dressing and makeup areas, trunks and costume racks, and a long table with assorted snacks. It was packed with people—some still in costume, some already in street clothes—congratulating each other, a big clump gathered around Remy. I spotted Dita at the edge of that crowd, next to a frowning woman who I decided must be their mother. The woman watched as Dita used a white towelette to wipe away the last traces of the smoky shadow and heavy eyeliner that went with her trapeze costume.

I'd messed up at my audition, but it hadn't been in front of a real crowd of paying customers. Dita must be mortified. So I walked over to her, waited for her to toss the makeup wipe, and extended my genuine sympathy offering. "Cotton candy?"

Dita blinked for a second, then looked at me like I was her savior. "Please."

She was about to step away to join me when her mother laid a hand on her arm to stop her. "This is your roommate?" she asked.

"Hi," I said, offering my non-cotton-candy hand to her. "I'm Moira. I'm so grateful to Dita and Remy for taking me in."

She shook my hand without any of the usual nicety you'd expect from a greeting. "Nancy was involved, I heard." She squinted at me, then shrugged, releasing my hand. "She's been good for my kids. Especially my older boy."

"Sure," I said. I had no clue what she was talking about.

"Let's go," Dita said.

"I'll walk you," the older brother in question, Novio, said, appearing beside us. And though Dita had a pinched expression, she allowed it.

Dita took an enormous bite of cotton candy. We had extricated ourselves from the postshow pack, or so I thought. But when I turned to introduce myself to Novio, I saw that Jules and Remy were trailing us too.

"Back off, you guys," Jules said. "Guessing she doesn't want to talk about it."

"We just want to make sure she's okay," Remy said.

"I'm right here, so you can talk *to* me not *about* me," Dita countered.

"I'm still sorry every day," Novio said quietly.

"I know," Dita said, around another bite of cotton candy. She swallowed and faced him. "It's not that. You're forgiven . . . I know it wasn't . . . you. It was Granddad."

I felt more and more like a trespasser in their private business with each step.

"Then what is it?" Jules asked.

Dita hesitated, and finally her eyes met mine before she turned back to Jules and her brothers. "I don't want to talk about it. I'll get over it. I promise." And then to me, "Thanks for the rescue attempt, even if it didn't work. My family is inescapable."

There was no real ire in it. She sounded, frankly, like she was okay with that.

"I hear you," I said. "But at least they're obnoxious about it."

Dita laughed, and though Remy said, "Hey!" in protest, I suspect he'd have hugged me for lightening the mood.

We stopped when we reached the Airstream. Dita took out her key, but then stepped back.

"It's open," she said. "Did one of you—"

"I definitely locked it," I said. Dita had given me an extra key that Thurston's admin had made earlier that morning.

"I haven't been back here since before our first show today," Remy said.

Novio shouldered in front of all of us. "Let me check it out."

He flipped on the light, and we followed him into the little cabin. It looked okay at a glance—or would've, if you'd never been here before. But someone had been here. Everything had been moved, and then *almost* put back where it was in the first place, or placed neatly somewhere it shouldn't have been.

Coffee mugs and dishes were the most apparent evidence; the cupboards were empty, the countertops full. The couch's throw pillows were all stacked to one side. But nothing broken, no destruction.

"Not again," Jules said.

"I don't know anything about this," Novio put in.

"We know," Jules and Dita said practically at the same time.

Their ancient history loomed like an elephant in the room for me.

"Can you tell if anything's missing?" Novio asked.

"Not so far," Remy said, and Dita nodded agreement.

We went through each small room. All of them had been hit. Or, rather, mussed. When we got to mine and Dita's, we found that the clothes in the closet were pushed to either side, a gap between them. And my suitcase was open.

I bent to check for the cash I'd tucked away in the bottom. No burglar would leave that, would they? I pulled it out and quickly counted. Every bill of the thousand was still there.

I looked up, the others crowded around. "They didn't take any of my money. But they obviously went through my suitcase."

Some of its contents sat neatly beside it on my mattress. The pillowcase had been removed from Dita's pillow. Glancing at the closet, I saw another distressing, methodical detail: the pocket of a pair of her pants had been turned inside out.

None of them said anything. "Are you going to tell me what this is about?" I prompted. "What did 'not again' mean?"

Novio left the room to go somewhere. Back up front, I guessed. Jules and Dita and Remy exchanged a glance, and Remy went after him. Then Dita spoke. "The coin, the one you said Nan mentioned to you . . . it was our grandfather's. Mine and Remy's and Novio's. He believed it was our family's good luck charm."

Right. Nan had said as much.

Jules's frown deepened. "Why would Nan mention that to *you*?"

"Just in passing," I said. "Keep explaining."

"Well," Dita said, pitching her voice low, "Novio was looking for it last year. He thought, uh, Nan Maroni had it." Her voice had gotten shaky, but she stopped and collected herself. "There were break-ins, worse things . . . But he was only doing what Granddad convinced him to do."

"Is this coin real? Where is it?"

"It's gone," Jules said quickly.

I didn't believe her, but it seemed I'd been caught in cross fire that wasn't aimed at me. Still, Nan had thought I might be here for the coin, so it was a good thing I had an alibi for tonight.

Remy returned. "They went through all of our rooms, and the bathroom too. The medicine cabinet stuff is sitting on the sink. Neatly."

"We better go report this to Thurston," Jules said. "He's always in his office after our last show."

We headed out, Dita carefully locking the door behind us. As we got closer to Thurston's trailer, it became clear that every light inside was on, the door wide open.

"That's weird," Remy said, which crossed out the possibility that this was normal.

"Nan?" Jules said.

The elegant older lady, the only person who knew my secret, was coming toward us from the opposite direction. Jules's parents were with her. They weren't headed for us, I realized, but were also on the way to Thurston's trailer.

"What are you guys doing here?" Jules asked.

Nan nodded to me, a brief acknowledgment. Jules's tall blonde mother answered in a vaguely Russian-infused accent: "Someone has been in our house while we were out tonight."

"Theirs too," Jules said.

Voices reached us from inside the trailer where we'd come to report the odd crime, now turning into an odd crime spree. Even though nothing noticeable had been taken, the would-be thievery made the night feel serious. In silent agreement, we crossed to the open door and entered. The Garcia mother, the one who'd considered me in the backstage tent, was inside with a man I assumed to be her husband.

"What are you doing here?" Dita asked them as we all piled in.

Books and posters lay on the coffee table in the living room, piled high but neatly stacked. The kitchen's cabinet doors hung open. The larger-than-normal interior of the trailer was not like it had been earlier, to say the least.

Thurston stood in the center of it all, and his eyes widened in surprise at our arrival. "You were hit too?" he asked, indicating the tidy disarray.

Dita nodded.

The Garcia mother spoke up. "The same happened in our home."

Jules's mom chimed in, "And ours too."

I moved around Thurston toward the desk to help make room for everyone in what had become close quarters. But then I spotted a piece of paper on the corner of the desk that wasn't stacked neatly like the others there.

A sheet of notebook paper, torn out, a ragged edge showing. It was folded in half. "What's this?"

"No clue," Thurston said.

I moved closer and picked it up. The message was brief. I shivered again, with a sense of deep wrongness.

"It's a note," I said.

"What does it say?" Jules's mom asked.

It said:

I want the coin too.

But before I could read it aloud, a crow with white plumage on its breast flew in through the door.

eleven

Caliban's dramatic entrance resulted in shrieks—from those who apparently either didn't recognize him or hadn't heard there was a pet bird in residence with the show's magician.

"It's okay!" I called out before they could swat him or something worse.

His eerie appearance made me expect him to grab the mysterious note and wing away into the evening. Instead, Caliban flew straight to Dita and grabbed a piece of genie-pink cotton candy stuck to the shirt she'd pulled on over her costume.

Raleigh bounded through the door before anyone figured out what to do about the bird other than look panicky and raise their hands to ward it off.

"Caliban," Raleigh said, stern. He held out his arm. The bird flapped over and settled there.

Color came up in Raleigh's cheeks as all of us in the room gaped at him. "Sorry about that, everyone. He flew away from me."

We were all quiet for a moment, and then Dita burst out laughing.

There was a stunned moment of silence before Thurston joined her. When everyone—myself included—looked at them like they were crazy, Thurston raised a hand and said, "What a night."

"This is serious," the Garcia mother said. "Someone has targeted all of us. Why?"

Dita and Thurston managed to pull in their laughter.

I still had the piece of paper with the ominous message in my hand. "The note says 'I want the coin too,'" I said, and held it up so they could see.

Any remnant of laughter vanished. Novio blanched and lowered onto the couch. His mother put her hand on his arm, sitting down beside him.

Nan had been quiet so far, but she spoke up now. "You went to that note quickly."

I bristled. "Whoever left this went through my things too. I've been working all night, and I went to the show after."

Thurston looked between us. "Why would you accuse Moira? You vouched for her."

Nan was taken aback. She'd clearly spoken before she thought it through. "Magicians are the most superstitious people I've ever met. I had to be sure she wasn't interested in it. Besides, Jules, didn't you tell me Roman's coin is gone?"

Remy and Jules avoided looking at each other, and I was probably the only one who noticed it. Jules's parents watched her reaction.

"We got rid of it," she said.

"Together," Remy said. "It's gone."

Thurston came over to me and took the note, peering down at it.

"They wanted you to know," I said.

"What?" Thurston's forehead creased.

"That's why they went through all your trailers, left the note. They couldn't have expected to find it, not really—a coin's so small. How could they unless they knew right where to look or got lucky? No, it's misdirection. They wanted you to know—whoever they are—that they don't believe it's gone. Probably hoping you'll try to move it or give something away in your reaction."

Remy reached down for Jules's hand, but neither of them spoke.

"You seem to have an awful lot of theories," Nan said.

"She might be right. I've heard some things," Raleigh said, bird still on his arm.

"You have," Thurston said, flat. "And were your things disturbed?"

"No," Raleigh said.

"Then what have you heard?" Thurston prompted.

Raleigh answered without hesitation. "There are rumors, whispers among some of the crew, about Roman Garcia. Rumors that he had a magic coin, very old. A coin that could make the bearer successful beyond their wildest dreams, give them the best luck in the world. That it was lost, but now might be found, as the saying goes. Do you think someone believes the stories? Crazy, right?"

"Crazy," Nan said. "There *was* an old coin. But these two say they got rid of it."

She said it with a hint of challenge to Raleigh, like she thought he might dispute that.

"I don't believe in magic, ma'am," he said instead.

I looked at the floor.

"Thank you, Raleigh," Thurston said, the CEO part of him visible in how effectively it closed the door in Raleigh's face. "Remember, discretion is the better part of employment."

Raleigh didn't protest. In fact, he retreated so quickly it was hard not to read his reaction as relief at the chance to escape. "Apologies for Caliban again," he said to Dita as he left. "Evening."

In his absence, the trailer felt airless and hot, thick with tension.

"Rumors and whispers," Thurston said. "Misdirecting us. I don't like it. Even if magic is real, it's not the problem. The hunger to possess it is."

Nan took a step closer to him. "If it's real? Has your mind changed? I thought you believed all that talk was nonsense."

Thurston waved a hand dismissively. "Nothing's changed. Raleigh is right. But we also know that rumors of this coin have created problems before."

"Tragedies, you mean," said Jules's mom, and her dad rubbed a hand across her back in comfort. "Lives taken."

Thurston looked chastened at being called on his softer wording. I didn't know the owner well enough to tell for sure when he was lying, but I wasn't convinced his clarification disavowing magic had been entirely true.

Which made me worried about standing here in the room with him.

Nan's caution in our private meeting returned, about how my magic could make other people dangerous to me. Now there were rumors and whispers and people who wanted some magic coin. It was a threat, plain and simple. To everyone in this room, but especially to me. Both because Nan wasn't convinced I was as innocent as I was, and because whoever was behind this, what they really wanted was magic.

While the smart money was on staying quiet, I spoke up anyway. "I don't understand, though. The note says they want the coin *too*. Does that imply that you want it, Mr. Meyer? Or someone else here?"

"It doesn't matter," Remy interrupted, with a note of finality. "No one is going to get it. If that's what they're looking for, let them look."

Jules had her arm tucked through his. "I don't like it either. But he's right, they won't find anything."

"Because there's nothing to find?" Thurston asked.

The Garcias' mother spoke now. "An old man's folly is all there would be to find. We have moved past this now. Let us not speak of it anymore."

Novio looked like he might throw up.

Thurston took in the room, everyone in various states of worry, and gave a thoughtful nod. "I'll have extra security added, particularly to keep an eye on everyone's trailers during performances. I won't have the rumor mill disrupting our season and putting anyone at risk. Not this year."

"Thank you," Jules said.

The next words were Dita's, soft. "Yes. I think I'm ready to call it a night."

"I'll come with you," I said, more than ready to flee.

No one was very talkative the rest of the night or the next morning. The Flying Garcias had yet another rehearsal after breakfast, which Dita had just trudged off to, looking murderous and martyr-like at the same time.

The midway would be on again in just a few hours, then the first Cirque show, then dinner, then more midway, then more Cirque. Then on to our next stop. These days would fly. Suddenly twelve weeks seemed like no time at all.

I pulled the sliding door to our bedroom closed and turned the lock. Then I sat with the heart-shaped penny in my hand. The metal felt slightly warm to the touch, and my own heart beat harder.

I held on tight, and thought, *Change back.*

I thought my palm was getting warmer, but I couldn't be sure.

I focused all my attention on the piece of metal, willing it. *Change back.*

Heat roared through me, and black stars pricked at the edges of my vision.

Somehow, I called on strength enough to unfold my fingers and fling the coin away.

And then there was nothing but darkness, and I fell back and back into its embrace.

I woke with Dita's hand shaking my shoulder. "Moira? Why are you sleeping half on your suitcase?"

I was alive. I blinked at her.

My mouth was dry. I forced out a response anyway. "Just not used to circus hours, I guess. How, um, embarrassing."

Dita held up the heart-shaped coin. "This was by the door. Is it yours?"

"Uh, yeah."

"What is it? It's like a gross little heart."

"A . . . charm."

She extended it to me. I trembled at the thought of touching it again, but I didn't have a choice. She'd want to know why, and I was already being weird, passed out in the middle of our teeny room.

I took it, and nothing happened. There was a slight heat to it as I pushed it into my pocket.

This entire experiment gave me a new data point. It reminded me of the first time I tried to hold my breath longer than I was capable of it. That had told me to train harder. This told me never try to change anything back. Yay me for figuring out my first limit?

"What time is it?" I asked.

"Time for work for you," she said. "If you're up to it."

"I am." I forced myself to my feet, looking down at my phone. She was right. I was almost late, in fact.

"I'm going to dinner—you're sure you don't need anything?"

I shook my head, and she grabbed her wallet and headed back out.

I started to gather my sleight kit. My phone made the little whistle that indicated a new e-mail message. I knew I should get going, but I clicked the in-box. The words *Birth Certificate* appeared.

Not a moment too soon.

My heart *beat-beat-beat* as I clicked to open the message and then again as I pulled up the PDF copy of my birth certificate. It loaded huge, so I had to adjust the size and pull the image around to get a good look at it.

There was Dad's name listed above *Father*, as it should have been (and a comfort to see, not that I'd considered the possibility that it wouldn't be him). Then I zoomed in on the mother's name.

Regina A. Ghost.

"That can't be a real name," I murmured. *Thanks for making it clear you didn't intend to be found, Mom.*

I shut the PDF and almost closed out my e-mail without seeing the new message.

The sender echoed that same weird name: *Regina A. Ghost.*

Holding my breath instinctively, I clicked to open it.

> My daughter,
> You are not where your father believes you to be
> or I would have had this message delivered in
> person. I have kept watch over you, in case this
> day came, but you managed to leave without your
> father knowing where you were headed. I will say
> it plainly so you can make no mistake: You cannot
> keep looking for me. Stop trying to find me. You
> only risk endangering yourself. I chose that name
> then because it is how you should treat me—like a
> ghost. Or you'll become one too.

My first communication from my mother, the loveliest assistant, part of the reason I'd ever wanted to do magic in the first place. And it was a brush-off.

Her message stung.

But I had made my decision on what to do. I wasn't the type to follow orders that came without logic. Witness my being here.

I tapped back a reply to Regina A. Ghost:

> Dear Ghost Mom Regina,
> I'm sorry you don't want to be found, because
> I really need to find you. Why would you keep
> watching if you didn't want to connect in some

way? Anyway, I'm already in danger. I blacked out trying to use magic today. I need answers from you. I need to understand how to control it. So I'll tell you exactly where I am, I'm on the road with the Cirque American. Please get in touch for real.

I hesitated, deciding how to sign off.

Sincerely,
Your daughter (whether you like it or not)

twelve

The Atlanta grounds were near a nice neighborhood with tall trees and generous sidewalks. I was on the latest of many walks around them, my next move eluding me. I felt stuck in neutral—my magic and my mother had refused to show up again for the past few days. After what happened when I tried to change the penny back, I half wondered if it was still within me.

Instinct told me it was, though. And that it would surge again with no warning.

For the remainder of our Jacksonville shows, the others had stayed quiet, not wanting to talk more about the break-ins when I'd made attempts to bring it up. The drive had been uneventful, and now I suspected Dez was avoiding me. There'd been no more private conversations, no more stolen kisses.

I shouldn't have cared, but that didn't change the fact that I did. Still, I hadn't sought Dez out. I was happy enough that his heart in his chest was beating.

But I needed to do *something*, I decided, besides waiting around. I wrapped up my walk and returned to the Airstream. Jules and Remy were holed up in his room; I could hear their muffled voices as I passed it. When I got to ours, Dita wasn't there yet. Tomorrow was our first day of shows here, but I had enough time before the midway began to squeeze in a visit to Nan. I wanted to tell her about the great mother-search setback and ask for advice. I could only hope she wouldn't accuse me of being behind the break-ins or being here for the magic coin again. I sat down to take off my sneakers.

Someone knocked at the front door. I assumed it wasn't for me, but Remy called, "Moira, it's Dez."

I jumped to my feet, then told myself to stop with the stupid surge of excitement. I hadn't kept carrying the heart-shaped penny. I'd buried it among my socks. That was the sort of cool logic I needed to employ here. Be cautious. Be governed by head, not heart.

I knew, *knew*, that it was a bad idea to get involved with him. I had *hurt* him, even if the effects hadn't been permanent. Next time they might be. And seeing him make that second heart around the random audience person, well, that had hurt *me*.

This was the last thing I needed.

And yet . . .

Anyway, he was probably here for nothing.

All of these thoughts were apparently not sufficient to keep me from stopping to slick on some lip gloss and run my hands through my messy curls. It barely helped. As always, without product to tame it, my hair went everywhere. And there was nothing to be done about my pale freckled cheeks—along with my height, the source of my Pixie nickname—which made me seem younger than I was.

Oh well. This was me. This was how I looked.

The lovely assistants had taught me this lesson without meaning to. Listening to them critique their beautiful bodies and faces, I had long since decided there was no bigger waste of time than worrying about looking like anyone besides yourself.

"Moira? You coming?" Jules asked, from right outside in the short hallway.

"Be right there."

Noble philosophy about looks aside, I resisted the urge to pinch some color into my cheeks like one of my romance heroines. I had a feeling Dez would have me blushing in no time.

I made my way into the hallway and past Jules and Remy. And then I stopped dead in the center of the living room. "Um, hi?"

Dez was dressed to impress. He had on black pants and a collared shirt, white against the brown of his skin, the throat open a little at the top. No tie—let's not go crazy; it was still Dez. But he'd gotten a haircut. And he was holding a bouquet of flowers.

They were from a grocery store, the plastic around them a dead giveaway. I didn't care. No one had ever brought me flowers.

"You're here for me?" I asked, though Remy had said he was.

"Yes." He was plainly struggling not to grin.

"Did you text me about going somewhere?" I asked, looking down in a panic at my jeans and ancient gray T-shirt. "I didn't get anything."

"No, I decided to stop waiting for you to text me," he said.

"You're so dressed up, and I'm . . ." God, I was really bringing the awkward here.

"You look perfect." He extended the flowers, coming a few steps closer. They were a riot of colors and varieties. Not red roses, for love, but it felt like they might as well have been. "These are for you."

Jules sighed dreamily behind me. I looked over my shoulder to see Remy elbow her.

As soon as I accepted the flowers, she rushed forward and snatched them away. "I'll put them in water. You go. Go."

Dez offered me his arm. After a moment's hesitation, I hooked mine through his. Though I had to let go again when we reached the narrow stairway out of the RV.

I used the break to take a deep breath, like I was about to do a straitjacket escape.

He stopped and picked up a small brown grocery bag he'd left on the grass outside.

"Where are we going?" I asked.

"It's a surprise," he said.

"I've never heard of a surprise date before. Don't you usually ask?"

"You might have said no."

"I probably should now."

So I surprised him by tucking my arm through his again. I inhaled, and he smelled good, a clean soap smell mixed with boy, like he'd taken a shower not long before.

"Are you sniffing my manly smell?" he asked.

"Maybe."

"Then my evil plan is working."

He was leading me toward the darkened midway. Everything was ready for tomorrow. There was an eerie sort of quiet to wandering the open ground in the middle of the deserted tents and booths. A light wind caused the tent fabrics to sway and crack occasionally, snapping back into place. The hush encouraged more quiet. Neither of us spoke to interrupt it.

As we neared the Ferris wheel, it flared to life, like a constellation come down to Earth right in front of us.

"Dez, is this for us?" I dropped my arm and gathered my hands in front of my chest. The motion was a little girl's, but I didn't care. I didn't feel like a little girl. I was on my own, eighteen, on a surprise date with a beautiful boy who had apparently arranged for us to have a private ride on the Ferris wheel.

"All tonight is for you. Come on," he said.

He directed me to the base of the wheel, stretching tall and bright above us. A wonder.

"How?" I asked.

"I've made some friends. I'm very charming, if you didn't notice."

"Oh, I noticed."

One of the friends was apparently the beefy ride operator. He tipped an imaginary hat to us, and Dez slipped him a handful of cash.

"Right this way," the operator said, only a touch of sarcasm in his voice.

He waved us to one of the enclosed metal cars, waiting with the door open. I entered first, and Dez slid in next to me. Close, so close, as the operator lowered the door into place, locking us into the car together. Like a very romantic cage.

"This is some surprise," I said.

He still had the bag with him, and he set it on the floor of the car between our feet. "Just wait." He failed to hide a small smile.

This was *too* romantic. I couldn't trust it.

"Uh-oh," he said as the ride began to spin, our car rising through the night air, giving us a view of the darkened midway and, beyond it, the Cirque camp spread out across the field. I saw a trailer door open, and a few lights switch on inside others. We were making a scene. A spectacle.

"What?" I asked, registering his uh-oh.

"A second ago you were biting your lip. You're supposed to be thinking about me. About how wonderful I am."

"You're almost too wonderful." I narrowed my eyes. I meant it. "Why would you do something like this? So . . . big."

He drummed his fingers against the seat, seeming nervous for the first time ever. "I could tell you would keep running away unless I made it impossible."

"I did not run away. I . . ." Okay, I'd pushed him away and taken off. Fair, but he didn't know the whole story. "That still doesn't explain why you're convinced I'm worth all of this."

The night wind wound around us, the car swaying as it traveled toward the top.

"My dad's nickname was Silver-Tongue, as in 'silver-tongued devil.' I get it from him," he said. "He believed in grand gestures, in turning on the charm."

"Believed, past tense?"

He nodded. "I don't know why you would think you're not worth this. You're obviously too good for me."

I didn't know what to say to that.

We reached the top, and the car dropped, looping around so we faced the other side of the grounds on the trip down. The big top loomed in our vision in this direction, the spires stark against the sky, and in the farther distance, the city's skyline. The night presented an unbearably romantic scene, even for a girl who professed not to be swayed by such things, who swore to herself that she didn't believe in them. Not really.

And then he took my hand.

There was this whole big world rushing up to meet us, and I had so many questions, but all I could focus on was Dez's skin against mine. Such a simple contact. He rubbed his thumb across the top of my hand, and then he released it. I wanted to grab his back, not ready to let go.

He raised his palms to the sides of my face and placed them lightly on my cheeks. "I'm going to kiss you now, if that's okay?"

I nodded, still stunned into silence.

I remembered to close my eyes at the last second, and then his mouth met mine.

We were kissing and spinning through the night, and it felt too good to worry about if I was doing the right or the wrong thing, the smart or the dumb one. His hands were still on my face, and this was not some gentle peck. This was what my romance novels described as "ravishing."

One of *those* kisses.

There might have been an untoward cheer from the operator as we flew past him and back around to the top side, where the ride slowed, coming to a stop.

I relaxed into the kiss until I felt heat surge within me, bright and burning, and had a momentary spike of panic—

Which Dez must have detected, because he eased back an inch or two and breathlessly asked, "You all right?"

"I just . . ." But it wasn't my magic. That wasn't the heat I'd felt this time. It could have been, though. I had no way to be certain whether something like this could bring it out or not.

I pressed back into the corner of the seat, as far away from him as I could get.

"You're running again. I think this calls for surprise number two," he said. "Though I kind of want to just keep kissing you now."

My cheeks flamed. *Danger, danger,* my brain said. My heart beat faster.

My heart didn't care if it was stupid to respond this way. It just did.

He bent to get the bag, and I looked out over the night. We were stopped at the very top of the wheel. The stars above were faint, because we were so near the city light. He extracted a cheap green bottle of champagne and two plastic glasses from the bag.

"Look out," he said.

And popped the cork, which zoomed out into the night. He handed me two glasses and clumsily poured some champagne into them, a little bit bubbling over onto my hand.

He blinked at me for a moment, serious. "To first dates," he said, accepting and then raising his plastic glass. He set the bottle on the floor of the car.

I lifted my glass, but my hand shied away when he went to tap his to it. "Dez, this can't be a date."

"It can't? *You* called it one first."

I opened my mouth to explain, but he cut me off.

"You should know this is the first date I've ever been on," he said, sheepish. "Ever taken someone on." He eased onto the seat beside me, leaving a gap between us, scanning the horizon. Was that color in *his* cheeks?

"I don't believe it," I said, sipping the champagne. I knew from comparing it to the few sips of champagne I'd had at special occasions with Dad that it was terrible, and yet, still, it somehow managed to instantly become my favorite champagne of all time, the best thing I'd ever had to drink. Ambrosia.

This was dangerous.

"I've had hookups, sure, but never a date." He paused. "We moved around a lot. I never met anyone that made me take the risk."

"What risk?" I frowned. The more I heard about where he was from, the more I didn't think it was any good.

"The risk of having my heart broken."

"Oh."

"I can tell it's not going to be easy. You're a runner," he said. "So thing two wasn't the champagne. I want to prove to you I'm serious . . . and I grew up around people who know how to seal a deal. There's something in it for you."

"What do you mean?"

"You came here to do magic, on a stage, like your friend Raleigh does, right? Not just card tricks."

Where is this going? "I want to eventually."

"I've watched you enough to know that's more important to you than any romantic gesture I could make. So, what if I helped you out? What if you could open for him?"

I shook my head. "Raleigh will still say no. He's not convinced I'm ready yet."

"Who said anything about asking him? You'll be good, right? I'll help you plan it. We'll steal his stage for just a few minutes. Get your chance for you," he said. "Just think about it."

I was tempted to say yes with every fiber of my being.

Dez set down his plastic glass and reached for mine. "I'm not going to kiss you again, not right now. And I think Jimmy will make us come down soon. I don't want to—I'd rather stay here, and not have to run the risk of you saying no to doing this again."

"I'll think about it," I said.

"Good."

We circled the world one more time before our feet touched the ground, and from the vision in my head of myself on Raleigh's stage, I already knew I'd say yes.

No matter how reckless or stupid I had to be to do it.

thirteen

I opened the front door and was greeted by three faces and two giant pizza boxes. Remy, Dita, and Jules were on the couch, apparently indulging in a late extra dinner.

"Finally! Jules told me you went on a date," Dita said. "Come save me from watching these two try not to give each other swoony looks, even though they see each other all the time. It's like they're in some kind of novel."

Jules had a pizza slice flat on one hand, in contrast to Remy's New York–style folded piece. She sniffed. "Please. We'd be in a movie, not a book. Black and white. I'm Katharine Hepburn, and he's Cary Grant."

"The Latino Cary Grant," Remy said, rolling his eyes affectionately. "He knew how to do a few flips," he told me.

"A few flips? He got his start in vaudeville." Jules shook her head as if she was surrounded by barbarians, then took a delicate bite of pizza.

"I sense a movie marathon in my near future," Remy said.

Dita gestured to the box, and I took a slice of cheese and eased down onto the floor in front of them. My technique at pizza was somewhere in the middle of theirs, a sort of half fold. I could control a deck of cards like a maestro, but I couldn't eat pizza without leaving a grease trail on my T-shirt. It was inevitable, like bad weather or the grave.

"*Soooo* . . . how'd it go?" Jules asked, rocking forward.

The evening with Dez had been confusing. And, alternately, like being hit by lightning. I could hardly say that. "We're probably better off as friends."

"Ha!" Jules shook her head. She pointed at the flowers. "Friends don't bring friends flowers."

"Some friends probably do," Dita said.

"Not many," Jules argued. "Unsatisfying report," she said to me, and took another bite of pizza.

I wanted myself off the agenda. Dez and I weren't something I felt comfortable discussing. I decided to change the topic to the Garcias' act. "Rehearsal going all right for you guys?"

A storm passed over Dita's face. "I'm hoping to take some time off. Maybe the whole week. Not just from rehearsing."

"Dita," Remy said, "I won't do the act if you aren't in it. And we have to do the act."

Uh-oh. I hadn't meant to cause this.

"Don't be that way," Dita said, glaring at him. "What if I need a break but don't want to mess it up for everyone?"

"You love being up there," he said. "You of all of us have always said it feels like flying. Even when Granddad was still around and coaching us, the worst days. You loved it. Why wouldn't you want to fly?"

"Maybe I can't anymore." She stood and stalked back to our room.

"Sorry," I said.

"You didn't know," Remy said. "It's a sensitive subject."

Jules tapped her boyfriend's shoulder. "Good job. Way to get a conversation going." Then, to me, "Do you have brothers and sisters? Are they like this? I just had my cousin."

Past tense and with a hard swallow after her question. I had Googled *Cirque American* and *Chicago* on my phone and read about the death. The sudden, tragic, accidental death. Obviously, they still carried it with them, just like Thurston had said of the circus as a whole.

"Not that lucky. No brothers or sisters," I said, neutral.

"Maybe you should go try to talk to her," Jules said.

It seemed like a weird suggestion. Dita and I didn't know each other that well yet. But . . . "I'll give it a shot. It's bedtime anyway."

I finished off my slice and got up. They didn't stop me, and when I reached the little hallway, I heard Jules say, low, to Remy, "I've been thinking, and I have an idea about the coin."

I shouldn't have wanted to overhear their conversation. But I didn't think they would notice if I lingered in the shadowy hallway, as long as I didn't make a production of it or stay too long.

"No," Remy said, keeping his voice down too.

"We can't leave it there. It'd be better to move it . . . Listen."

They were talking about the mysterious coin. I should stop listening. I should *really* stop listening. This was wrong.

Remy said no again, and I heard him climb to his feet. Before he could catch me, I turned and hurried the rest of the way to our room. Getting busted would have served me right, but I made it.

Dita lay on her bed, staring up at the ceiling.

"Families—am I right?" I said.

"I don't want to talk about it."

There was no wiggle room to misinterpret. She didn't want me to attempt to coax her into talking or provide a willing ear. She didn't even look away from the ceiling. But I spoke anyway. "I hang out at a theater back home a lot. The women there like to give advice—to each other, to me. It's nice. The way they're always there for each other, for me. I'm pretty sure they'd tell me to say 'That's fine, Dita,' and back off, so that's what I'm going to do."

She blinked, and I could see her eyes were watery.

I stayed at the door. "But they would tell you that talking about it to someone you don't have so many emotions wrapped up with, like someone who's not a member of your family, might make you feel better about whatever it is. I'm still backing off. But when you're ready, I'm here."

She drew in an audibly shaky breath and sat up. A tear trailed down her cheek, and I hated the thought I might have made her cry. But I didn't think it had anything to do with me.

"What about you?" she asked. "Something's going on with you too. You never talk about your family, not really. Or Nan's interest in you. And you keep letting Raleigh brush you off about opening for him. I'm also here whenever you're ready to tell all."

"Touché," I said. "I guess we're the secret-keeping twins."

"Ha, no. That's Jules and Remy."

How right she was, after what I'd overheard. "I think I'm going to let Dez help me sneak onto Raleigh's stage and perform."

She gasped. "Will Raleigh freak?"

"Almost certainly."

"Good for you," she said. Then she sighed. "I do love flying, I just . . . don't seem to be able to do it anymore. I get up there, and I feel like myself right up until I don't. You ever feel that way?"

"Remember my audition? I think everyone feels that way sometimes in front of a crowd."

"It's not the crowd. It's . . . I'm afraid now. I never used to be, but now I am. And I don't know how not to be, how to make it feel like it used to, being up there. Like I didn't have to worry. Like nothing would go wrong. You can't fly and be afraid to move at the same time."

"I'm gathering you all lost someone close to you." What Jules's cousin had meant to Dita wasn't clear to me, but he'd meant something. "It could just be you need more time to go by."

"It's been almost a year." She said nothing else.

"Maybe what you need is to reinvent yourself a little," I said. "Feel like someone who's still you, but different too. For starters . . ." This was none of my business, but we were friends. I owed her the truth. "You don't look like yourself when you're performing. What if you did?" My eyes flicked to the closet. "You might feel better if you looked like you. Outside in, fake it to make it, and all that."

She followed my gaze to the neatly hung rows of men's clothing. "My mother would die."

"No, she wouldn't. She might freak out, but she won't die."

"Hmm," Dita grunted.

"I need to visit the costume trailer to get a mask made anyway," I said. "Some costume improvement of my own. You'll come too? Our secrets, for the time being."

"I like it," Dita said. "Secret-keeping twins."

Dita hesitated another moment and took another longing look at her closet. "If we go see her tomorrow, I'd say she could have something in a week—probably by Memphis."

"Memphis it is. We play it cool here, and then *bam!* We make our moves." Raleigh would never see my plan coming, not with Dez's assistance.

"Partners in crime," she said, offering me her hand. I shook it.

"I feel like we should go smoke cigars or something," she said.

"The handshake is a classic," I said.

For the first time that evening, I felt certain I was headed in the right direction. Dita had put it best: you couldn't fly and be afraid of moving at the same time.

fourteen

The next day I was headed to the Maroni trailer for my conversation with Nan when I bumped into—literally, to my horror—Dez. He came out of nowhere, and we collided.

He put his hands on my arms, steadying me.

"Was that a ploy?" I asked. "Have you been waiting around?"

That grin I wanted not to like returned. "Someone's in a mood. Why would I be waiting around here?"

He looked around, and his eyes settled on the Maronis' RV. He lowered his voice. "People say things about Nan Maroni, you know."

Dita had said as much, but it felt wrong to gossip about her. "So I've heard. They probably say things about me. And about you too."

"If they were saying things about you *and* me, I'd like them better."

Gah. My cursed heart couldn't help responding to this.

"Don't blush," he said. "Though it is cute. You don't want to hear the gossip? Everyone likes gossip."

"Fine. What do they say?"

"That she has magical powers."

I should've guessed this was what he'd say. "She doesn't seem like a witch to me," I said, careful. It was too close to home.

"Me either," he said. "Enough about her. I'm more interested in you. Did you decide yet?"

He might as well be doing the boy equivalent of batting his eye-lashes. This level of charming should come with a danger category designation like a hurricane. *We've got cat-five flirting developing in the middle of the Cirque camp.*

"Yes," I said. "Memphis work for you?"

"Memphis it is." He grinned. "You want to hang out now? Discuss the details?"

I could hardly tell him I was here for Nan. "Right now I'm going to see Jules."

"I know a brush-off when I hear one. See what you can find out about Raleigh's schedule, when he gets to his tent before his act. I'll do the same for the assistant, and we'll compare notes. Talk to you soon, lovely Moira."

He smiled at me, and I braced for another kiss, but he sidled off when I didn't stop him from going. *Argh.* I pulled myself together, completed my journey, and knocked on the door to the Maroni RV.

"It's open. Come in!" Jules called.

The family was watching an old movie together, or hanging out while Nan and Jules did, anyway. Their father, Emil, gave every appearance of napping. Novio Garcia was there too, with an air of Zen suffering, in a kitchen chair pulled over to the side of the couch.

Jules had the remote next to her. She started to pause it and get up. So I had to awkwardly say, "I'm here to see Nan."

Nan rose. "I'll be back in five minutes. Keep watching. You know I can quote the entire thing from memory."

Jules looked between us with interest but settled back into the couch.

Nan met me outside on the grass. I was a little worried Dez might return and spot us together, but the coast remained clear.

"What is it?" she asked.

"I started looking for my mother."

Her eyes widened in surprise. "Did you find her?"

"She put a phony name on the birth certificate: Regina A. Ghost. And then she sent me a message. A clear one." I pulled up the e-mail on my phone. "She doesn't want to be found."

"What woman would do such a thing?" she asked. "Use a fake name on a birth certificate?" An unfiltered response, because she added, "Sorry. If she's Praestigae, that might explain it. The secrecy."

"I still don't get what that means. But she somehow knew I'd requested the birth certificate, and she didn't like it."

I held the phone out for her. She peered at the screen.

"What a strange woman." Nan shook her head slowly, considering. "Has your magic presented again? Have you tried to call on it?"

We were speaking softly, but I still looked around to confirm that no one was paying attention to us. Dez had that ability of popping up unexpectedly. There were a few people crossing the grounds nearby, but they seemed safely head-in-the-clouds in their own worlds, unconcerned with ours.

"It came back the other day." When she frowned in concern, I explained. "It was okay. Barely. It was during a performance. I was in a straitjacket. But I was able to rush through the end."

Her mouth was slightly open. "In a straitjacket?"

"Doing an escape. You didn't think I was all about card tricks, did you? Anyway, I made something out of a regular coin." I had the heart-shaped former penny in my pocket. Much as I wanted to toss it, I felt like I should hang on to it. When I held it, it was almost like my palm heated again, just barely. Not enough to freak out over.

But like the little copper heart had a spark of life in it.

"May I see?" she asked. No badgering like that first day in the tent.

I produced it, rolling it out to the end of my fingers and showing it to her.

She didn't take it, and I was relieved not to have to hand it over. She squinted.

"Were you visualizing this when it happened?" she asked. "It is a heart? The real kind?"

"I wasn't. I was thinking about the person who gave me the penny." I didn't elaborate on who that was. "He, um, had heart pain. No lasting effects, though."

"So much detail for an accidental creation." She paused. "I wish we knew more about your limits. Your mother's reluctance to be found seems like an important part of the puzzle. Can you talk to your father about her? Are you still in contact with him?"

Dad. The reason I was here. The only person I could guarantee to have some kind of answer. "I was afraid you'd say that. Yes, I am. I'll call him."

"Let me know if there's anything I can do," she said, and started to go back inside to her movie.

"Wait."

She stopped.

"This coin everyone is searching for," I said. "Should we be worried about that?"

"I hope *everyone* isn't searching for it." Her face darkened, and there was a distance to her answer, like she was reliving the past at the same time she spoke. "Jules promises me that no one will find it, and I have to believe her."

"But if someone did find it . . ."

"The coin in and of itself holds lucky magic—it protects the holder—but only if they use it, keep it on them. Like all magic, even an object of good can boast a double edge, a sharp one. It can corrupt. It can make the wearer feel untouchable. That's why it's a good thing it's gone."

But the coin wasn't truly gone. Remy and Jules knew where it was, and Jules had some plan to move it. I kept that to myself. Their secrets weren't mine to tell.

Nan's next words sent guilt spiking through me. "You must tell me if you hear anything about it. We can decide what to do. These people would be a danger to all of us."

"I should tell *you*, not Thurston?" I had gotten the distinct sense the other night that she didn't fully trust him.

"You're too smart for your own good. But, yes, Thurston believing in magic would not be a good thing. I don't want to encourage him to start."

"Why would it be so bad for him to know?"

For anyone to.

"You might think those tidy break-ins were nothing much to worry about, and perhaps you would be right. But they were a beginning. People will do things to possess even a fraction of magic. Thurston is a good man, but he is curious and powerful. I would rather he stay a good man, with limits to his power."

"Okay," I said, nodding. "No word to Thurston. If I hear anything that makes me concerned, I'll come straight to you."

That wasn't a lie. I wasn't concerned about what I'd overheard. To be completely honest, another item of magic on the loose seemed like a welcome distraction for anyone who would potentially notice mine. It was a threat that there were people looking for magic, and misdirection could be as powerful a tool as any magic coin.

Looking satisfied, Nan glided back to the RV and disappeared inside.

I took my phone out of my pocket as I walked away and considered the little voice-mail icon. It had been lit up since that morning, a tiny numeral one superimposed over the audio reel symbol. I pressed to play it, holding the phone tight to my ear. Even if it hadn't said who the missed call was from, I already knew who it would be.

I'd been dodging Dad for almost a week now, hadn't I? Texting back with first the address in Ithaca, then sending an e-mail about how busy I was. I still hadn't come up with a Dad strategy for the delicate operation of asking him about my mother. He would want to fly straight to me, and that obviously couldn't happen. Not yet.

For so many reasons.

None of this made it any less nice to hear his voice. "Moira, sweetheart, it's Dad. If you're mad about what happened before you left . . . I should have been nicer about it. But call me, all right? I'm having daughter withdrawal over here. Also, I need to complain about everyone at the theater. And I have to take the little quiet guy on a tour of my private collection, which you know I hate. Oops, I'm now actively making a case for you *not* to call. I hope you're learning a lot and having fun. But not too much fun. Call me. Okay, bye, love you."

I didn't want to hurt him, and asking about my mother was going to do that, at a minimum. He was a good dad. He cared. I thought even his prohibition on magicianship came from a place of wanting to protect me from the slings and arrows of the world—or, more accurately, from failing at achieving something he viewed as smoke and mirrors, an impossible mirage.

I deleted the message after I finished playing it back, but I didn't return the call. Not yet.

I'd just finished a coin trick and was waiting for Raleigh to make his twenty-minutes-early arrival for his second performance. It would be three days in a row, if he showed, good enough for me to proceed with the plan that Dez, Dita, and I were concocting for Memphis.

The head costumer, a colorful eccentric named Sunshine, had been all too happy to get to work on a new costume for Dita, and to create a mask for me that would make me look like I'd "stepped out of a magical dream." She'd clapped her hands and said, "Cat eyes."

As Dez had suggested, I'd been observing Raleigh's arrival and departure times, stationing myself near his tent before each of the two performances he did during each midway session. (More than two would be death for a magician—too much risk of someone returning a third time and seeing how the illusion was created.)

Scanning for Raleigh, I turned to take in the crowds coming my way and saw Dez instead. He was having a serious conversation with the devil-bearded man who'd been dealing on poker night, Rex the family friend. Tonight he wasn't in a suit coat, but he did sport an old-fashioned hat. Not a fedora, but something like one. Brandon was with them, listening intently.

Dez said one last thing, then left the two of them behind.

And spotted me.

"My favorite person," he said, sidling up. The almost-fedora moved away in the crowd behind him. "How are you doing?" he asked.

The question struck me as sincere, not just polite.

"I've been better, I've been worse."

"Too bad," he said.

"What does that mean?"

He smiled at me, and my heart responded immediately by speeding up.

"Don't doubt me so, Moira. I like you. I'm proving it. I only meant that your answer sounded like you could be doing better. I hate to hear that."

"Oh. Did you find out about the assistant?"

"Yep. She shows up as close to curtain as possible. Five minutes early, max."

In the distance behind him, I saw the Ferris wheel spinning through the air. Dez would have to get back to his own stage soon. And Raleigh chose that moment—right on schedule, actually—to pass by us, pulling on his stage jacket. He stopped and frowned at the two of us.

"Ready to let me open yet?" I asked sweetly. It was worth a shot.

"Keep asking." But he added, as he always did, something to string me along. "It'll happen someday."

I sighed. Pure theater.

For a moment, it seemed like he might say something else, but in the end he just shook his head and went on around the back of his tent.

Our plan was solid. It would work. On our first night in Memphis, Dita was going to distract Raleigh—she was going to ask his advice on suit cuts for future variations on her new costume, something male magicians knew a lot about, in exchange for teaching him how to tie bow ties perfectly.

"Have you figured out what trick you're doing for your big debut?" Dez asked. "I saw you in the straitjacket. I hope this one'll be less painful?"

Behind him, the arms of the Ferris wheel stopped, shining in place in the night sky. "Why would an audience want to watch something easy, Mr. Knife-Thrower? Would that make them feel like they'd seen something beyond what they could do?"

"People like tricks." He refused to cede the point.

"People like daring."

"You're doing something scary is what you're telling me?" he said.

"I'll be using the straitjacket again. And I'm bringing my own coffin," I said, enjoying the way his mouth had dropped open in surprise. "Don't worry. I'll teach you your part before I climb into it. Any problem?"

He swallowed, then grinned. "For you, anything."

"Famous last words."

fifteen

When I emerged from the dressing room into the costume trailer's small sea of fabric, sequins, zippers, and feathers on the day of our first Memphis shows, I was still glowing from the effect of my brand-new mask.

Dita was in the other dressing room. We'd agreed to keep the results of our costuming experiments a surprise for each other too, until that evening's performances.

"Do you like it?" Sunshine asked. The head costumer was in a flowy, flowery dress she'd almost certainly designed and sewn. Her multihued hair was piled on top of her head in a precarious twist adorned with sequined bugs she'd also clearly made herself. Before I could respond, she called out, "Dita, you have to tell me if anything needs adjusting! I'm assuming the silence means you're in love with it!"

There was no response, but the costumer seemed unconcerned by this and turned back to me. "Well?"

"It's perfect," I said.

And it was: black, sparkly, mysterious. I felt more magical the moment I put it on. The eyes were cat-shaped. As I'd requested, it hugged tight to my face, the light plastic lining shaping itself to my skin from above the eyes to the apples of my cheeks, so it wouldn't create any issues or get displaced when I pulled the straitjacket on and off. Not unless things got uncharacteristically violent.

"I knew it would be," she said, not cocky, just confident in her abilities. "Let me know if you want me to improve upon your jacket. I have some ideas for hidden pockets I want to test." She maneuvered away through the racks to supervise one of her staff, hard at work at a sewing station that clacked and buzzed.

Dita stayed quiet in the dressing room, and I decided not to bug her or rush her. I was eager to see how her new costume had come out—but not enough to violate the sanctity of our pact.

The costume trailer was apparently always busy. People kept ducking in and out to pick up alterations, and now Jules waltzed in, drawing attention like she always did, even though she was in simple practice clothes.

"I'm here for the fix-up," she said.

"Just a sec, princess," Sunshine said.

Jules sighed and shifted from foot to foot, looking around . . . Her eyes landed on me, and she smiled and came over. I knew Dita wanted to keep the costume thing quiet until later.

"Hey, what are you doing here?"

I was saved from answering by Dita's voice. "She's with me," she called from inside the dressing room.

"And what are *you* doing here?" Jules asked, interested, fixing on the curtain.

"None of your business," Dita sang out.

Jules looked almost injured. From behind the curtain, Dita amended: "Sorry, I didn't mean it like that. I'm trying on a new costume. Don't tell, though, not until tonight."

"A new costume?" Jules asked. "You're wearing it tonight?"

The costumer swooped through the racks to us and passed Jules a garment bag. She also made clear she was eavesdropping. "So it fits! I knew it would. I can't wait to see it on."

"Me too," Jules said, accepting the bag.

"Now go," Dita said, "and *don't tell*. I don't want to have to fight about it with Mom. It's going to be a surprise. No one will see it until the act."

Until it was too late for anyone—read, her mom—to stop her from wearing it.

Jules shrugged, but there was still an odd look on her face. "Not telling. And going," she said, and she did, with a nod to the costumer.

After a few more moments, the curtain to the second dressing room slid across its wobbly rod, and Dita finally stepped out. A garment bag was draped over her arm. I wasn't sure at first why she'd shooed Jules so forcefully, but then I noticed that her face was blotchy. I'd have thought she'd been crying and wanted to hide it, except for how bright her brown eyes were. They danced. It was the kind of ridiculous thing someone would think about the duke in one of my borrowed romance novels, but that didn't make it less apt.

"Do you like it?" I asked. "I think you like it."

"Of course she likes it," Sunshine said. "This may be my favorite costume I've ever designed. I can't wait to see it tonight."

Dita ducked her head a little. "It makes me nervous how everyone will react."

"If they aren't idiots, they'll love it," Sunshine said. "Now get out of here and let us work."

The late afternoon Memphis skies rained sun down on us outside. "You're clear on tonight?" I said to Dita.

"Are you sure about going through with this?" she asked.

"Yes, I am absolutely convinced. Raleigh might let me do this in a month or two, when the season's wrapping up. But that will be too late." I couldn't afford to play it safe. A success onstage would give me the confidence to finally call Dad.

That was what I was telling myself at least.

She swung the garment bag around. "I know my part. I hate to miss your show, though."

Dita would have to miss it if she was going to be on Raleigh distraction duty.

"You'll catch it next time," I said. "Yes, I'm assuming there will be a next time."

"And Dez is your assistant. By the way, are you just making out, or is it serious?"

I made a face at her. "Brandon's helping too, with crowd control and sound design." When Dita looked at me with a question on her face, I said, "Gathering in people to watch and starting the music. Helping doesn't mean anything serious."

Except in Dez's case. I knew he meant it as a testimonial to his dedication to pursuing whatever was between us.

"Whatever you say. Just don't die *or* lose track of time tonight—I need you there to protect me when Mom sees this costume." She didn't sound as nervous as before. A big grin appeared, creasing her face and showing off gleaming white teeth. I'd never seen her like this, with joy spilling out.

"I wouldn't miss it for the world. Also, dying is for when we're eighty. I'd rather be"—I lifted my hands to frame the words—"the Miraculous Moira, the girl who cheats death."

I visualized the glass coffin I'd escape from in my mind. Everything would go exactly as planned.

Except that night Dez was late.

The dimly lit backstage area of Raleigh's tent featured two dressing tables with makeup out on them, some trunks and racks, and other random detritus that tended to accumulate in the prep area for a show. I paced around the edges of my glass coffin, a final check for any gaps or problems that I might have missed when I'd assembled it in the shadows back here a few minutes before.

The medium-sized trunk the coffin was stored in when it was collapsed sat nearby. My phone was in the cradle of the Wi-Fi speakers on top of it, ready to blare out my sound track.

Brandon had been right on time, twenty minutes ago, and was out front luring us a crowd. And there was—thankfully—no sign whatsoever of Raleigh. Or his assistant, who *never* came to work early. She seemed disgruntled about having to show up period, anywhere, on anyone's schedule but her own. We should be safely onstage before she appeared to apply her makeup and don her voodoo-queen costume. Assuming Dez ever got here.

He rushed in through the tent flaps then, and I turned my back to him so he wouldn't see my relief that he'd shown up.

Whew.

"I forgot to ask before . . . What if you can't get out?" His question was breathless. "What do I do then?"

The last thing I wanted was Dez coming near the coffin after I was locked inside. I was letting him be my assistant, but I wouldn't risk hurting him again.

"I will get out, so don't worry about it. I can hold my breath for up to five minutes, but I won't need to." When I'd first started, I'd practiced getting out of the straitjacket in a small space by finding a stray phone booth left over from ancient times. I'd held my breath and simulated with the straitjacket unbuckled many times in my room at home. My room, where the bulk of my walk-in closet's walls had been covered in blueprints and sketches and designs for various illusions I had in mind—hidden by my clothes. Dad never bothered to go in there. And Dad's suppliers never questioned why I wanted something made or any questions I had.

"Stop ignoring me," Dez said.

I finished my inspection and turned to him with a smile.

"Um, wow," he said. He wore the oddest expression. And that was hardly his most articulate sentence ever.

"What? Do I have something on my face? Am I bleeding out my eyeballs?" He still just stood there. "Do you have brain fever?"

"I might."

"I hope not. That would be inconvenient. You're my lovely assistant. All you have to do is"—I ticked the things off on the fingers of my right hand, in case he'd forgotten—"make sure the straps are tight, hold my arm as I get into the coffin, then cross the stage and hit the clock timer. Oh, and make sure Brandon starts the music on cue." I had one finger left, so I added, "And look pretty. Got it?"

"I always look pretty," he said.

Tonight he wore a vest with nothing underneath and snug black pants, an outfit that looked like something out of one of those male stripper movies. I couldn't dispute what he said. He did look pretty.

That didn't mean I couldn't protest. "Stop gaping at me. Are you sure about the brain fever?"

"You . . . That mask," he said. "You look like a superhero."

"No, I look like a magician."

When I turned my back on him again, I smiled wider. I could be a superhero magician, like Zatanna, in comic books.

Brandon appeared from the other side of the curtain. He always seemed mellow to a fault, so the nervous energy radiating off him was striking.

"Everything set out there?" I asked.

"I got your crowd," he said, tugging on Dez's arm. He whispered something into his ear, and I tried not to be offended.

Dez had a grave expression, but when he saw me looking, he pasted a smile over it. Brandon, done with whatever he'd had to say, disappeared back behind the curtain to his post.

"What was that about?" I asked.

"He just wanted me to know there's a good crowd."

I must have telegraphed my skepticism.

"No, really. We probably should get moving."

He was right, and their shared concerns were none of mine.

"Showtime," I said.

He hurried around to the far end of the coffin, which had slides on the bottom to allow us to move it more easily. Once we had it in place, we only had to turn the bolts again so it wouldn't move. I held the curtain aside, and Dez pushed it onto center stage. I put the oversized clock in place beside it, and shook out the straitjacket. The lighting was already set, moodily dim, but bright enough on the coffin to show every tortured movement I made inside it.

Brandon ducked in at the back of the empty tent.

"Let them in," I told him.

Brandon hesitated. "You're ready?"

"Go ahead," Dez said.

At Dez's word, Brandon actually moved to do it. Annoying.

As the first people wandered in to take their seats, I remembered I shouldn't stand here gawking. I waved for Dez to follow, and we went back behind the black curtains with Raleigh's spooky designs on them. That meant Dez stood right behind me. The heat of his body seemed to penetrate through my light black clothes, thin and flexible enough to allow room for maneuvering in the straitjacket. I smelled that boy/soap smell, with a little sweat mixed in.

"I like the mask," he said.

His mouth was near my ear. And I . . . didn't run or stay still this time. I angled my head the slightest fraction to the side, so that his lips pressed gently against my neck.

The result was a small noise from one of us—me or him, I couldn't swear which of us made it. Not and be right.

Maybe it was both of us.

I stepped away, not wanting to, and peered through the curtain. "Full house," I said, swallowing. It was. Every row filled. Brandon might be annoying, but he was good at rustling up a crowd.

A woman in the front row with long brilliant-red dyed hair—no one's hair was that shade in real life—fixed her eyes right where I was, having seen the curtain shift. I dropped it. Amateur hour on my part.

"Moira," Dez said, "I want to kiss you."

The fact that I wanted that too scared me. *Distraction. Misdirection.* They were for other people, not for me. I had a goal.

"Not now. We're on the clock," I said. "Just look pretty."

"For you, anything," he said, an echo of his earlier words.

"What are you doing here?" Raleigh's assistant wasn't *always* so late apparently. Of course this would be the day when she discovered promptness was an option.

"Um." I pivoted on my heel and then forced myself to channel Dad when he was in show mode. "I'm opening for you."

There must have been enough authority in it that she believed me. She shrugged. "Whatever."

In case Raleigh showed up early like she had, I said, "We're on."

Dez held the curtain to one side so I could step through. I lifted a hand high in the air, the straitjacket dangling from it as I strode into view of the crowd.

The audience applauded. All except that woman in the front row, who was cool and expressionless. I knew the type from Dad's shows—a critic who would have to be mightily impressed before she gave a hint of appreciation. She had bare arms and a tattoo on her bicep, a snake wound into some odd shape that was roughly oval.

I'd heard Dad tell Raleigh once that if there was someone in the audience obviously trying to see how everything was done, focus on that person. If you got them, you would get the rest.

Be a judge, I thought at redheaded snake lady. *I'll win you over.*

When the rest of the audience quieted, I began my patter, walking up and down the stage as I did so. "Adelaide Herrmann, known as Addie to her friends and family, performed as the Queen of Magic for decades in the early 1900s. Following the death of her husband, the legendary Alexander Herrmann, she kept the show alive. Though she was carrying on his legacy, she also built one of her own. She could disappear in full view of the audience, and she reportedly once caught six bullets on a stage in New York. Sadly, she is mostly forgotten today, but she was the first female magician of the period—and one of the only women in magic history—to become successful as a solo star."

I walked over to Dez. I could feel that I had the audience's attention, if not their full investment yet. I held out the straitjacket, and he accepted it.

"Can you confirm this is a legitimate straitjacket—no tricks?"

He tested it as we'd discussed, pulling at the fabric and the straps to demonstrate.

"Satisfied?" I asked the crowd.

The snake tattoo lady's arms remained crossed. But the rest of the crowd seemed with me, murmuring assent. I raised my arms, holding them out in front of me.

Dez pulled the jacket over them, sliding it slowly into place. He looked at me with enough intensity that he was *a* distraction. Not a distraction *for* me.

Moira, I want to kiss you.

He kept watching the crowd too, but his eyes always returned to me.

My cheeks went warm, and I returned to my patter. "Addie Herrmann would never have done such a violent escape as the one I'm about to attempt. She was a graceful performer, known for moving like a dancer. I hope to infuse this evening with some of her loveliness."

"You will," Dez murmured, and the heat in my cheeks grew.

The woman in the front row smiled a little, though she couldn't have heard him. It was a positive reaction, though, so I'd take it.

I continued. "She moved like a dancer because that's what she began as. Much like me, she practiced in secret as a teenager, because her family wouldn't approve of the pursuit. Dancing, in her case, stunts like this in mine." When I looked pointedly at the glass coffin, the crowd laughed. "Girls will be girls," I said, and they laughed more. Even the snake woman smiled.

"When she was discovered, she became part of a revue. Then she went on to become a velocipede rider—what we'd think of as a bicycle racer, which was fairly scandalous at the time—before meeting and marrying Herrmann the Great. With him, she helped create the stage show as we know it now." I indicated the tent. "With backdrops and with music, the great illusion made into art. And in her own show, Addie Herrmann never spoke, always performing silently to music. So my illusion will also be silent. I will not speak once I enter the airtight coffin you see on the stage, which will be sealed with me inside it. The air within will be expelled—you'll hear something like a pop and then a puff—and then I invite you to hold your breath while I attempt to escape. See how long you can last. This is no trick. The small confines, as you can see, will make getting free more difficult. Holding my breath while struggling to escape, even more so. But Addie deserves a fitting tribute."

I stopped speaking and put my back to the crowd so they could watch as Dez buckled the straps.

The tent was absolutely silent. He finished and stepped away, toward the coffin.

"If we are lucky and my performance is a pleasing tribute, maybe she will communicate with us, in one way or another." I stalked across the stage to Dez, who held the coffin lid open. Music poured from speakers backstage, cued by his friend. At least he got the timing right.

There was no way I could have felt Dez's hand through the canvas as he held my arm to assist me while I stepped up into the coffin. But I could have sworn I did.

The weight of the audience's attention lay blanket-heavy over me as I reclined inside the glass container. My movements weren't awkward, only because of my hours upon hours of practice. With a shake of his head, Dez looked down at me and then lowered the lid into place. The closure clicked, catching.

I closed my eyes, acclimating to the feel of the tight confines around me.

I took a deep breath in and held it. I reached out with one of my feet and pressed a button. Air gasped out of the coffin. I held my breath, and I hoped the audience did too.

Then I started to work my way free.

I turned to my side, bracing my left shoulder against the underside of the coffin. My face was pressed nearly to the glass, but not quite. I forced my lower arm to push against the fabric of the straitjacket.

Doing this while holding my breath made it more difficult because releasing that breath was usually what gave me the slack I needed. If I released mine too early, I'd be gulping in oxygen when I stepped onto the stage. That would hardly be a marvel, and not even close to a miracle.

Through the glass, I could see some faces in the crowd, including the snake woman's. She simply watched, but other people were holding their breath or had their hands in front of their faces. They weren't chattering. They were on the edge of their seats.

Exactly as I wanted.

I flipped around to get a better angle, using a little too much energy. I had to wriggle to get back into a place where I had enough leverage to work against the straps.

There.

Arms free. Now to undo the buckles. I reached around behind me and—

No, no, no. Not now.

My palms went hot as fire.

sixteen

My fingers burned as they worked the buckles, on fire as I tried to get them loose before something disastrous happened in full view of the audience.

If only I could plunge them into ice water.

I shouldn't have thought that. I should have thought anything else.

Because I knew what I'd done as soon as the first icy drop touched my jaw.

As I fumbled with the buckles, more water came.

Freezing water came from below, rising around me. More and more of it. I was surrounded, and the canvas of the straitjacket soaked through in seconds, growing heavy. Weighing me down, down, down.

It was far heavier than the weight of the audience watching. Heavy enough to drown me.

Squinting, I attempted to look through the water—swiftly filling the coffin—at the audience. I caught a glimpse of the red hair of that woman, still seated. But some people were standing. There were gasps, open mouths.

They'd all forgotten to hold their breath. And so had I, in the moments when my magic showed up. My magic had always transformed, not created. Now my magic was using the breath I'd released to make my wish into reality.

The icy water had filled the glass coffin. My lungs began to burn as badly as my hands did. My heart was on fire too.

I couldn't last much longer.

I had to get out of here. And I'd told Dez not to break me out.

Usually when I did a trick or an escape, I was calm and methodical. You had to be. Being rattled—or rattling yourself—could mean certain death. Metaphorical and literal.

How much smaller the coffin felt, filled with water. I should have floated up, but I was pinned to the bottom by the straitjacket's weight.

You can't breathe, but you have to think.

There, a tiny piece of calm in that thought. In the ability to think. I grabbed onto it and pulled it to me. My hands and my lungs were still burning, but I remembered the heat in my hands was there for a reason.

It was my magic.

My magic was killing my illusion. But could it save me too?

I closed my eyes, hot pain racing through my body, and I envisioned the straitjacket transforming—not entirely into something new, but into a larger version of itself. A version loose enough that I could move. It felt almost like some strength poured into me. Not something I created, but some extra strength from outside.

I drank it in.

And when I shifted my arms, testing my limits, the extra room was there.

Quickly I brought my arms up and undid the buckles with motions half-frantic and half-practiced. I got the straitjacket off.

The heat in my fingers was receding, but if I stepped out of here right now, like this, everyone would see that I was near-drowned.

So I brought my hands up and covered my face below the sparkly mask. *Still in place,* I thought semi-hysterically. *Well done, costumer.* And I imagined a pocket of air in front of my face, pressing back the water. My hands on their own wouldn't have been sealed tight enough to keep water from slipping through, but my magic did as I asked, because as soon as I felt the water around my mouth evaporate, I opened my lips and sucked in air. Those blessed breaths, shallow and then deeper, returned me to myself.

I was going to make it.

I pulled the straitjacket out of the way, thrashing against it to get it to one side.

The crowd was noisy enough for me to hear them through the glass. There were some claps, but more exclamations.

I looked up at the coffin lid, feeling almost normal, almost recovered. My lungs still burned, but less every moment.

When I stepped out of here, I'd be able to breathe freely again. I'd *be* free.

I focused on the words that had appeared above me, revealed by the moisture. The final element of this stage illusion.

Then I reached up and pressed on them, pushing the coffin lid up and open.

Hands grasped it immediately—Dez's—and that was good, because my strength faltered.

He kept it propped open like I'd instructed him to, but he wore a troubled expression. He must have known something had gone wrong.

Later. Deal with that later, I told myself. *Your cup didn't empty and break.*

I ignored him and pulled myself up, then onto my feet so that I stood upright in the coffin. The water sloshed around my ankles, hitting my lower calves.

The applause drowned out the mournful music, and then the violins stopped. There was a hiccup of quiet before the applause grew louder. I scanned back to the red-haired woman's seat and felt a moment of insult: she was gone. She'd left. Why did that bother me?

Well, her loss, I thought.

Dez offered me his hand, and I took it, climbing from the coffin onto the stage.

Releasing his fingers, which felt so warm in mine, so normal, so safe, I walked to the front and center of the stage. I raised my arms overhead and then lowered my torso into a deep bow.

No one, with the possible exception of Dez, seemed to have realized the icy water soaking my clothes and skin wasn't a planned part of the act. And no one was registering any disappointment that according to the prop clock, I'd been in there for almost three minutes. An eternity compared to the two minutes I'd intended.

The last remnants of panic faded, and I straightened and swept a hand toward Dez, or more precisely, toward the coffin lid.

"She must have been pleased," I said, throat straining to make the words sound normal. They almost did.

Traced by fingertip (mine, not Addie Herrmann's) were the following words:

Greetings
from one Queen of Magic
to another

Backstage I was met with a furor of a different kind.

Dita hovered near the back entrance. "Moira, I—"

"What do you think you're doing?" Raleigh spoke over her, confronting me before I had so much as a chance to sit. Or dry off.

He was in his tux and tails, his spooky top hat making him loom even taller. A black-and-white-striped bow tie hung loose around his neck, part of the distraction plan.

He should have been an intimidating sight, but suddenly I had no intention of apologizing. My magic had come, surged out of control, and then I'd controlled *it*. Not easily. But I had.

"Opening for you," I said, crossing my arms in front of myself, for warmth as much as in defiance. My skin was all-over goose bumps from the water's chill. But I refused to appear cowed. "You better get out there. The crowd is all warmed up. You don't want them going cold."

Raleigh glowered at me. "Moira Mi—"

"Miraculous, I know." I cut him off before he could say my real last name.

He shook his head, lids lowering in a lazy way that registered as a warning. He pulled the bow tie from around his neck and tossed it at Dita, who lunged forward and caught it. "That's why you offered to chat bow ties with me? To distract me, so she could do this? Horn in on my act?"

"That's not exactly it," Dita said.

"She only did what I asked. You can go, Dita." She took the chance to bolt. I didn't blame her.

"You're not seriously guilting me over this, are you?" I said, shaking my head at Raleigh and narrowing my eyes. "Do I need to remind you how *you* got your break into magic?"

I didn't mean Dad—or not just Dad, anyway. Raleigh had managed to hide from the custodians and stay overnight in the theater. When Dad showed up to rehearse a new illusion with some new assistants from the agency, Raleigh had revealed himself with bluster and asked to show Dad a trick. It was part of how I got the idea for unveiling my talents to my father. Why not show him, like Raleigh had? Only later did Dad find out Raleigh didn't have any place to stay and would have had no money to get back to New Orleans if it hadn't worked out. He'd hitchhiked all the way across the country.

He knew what it meant to want this.

"That's different," he said. "I had no other options."

"Neither do I."

Dez had stayed quiet, but he spoke up now with a calm that made me uneasy. "You shouldn't yell at her. You should just be worried about trying to top what she did out there. Good luck. You're going to need it."

The two of them glowered at each other. Having someone truly in my corner was nice.

Brandon, with good timing for once, breezed through the curtain, pushing my coffin ahead of him. "Stage is clear."

"Fine," Raleigh said finally, and shrugged his shoulders high. Then he released them and shook off the tension. "We'll finish discussing this later."

He snapped his fingers at Brandon, who hopped to and helped maneuver the cabinet that had Marie and Caliban inside it already out onto the stage. Raleigh didn't so much as glance in my direction while he waited for his moment.

As soon as Dez's friend came back through, Raleigh glided past the curtain, doing something that earned him a hearty round of applause almost as soon as he appeared.

Now that Raleigh was gone, my hands were shaky. So was my body. *Wait, no.* The problem was the cold. I was shivering. The chill ran all the way through me, as soon as I allowed myself to feel it.

Dez put his arms around me, pulling me in close to him. I didn't protest. Every molecule of my skin was screaming to get as close to his warmth as possible. "You're freezing," he said.

He looked around for something and settled on a robe beside one of the dressing tables, which he shuffled us over to without releasing me. He picked it up, billowed it around my shoulders, and pulled it close.

"Just get warm. Then you can send me away and go take a hot shower." His lips quirked up on one side. "And not just hot because you'll be in it. Too bad I have a show to do too, you know."

"Don't be . . . ridiculous." My teeth chattered the tiniest bit, and I went quiet, absorbing the warmth.

"The water," he said. "Where did it come from? That's some trick you've got. I don't see any way for it to be there."

There was no denying the surge of victory that standing on that stage and hearing the applause had brought. But being trapped in that water had been terrifying.

I didn't want to lie, so I didn't. Not exactly. "It is, isn't it? Some trick."

He ticked his head to one side. "A magician never reveals her secrets?"

I should have thought of that. My brain needed to kick back into gear. "Do you think Raleigh will let me perform again?"

"I think everyone who watched you will be talking about nothing else."

"Did you see that"—I paused for a small chattering of teeth—"lady who left? With the red hair. She wasn't im-p-p-pressed."

"No," he said. "I saw an audience that was obsessed, who'll be talking about it for days, like I said. And that kind of talk has a way of getting back to the boss. Thurston will know by the end of the night. But . . ."

"What?" I asked, afraid. The troubled look Dez had worn when I climbed out of the glass coffin was back.

It was too dark for me to see his eyes, but I could hear the concern in his voice. "That was an illusion, just an illusion, right? You weren't in danger?"

I coughed. "This from the boy who threw a dozen knives at me?"

He didn't budge. "You weren't in danger then. Were you tonight?"

I struggled to come up with the right words. I didn't want to lie to him, but I couldn't blurt out that I possessed real magic. In the end, I didn't have to. Brandon reappeared and cleared his throat loudly. "We have a paycheck to earn," he said.

"Thanks for your help," I told him, only somewhat grudgingly.

"That was badass," he said. "But it was charity. So we better go, D. Can't risk getting fired for your . . . friend."

That quick, I was back to not liking him again.

Dez gathered the robe around me tighter, transferring the fabric he held to my hands so it would stay in place. He whispered, "Moira, I still want to kiss you." He pressed a quick kiss to my lips before I could have stopped him.

Trouble was, I wouldn't have. I was alive, my heart was beating, and the soft press of his lips to mine only left me disappointed we didn't have time or space or privacy for a real kiss. For more.

And then I knew I was absolutely in danger, standing here, right now. I was done protesting. My feelings were real. I'd have to trust his were too.

"Well?" he asked, hesitating. "Were you in danger?"

His friend throat-cleared again.

"Not so much in danger," I said, tapping his shoulder, "as playing with fire."

"You mean me." From his careless smile, I assumed he bought it. He left, disappearing through the back tent flap when Brandon lifted it aside.

I figured we were even. He'd lied to me when we met, about that stupid knife heart. A lie for a lie. Mine was almost the truth—except for the not-being-in-danger part. I was deep in it.

seventeen

I waited until my teeth stopped chattering and the goose bumps disappeared from my arms, but I took off before I had to face an angry Raleigh again. I didn't want him to sic his crow on me. I knew I needed to give him the space to cool off, *then* I'd plead my case. I kept my fingers crossed that he had a good show. The boost of a well-received performance might help soothe away his anger.

All this meant that I navigated back to the Airstream in my chilled, damp clothes. The memory of that redheaded snake lady returned, and I wondered why I was still thinking about her, a random audience member. I stopped in my tracks.

The why smacked me in the face so hard it almost knocked me down.

Nan Maroni had said that the magic in her tarot cards meant they always told the truth. According to her, I'd transformed the Magician card into my story. There'd been two figures I couldn't identify on it, along with me and my dad.

One of them had been a woman with long red hair.

That's crazy, I told myself. *There are a lot of women with long red hair.*

But this one had sat in the front row, acting strangely. And there'd been that moment while I was trapped in the box when it had seemed that a push, some aid came from outside to lend me strength.

Was that woman my mother? If so, why would she bother to show up and then just leave?

I hurried through the dark. I wanted to get changed and go looking for her. Maybe she was still here.

Except I didn't have to. When I got to the Airstream, the woman was waiting beside it. She glanced around.

"Nobody's with me," I said. "We can go inside, if we need privacy."

How I got out the words so calmly was a mystery. My knees were shaking.

"No," she said, her voice quiet. "I can't stay long. It's too risky. You know who I am?"

Her surprise that I might have guessed was plain. I walked closer, my heart stuttering with each step. "You're her. My mother. The ghost."

A thin smile. "That's why it's too risky," she said.

She was beautiful, with a heart-shaped face, and a light dusting of freckles not so different than mine. But up close, bathed in the light of the security pole nearest the Airstream, she looked paler, weaker, than she had in the tent. The bright red of her hair took on a brittle cast.

"Because you're one of the Praestigae?" I hoped I'd said it right; endless Google searches had convinced me only the term was originally Latin. It didn't show up in relationship to any secret societies—criminal, magical, or otherwise.

"Never say that word again," she said. "You don't know what it means."

"Tell me, then," I said. "Why did you leave? Why are you here now?"

Voices reached us, some people returning to their RVs after the midway. She flinched.

"It's nobody," I said, relieved when no one came into view. They must have been headed to another row. "Why are you here?"

She glanced around again. "I wish we could have hours to talk," she said, speaking more quickly. "I wish I hadn't been forced to leave you. But . . . I did it for you. So you could choose your future. Your dad's been good to you, hasn't he?"

I nodded.

"The man who would have raised you otherwise . . . Count yourself lucky. He can never know about you. That's why I'm here—you should leave the past in the past. You shouldn't be here. You are not meant to be Praestigae, so do not say it again. The night could be listening. You have to promise me."

I knew I didn't owe her anything, but she sounded near-panicked. "I promise."

She lifted a hand like she might reach out to touch me, but then dropped it. "I didn't want the life for you that I have. I saw your life unwinding before me, a dark road, and so I tried to make sure it would be in the light instead. I came to warn you. To tell you to be careful. Your magic is strong, but it does have limits. I came here to tell you . . . you should go home. You might be discovered here."

I ignored that part. I wasn't going anywhere. "Nan Maroni told me about magic. She said it's like a cup. If you empty it and it breaks, then you don't get any do-overs. You die. But I don't understand *how* my magic works. It just . . . happens."

"Nancy Maroni knows about you?" She blinked at me. "About what you can do?"

"She figured it out. She's where I heard . . . that word." My mother seemed stricken by the news, so I added, "I don't think she'll tell anyone. But wait. Why would I be discovered here, as opposed to at home?"

She motioned from the top of her head down to her shoulders. "You can see how tired I look, out here. I am *allowing* you to. In the tent, you saw the me that is an illusion. The me I must keep presenting to my people. My cup—as you put it—is almost empty. I do not transform anymore. I create illusions, because it takes less magic." She reached out with her hand and touched my arm. "The reason you're in danger of being discovered is because we are looking for something here that used to belong to us. There were rumors last year, then more recently, that it had surfaced at the Cirque American. A coin from the Circus Maximus."

"Why do you want the coin?"

"It's sacred to the Praestigae. And, with it, I can keep using magic. It will fill me up. Without it . . ."

"You die?"

Oh God. The Praestigae were the ones looking for the magic coin. My mother needed it.

"I am their . . . only magic user left. That is why they can never find out about you. Now you understand why I have to go. Why we can't know each other."

I wanted to grab her, refuse to let her leave. "But I still have so many questions."

"I don't have time to answer them." She took my hands in hers. "I am proud of the young woman you've become. Your magic, I bottled it up with an old charm—it was loosed when you came into contact with another source of magic. We never thought you would."

"We?"

"Your dad and me."

So he knew. He knew, and he'd never said a word.

She hurried on. "After tonight, I think your magic will come when you're in danger, until you can control it. You can't let anyone know you have it. If *he* finds out about you, I'm too weak to protect you."

"He who?" I asked, trying to keep her here, just a little longer. But my questions weren't the only reason I didn't want her to go. I never thought I'd get the chance to talk to my mother. And now, for it to be over so quickly . . .

"Better that you never know." She squeezed my hands. "You shouldn't be doing those escapes, not here, and not until you learn to control your magic. It's not safe. When you *must* use magic, you have to guide it. Otherwise, it will do whatever it wants. It can consume you. And the more you use it, the more it'll change you." Gently, she slipped her hands from mine. "I have to go."

I resisted the urge to argue. I couldn't give up doing escapes. So I asked, "Will I see you again?"

She gave a sad smile. "Not if we're lucky."

And then she released my hands and walked away from me. I hesitated. I rushed around the Airstream after her. But I saw no one. Whether she was hiding from me or not, casting an illusion, something told me I wouldn't find her again unless she wanted me to. I didn't think this evening could get any weirder.

My phone buzzed with a message from Dita: You still alive? Don't forget to come over.

Crap. I had to go to Dita's costume unveiling. What I wanted to do was call my father and demand he tell me the truth.

I wrote her back: Be right there.

I had a little time. She'd told me she wouldn't come out of the dressing room until right before she and her brothers went on.

I let myself into the RV.

I just met my mother.

My mother, who claimed she left to protect me. Who'd forbidden me from saying the word *Praestigae*. Who was worried some guy she answered to would find out about me. Who said I shouldn't do escapes.

My mother, who would run out of magic without the Garcia family coin. Which used to belong to the Praestigae and was sacred to them.

I didn't think the Garcias were connected, so that part didn't make sense. But then, none of this did. Neither did magic being real.

I dug out a clean, dry outfit and changed into it. Walking in the night air had dried my hair at least.

Dad had known. All this time, he'd known I had magic hidden inside me, just waiting to come out.

I took out my phone and called him.

"Moira? Is everything okay?"

He sounded alarmed to hear from me, and I realized why. It was intermission. He was midshow.

Well, then we could both be alarmed. I leaned against the wall beside the closet. "I'm not sure."

"You didn't call right now to avoid having to talk to me for more than two minutes, did you? I miss you, sweetheart."

"The story you used to tell me about my mother. Do you know anything else about her?"

Shocked silence stretched between us. In it, I heard the familiar noises of the Menagerie backstage behind him. The managers for the various departments called out to each other. Some of the assistants joked around, laughing. And, for a second, I felt bad about springing the question on him.

But he'd lied to me. My whole life. I'm sure he must have thought it was for the best—my mother clearly must have agreed—but still.

The deception hurt.

"You've never asked about this before. Why now? Maybe I should come see you."

I stood straight, sensing disaster approaching. I hadn't thought this through. He could still force me to come home, blow my cover here. Now more than ever I had to stay at the Cirque. That magic coin was here somewhere. Jules and Remy's whispered conversations were proof. My mother might want me gone, but I wanted answers and I didn't want her to die. And I wanted my future. As a magician.

Nan's original suspicions about why I was here meant no one could find out I now wanted to know where the coin was too.

Dad and I coming clean with each other would have to wait. "I'm sorry," I said. "I've just been wondering. It's nothing to worry about. Go finish your show. We'll talk more soon."

There was a long pause. A woman's voice said, "Mr. Mitchell?" in the background. He ignored whoever it was.

"Moira, I love you. If I could give your mother to you, I would. I would give you anything."

It was the way he said it that made a sudden anger spike within me. He said it like it was true.

"I know, Dad. Love you."

I sank to the bed and sat in the near dark for a few minutes, hoping for a bright idea to present itself that would allow me to look for the coin without betraying the Garcias or the Maronis.

My mother had abandoned me to keep me safe. But she seemed convinced I was as far from that as possible here.

Too bad. I wasn't leaving.

eighteen

The flash of a metaphorical lightbulb overhead didn't come.

Eventually, I had to get up and make my way back through the cabin to the door. I remembered the break-in at just that moment. The back of my neck tingled, like it could sense that someone might be watching me, maybe even my mother's mysterious *he*, waiting right now in the darkness.

I carefully locked the door behind me, then I turned and saw a security guard sweeping a flashlight across the grass.

Those must have been the eyes I'd felt watching me. Right. I had no reason to become completely paranoid. Or every reason?

I crossed the grass toward the main tent and its riotous noise as quickly as I could without running. No matter what was going on with me, I still wanted to be a good friend to Dita.

When I reached the big top's backstage entrance, some of the clowns were hanging out in a cluster. As usual, one was smoking a cigar that reeked.

"There you are," he said. "Remy said to tell you that you're late and Dita won't come out until you get here."

Some friend you are, Moira.

"Thanks," I said, and ducked inside the flap.

Backstage was packed with glittering performers, off work but still hanging out. The music that went along with the Maronis' wire act wafted through from the main tent. I scanned for the red-and-black costumes of the Garcias and spotted them in the corner. I wound through the crowd toward them. Remy spotted me.

"Finally," he said. "Dita, she's here. You can come out now!"

"Send her inside," Dita's voice called from within a makeshift dressing room, curtain strung across its opening.

Their mother stood beside a makeup table nearby, frowning at me, or possibly at Dita. Novio nodded to me from his position next to the scantily clad blondes who performed with them.

I took the curtain and held it tight so no one could see inside, and then I was behind it.

"Oh my God!" I exclaimed, turning and getting a look at her.

"What?" Dita pulled at the edge of her sleeves and shifted from foot to foot in a pair of sequined black slippers. "Is it terrible? I have time to change back into the usual one."

"Don't even consider it," I said. And I didn't have to pretend anything.

Her short hair was slicked back tonight, and she'd lined her eyes with heavy black liner. Her lips were painted a neutral pink. The effect was dramatic on its own.

But the costume was the star. The formfitting material covering her legs was cut like her brothers' costumes. But where the boys' necklines plunged to deep Vs that left their chests exposed, the costumer had given Dita a faux vest with a modest V at the top. Flat black sequins outlined the red that shaped the vest. It could have looked goofy— maybe should have—but it didn't. It was striking. Despite the snug fit, there was nothing overtly sexed-up about the costume, unlike her previous one. A singular look for a singular person.

"You look like a dapper daredevil," I told her. At her uncertain shifting, I said, "That's a good thing. It suits you. You look *great*. The dapperest daredevil in history."

In the distance, the music for the Maronis cut out and applause swelled. Thurston's voice boomed, the words indistinct from this vantage point. Outside the curtain, Remy said, "It's time, Dita. Come on."

"Everyone's going to love it," I said. "You do, don't you?"
That grin from earlier, joy included, showed up. "I do."
"And do you feel less afraid?"
Her grin left. But she said, "I think I will."
"Go on, then. Knock them dead. Ready?" I grabbed the curtain so she could make an entrance and jerked it to one side. She took a breath and then launched herself out of the dressing room to join her brothers.

"Looking good, sis," I heard Remy tell her, and she glanced over her shoulder one more time, grin still in place.

They jogged toward the main entrance to the ring.

Their mother stood where she had this whole time, her arms still crossed. "This was your idea?" she asked me.

"She looks amazing, doesn't she?" I said, and then got out of there.

I scurried to find a place to watch their act, hoping the costume change would pay off in boosting Dita's confidence level tonight yet still feeling overwhelmed by the entire evening. Jules was standing by the side entrance, where there was a small curtain to conceal performers while allowing them a view of the ring. The clowns from outside were there too.

"I love the costume," she said. "I gave her the slippers. I wasn't sure they'd go. But she's wearing them."

"They look great."

Jules nodded, biting her lip, and we turned to watch the performance. The Garcias and the twins preened on their platform perches, and Novio was already swinging back and forth. Jules looked as nervous as me, waiting to see if Dita would make her somersaults and catch this time. She hadn't yet, not since the season began. Every night had been off.

I'd even stopped staying to watch, sensing that Dita would rather I *not* see her fail over and over again.

The twins went first, as Thurston did his usual spiel about the act and Goddesses of Beauty and Love Brothers—apparently the Garcias' infamous granddad had been the one who came up with this, even going so far as to have their mother name the siblings Romeo, Casanova, and . . .

"And now, the chief Goddess of Beauty herself, lovely Aphrodite," Thurston said, and the band played Dita's sensuous theme music. She stood on the platform, straight and tall in her new costume.

And suddenly I couldn't stop thinking about the magic coin. Where had their grandfather gotten it, if it used to belong to the Praestigae?

Dita's head went down for a second, like she was losing her nerve, and Jules grabbed my arm. "Ouch," I said, and her grip loosened, but she held on.

Novio swung back and forth, watching the platform. Remy said something to Dita. And, finally, as we watched—as everyone watched—she lifted her arms and ably accepted the swing flung her way, and then she was off the platform and hurtling through space.

She swung back and forth, like an extension of the trapeze itself, moving smoothly, quickly. Easily.

"She's going to do it," Jules said, almost squealing in my ear.

I hoped as hard as I could she was right. *Come on, Dita. Come on. You got this.*

Above us, high in the air, Dita released the swing and spun into a tight ball for her somersaults—one, two, three of them! She came out cleanly, as if it was as easy for her as breathing, and grabbed her brother's wrists.

Novio's teeth flashed above us. So did hers. They were both grinning big enough to fill the tent.

"Have you ever seen anything more lovely?" Thurston boomed, happiness in his voice. "And wait, what's this? A repeat performance for us? How will we resist her charms?"

Because instead of calling it a night and spinning down into the net, Dita went back to the platform and repeated the entire sequence of events. In fact, she did still another triple somersault after that before she finally ceded the air to Remy and his final quad—which he made too.

Somehow, though, when Jules raced out to join them and they took their bows, I knew all of the Cirque people gathered around the side curtain were cheering for Dita.

All except her mother. She should have been pleased. But when I looked over and saw her greeting her kids, her lips were pulled tight.

"You were incredible!" I said to Dita as soon as she was close.

She was sparkling, laughing, breathing hard. Remy slapped her shoulder. "Three triples," he said, like he was dumbfounded by it.

"Says the boy who does a quad every night," Dita said. But I could tell she was proud of herself.

Jules rushed in then. "Congratulations! New costume *and* back in fine form." Remy slid a look at Jules, but she just beamed back at him. Her arm was looped around Dita's shoulders.

"Thanks for the lucky slippers, Jules," Dita said, and I thought I saw her smile falter briefly.

"You're supposed to be a Goddess of Beauty," said a woman's voice, cutting through the celebration like a sharp knife. We all backed away from it, which had the effect of ceding the floor to Maria Garcia. "You look like a boy."

My mouth fell open. But not for long. Fury blazed up, and I searched for the words to defend Dita, her mother be damned.

Dita didn't need me to come to her rescue, though. "No," she said, the word heavy, like it made her sad to have to say it. "I look like myself. I *feel* like myself. For the first time in months. I'm not that little girl who will do whatever you say anymore. I can't."

Novio stepped up beside her, their shoulders touching, and Remy followed suit. He stood on her other side. A united front.

"You don't have to," Novio said. And then to his mom, "She looks great and she performed at the top of her game tonight. You can't ask for more than that. And if you do, you sound like Granddad."

That seemed to steal all the air right out of Maria Garcia's lungs. She looked chastened, even guilty. The tightness in her mouth curved in on itself, her entire body contracting. "You are right. I do sound like him." She swallowed. "I'm proud of you, my beautiful Dita. Ignore me. I forget sometimes that we don't have to please him anymore."

"We never did," Dita said.

But none of them seemed to believe that.

This Roman Garcia must have been some piece of work. Dez was up on all the circus gossip; I hoped maybe he could give me some intel. But that was for later.

I caught Dita's eye. "We did it."

"Partners in crime," she said.

And she had managed her act—unlike me—without almost drowning. A definite win.

Thurston walked out of the ring, everyone making a path for him. He came straight to us. "Well done tonight, everyone," he said, and his eyes settled on me. "I heard a story during intermission from Dez. You'll do that act every night before Raleigh's performances?"

Was he really asking me if I would open for Raleigh?

My mother had said I shouldn't do escapes anymore, not until I could control my magic . . .

But I couldn't turn this down. This was my dream, what I'd come here for. My future in the spotlight.

"Yes," Dita said, her laughter back, "she'd love to."

Thurston's eyebrows lifted. "Are you sure that you're up for it?"

"Yes, I'd love to," I echoed, wishing I sounded more enthusiastic.

"Then it's settled."

He left us, bestowing one final beam on Dita.

Of course, it was possible I'd turn air into burning sand next time. And I'd forgotten to ask whether anyone had checked with Raleigh about this new development.

But I wouldn't spoil our victory celebration by bringing up all the things that could still go wrong, not when they were secrets I had to keep. I'd just obsess over them instead.

nineteen

The answer to whether Raleigh knew about Thurston's promoting me to his opening act got answered pretty quickly the next night when I showed up.

"Don't bother asking, Pixie," Raleigh said. "No, I didn't get a vote. Believe me."

The fact that he was still ticked at me was unfortunate, because I needed to know more about the coin and I'd planned to ask him. He told us he'd heard stories the night of the break-ins. But I knew Raleigh well enough to know he wouldn't be sharing anything with me until he stopped being mad.

He continued, "And *you* are trickier than you seem."

That was for Dita. She had tagged along to apologize.

Ouch on both counts.

"Raleigh, you know I respect you as a magician. You could try doing the same for me," I said. "Dita was just helping me get a break. I don't want to take your place. I swear."

Dez swung through the flap of the tent. He had on his vest, his chest bare beneath. Distracting. He raised his hands and said, "For my next trick, I'll turn this guy into . . . a guy who's happy to have a kick-ass opening act."

Brandon, following Dez, laughed, probably at the word *kick-ass*.

Dez smiled at Dita. "Congratulations to you for last night too, I hear."

"Um, thanks," Dita said, fidgeting, obviously a little embarrassed at the flattery.

"I heard that too," Raleigh said, softening.

Dita said, "You did need to learn how to tie bow ties the right way."

"True, your way is easier," Raleigh admitted. He waved toward the exit flaps. "I'll be back for my set."

I shrugged. "Your loss."

After saying it, I immediately wondered if I should have tried a different tactic. I didn't want him to get upset enough about this to call my dad. I made a promise to myself to be nicer.

"What's wrong?" Dez said, coming closer. "You're doing that thing you do with your lip."

"What thing?" I asked.

He lifted his hand and put his fingertip gently on my lower lip. "Chewing on it. I understand the impulse, but . . ."

I heard a choking sound and looked over to see that Dita's eyes were as wide as the clock face that counted down my escape onstage. They met mine in a way that could only mean *I want to know* all *about this later.*

Dez widened his smile to include both of us and dropped his hand. "I shifted my showtimes so Brandon and I could help out again. I promise to look pretty. Assuming you want me."

Oh, did I. My cheeks heated, and I said, "Please stay."

My escape went as planned that night. Well . . . except for a white-hot flare of magic as I started to work free of the straitjacket.

Panic rose as I stared up at the glass lid of the coffin, and I thrashed against the fabric, burning up. *You have to guide it,* my mother had said. And so I did, visualizing my magic providing an assist as I undid the buckles and the straps. I surged free to a standing ovation.

Maybe my mom didn't know everything. Or maybe I was being an idiot. But I basked in the applause, like I'd earned it all on my own with no magical help.

I swore using the magic wouldn't change me. I wouldn't let it. I couldn't be who I wanted to be without performing.

Dez pulled me aside after I left the stage, frowning. "Where was the water?" he asked.

Oh. Right. He would notice that.

"I can't do it the same way every time," I said, dodging. Not quite a lie. "You might figure out how it's done."

"I'm beginning to think I'll never figure *you* out."

"Good. I don't want you to." That at least was the absolute truth.

"Too bad I can't seem to stop trying."

"My resistance is futile?"

He pulled me against his chest and gave me a kiss that promised more to come later.

"What resistance?" he asked. "You coming to watch my act?"

"Wouldn't miss it."

Then we were off, him to throw knives, and me to admire him while he did.

I was smoothing on lipstick backstage at the magic tent when Raleigh poked his head in—early. "Figured it's probably time to check out my opener," he said. Then he disappeared, presumably to find a good spot in the audience.

This meant we were back on speaking terms. He'd held out longer than I expected, so my relief was beyond genuine. We were in Saint Louis, our third day of shows here, in fact.

Good, I thought. I needed to talk to him. I'd riffled through our RV trying to locate the coin, feeling like sneaky scum, and I kept continual watch for my mother at performances. No surprise—I hadn't seen her again.

These first few weeks of the season had gone by so fast. If this was considered a more leisurely pace, I didn't know how people in other touring shows survived. It felt like as soon as we started doing shows, we were back on the road, catching our breath for a half second, and then on to more shows. Only two months were left until the end of the season. I didn't have a clue how long my mother had—but how could I not try to help her? Besides, then I could see her again. Talk to her again.

Maybe this was what being an adult was like. Not the in-control knows-everything feeling everyone pretended it was, but the constant sensation that everything was moving too fast and there was no way to slow it down.

Dad had sent a giant bouquet of flowers and a gourmet food basket to Amber's address in Ithaca. Her voice-mail message had said, "I feel guilty eating this. But I'm still going to. Call your dad."

Dez came in, so I knew it must be time to go on. I set aside my worries, something I was getting better at. Denial, my new friend.

"Ready?" he asked.

"Always," I said.

We went out onstage together. I launched into my now-practiced patter, spotting Raleigh at the back of the tent. He stood in the corner behind the last row, arms crossed.

Dez helped me into the coffin, as usual. And as usual, his touch set off butterflies within me. We were getting closer. But I couldn't shake the feeling that he didn't know me at all.

I pushed the button with my toe to expel the air and worked to get free. The heat of my magic burned through me, a searing flame I was almost used to, though it hurt every time. But no water appeared from thin air, and I guided the magic through my arms and fingers, making my best time yet.

The crowd applauded once I was successful and bowing before them—and Raleigh joined in before slipping out to get in costume and persona.

"Not bad," he said when we rejoined him backstage. His assistant was there too, prepping the cabinet. Dez and Brandon left again to wheel off my equipment.

"Thanks," I said, though it was hardly high praise.

"You'll need to come up with something new before long. People will get tired of it. More importantly, you will."

He might be right, but he was one to talk. I eyed his cabinet, where his assistant nodded to me before stepping inside. Caliban was with her, as ever.

"I am working on something else," he said. "It's just busier here than I expected. And buying equipment is expensive."

"You don't need to justify anything to me. I'm just grateful for the chance to be onstage. And I'm almost ready to test out a new illusion." I hadn't showed it to anyone yet, because I lacked a few supplies and I would need help to pull it off. This illusion would see me suspended in the air, precarious in a different way than in the coffin, and potentially much more dangerous.

But I was convinced I could handle it.

Raleigh pulled on his jacket and straightened the sleeves.

Dez and Brandon were still clearing the stage, so I chanced asking the real question I had for him. "Hey, you heard any more about that coin? The, um, magic one? I'm curious about it—whether anyone thinks it's real."

He frowned. "Like father, like daughter, I guess?"

I blinked. "What does that mean?"

"You know. All that stuff your dad collects." He made spooky spirit fingers. "With supposed powers. Oooooh."

"He does?"

He gave me a skeptical look. "Yes. You've been in the warehouses."

I'd been in *the* warehouse. Singular.

"Oh, that stuff. Right." Dad had been keeping a lot more secrets than I'd even realized. "So, you hear anything else about the coin? Any idea where it is? Dita worries," I added, feeling like dirt for using her name.

"I wish. I see the security guys around, and I don't think there've been any more break-ins. People still talk, but they don't say anything new."

"Really? What do you hear them saying?"

Raleigh shrugged one shoulder, sleek in his tux. "Just that it's real, and that they're looking for it."

"They who?"

"The mysterious 'they' who are never defined. You're awfully curious about this, Pixie."

I was about to ask more anyway about whom he'd heard discussing the mysterious *they* and the coin, but Dez came back. He looked between the two of us with some suspicion.

"What are you two talking about?" Dez said. "You both look dead serious."

"Nothing," Raleigh answered.

"Whatever," Dez said. "I gotta go. You coming?"

He meant to watch his act. "Of course." He tugged on my shirt and gave me a quick kiss. I didn't let myself worry about the fact that it was obviously for Raleigh's benefit as much as mine.

Raleigh said nothing. The magician code meant he'd expected me to return the favor and watch his set. I went with Dez anyway, my new loyalty asserting itself.

He rewarded me with a grin when we got outside. "That guy likes you," he said.

"No, he's just being big-brotherly. Besides, I like you."

"Good."

Brandon was ahead of us in the crowd, and he'd stopped to talk to someone. It was that man from poker night. Weird, creepy Rex. He wore the same fedora-ish hat as the last time he'd made an appearance.

What was equally weird was that Dez stopped cold when he spotted them.

"Dez? What's wrong?"

He stood frozen for another second, then seemed to relax. *Seemed to* because his shoulders were still tight, but he forced the tension out of the hand that was in mine. Magicians notice these things.

"Nothing," he said. "I'll see you after, okay?"

He kissed my cheek again and took off, heading straight for Brandon and Rex. The man reached out and took his shoulder when he got to them. It was impossible to tell from my vantage point whether the slight shake he gave Dez was affectionate.

The three of them disappeared between the side of the contortionists' tent and the stage.

Huh.

I found my way to the back of the crowd that was already gathering to watch the hot knife-thrower do his thing. Dez and I were new, I told myself, and we hadn't even really had a "define the relationship" talk yet. Him talking to random family friends in unusual hats was none of my business.

Neither was my talking to Raleigh about the coin any of his business, for that matter.

Dez was late coming out, though, which was odd. He usually appeared onstage right at 8:50, punctual to a fault.

When he finally arrived, five minutes late, I went still in shock.

He had a cut that seeped blood on one cheek, and his left eye was rapidly turning purple. "Got into a fight with my equipment manager," he said, with a grin that might have fooled the audience, but not me. "You should see the other guy."

Brandon, standing at the side of the stage, appeared fine. Something told me creepy weirdo did too. He'd hurt Dez, for some reason.

I changed my mind. This *was* my business, whether Dez wanted me to stay out of it or not.

twenty

I retraced my steps and ducked off the midway between the same tent and stage where I'd seen Dez, Brandon, and Rex disappear a few minutes earlier. This was the way to the back of Dez's stage, where I'd wait for him to finish his act—and hope his busted eye didn't throw off his aim.

He hardly even needs to see to throw accurately, I told myself. *That's how good he is.*

Small comfort. I also kept my eyes peeled for any sign of Rex. He was nowhere in sight.

Intuition—and what I knew about Dez—told me if I didn't catch him immediately after he came offstage, he'd avoid me entirely. Waiting gave me time to roll around in my head the new fact about Dad being into magic items and having a warehouse I knew nada about. My whole life was beginning to feel like a lie, and somehow that made me more determined to talk to Dez. To be there for him.

To make this relationship one true thing . . . if I could.

A few minutes later, the crowd erupted into sustained applause, which meant Dez was finishing up. A fact confirmed by Brandon descending the set of steps that led down from backstage a few minutes later. "Sorry, cutie. He gave you the slip."

"What?"

"He went off into the crowd, signed a few autographs, and bolted. Must've known you'd head back here."

"Where can I find him?" I asked.

"Nowhere tonight. He'll let you find him when he wants to be found."

Argh. Boys were maddening.

I pressed Brandon. "Is that guy gone? Dez isn't going after him, is he?"

He hesitated. "He's gone. And Dez wouldn't go after him without me."

That was a relief, at least. "What happened?"

Brandon tilted his head back and stared up at the starless black sky. We were alone, so there was no reason for him not to answer. Then he said, "He's my brother. You're not."

"You two are brothers?"

Brandon looked back at me and snorted. "No, but we might as well be. And that means you need to leave it alone."

"So you're not going to help me. Do you have the phone tonight, or does he?"

He shrugged. "He does, and now I have to go clear the stage. Leave him be tonight, 'kay?"

I didn't bother answering. He headed up the stairs again, and I was already tapping out a text message to Dez: We don't have to talk about why you have a black eye if you don't want to, but I want to see you.

I waited a long minute, staring at the screen, willing him to respond. Nothing.

So I added: I care about you. ♥

That did get a response: Your mistake.

I tried a couple of times more: Tell me where you are. I'll come meet you.

Brandon returned with a duffel bag, undoubtedly full of knives. "Just leave him be. No one wants to see their girl when they just got beat down. He's got bigger things to think about tonight."

After waiting longer than I should have, I gave up and went to bed, deciding I'd track him down tomorrow. I just hoped he was okay when I did.

He dodged me the whole next day. Didn't respond to the texts I sent. And then he didn't show up to be my assistant. Raleigh loaned me his, and I had to admit she did an excellent job.

But Raleigh had made it clear she couldn't do it permanently.

I could find another person to fill in as my assistant, no question there. But I wasn't willing to give up on Dez. Despite his managing to dodge me after his act again, twice. He wasn't going to escape from this escape artist so easily.

Nonetheless, locating Dez was proving far more difficult than it should have been. He was a no-show at the dinner mess. And I had no idea where he slept—something that should have occurred to me before now. He'd always come to me, and I'd never thought to wonder.

I waited until after the evening's last show and wandered around the Cirque grounds through a relatively sedate night, looking for the fire-pit-slash-party edge of camp. My best bet to find him.

A few people had their RV doors open or sat outside in clustered camp chairs, drinking together. I searched each mini-gathering I passed for a familiar grin. Finally, I found one—if not the one I was looking for.

Brandon was at a card table set up for a poker game along the edge of the grounds. The only places that I hadn't checked yet were the province of the big trucks and equipment haulers arrayed behind the poker game. The table was a mix of workingmen and a few people I recognized from the Cirque performer families. The Garcias' quiet father was there. I was relieved to see that Dez's family friend wasn't.

I didn't want to interrupt, but I had little choice. I tried to be as inconspicuous about it as possible, circling around to kneel behind Brandon.

I tapped his shoulder, and he grunted. "What?"

"Where's Dez?" I asked.

He shrugged the shoulder closest to me and said over it, "How would I know?"

I sighed. "Can we talk for a sec?"

"Nope," he said, "I'm busy. Your boyfriend will have to wait. If he still is."

"Can you at least tell me where he might be? Where do you guys stay?"

That stiffened his arms for a second before he relaxed again. "Keep walking," he said, "and you'll see."

He didn't glance at me or follow up in any way, so I stood to leave. "He means back that way," a random guy watching the game told me, pointing toward the big semis.

"Got it," I said, though I didn't.

But I could hardly march back in the direction of the Cirque now—I didn't want to leave this unfinished with Dez. Maybe the two of them had a cute tent they pitched back here or something. That wouldn't be so bad, even if it meant the lack of a real roof overhead.

There was a line of porta-potties back here, and outdoor showers hooked up to a water line. I passed them and made for the big trucks. Surprisingly, there were lights on in the backs of the semis closest to the makeshift plumbing. Multiple sliding doors ran along the side, some open and some closed.

The first open door showed a glimpse of a single-sized bunk with rumpled sheets crammed against a partition, a pole for hanging up clothes, and no other room to speak of.

These semis weren't for hauling equipment. They housed miniature living compartments.

I checked in each open door as discreetly as I could, nodding to crewmen as I passed. Most of them, already asleep, didn't nod back. The doors were left open to admit night air. No one had air-conditioning, though a few had fans rigged up in the corners.

Dez wasn't in the first truck, so I kept going to the next. The same story along this line of sleeping compartments—a few people sleeping, others with their doors closed.

I neared the end of the truck. One door closed, and one last open one.

"Dez?" I asked softly, sensing he was near. Hoping he was and hoping he wasn't. I knew he probably didn't want me here.

"Shit," he said.

Guess I was right.

I paused. I couldn't see him yet.

Obviously, I didn't care that he lived in this tiny space. That these semis existed was another part of circus life I hadn't known about. I hadn't even considered that Dez didn't have a nice place to stay. My alternative to the Airstream had been my convertible, and I'd thought that wouldn't be comfortable enough. I was a pampered princess, I realized, in a way I'd never understood before. I felt ashamed of my obliviousness.

I took another step.

"Welcome to my humble abode," he said.

He was sitting up against the makeshift metal wall behind a small cot, like he'd been staring out into the nothingness of the night before I arrived.

He reached over and pulled the chain on a desk lamp sitting precariously on top of a battered red dictionary on a shelf over the bed.

The light revealed a swollen eye with impressively, painfully multihued bruising around it. There was also a tint of red on his cheeks.

Him blushing instead of me, for once, and I hated it. I hated what I suspected was the reason for it.

"Don't you dare feel embarrassed." I paused. "Can we talk here? Can anyone hear?"

I knew a little about my dangers, but I didn't know the first thing about Dez's.

"Brandon's out running a game," he said. "No one else would be able to. But I'm not really in a talking mood."

"Too bad." I eased onto the cot and swung my feet up, sitting cross-legged beside him. He didn't mirror my posture, leaving his legs stretched out beside mine. Not touching, but so close that it had to be a decision for them not to.

"You came to break it off, didn't you? I can save you the time." He raised his hands and made sarcastic air quotes. "'We aren't right for each other. Two different worlds. Fun while it lasted.'"

The words were clipped. I'd never seen him like this.

"Wrong. I came to tell you that I don't get brushed off this easy. Dez, I may be stupid. I know I shouldn't want this, but . . . I don't want to break anything off. Not with you." I took a breath. If I was brave enough to seal myself into a coffin . . . "I came to make this real."

He shifted forward, away from the wall. Toward me.

"And I came to see if you're okay. Why'd that guy hit you?"

He surged forward, and his other hand cupped my cheek, and he kissed me. His lips crashed into mine, but it was a pleasant pain. This kiss had darkness in it, and frustration, and wanting. And it felt true. True in a way our others hadn't. In the way I wanted with him.

I kissed him back the same way.

Danger, danger, my brain said. My heart beat back its response: *Shut up. Shut up and kiss the boy.*

I pulled back first. "Why was that guy here again? He doesn't seem like much of a family friend, doing this." When Dez's expression darkened, I added, "Not to such a pretty face."

I gingerly touched the unmarked skin below the bruising. And then I moved beside him, our bodies touching from our shoulders to our calves, hanging off the side of the little bed. We faced the small sampling of clothes draped over the top of the bar, including his tanks. The only nicer piece of clothing there was the suit from our date.

"I don't think our families are much alike," Dez said. "Can't we just go back to kissing?"

Ha. You have no idea. "We can, as soon as you explain. How you grew up . . . that's not your fault."

"I should have texted you back," he said.

"So make it up to me. Tell me now. Why did that guy hit you?" I didn't ask why Dez would let him. That guy had given off a deep feeling of wrongness about him during my one close encounter. I wouldn't encourage Dez to fight him.

"I owe him something. My dad owed him something."

"Money?"

"Worse. Loyalty."

That *was* worse. A sudden thought occurred to me. "You aren't here looking for a magic coin, are you? One that belonged to the Garcias?"

Long moments stretched with no glib reply. Probably I shouldn't have asked. Could Dez be one of *them*? The Praestigae? It was impossible, right? But . . .

"You should be careful who you mention that to," he said.

I wasn't letting him off the hook. "Should I have mentioned it to *you*? What do you know about it?"

"What do *you* know about it?"

"You realize you're acting really weird, right? Are you looking for it?"

"No, but I've heard a lot of chatter about it," he said. "The way you do in places like this. Rumors about last season, about this famous coin surfacing that means easy street for anyone who has it. There are people who are convinced that it exists and that it gives good luck. People always want something valuable."

In some ways, it would have been less complicated if he'd said yes, he was looking for it. My mother needed it. He might even have had the answers I longed for. Of course, my mother was also convinced that the Praestigae finding out about me would be a disaster.

"How did you hear about it?" he asked. "From Nancy Maroni?" He dropped the name casually.

That set off a string of doubts: He wasn't lying to me now, was he? He could have just pretended that he'd never even heard of it. But he hadn't—which meant he probably *wasn't* looking for it. Or he was lying to me again and I was a terrible judge of character making a huge mistake.

No, I want this. Him.

"I heard it belonged to the Garcias," I said. "And *they've* heard that people are looking for it." Except that possibly made it sound like *they* told me about the coin, and implied that I thought it was real. That was too much to give away. But the leap he made was a different one.

"Then they don't have it?"

I shrugged. "How would I know? And why do you want to know anyway? Do you believe what you've heard? That it's real, and that it can do, um, magic?"

I had no idea why I was asking him this. I was begging to get caught.

"Sure."

Not the response I expected. I straightened. "You do?"

He put his hand on my cheek again. "I keep telling you, where I come from, it's not like wherever you're from, lovely Moira. We believe in fairy tales. Magic coins, fair ladies, evil witches, tyrant kings, and benevolent queens."

"Very funny." I couldn't tell if he was joking. He had mentioned the rumors about Nan to me too. "Anyway, handsome prince, you promise you won't disappear again? That you'll be honest with me?"

"I'll do my best." One side of his lips quirked, and then I got a full grin. "I'm happy you didn't come to break up with me."

I thought when he moved again, it would be to kiss me. But he pulled at my limbs, until we lay down beside each other in the little bunk, spooning, his front folded against my back. We could just barely fit, sideways. The embrace should have felt stifling. Instead, I felt safe.

More of this, my heart said. But *danger, danger,* said my brain.

Dez pressed a kiss to the crown of my head, and his fingers traced a lazy circle on my hand.

"I'm glad you came," he said.

"I'm glad our cards are on the table," I said, wishing mine were.

I didn't try to read the meaning of his sigh against my hair.

twenty-one

The hardware store aisles gleamed around us, packed with hammers and wrenches, nails and bolts. Normally, I'd have ordered what I needed for my new escape illusion from one of Dad's suppliers. But that had been a lot easier when I was having things shipped to the condo or the theater, and then peeling them off as needed.

"What are we here for again?" Dez asked. His eye was almost back to normal, with only faded bruising around it. A red line where his cheek scab had been.

He'd ridden with me on the drive here to Kansas City for our shows through the Fourth of July. In fact, we'd spent an insane amount of time together over the past week. I should have been sick of being around him, and wanting to be alone, if only for a few hours.

But I wasn't and didn't.

I was in deep trouble with this beautiful, rakish boy. Hanging out with him almost made me forget about the revelations from my mother. And Dad's secret warehouse. Almost. Nothing kept me from worrying about my magic and what would happen if I couldn't control it during the illusion I was planning.

Becoming a magician was still the most important thing in my life. I'd poured all my excess energy into developing this new escape. My most spectacular yet.

And, yes, the riskiest. But I wasn't telling anyone that part.

"Lovely Moira? I asked you a question," Dez said. "Are you obsessing about my good looks again?"

"Something like that," I said.

He leaned in and gave me a quick kiss. Easy and familiar. Which had the combined effect of being disconcerting. I was falling for him too hard. The girls at the theater would have urged caution, even if Dita and Jules seemed to approve. (Jules especially—he'd gotten her right at the start with the flowers and the solo Ferris wheel ride.)

Dez swept his arms to indicate the entire store around us. He was in his usual tank and beat-up jeans. "So, what are we here for? Because I would like to be somewhere else. Somewhere with just the two of us."

"Shut up," I said, knowing my cheeks had gone up in a flare of May Day red. His arms were distractingly delicious from all that knife-throwing. "You're assisting me today. We're working."

"Ready and willing. So . . ."

I started walking up the aisle again. "Chains. We're here for chains."

When he didn't respond right away, I looked over my shoulder. He was standing in the middle of the aisle. "Kinky," he said.

My cheeks, my cheeks, my cheeks are on fire. We don't need no water; let me do a disappearing act. Poof.

"They're for my new illusion, gutter mind."

"Oh," he said with a shrug, and advanced. When he got close, he spoke into my ear. "I love messing with you."

I rolled my eyes. "Romantic interlude over."

Besides, we were at the section of locks and chains. There was a display of various chains hanging lengthwise. I ran my fingers over them, testing the size of the links and the weight of each one thoroughly.

"This one's nice." I wrapped the promising silver chain with tight links around my forearm and tugged to see how it felt.

"You're going to use those?" he asked. "Why call it an illusion and use real chains?"

"An escape illusion. This is for the escape part. What else would I use? I left my good chains at home." I didn't look away, thoroughly absorbed in deciding which would work best. This new illusion was going to be grand, outdoors, and bar-raising for me—assuming I was able to convince Thurston to let me do it.

He had let Jules walk above cities, so I figured it should be fine. I just had to pull it off perfectly when I demonstrated it for him. That was the key to getting his approval.

"Um, you could use fake chains? Some sort of magic-shop fake ones? Or just stand on the ground and do card tricks?"

"Gross," I said. "That's not the kind of magic I do." I paused. "I mean, I do employ certain tools and tricks, but you need the major elements of an escape to be real these days. People are too savvy to believe what happens behind a curtain is real now. They want to see something they never thought they'd see up close. Like a girl escaping from chains"—I smiled—"while suspended upside down from a burning rope."

I looked around the store. "Speaking of which, we need to pick up some heavy-duty rope too."

"Suspended from how high?" His arms were crossed in front of his chest.

"I thought I'd start with a dozen feet."

"Oh, just enough to break your neck."

I narrowed my eyes, focusing on the chains in front of me. "I don't plan on doing that. Why the sudden attitude change? You helped me get my break."

"I know. What was I thinking? I don't like the idea of this one."

"You're scared. Aw, that's sweet. But I'll be fine." Unless I magicked the rope into water and fell to my doom. But I'd gotten better at guiding the magic, at ignoring the pain.

"I just don't want anything bad to happen to you."

"I could get hit by a bus outside." I struggled to keep my voice casual, but I was irritated by this line of conversation. It felt like a cousin of the same sexism that had prevented Dad from being able to see me as a potential magician, like him. "I'm good at this stuff, you know? I've been practicing for years. I've put in the time. I know how to design an illusion. I would never plan an escape I thought I couldn't do. Putting yourself in real danger in front of an audience is unethical."

I was parroting things I'd heard Dad say in lectures. And I was lying again. This was the same kind of unethical as magicians pretending to have supernatural powers—which was weighed down with irony now that I really did have them. I still wanted to do magic *my* way, but my mother had been right about one thing: doing escapes seemed to make my actual magic show up.

"That first night, with the water—was that safe? You haven't done it again. You had a close call, didn't you? What happened?"

Of course it hadn't been safe. It also wasn't part of the illusion. I couldn't tell him that. Part of me wanted to, more than anything. But it wasn't smart.

And I was always smart.

"I'm standing here, aren't I?" I whirled back to the chains and picked out a long strand. "I think this is thick enough to be dramatic but not so thick as to completely impede my movements. I brought my own locks, just in case. I've been toying around with this idea for a while."

"You're the expert," he said.

"Yes, I am."

I went to get the owner of the hardware shop to cut the length of chain I needed and then some rope. While he did, Dez prowled around the edges of the store.

He rejoined me at the checkout counter. "I should make you empty your pockets," the balding owner said, addressing both of us.

My jaw dropped open. "I'm a customer."

"Not you. Your friend." He spoke more clearly to Dez the next time. "Don't think about taking anything out of here, young man."

"No plans to," Dez said calmly. Like the guy hadn't accused him of being a thief. "I apologize. It's an old habit."

I forked over a credit card with a clumsy hand, and the guy ran it. "Thanks, Miss—"

I snapped back to attention and cut him off. "Moira's fine." I scribbled on the receipt. I hadn't even considered that my card had my real last name on it. Sloppy.

"No harm meant," Dez said, smiling one of his more inscrutable smiles as he picked up the box the guy had stowed my chains and rope in.

We hit the sunny sidewalk outside, heading toward the parking lot and my convertible.

"What's an old habit?" I asked Dez.

"You don't want to know."

"No, I do. I really do."

He stopped walking and looked at me. "Casing the place. Figuring out where the cameras are." He started moving again, and I trailed him. "And your last name's Mitchell, not Miracle, based on your credit card. I figured Miracle was a stage name, but it's good to know for sure."

We were at the car. I unlocked the doors and got in, buying time to figure out how to respond.

Dez thumped the trunk, and I pressed the button to open it. He loaded the box and got in the passenger seat.

I sighed, looking at him. "I want to trust you." Those brown eyes were all too known to me these days. Yet there was obviously so much we *didn't* know about each other.

"We can't always get what we want."

No kidding.

"Look, back there," he said. "That's something I'd rather not talk about."

How could I press harder, given the secrets I was holding back from him?

"Talking is boring anyway," I said.

And then we were kissing, his hand winding up into my curls. He'd admitted he was checking the place out, that it was habit. But I was the one not being trustworthy.

I told myself I didn't have a choice.

twenty-two

I looked down from my vantage point, standing in a car on the Ferris wheel's next-to-lowest arm. A rope was wrapped securely around my ankles and tied off to the other end of the car.

"You're sure this is safe?" Dez asked from the ground below.

"That again?"

Jules had volunteered to do the honors of lighting the flash powder that would slowly, very slowly, burn away the rope fibers—leaving me plenty of time to escape from the chains draped all around me, secured by locks.

Dez would take over her duties next time, assuming Thurston approved of me doing this escape when the midway was open. As expected, he *had* wanted to see the new act before he gave it the okay, since it would require stopping operation of the ever-popular wheel for a few minutes. Still, it had seemed like the most logical choice for something to tie on to in a dramatic way, in the absence of any five-story buildings like the kind Houdini and Dorothy Dietrich had used for similar escapes. And I had a soft spot for the Ferris wheel, site of a certain first date.

Plus, I thought Raleigh would be relieved to have me out of his domain.

Or not.

He stood in the background, behind the others who had gathered to watch. Thurston was there, of course, along with a motley assortment of Cirque folk, and the familiar faces of Dita, Remy, and Nan. I'd been surprised when Nan showed up, elegant as ever. Dez was in the front of the pack.

"You're sure this is good?" Jules said, eyeing the rope. "I could ask Dad to check it out. He always gives my wires a look."

"I appreciate the offer, but it's good. I've had some practice with knots." No need to divulge that my practice before today had been piecemeal, mostly involving tying knots I could then undo or experimenting in the theater with tie-offs when no one was around. I had gotten good at slipping out of handcuffs while suspended from one of the wires in the theater—right side up, so I could abort if anyone came along. Doing a more formal version like this had been the goal all along, but those stolen sessions had been far simpler.

Easy isn't what the audience wants.

I sucked in a breath and lifted one of my arms. It was chained, but Jules would also close the lock that would bind it against my body. One of the sound guys had given me a clip mic, to help with projecting my voice.

"You might think this escape is a hat tip to Houdini. But, instead, I want to dedicate it to one of the best-known stage performers of her time, Mercedes Talma, also known as Talma, the Queen of Coins. My sleeveless costume is a nod to her performances." I flourished with my fingers and produced a prop gold coin. Then three. My audience gave me a smattering of applause, and I tossed the coins down to them. The inside of my black shirt and my pants contained a few hidden pockets packed with similar worthless prop coins. I had to hope I'd calibrated right not to release them until the big finish.

I continued. "You've probably seen her on old posters, rising off a table draped in a sheet. She was the woman used by her husband, Servais Le Roy, when he invented the levitation trick. But she soon won top billing of her own, and Houdini himself gave the thumbs-up to her mastery of sleight of hand with coins. Once, reportedly, muggers made the mistake of accosting her on the city streets—she kept producing coins until they were convinced she was magic, and they ran away. My feat today will be a bit of a metaphorical twist on the same. These chains symbolize the protection of gold and valuables. Escaping them before the rope burns will be all the more difficult—but what if I told you to think of this like a heist we're embarking on together? I will get through the locks and chains, and deliver the valuables to you. Hopefully, with just the mystifying touch Talma herself employed during her thirty years on the stage."

I held my arm in against myself, positioning it so there'd be a small fraction of extra room. "Would you do the honors, Jules?"

Stage magic happened in those small fractions, the secret pockets of reality no one bothered to pay attention to. "And will you assure everyone that the chains and locks are real?"

Jules tested the chains that looped around my arms, torso, and legs. Then she secured each of the five locks with the master key.

I hadn't made things easy on myself. I expected my magic to show up, like it usually did these days during an escape, but I planned to guide it, as my mother had said—not to rely on it—to accomplish this feat. I'd gotten better at doing that. I hoped.

"Stand back," I cautioned.

Then I stepped off the arm of the Ferris wheel into nothing.

I plunged through the air, the rope yanking tight at my ankles.

My small audience's collective gasp was gratifying music to my ears.

I'd practiced a few times with Dez earlier that day, on how to time the step and the fall so nothing got dislocated. That didn't mean I'd done it enough to make it as familiar as producing the coin from my palm had been.

I dangled at the end of the rope secured around both my ankles. Taking a breath to get my bearings, I spun in the air, bound in chains.

The head costumer had suggested making a velvet lining to go between my ankles and the rope to make it more comfortable. *Comfortable* wasn't really the word I'd have used, but at least it only dug partway into my flesh.

"Fire!" I called out.

Jules muttered something above, but I couldn't make out what she said. She took the automatic lighter I'd provided—as if she was about to light me like a barbecue—struck it, and held it next to the rope.

The flames were dramatic, the flash powder providing an extra burst and a pop. Another gasp from my small crowd. The strangers in it applauded. I saw Brandon join Dez, shaking his head and gaping at me like I was crazy.

It was Dita who called up this time. "Are you sure this is safe?"

I grinned dizzily, blood rushing to my head. "Now let's complete this heist," I called out.

I worked against the chains. The warm metal pressed into the bare skin of my arms, baking in the sun. The chains pressed less firmly into my torso. I'd have imprints later from the coins concealed there.

My head pounded like the world's worst migraine, and I crooked a bit at the waist to hold it up. A little dizziness wouldn't kill me. A lot might.

At least there's no magic heat yet, I told myself.

I fought to get my neck at a good angle. The wind and my own motion sent me rocking like the more violent pendulum of a clock. Back and forth in the air, back and forth . . .

I had a thin pick just inside a hidden pocket at my waist to help with the locks—two of them would fall away when the chains did, not as secure as they'd appeared—but I had to loosen one of the coils enough to get to the pick before it could help me out.

Which would have been much easier right side up.

My breathing grew shallow. I *was* in danger. I'd rushed putting this together.

I had to get out of this.

I exhaled and punched one arm through a loop in the chains. The rope above sizzled and popped, and Jules called out: "A strand just gave. Hurry, Moira!"

One of the locks Jules had secured was of my own design, and I shook it off, letting it fall to the ground below. The crowd cheered.

Sweat dripped into my eye, stinging. *Stay focused.*

As the rope swung, my magic arrived, roaring to life. Still, my heart thudded with the certainty that I was in danger of failing this escape.

My hands heated against the chain, and the chains absorbed it, every link consumed by a fast-moving wave. I was wrapped in the coils of a snake made of fire. A snake like the one in my mother's tattoo.

The overheated chains squeezed me tighter, forcing my breath out. I fought to suck in more air. Enough to keep going.

I wasn't guiding the magic. It was in control.

"Moira! Everything okay?" Dez, of course.

I gave a shaky thumbs-up with the closest thing I had to a free hand.

"Second strand!" Jules called, almost shrieking it. "Gah!"

The rope let go some traction, jerking against my ankles. I fell. Only a few inches.

But I was running out of time.

And burning up.

My blood boiled, and I did what an escape artist should never do. I began to focus on every way this was going wrong.

About how the chains around me were too hot, and I couldn't make them not be, and how when the audience pulled them away from me later, they'd see the imprints of the chains scorched into my skin. In this vision, I lay twisted on the ground, eyes staring up at nothing.

Morbid. So morbid. Don't turn into the audience. It was Dad's voice, not mine, that I heard in my head. *They might want a dramatic failure, but they can't have one.*

"Moira?" Dez again.

"Just a sec," I grumbled through a burning throat.

I stopped moving and closed my eyes. And I banished that vision of myself dead. I ignored the heat burning into me and visualized ice coating the chains. I strained to transform the heat, to draw on my magic to help me. To guide it, the way I'd thought I was better at now.

Come on. Do it.

The heat eased a fraction. I moved, and . . .

My arms slid through the chains like they were water and I was cutting through the waves.

I heard another lock fall and hit the ground with a dull thud, even though I wasn't sure I had gotten to the pick, and then another. A length of silver chain followed them to the ground, and my eyes locked on it in wonder. A little in horror.

My entire body felt like a live wire, like electricity, like I was the fire, I was magic itself, and nothing that was real could hold me.

Oh, Houdini, if you could see me now. The truly unholdable girl.

I wanted to laugh or scream, make some noise that proved I was still alive, but I didn't. I found the pick, undid the last true lock, and cast off the final chain.

As if on cue, Jules shrieked again: "It's almost through!"

A flash of motion below, and someone produced a net from behind a tent. That was not the plan.

"As promised," I shouted, "the contents of the imaginary safe we just robbed! In Talma's memory!"

I triggered the release mechanisms with quick, clever fingers, and as the gold coins showered down, I heaved myself up to grab the rope above where it was burning. Then I swung over to the arm of the Ferris wheel and landed safely on the metal.

The rope gave at that moment, burned through, the length that had supported me dropping to the ground.

That couldn't have been more perfect had I timed it.

The crowd called out, cheering and clapping. I waved, like Dad would do from the top of the theater.

Jules climbed down from the car and grabbed me. She clutched me, like she still wasn't sure I was safe.

"That was terrifying," Jules said, beaming at me. "I loved it."

You barely made it, a little voice inside me said. But the applause below drowned it out. I had done it. I'd successfully resisted my magic's takeover and made it work for me.

"Come down and accept your kudos," Thurston said, producing a bottle of champagne from somewhere and popping the cork. His assistant held a clutch of plastic flutes.

I didn't meet Dez's eyes until I was on the ground. He was smiling, but there was something else behind his expression. Intense suspicion. He took one of my coins and flipped it into the air, catching it again. I kissed him on the cheek, quick, before he could say anything.

Not that he did.

Nan met me at Thurston's side. She took my elbow and kept a placid smile pasted on while she spoke. "That was not just skill, Moira. You must be careful."

I didn't want to hear it, so I turned to Thurston. "Champagne, you said?"

"I know you're underage, but you're not as young as this one." He eyed Jules, in a half embrace with Remy already.

Brandon took one of the plastic glasses of champagne and handed it to Dez, then another for me. They were also underage. Raleigh accepted one too, but he simply downed it and left.

Thurston didn't seem to notice. "To a great escape!" he said, lifting his glass. "And to the magic of the Cirque!"

Nan frowned at that wording, but she took a sip anyway.

We all plastic-clinked, and then Dez pulled me off to one side. "Was the effect what I wanted?" I asked, only because I knew the answer was yes. Sometimes you want constructive criticism, but other times you just want to be told you know what you're doing. After how close that had been, I wanted to hear nothing but praise.

Dez had an intensity to him that didn't mesh with celebration. "You almost didn't make that, did you? Why are you pretending?"

I went still. "What are you talking about?"

He shook his head. "Stop pretending that was safe. You want me to watch you get hurt?"

I held out my arms. "Do I look hurt?"

Okay, so there were marks from the chains on my skin, but I was fine. *I was fine.*

"Not yet," he said.

I gulped another drink of the warm, dry champagne.

Thurston called out, "Moira, can I steal you for a sec? I want to hear how you make the flames on the rope so dramatic. I wonder if we could use that trick elsewhere."

Dita, beside him, was nodding and smiling. "She always says my costume looks like a daredevil's," she said. "Maybe it could be something special I use in our act. We could make my swing look literally smoking hot?" She swallowed her smile, then added, "A little extra before our remembrance on the third."

"Go on," Dez said. "Go talk to the people who can't tell you're risking your life. I'm not one of them."

I watched him walk away. He didn't understand, because he couldn't. I'd been fooling him all along.

twenty-three

I didn't always make my way over to the big top at night. Only occasionally, when I wanted to catch one of my friends' acts. I did the next night for the last show of the day.

There had been a soft murmuring about these July holiday shows among the performers who'd been around last year, ever since we arrived. And Dita had made it plain that her desire for a special addition to her performance on the third was related to the absence of Jules's cousin. It was the anniversary of the Cirque's loss.

Dez had said he had "things to do" after his knife act. I hadn't argued. Neither of us was ready to apologize yet.

I figured he'd get over it before he had to take on Jules's role for the real live encore of the burning rope escape when we got to Dallas.

Entering the backstage area, I encountered the usual bustle and tumble of bodies and activity. To an outside observer, it might seem like there was no difference between this day and any other. But there was an undercurrent that wasn't usually present, and Dita had been possessed by a stormy moodiness earlier. The circus was built on risk, on taking chances. But today, everyone wanted to make it through the day a little more than usual—with no incident or accidents, like the tragic one they'd witnessed a year ago tonight. Thurston was throwing a "wake or a remembrance, whichever you prefer to call it" in the mess tent after this show.

I reached the Garcias' area as they were preparing to head out. Dita had some flash powder I'd given her, and she was going to employ it at the start of her trick. She'd been defiant about not wanting to wait to incorporate it. She was determined to use it tonight.

"Hey," I said to her, "you all set? Sure you don't want to hold off and practice a few more times?"

I had no doubt she'd do great with it—she had been performing at top capacity since her costume switch and, unlike me, didn't need magic to do it—but I also didn't want her to feel like she *had* to use it. There was little danger in it, but navigating through the burst of smoke might prove difficult at first. On a day when everyone else was being extra-careful, she wasn't.

"You sound like one of my parents," she said. "Sam was a born performer. He would want me to pull out all the stops."

I nodded. It was the first time I'd heard her say his name.

The audience erupted into applause, and Remy waved Dita over to the starting point. "See you after," I said.

I joined the small gathering of people at the side curtain to watch, nodding to Raleigh hovering at the back. There weren't too many onlookers this evening. Whether it was due to superstition or eagerness to get the party started was impossible to say. Probably both. Thurston did his usual banter, and the Flying Garcias sailed up to their posts and began flying through the air in turns.

Dita raised her hands and clapped her palms together, and special-effects smoke billowed around her. The audience cheered as she grabbed the trapeze and swung out through the smoke. In her black and red, she was like a daring devil emerging from some fiery dimension. She built speed, blazing back and forth. And when she let go of the bar, not a soul in that room doubted she'd make the somersaults. She did one, two, three perfect spins, then latched onto her brother's wrists.

I never doubted she'd make it these days, not since the first night I'd watched her achieve a triple. She might not have been born on a trapeze, but she'd been born into a family who put her up there quickly enough that she might as well have been.

After the last bows were taken, the Garcias rejoined us back-stage. Dita's mood had lifted a fraction. There was an almost-smile on her lips.

Raleigh appeared as we made our way over to the family's dressing tables.

"Party?" I asked Dita.

I knew I should try to make things right with Dez, but I also knew I shouldn't ditch Dita when she was feeling vulnerable.

"Let me do a quick change." She paused. "I won't want to stay long."

"You don't have to go at all."

"No, I do. I want to."

"Sam would go," I said, just for her.

"He would. So I will," she said. "It's nice to hear his name again."

Her eyes were bright, shining with unshed tears.

She slid the top drawer of the dresser open and began pawing through it. "What in the . . ." She reached farther into the drawer.

The inside was a messy jumble of bow ties and undershirts, a rum-pled men's button-down, stray sequins, and gym chalk. The arrange-ment, or rather the lack of it, was odd. Dita was unfailingly tidy. I was neat, but I often worried I was still too much of a slob for her to happily share a tiny room with. She never left anything out that could be put away.

"Somebody's been in here," she said. After checking the contents, she pulled out a folded piece of paper jammed at the back. She unfolded it, skimmed it, and said with pain, "Not today."

I reached over to take the paper from her. Remy and Novio had been chatting, but they turned to face us now. "What is it?" Raleigh asked.

"Another note," Dita said. I showed it to them.

I want the coin. You Garcias know where it is.

Novio's face went hard, and before he could stop himself, he punched the mirror on top of the dressing table. The glass shattered, and the noise attracted the attention of the few people still lingering backstage.

"What is this?" Thurston said, hurrying over.

Novio was contrite already. "I'm sorry," he said to Dita.

She shook her head. "Don't be. I feel the same way. I wish I could punch someone. That drawer was all nice and neat earlier. Someone went through it while we were out there."

I handed the note to Thurston, my pulse racing. *Had my mother left this? Or someone with her?*

"This is unacceptable," he said.

"I hate that coin," Dita said, with a frustration in her voice that I'd never heard.

Remy spoke up, solemn, "It can't hurt anyone now. I promise."

"But whoever left this might," Dita said.

Remy couldn't argue that.

But Raleigh spoke up. "Seems like more misdirection to me," he said. "I'm sure you're safe."

Dita stood for a moment, folding in on herself. Then she sprang into motion, plucking a shirt from the messy drawer. "Enough. I won't let this person ruin the day." She stalked toward the makeshift dressing room. "Let's go to the party."

Thurston refolded the paper and slipped it into his pocket. "I'll see you all there," he said.

"I'm not up to it," Novio said, and no one tried to convince him differently. He disappeared out the flap into the night.

I knew Remy would take off to consult with Jules, but I wanted to question him before he did. "Remy, hold up," I said.

I began to tidy Dita's drawer, hoping I was guessing correctly at the order in which she liked things.

"I need to go," he said.

I stopped what I was doing and pulled him away for a private conversation. The situation was awful, but also an opportunity. Raleigh stayed put, watching speculatively as I steered Remy outside.

"Where did you two put the coin, you and Jules?" I asked. "Are you positive it can't hurt anyone? That no one will find it?"

My mother needs it, I thought.

A muscle in Remy's jaw twitched. "I don't know what you think you know, but don't worry about it. It's not hurting anyone. Whoever this is"—he waved a hand to indicate the note-leaver—"will get bored and move on. They'll never find it."

"There's no way you can know that," I said. "Maybe you should move it."

Then I could watch and see where he and Jules went, and send a message to my mother through that ghost e-mail address or something.

"No," he said, "it's good where it is. Don't worry about it."

I did what I seemed to do best these days: I lied. "Good. See if Jules can make Thurston less suspicious."

With a nod, Remy left. I rejoined Raleigh and finished up with the drawer.

"Where's your shadow?" Raleigh asked.

"Busy," I said. "I think he's washing his hair."

"I told you to watch out for him."

Funny, I thought. *If you knew what he was mad over, you'd probably be on his side.*

"He didn't have anything to do with this, if that's what you're thinking." That much I felt certain of. No way he'd have come around here when I was present, not while being so mad at me.

"I wasn't," Raleigh said neutrally.

Dita slid aside the dressing room curtain and came over to us. Her short hair stood up as if she'd run her hands through it, and her cheeks were blotchy. Of course they were. She'd been gone longer than just changing would have taken. The shirt she had on wasn't as crisp as usual; whoever had messed up the drawer had wrinkled it.

"You were great tonight," I told her. "And the day's almost over."

"But it's not over yet," she said, glancing at the dressing table.

The rest of the night passed unceremoniously, though the party was the least party-like event I'd ever been to. We all left early, and I slept uneasily, dreaming of a lost coin.

twenty-four

Our last day in Kansas City passed with no further disturbances, and with little conversation between Dez and me. My mom had said I wouldn't see her again unless we were unlucky, but I craved her guidance. My magic had almost caused me to botch the Ferris wheel escape—and no matter what I'd said to Dez, the consequences would have been very real. My magic career would have been over before it began.

Now I was on my way down the midway to do it again, this time in front of an actual audience. We'd arrived in Dallas two days ago, and Thurston had added an extra daytime performance to our dates here. We were all to be on three times a day. A grueling pace that still left plenty of time for me to think as hard as I could, in case she could hear me: *come see me again, Mom.*

Thurston had also decided that today was the day we added my dangling chain escape to the midday show. Doing it more than once a day would make it too ordinary. It would be my debut as a featured performer for the Cirque (not just Raleigh's opener), kicking off the opening of the Ferris wheel.

I could see the crowd gathered around the wheel as I approached. I'd texted Dez, and he'd confirmed he would meet me at the car at the end of the second arm with the rest of the supplies and the lighter. He was in charge of tying the rope, to the ride and to me, in addition to lighting it on fire. He'd been a quick study with the knots.

Despite his showing up to help, he had taken off immediately after each rehearsal. I missed him, but I wanted him to break first. I refused to apologize for going after my dream.

The crowd wasn't a surprise, but Thurston waiting in costume near it was. He waved me over. "I thought it might be good for you to know something going into this performance."

I took a moment's pause, figuring it must be something bad. "Can't it wait until after?"

"You are all so dire all the time," he said, shaking his head. "I just wanted to say I was wrong about you. The Cirque ticket hotline has started to get calls not just about when Jules's next walk is, but about when your next escape is. We added your schedule to the website. I thought you'd like to know. Your legend is spreading."

A thrill raced through me. He smiled at me, and I smiled back. *I was doing what I'd come here for. For real.*

Still smiling, I finished my journey to the Ferris wheel and clambered up the spoke to the spot where Dez waited. He sat with his legs out on the metal. "What's wrong?" he asked.

"Nothing's wrong," I said. Except that I wished he'd say he was sorry for overreacting, and that my mother would show up.

I swept my gaze over the crowd below. There were a lot of people, but I saw no brilliant-red hair.

"Ready, then?" Dez asked. "Unless I can talk you out of this."

"You can't. I'm more than ready." I held out my arms, and he assisted with the application of the chains. My body wanted to lean into him, so I made myself stand straight. His face came nearer as he clipped a small mic to my T-shirt collar.

One quick move and I could be kissing Dez.

Our eyes met, and I knew he was thinking the exact same thing. But we were both too stubborn to cave.

The crowd murmured, watching me get bound up in the metal chains. When we were all but ready to go, I stepped up onto the edge of the car. It would add a few more dramatic feet to the drop—and yes, I did it to goad Dez.

Nerves kicked up within me. He hadn't been entirely wrong about the lack of safety. The first time was a close call.

This one wouldn't be.

I spoke, the mic picking up my voice. "Welcome to this illusion in honor of one of magic's great ladies, Mercedes Talma. Not an escape artist, though she could have been . . ."

I ran through the whole riff, setting up the fake heist. The late afternoon was beyond warm, heading toward blistering, and the chains were already growing hot against my skin. The sound guys had insisted on the tiny mic, even though I wasn't sure it would survive my writhing.

"Do the honors, lovely assistant," I said to Dez. He didn't preen, only turned the keys in the locks, but the audience still cooed with delight. He tested the chains so the audience could see they were real.

"Set?" he asked. His eyes were so brown, his pupils made tiny by the sun.

"Set," I said, jumping off.

As I fell, I spotted the unmistakable red of my mother's hair in the crowd.

It was enough to distract me from turning to break the speed of the descent, and so the force with which the rope tugged me up by my ankles sucked the wind out of me. My lungs burned, emptied of air. My torso throbbed with searing pain. My ankles protested, the rope cutting in.

All I could think was, *What is she doing here?*

I blinked to keep tears from my eyes, not because I didn't want anyone to see—though I didn't—but so I could look for her.

"And now . . ." Dez said above me. There was no way he could have guessed the extent to which that drop had hurt.

"Fire," I managed, a bit strangled.

He lit the rope.

Shit.

I was spinning, trying to recover my wits and steady my breathing and search each face below me for her all at the same time.

There.

I snagged her standing at the back of the crowd, far enough away that I had to crook my neck at an incredibly awkward angle to see her. Her arms were bare, and I'm sure her tattoo would have been visible if I hadn't been upside down and fifteen feet in the air.

"Moira?" Dez called down softly. "Something wrong?"

He probably wanted me to say yes. But I had to talk to her, to find out why she'd come. So failure was the one thing that was *not* going to happen.

"Just busy," I called up, and began working, no matter that my body still screamed from the harsh drop. The special-effects smoke stung my nose—though not as much as the real stuff would if I let the rope burn through. I called on my magic quick, wanting not just to get free, but to do so faster than ever. I told myself it wasn't about impressing her, but about catching her.

I'd never successfully summoned my magic. It had always just showed up.

This time was different. As soon as I called for it, the heat of my magic unfurled within me . . . and I felt triumph in the success. My magic had come, and now it would free me. I guided it to the first set of locks, wriggling against the chains—

The shove of an outside force knocked the breath out of me again. But not just my breath. That force, strong and solid, pressed against my magic until I couldn't feel it anymore.

I called for my magic again, and nothing happened. It didn't come back.

Panic set in. I searched for my mother, hoping she could help. I was wasting valuable seconds while the rope above me burned.

My eyes found her, and she gave me a brief, disapproving nod. She raised a finger and pointed to her chest.

It was her. She was the outside force.

She had used some of her finite amount of magic to keep me from mine.

I took shallow breaths, my lungs burning again.

I called on my magic, and when it started to respond, I felt her push once more. *How much power is this taking from her?*

I couldn't risk her running dry, not because of me. I'd have to get out of this on my own. I twisted, unable to ignore the pain. The clip mic caught my every gasp and grunt.

The crowd below was riveted—and cringing. I ignored them, ignored her, and Dez above.

He wouldn't interrupt, not after the way I'd acted.

Finally, I got to the first lock and managed to get it undone. I fumbled for the lock-pick tool hidden at my waist and palmed it . . . just as a strand of the rope gave way to the fire.

I dropped, and the tool flew into the crowd. They'd see it. Worse, I'd have no help unfastening the next locks.

I tried to call my magic again, praying it would respond. This time my mother let it come. My limbs heated, blotting out the aching pain, my ears roaring with life as I imagined the metal twisting and turning for me. I imagined it melting away.

The rope dropped another foot. "Last strand," Dez called out, the concern in his voice plain. "Bring the net!" he shouted.

"No!" I had one last chain to get clear of, but I went ahead and triggered the prop coins to make myself lighter. I realized afterward that I hadn't said my line, so I added, "And that's how you do a heist" as I twisted my fingers against the last lock. It plummeted to the ground, and I swung up to grab the rope so I could swing to safety.

"Ah! No!" I swore as I almost grabbed the burning part.

I reached again, higher . . .

I saw the last strands of rope burn through, and then I was falling fast.

I hit mesh with a jolt and bounced back up into the air.

The net Dez had called for had saved me from hitting the ground. From a broken arm, or a broken neck. Or worse.

My face burned with humiliation.

The crowd seemed baffled, but they were applauding anyway. I leapt free of the net, looking for my mother. She caught me, holding tight to my arm, and said urgently into my ear, "I told you to stop this. To leave. But here you are, still taking risks you can't afford to."

"I've been looking for the coin, for you . . ."

"Stop." She gave me a soft push, but there must have been some magic in it. The ground seemed to waver beneath my feet, and I fell back into the mesh.

"Wait!" I said, forcing my way out of the net. I tore through the crowd, searching for her.

Dez caught up with me and grabbed my arm. "What are you doing?"

I continued to scan the crowd. "Did you see her?"

Dez put a hand on my shoulder, stopping me. He was pale, but also furious. "I don't know what you're talking about . . . Or what you're thinking. I can't watch you keep risking your life!"

Oh God, what was I *doing? He's right. I almost died.*

Because my mother had distracted me, and then prevented me from using my magic. But still.

The same magic she'd told me to stop using. This visit had been to deliver a message: *I told you to stop.*

"Nothing to say," he said. "What a miracle."

"Dez, wait!" I called to the back of his head as he vanished into the crowd.

There was nothing left to do. If I wanted him on my side—if I wanted him, period—I'd have to tell him the truth.

twenty-five

Still spooked from my mother's latest abrupt appearance and disappearance, I tracked Dez to his bunk later that evening, after he was done for the day. I needed one person to understand.

No, I needed *Dez* to.

Hitting the ground wasn't the only thing the net saved me from. It was the thing that saved me from losing my job. While Thurston was no longer a fan of this particular escape, he agreed to let me continue opening for Raleigh. I had a couple of days off, though, due to back bruising and Thurston wanting to make sure I didn't have any hidden injuries.

It was going to be a relief to tell Dez the truth; I'd almost forgotten how to, and in so short a time. Maybe using magic did change me.

When I reached the semi, Dez was flat on his back in bed, worrying one of my gold prop coins in his fingers. He tossed it up into the air, caught it, and rolled it between his knuckles, then repeated.

I stood there for a long moment, searching for words and coming up with none. I wondered if it might be better off just leaving . . .

"Yes?" he said.

"How'd you know I was here?"

"Your shadow. You're looming."

I decided to take the fact that he hadn't told me to leave as an invitation to stay. I eased into the sleeping compartment, overheated from the day's sun, and sat at the end of the bunk. "I need to tell you something."

"What is it? Some ethical argument about why risking your life is okay? I seem to remember you saying that it wasn't. But that's what you've been doing."

I'd never seen him quite like this.

"No," I said. "I came to say you're right. And to explain. Why I thought it was okay."

He sat up, his expression one of disbelief. "You made me light that rope on fire, and then I stood there watching you struggle. If I hadn't . . ."

My throat went dry as I remembered. If he hadn't been there and called for the net, I wouldn't be sitting here. I'd be lucky if I were conscious. Calling for magic and having it not show had been terrifying . . . Mom's lesson had been harsh. She'd made her point that I couldn't count on being safe here. But that didn't mean I agreed with her conclusion that I had to go. I couldn't.

No, I *wouldn't*.

"I owe you an explanation," I said.

"This should be good."

I remembered how I'd worried about his black eye, knowing that weird creep had given it to him. Observing as I hung in midair about to fall would've been worse for him. No wonder he was so mad.

I probably shouldn't have been telling him anything I was about to. But "probably shouldn't" wasn't stopping me much lately.

I cared for him, and he cared for me. I had to make this right.

"Moira?" he said, a note of exasperation in his tone.

"I learned magic in secret because I didn't feel like I had a choice. My father . . . he caught me once when I was twelve and flipped out. Said women can't be magicians. When I tried to show him this summer, he still wouldn't listen. You've heard of the Mysterious Mitchell, Master Magician?"

"*That's* your dad? You must be loaded."

"He's a powerful guy, hard to disagree with. So that's why I'm here, the fake name, all of it. I'm doing this whether he wants me to or not."

"You don't have to risk your life."

"That's not the whole story," I said. "You told me once you believe in the kind of thing I'm about to tell you. Though I sort of thought you were joking."

"What kind of thing?" He tilted his head.

"In the Garcias' coin, that magic is possible."

He said nothing.

"That's what I came here for tonight: to tell you I can do magic. Just since I got to the Cirque. It's all new. I barely know what I'm doing, but I'm definitely using it," I said, babbling. "And by *it*, I mean magic. Actual magic. Which shouldn't even exist."

He raised a hand, like he was warding me off. "You shouldn't be telling me this."

I was semi-surprised I hadn't gotten a *What are you talking about?* But not entirely. "No kidding," I said. There was no going back now. "But how can I not? I don't want to lose you. Not over this—I feel like I have to tell someone, and I trust you."

"Even though I told you not to."

I nodded.

"You can do magic," he said. "Like what?"

"Mostly, I, um, transform things. I can prove it, if you're willing to believe me."

He raised his eyebrows. "You're going to do magic right now?"

I shook my head and fished in my pocket. "You remember the day you had your heart pain? I was a little mad at you, and apparently my magic decided to lash out at you."

"*You* made my heart go crazy like that?"

I unfolded my palm and showed him the heart-shaped penny. "This is the penny you gave me. It looked like this, um, after the event happened."

"It's a heart," he said, dumbfounded.

"I think maybe it's yours? A version of it." "In for a penny, in for a pound," as the saying went. "I was worried after that, well, that I . . . that I might hurt you. It's part of the reason I tried to keep my distance. Not very successfully."

He blinked at the heart-shaped penny. And said nothing.

How had I not guessed he wouldn't take this in stride? It would be too much for anyone. I dropped the copper heart and buried my head in my hands. "Oh God, this is a disaster. You think I'm a total freak. Kill me now."

And then he . . .

He laughed.

I heard it, and my head came up. He was doubled over. Laughing. "It's just . . . magic. You can do magic. And I . . . I had no idea."

I wanted to punch him.

Maybe he could see that in my face, because he sobered up fast.

"I don't think you're a freak," he said. "I missed you."

He leaned forward, reaching out for me. I met him halfway, and we kissed, soft and sweet. He smelled like Dez with a faint hint of sweat. My brain gave up. I would have told him anything. I would have forgiven him anything.

We parted.

He pulled me further into the compartment, and we sat facing each other. "This magic, though," he said, "you mentioned that you haven't had it long. Does anyone else know about it?"

"Magic is inherited, I guess. I had never met my mom, but she showed up at our show in Saint Louis. The woman with bright-red hair and a snake tattoo—did you see her again today?"

"She was there today?" His surprise was plain.

"She probably didn't want you to see her. She, um, stopped me from using my magic at the beginning of the escape today."

"Why would she do that?" Dez demanded. "You were almost hurt."

"She told me to stop doing my escapes before . . ." Might as well go all in, even if it meant breaking my promise to my mother. "She's a member of something called the Praestigae. Have you ever heard of it? Them, I mean."

He looked at me like this was too much to take in. So far, he'd taken everything in relative stride, but I was afraid he'd say yes or that he'd tell me to get out.

"Never," he said.

"Apparently, there's only so much magic everyone has, and she's almost out. She's the one who needs that coin. But I think there are more people looking for it, not just her."

"Hmm," he said, frowning. "Why doesn't she want you to do escapes?"

"The only-so-much-magic thing, and that I barely know how to use mine. It tends to show up during escapes, and she wants me to be careful. I thought I had it all under control, but then . . . the other day . . ."

"And today?"

"Yeah," I said, "but only because she kept me from using it."

"I still don't get why she would do that."

"Probably just because she told me not to, that it wasn't safe. That I had to be careful. She doesn't want any of the Praestigae to know about me."

Dez shook his head. "Moira, she's right. You can't keep doing these 'illusions' if they're dangerous."

I straightened my spine. "I can and I will. I just have to learn how to control my magic better, be more careful for now. I'm not going to give up on my career. Not for anybody. This summer is my chance to be a magician . . . So will you still be my assistant?"

He considered it for a long moment, and I wasn't at all confident that he'd agree.

"On one condition," he said. "That you find a trick where I never have to watch you almost break your neck again."

Thank God he said yes. "I know just the thing. It'll take a few days to put together, though."

I didn't elaborate. I kissed him instead.

I woke up feeling hot and sweaty and . . . wonderful. Dez was wrapped around me. That was the wonderful part. The less wonderful part was that the sliding door was still open, potentially revealing us to the view of any random passersby.

This was a pressing problem, because what had ripped me from sleep was a whole lot of sounds, and now that my eyes were open, they saw bright sunshine. Everyone would be awake and moving around out there. I heard guys calling to each other, and a couple of women laughing in a distance that was not that distant.

No one was staring in at us, at least. I attempted movement, and Dez held me tighter. "No," he said. "I'm having the best dream."

I turned over, still on my side, to face him. Somehow I managed this without tossing him off the tiny cot and onto the small length of floor. I wore one of his T-shirts, and he was without one. We'd fallen asleep before things had progressed too far, but we'd gone far enough.

"Oh," he said, eyes opening, "it's not a dream."

"Good morning, flirt," I said.

He kissed the tip of my nose. "It was a good night too."

"I should get going," I said.

"We have shows later," he said. "Things to do."

His face angled closer, and I blurted out in horror, "My breath is terrible, I'm guessing."

He pressed a quick, soft kiss to the corner of my mouth. "So's mine, I'm guessing. See you later?"

"Safe bet."

I knew I had a stupid grin plastered across my face. He knew I had magic, and he didn't care. He hadn't called me crazy or a freak. I breathed easier, having told him the truth.

I extracted my limbs from his as gracefully as I could—not very, as it turned out—and slid to the end of the bed, preparing to face the outside world. I pulled my jeans and sneakers on. But before I could quite make it the rest of the way into the daylight, his hand lightly grabbed the back of my shirt. I mean, his shirt.

"Moira? I'm glad you told me. But you probably shouldn't tell anyone else."

"No kidding. Agreed."

He let me go. I completed my exit, feet hitting the ground.

Annnnd so, of course, the first person I saw was Brandon, grinning at me. How could Dez's grins be so charming and Brandon's so mocking?

"Morning," I said.

"Guess you found him. Walk of shame!" he hooted.

"I have nothing to be ashamed of," I countered, waltzing past him.

"Hope you didn't forget your panties," he called out.

I stopped, glaring at him, and my palms heated. I could feel anger roiling on the horizon, like kindling waiting for me to add flame. Now that I could call my magic and have it respond, it seemed I'd have to be careful not to use it accidentally.

Dez emerged from the trailer. "Do you want me to punch him for that?"

I breathed deep, willing the magic away, and put on a weak smile, relieved that it had worked. "You might hurt your hand."

"I'm only not because you said so."

What I'd meant about the lack of shame was true. So what if we hadn't really spent the night together in that way? I wouldn't have felt any different if we had. That was antiquated nonsense, making girls feel cheap for having sex, when everyone pretended like it was perfectly fine and the most natural thing in the world for boys.

My mother was right about one thing, though. I would have to be careful with my magic in a world with this many things to be angry about.

twenty-six

Raleigh's backstage area was empty when I arrived the next night.

I had used my Thurston-mandated days off to order the extra supplies for the new illusion I'd mentioned to Dez. Now I intended to poke for a little more detail on Dad's fascination with magic objects. I needed to have a talk with him, but I wanted more context first.

I could hear Raleigh onstage. He was at Marie Laveau number three, the granddaughter, in his patter. I sat down in the assistant's chair to wait for him. His spare hat was propped over the corner of the mirror, and there were a few small pots of men's makeup along the top, to prevent shine and accentuate the eyes. His assistant's robe was balled up on top of it.

The crowd erupted into applause, and Marie came back through the curtain. "You," she said, and shrugged. "Don't mind me. He's signing autographs." She reached behind me and plucked up her robe, throwing it on. Then she left.

Raleigh would appear any second. I started to get nervous.

Here I'd thought Dad was as transparent as it got, father of the year aside from his not supporting my dream. Would I be happy to know more about the secrets he'd kept from me, or would I wish I was still in the dark?

Raleigh breezed in off the stage, humming under his breath. It must have been a good show. Caliban sat on his left forearm.

"Hey," I said.

"Wasn't expecting you tonight." He reached up with his other hand to loosen the bow tie at his neck, and I frowned, recognizing its black-and-white stripes.

That was the bow tie he'd tossed back at Dita the night she was on distraction detail.

"Did Dita give that to you as a present after?" I hadn't realized they were that friendly.

Raleigh paused midstep. "Moira," he said. And then, "It's not what you think."

"I'm just curious where you got it," I said.

But his reaction made me pause. What did he think I was asking him?

Hold up a second, I thought. Was it possible that Raleigh had been the culprit behind the note? "Did it come out of her drawer backstage?"

Why would he be wearing it if so, though? This whole situation had become unexpectedly bizarre. I waited for his perfectly logical alternate explanation. There had to be one.

Raleigh gestured with his hand so that Caliban jumped over onto the dressing table. He took off his top hat. "Don't blow this up. I'm . . . mostly . . . working on this for your dad."

"Working on what?"

"You know how he is. He wants that magic coin. I was the one who told him about it—that was why I came out to Vegas. I owed it to him to tip him off."

This was not the explanation I'd hoped for. "Raleigh, I never knew Dad had a collection of magic stuff. Not of stuff he thought was real magic. Not until you mentioned it."

"Crap."

"Yeah." I watched his face so I could catch any glimmer of a reaction. "Do you know about the Praestigae too?"

"The what?" Raleigh frowned. "Sounds like some of the gibberish he's sent me looking for, but I don't know that one." He didn't look like he'd ever heard the word before. No hint of familiarity. "Look, your dad probably didn't want you to know he believes in this mystical junk. I don't. I just pick it up for him when he asks. He pays me well for it."

"I really wish you hadn't been the one to leave that note." I had to tell. There was no guarantee Dad would hand over the coin to my mom. I couldn't risk him hiding it away.

Nan Maroni would take care of this, though, if I tipped her off. "Raleigh, I'm truly sorry . . . I promised Nan Maroni I'd tell her if anyone was after the coin. She got me a job here."

"*Craagh,*" the crow said.

"Fine." Raleigh shrugged, still seeming unconcerned by my finding out he was involved in this. "But I can only talk if Thurston's there. And I have to feed this beast first."

Requesting that the boss attend his confession was a surprise, but not one I could deny without seeming suspicious myself.

"So I'll meet you at Thurston's trailer after the show then, with Nan," I said, hoping she'd agree to come. "I'll get his assistant a note saying that we need to see him."

Raleigh nodded.

Nan wasn't going to like this. Not any more than I did, if for entirely different reasons. Guilt spiked in me. Raleigh was a friend.

But even after that stunt my mother pulled, this was her life on the line. And I'd be lying if I said knowing Dad was part of it didn't make it worse, another giant reminder of the secrets he'd kept from me.

Dez and Brandon still shared a phone, and I had no idea which one of them would get the text I sent. So I worded it carefully: Have to go to a meeting with Raleigh. In touch later. Brandon, tell Dez if this is you.

Before I could call up a new text for Thurston's assistant, a reply buzzed: Sweet. Will tell him.

Brandon.

I sent the production assistant a message for Thurston, asking that he meet us and adding that she should treat it as confidential.

Nan and I neared Thurston's trailer. The door stood open, so it looked like he'd be waiting. Hopefully, with Raleigh.

"Sorry I volunteered you to be here," I said, praying that she took my motivations at face value. That Raleigh did too.

"It's my own fault. You just did what I told you." She threw her shoulders back a fraction. She had a wide-legged pantsuit with a flowing top that played up her regal elder angle. "I can help with Thurston. Just follow my lead."

Nan didn't bother pausing to knock or call out; she just glided up the steps into the RV, and I followed. Raleigh sat on the couch in the living room area. He'd ditched his coat and rolled up the sleeves of his white shirt. The bow tie was gone.

He nodded to me. Brief. Nervous.

"Evening, ladies," Thurston said. "I just got here. This magician with a hangdog expression was waiting for me. So I'm curious about the purpose of our meeting . . . But first, can I get you anything?" The question was for Nan.

"Nothing but a chair," she said.

Thurston hopped to the kitchen and brought one back, setting it across from Raleigh. I took the seat beside him.

"Why are we here?" Thurston asked, bringing over a second chair for himself. "This inquiring mind wants to know."

Nan nodded to me.

"You're not going to like this," I said.

"Then it sounds like I definitely need to hear it," Thurston said.

"Okay, well . . . Raleigh was the one who left that note in Dita's backstage dressing table," I said. "He's looking for the coin."

Thurston wore a look of shock, but it didn't last long. His eyes narrowed on Raleigh. "Explain."

"I will," Raleigh said. "When you brought me here this summer and told me the story, I agreed to take your extra assignment to find it. I may have also talked to the person I've done this kind of 'finders, keepers' for in the past . . ."

"Keep going," Thurston said.

"I don't like failure," Raleigh said. "You asked me to find out if this coin was real, if it had powers. But without directly asking anyone. So that's what I've been—"

"Thurston," Nan said. "*You* are behind this?"

Thurston stood. "I asked Raleigh to quietly pay attention to rumors and try to find it. I did not tell him to scare anyone or to cross any lines." He zeroed in on Raleigh. "In fact, I told you the opposite. Did you forget?"

"There were more rumors," Raleigh said. "And I thought someone else might be getting close to finding it. I did what I thought you'd want."

"But you didn't ask me," Thurston said, "or I'd have told you not to." He rubbed at the back of his neck. "And on that day. Poor Dita." He stopped. "Did you leave the note in here too?"

"No, that wasn't me," Raleigh said. "It just gave me the idea. The break-ins that night weren't me either. I'm telling you, there are other people looking for the coin."

"Who?" Nan asked.

"I don't know. They're better at hiding their identities than I am, clearly." Raleigh looked disgusted with himself and then glanced at me.

I got the message loud and clear. He could have told them I was my father's daughter right away. He hadn't, though. And unlike Raleigh, I knew who the others after the coin were. Or I thought I did. Maybe I'd bought them more time.

It didn't make me feel better about selling out a friend.

"I suppose I should thank you," Thurston said.

"For?" Raleigh asked. "I haven't found anything."

"For making this straightforward," Thurston said. "I'll give you severance pay to cover the entire summer, and the assignment. But you're fired."

"*What?*" Raleigh and I said at the same time. "That's not fair," Raleigh went on. "I was doing what you asked."

"No, you weren't. I can't keep you on after finding out about it, even if I wanted to. It wouldn't be fair to everyone else. My stars—my friends—expect me to protect them. I'd fire myself for contributing to this, if I could."

"But now that we're clear, it's good," Raleigh tried.

The former CEO in Thurston was in full effect. He might as well have been wearing a business suit instead of a ringmaster's tuxedo. "No. And it's effective immediately."

Raleigh wasn't willing to give up. "But you can't do this. There's another show tonight."

Thurston looked at me for a long moment.

I hadn't meant to get Raleigh *fired*. "I don't think Raleigh meant to scare Dita," I said. "Maybe you should think this through some more."

Raleigh cut in. "Don't be ridiculous. She's not ready."

Thurston ignored him. "You're promoted to head magician, Moira. Also effective immediately."

Raleigh's jaw worked. Mine dropped open. It was the showcase I'd wanted, but not like this. My mother definitely wouldn't like me being even more in the spotlight or the things I'd have to do to stay there.

"Huh, Pixie, guess everything worked out just right," Raleigh said. "Congratulations."

"I never wanted this."

"Uh-huh," he said, standing. "I'll just be going, then."

I wanted to follow him. Apologize for . . . something, for him leaving and for me taking his place. To appeal to his better nature about not outing me to Dad in retaliation. I also wanted to know why he'd taken the bow tie and then worn it.

But Nan gave me a slight shake of her head, and I stayed put.

"Thank you for bringing this to me," Thurston said. "Why did you come as well?" he asked Nan. Then he pulled out his phone. "Just a second—I better alert Jane."

He called his assistant and explained that Raleigh would be leaving, and to pay him for the remainder of the season. He added that Moira Miracle had been promoted, and asked for a poster to be produced to put up outside the tent.

"You won't spread the word about this, will you?" I said, unable to stay quiet. "Ruin his career? I've known Raleigh for years. He's a good guy."

"I won't. I played too much of a part in it." He scrubbed a hand over his face. "Is this day over yet?"

"Thurston," Nan said. Her voice was firm. "You shouldn't be getting mixed up with this idea of magic. I was under the impression that you thought it was all fantasy, wild tales."

Thurston's eyes flicked between me and her. "You're comfortable talking about this in front of Moira?"

"I am," Nan said.

I hoped that didn't pique his interest in me. I had no idea how she was planning to play this.

"I didn't buy any of it. I thought Roman Garcia was a bitter old man, who wrote me letters about things *he* believed. But I didn't put any stock in them." Thurston angled his body toward Nan. "But then, over the summer, I thought back over last season and some conversations I had with Jules and Remy. And I started watching videos of her performances. Jules had it, didn't she? That coin? That's part of what I interrupted after that last show of the season, something to do with it. It *is* magic, isn't it? That's why you asked the two of them what they'd done, after the break-ins."

Nan was very still. I waited to see how she'd respond.

"I thought you didn't believe the stories about me." She gathered her hands in her lap and looked straight at him.

"I don't . . . other than that you were poorly treated."

"The coin is part of those stories. I'd rather you not believe in it either."

The two of them stared at each other.

"I'm sorry to disappoint you, truly," Thurston said. "But I think I do believe."

"So this is all about your boundless curiosity." Nan's eyes flicked to me and back onto Thurston. "Okay, then, while I hate to say this in front of an employee . . . who obviously I would not speak in front of if there was *anything* to this . . ."

She paused, but neither Thurston nor I could have mistaken the pause as a place for us to jump in. I could see how radiant she must have been as a performer as she called up her full authority. How arresting it was when she spoke again, like this was a performance.

"You are a fool."

I couldn't speak for Thurston, but I hadn't expected that. He shifted in his chair.

She continued, majestic in making her case. "Magic is for the super-stitious. For people who believe in ghosts and fate and things that go bump in the night. For people who want a reason to fear others. So I could read the cards? So my mother could? Somehow we became people to fear. It does disappoint me you would be one of those people, but it disappoints me more that you would put your people at risk. People like Dita Garcia. Like my family. What happened last season was all about people searching for that coin. Your joining the hunt will only make more people want it. So you are not just a fool, you are a dangerous fool. Will you stop?"

What a performance it was. I wanted to applaud. I could only hope it was a successful one.

Thurston took a moment, perhaps to see if she had more to say. She waited for his answer.

He didn't give one, at least not exactly. "You aren't worried about these other people Raleigh mentioned finding it?"

"No," she said, though *that* had to be a lie. "I am not. The only reason I worry about it at all is the *stories* people tell about it. Stories have power. Superstition can kill."

The last word hung in the air.

"What do you think?" Thurston looked at me. "Do you believe in magic?"

I hadn't been prepared for the question, not from him. So I said something close to the truth, close to the things I'd said to Nan when she told me it was real.

"I believe magic is a trick, a pretty lie."

"She's a wise girl," Nan said. "Sometimes. Is this matter closed? Have I answered your curiosity? Will you stop?"

"Your wish is my command." He smiled at her. "I know I said I believed, but it was more of a wondering. You won't hold it against me? You'll still come for a drink now and then and tell me stories about the good old days?"

"And the bad ones." Nan smiled faintly, but the smile didn't touch her eyes. "I wouldn't mind a sip of something right now."

"My pleasure." Thurston got up. He motioned toward the door and said to me, "You'd better get going, hadn't you? You have a new show to start preparing."

"Keep all this quiet, dear," Nan said.

"As a mouse," I said, and then hesitated. "I can tell Dita, though, about Raleigh?"

Nan gave me a discreet nod, and I got out of there.

I stood outside in the night air, processing. I was now the Cirque's head magician. So why did I feel doomed?

twenty-seven

When I stepped into our room, Dita was propped on her side with earbuds in, watching something on her tablet. She already sported a pair of plaid pajamas.

I'd needed a walk to decompress and think through the conversation in Thurston's trailer. I wasn't ready to talk to Dez about what happened yet, for reasons I wasn't clear on. I should have been. But . . . I wasn't.

During my wandering, I'd passed a Mexican bakery that was still open up the street, and gone in to select a giant white paper bag full of many delicious things. I approached Dita and shook the bag to get her attention, opening the top and holding it in front of her.

She popped out an earbud.

"I come bearing sweets," I said. "Take one. You're going to need it."

Dita's fingers darted out to pause her show, then she removed her other earbud. She took a small wedding cookie and crunched it. "Why do I need it?"

"I have weird news."

She waved for me to hold the bag open again, and I set it down beside her. "I'll take a reserve cookie, then," she said.

I settled on my bed. "You know when you made me promise to tell you if there was any strange or secret stuff going on?"

She swallowed, and went still. "Yes."

I sighed. "Raleigh was the person who went through your drawer. He left the note."

"Raleigh?" she asked.

"Yep, he was looking for the coin"—I hadn't actually clarified that I was allowed to tell her about Thurston—"this whole time. And now he's been fired. I'm taking his place."

"Raleigh was looking for the coin." She shook her head in wonder.

"He was sorry that he scared you," I said. I assumed he was. He wouldn't have done that on purpose.

"I hate that coin," she said, repeating her words from that night. She added, "I wish we could toss it in some ocean, destroy it forever."

"I can understand why." *But don't do that,* I wished. *Please don't do that.* I wanted to ask if she had any idea where Remy and Jules might be stashing it. That would be too obvious, though.

"How would we even know it worked anyway?" Dita said. "It'd probably wash back up." She straightened her blanket over her legs. "Thank you for telling me. For not keeping me in the dark."

Lucky for me, she didn't ask whether anything else strange was going on. But I felt entirely awful that I was still on the lookout for her hated coin—with no intention to destroy it.

The next afternoon, I managed to snag a moment alone in the Airstream before the others returned from lunch. I'd spent the morning rush-ordering supplies for a new illusion. Now I stared at Dad's name in the contacts list on my phone.

Some part of me hoped he'd heard through the magic grapevine there was an amazing new magician at the Cirque American, and discovered it was me. That he'd immediately recant, convinced by the buzz and then by seeing me perform. And then he'd explain why he'd kept my ability to do real magic a secret all these years, along with the warehouse I'd never been told about.

I pressed his name to call him. It was a couple of hours before he'd leave to get ready for his evening performance, a good time for him. He should be at home. He'd be eating some kind of lean protein and boringly healthy steamed vegetables.

"Moira?" He was out of breath when he answered. "Sorry, I forgot my phone in the study."

His study. I pictured it—he'd be standing by his big desk. Rare playbills featuring the most famous magicians of history filled the walls, trapped in heavy frames from which they'd never escape. The Great Houdini draped in chains, Howard Thurston surrounded by the supposed spirits of the dead, Harry Kellar with his similar army of red demons, Carter the Great pretending to be a friend of the devil . . . and Dad, from his first year as a headliner, flanked by spotlights and excerpts from rave reviews.

All of them were men.

"A little cardio never killed anyone," I said.

He laughed.

We transitioned to awkward silence.

I could hear him sit down in the throne-like leather chair. One of the wheels always squeaked when it moved.

"You mentioned you had to take somebody on a tour of the collection," I said, easing down on my mattress. "How'd that go?"

"Did I? When was that?"

"A voice mail. Where'd you take them?" My free hand had balled into a nervous fist without my meaning it to. I relaxed my fingers.

"The usual highlights—Houdini's straitjacket and milk can, Carter's cards."

"No, I mean which warehouse?"

Crickets.

"Raleigh mentioned you had more than one."

"Moira, what is going on? First you ask me about your mother, now this."

I don't know, Dad, I thought. *Did you lie to me for seventeen years?*

But even with catching Raleigh and with my mother's casual confirmation that Dad had known, I had doubt. This was my dad. We'd always been close. He couldn't have meant for me to find out these things this way. I wasn't ready yet to blow up our relationship. Not over the phone.

"Nothing—I just thought maybe you got some cool new stuff," I said. "Don't be so worried. You know you're my favorite dad."

"And you're my favorite daughter. So . . . when can I come see you?"

Crap.

"Now's not really great. It's busy."

"I'll just fly up for a day—you could take one day off. Or even a couple of hours for lunch. I can catch a red-eye. I could be there tomorrow."

I forgot how hard it was to dissuade him once he was set on something. A big part of being a magician was figuring out ways to do the impossible, to solve problems. I hadn't figured out how to solve my problem with Dad yet. Raleigh was undoubtedly headed back to Vegas and might well tattle on me when he got there.

Then again, if Raleigh told him, he'd be doing me a favor. Giving Dad time to get used to the idea before we had it out.

"Um, not this week—maybe in a couple of weeks?" I searched for a story. "We have a break, and I was going to go home with one of my friends here. She lives out west, so it'll be closer for you."

He grumbled but finally said, "I can wait a little longer. Send me the details as soon as you have them. How is it going there?"

"I like the work, and the people. I think it's what I'm meant to be doing. But I'm still learning—every day. It's not easy, obviously."

Wow, that was so vague I was sure he was bound to call me on it, but instead he turned into philosophical Dad. "Nothing easy is real. You know how I hate sayings, but 'Easy come, easy go' is one I've always put stock in. How can you expect to hold on to something you never had to work for? Find that thing, the one that feels right to you even though it's hard. Work that you love is a gift."

It was good advice, and I was terrified I'd start crying. I missed him. And I already had the thing: magic was mine.

"Dad." I put my best dose of daughter in it. "I go away for the summer and you turn all squishy. Please tell me you're not writing a self-help book."

"Very funny. You know I hate that stuff."

"If you were more actualized, you might feel differently."

"What does that even mean? We are already actual—actual people. It's meaningless."

I missed this. Cranky dad, conversations like this.

"Your advice was gold. I miss home sometimes. The theater, the girls backstage, you."

"Thank God," he said. "I keep waking up in the middle of the night from these terrible dreams where you become one of those independent kids who never visits me. Where I'm like this awful burden you realized you never wanted to go back to as soon as you got away."

"You'll show me this other warehouse when I come home, right?"

Of course he wouldn't, if he thought it would awaken my magic power.

"I can't wait," he said.

Smooth. But then he had plenty of time to get yet another warehouse, or move whatever objects he had in there. I hated being suspicious of him. Of myself. Of *everyone*.

The real question was: How long could I put off telling him, should Raleigh decide to keep his mouth shut?

Not much longer, not unless I wanted him to find out with no warning in a month when we hit Vegas for our final dates.

❖ ❖ ❖

The less than desirable circumstances of my promotion didn't keep me from feeling a thrill as I donned my mask at what was now my dressing table a few days later and prepared to take the stage for rehearsal. My stage. It was a guilty thrill, but a thrill all the same.

When I navigated around the curtain, Dez already stood on the far side of the stage.

He leveled a gun at me. "You're sure this is safer?" he called over.

"You're sure you loaded it with the dummy round?" I countered. "Let's do this, then."

A clear pane of safety glass sat in a frame between us to serve as proof to the audience that the actual bullet I'd catch in my teeth had been fired. It wouldn't have been, of course.

All the new equipment I needed and posters about my debut had arrived in time for our dates in El Paso. My first performance was tomorrow, and I was grateful we were back to two shows a day here instead of three. I had a feeling this one—combined with the coffin escape for the late show—would wear me out.

The only reason I could even contemplate putting it into my repertoire after a week's work was my knowledge of Dad's version of it. The bullet catch should always be an illusion. Twelve magicians were reported to have died doing it. Most of the ones who lived were smart enough to fake it—not that it was entirely safe, but it was *safer*. And this would definitely be safer than the hanging-upside-down escape had been. I'd be using the smallest bit of magic in a very focused way.

My mom might still protest, but I didn't see any way around it. I could call magic consistently now, but I was convinced it would show up regardless during big illusions or escapes. So embracing and guiding it was the safest option.

If she came to see me again, I could explain the favor I'd done catching Raleigh and ask how I could help with her problem.

For this illusion, I'd rush-ordered enough sheets of safety glass to take me through the end of the season, along with wax bullets that looked like real ones to the eye and would break through the glass, but which would dissolve before they reached me. Getting the firearm, real bullets for me to produce at the end and some safety goggles had been beyond easy. We were in Texas, after all. My credit card worked, and we'd walked out of the store with the handgun now in Dez's capable grip.

Dez, it turned out, was a crack shot—another talent his unsavory childhood had left him with. "Other kids had coloring books. We had contests to see who could shoot the most Pabst cans off a fence. I killed at target practice." Which meant, at least, I didn't have to go around the grounds looking for an expert marksman or markswoman to help me out. Even a wax bullet could do damage if, say, fired wildly into the crowd.

The real crux of the trick, the thing that would flummox anyone trying to figure it out, was how I planned to produce the marked bullet. There would be no contact whatsoever between Dez and me once an audience member scribbled an identifiable marking on the wax one. We didn't need any contact. I was going to transform the real bullet that would be stored in my cheek so that it matched the wax one the audience member had drawn on. I'd been practicing every night—drawing a design on a bullet—and then holding a fresh bullet in my palm and transforming it to match the first. Then I'd confirmed I could reliably do the same thing with the bullet in my cheek.

I could.

It was the penny shaped like a heart that gave me the idea. My magic seemed to like when I directed it to do something small and intricate. Even if it still mostly felt like being possessed by some force with a mind of its own, it was a force that was willing to listen.

So I ran through my prepared spiel, leading up to my final lines before the firing. "Can we please have absolute silence in the tent? And everyone, no matter what happens, please stay in your seats, for your own safety."

I donned my safety goggles, slipping the plain bullet in my mouth as I put in a mouth guard for show. Dez put his goggles on too. All these layers of glass between us were like some metaphor I didn't care for in that moment. He might as well have been aiming for my heart. He'd hit it.

Dez raised his hands again, sighting toward me, and I saw him click the safety off.

You trust him, right? Not to shoot you?

Of course I do.

He fired.

The shot cracked like lightning through the tent.

The glass fractured in the center, and I willed the bullet in my cheek to change to match the one with Dez's scrawled initials on it, visualizing it in great detail. My whole body grew hot, like it always did when my magic came, and the metal of the bullet seemed to boil against the tender skin inside my mouth.

The moment of truth.

I removed the mouth guard, produced the bullet between my teeth and turned to the not-really-there audience. I spit it into my hand.

Dez had put down the gun and walked over. At this point in the show, I'd invite the audience member to inspect the bullet and confirm it was the same one they'd marked. Dez leaned over and examined it, then gave a low whistle. "That is some freaky mojo," he said. "Also, I hate this trick."

I laughed. "Why?"

"I don't like shooting at you."

"That's a good thing. But I'm right here and just fine."

"Yes, you are," he said. "We good? You want to do it again?"

I considered. "No, I feel like I've got it."

He hesitated. "Could you make a coin like the missing one? The way you make the bullet look the same?"

I blinked, then shook my head. "No, not without seeing it first. And it probably wouldn't have the magic Mom needs anyway, the copy."

"Right. Just a thought." He kissed my nose. "So we're done, then?"

"Why? You have plans for us?"

Dez took both my hands in his and swung them. "I wish. I have plans with Brandon."

My grimace was inadvertent. Dez laughed at it. "He's my friend. And he wants to go out into town. I promised."

El Paso was right on the Mexican border, with Ciudad Juárez on the other side. Who knew what the boys would get up to?

"Abandon me. See if I care." When he looked briefly uncertain, I said, "No, it's cool. Go on. I should rest up for tomorrow anyway."

"Good luck," he said, leaning in for a kiss. My lips lingering against his felt like the moment the bullet left the gun, loaded with possibility . . . and danger. I'd told him all my secrets, but I sensed he still had plenty left.

When he pulled back, he said, "I . . ."

Was he about to say it? I love you?

I wanted it, and I didn't want it. But I wanted it more than I didn't.

"I'll see you tomorrow," he said.

So that was me projecting. The letdown told me how much more I'd wanted it. "Don't get too wild. I need you to come prepared to aim true."

"Oh, I will."

He gave me a deadly grin.

twenty-eight

Backstage the next evening I smoothed on classic red lipstick and went over everything mentally one final time.

The bullet catch was dramatic enough that it could—and would—stand alone tonight. I didn't want to have to think about any other props or sleights, not until I'd done it successfully a few times in front of the crowd. These tents were on the small side but still held about fifty people at maximum capacity.

Thurston was thrilled about the act. He'd added an extra insurance rider—assuring me it was nothing after what they paid for Jules's walks—and had a sign produced for the outside of my tent.

SEE THE **MIRACULOUS MOIRA** PERFORM THE **DEADLY**

BULLET CATCH

EXCLUSIVELY ON THIS STAGE **TONIGHT!!!**

I expected a packed house.

Dez came in, and I did a double take. He'd worn his suit. I was touched by the gesture. "You're looking sharp," I said.

"That's where 'sharpshooter' comes from," Dez said. "Well-dressed men like me."

"It was so much better before you opened your mouth."

He moved in close. "That's what *she* said."

I rolled my eyes, and he kissed my cheek, just below my mask. "Don't want to mess up your lipstick. Not this early in the evening." I willed myself not to blush. "Did you have fun last night?"

"No. I missed being with you." He said it straightforward, not like it was part of the flattery game he was so good at playing.

"Oh." I fidgeted. "We'd better get out there."

"Your public awaits. Where's the box?"

I picked up the small gun box with the handgun and the dummy shot locked inside. Dad had always been religious about this safety measure, so I was doing the same. I'd kept it hidden away in the closet of the Airstream, and I checked now to make sure that the gun and the dummy round were all set before relocking the box to hand off to Dez.

He accepted the case and the key to it, and held aside the curtain so I could go out first. One last deep breath, a straightening of my shoulders, and I put on a smile for the audience. Then I stepped out from the curtain to take the stage.

I paused. The gun case nudged my back, since Dez was coming out behind me.

There were more people than I'd ever seen in this tent. Standing room only, which was probably illegal. It seemed like a monster made up entirely of eyes, all on me.

Keep going, I told myself. *The audience isn't a monster. It wants to be your friend. Get it on your side.*

I smiled. When I spoke, I projected. I'd never needed a mic before in here. "Good evening and welcome. I'm the Miraculous Moira. I can't imagine what's brought so many of you here tonight."

There were a few nervous laughs.

I couldn't help feeling like this audience was here in case they might see a tragic death on the stage, the morbid factor in full effect. Oh well. Magicians counted on it.

"Wait, I can. You want to see a miraculous feat, a girl escaping death, and I'm too happy to oblige." I nodded to the sheet of glass set into its frame to my left. "On this stage, you'll see a hole in this glass, which will serve as proof that a bullet was fired—at me—on this stage. This handsome devil over here will be doing the firing." I nodded to Dez, who nodded back and shot the audience a grin. "And one of you will mark the bullet. That audience member will then confirm it's the same bullet that I catch . . . in my mouth."

There were a few surprised "oohs."

I raised my hand and crossed my fingers stagily. "Hopefully."

That got a smattering of laughter and some light applause. The audience was coming along.

Dez held up the gun case, then set it on the ground and unlocked it. He removed the pistol and began to check it out. Even though I'd already done so earlier, it offered more evidence to the audience in support of the reality of what they were about to see. And it gave them something to watch in addition to me while I did my setup.

"But first, while my lovely assistant makes his safety check, I want to tell you a story. So many of the women whose work allows me to stand on this stage before you have been largely forgotten . . . by the men who write magic history. I'll be dedicating tonight's performance to two women from Georgia who made a sensation in the late 1800s with great feats of strength and controlling metal."

They wanted to see that bullet fired, but they could listen to this first.

"The first was just a teenager when she performed, after supposedly gaining powers during a lightning storm. Powers to make those around her believe she was a 'human magnet.' She was Lulu Hurst, also known as the Georgia Wonder. She only performed for a short time, but she managed to inspire a successor who ended up surpassing her feats— Annie Abbott, who performed as the Little Georgia Magnet. Both these women could move metal objects onstage while three strong men tried to prevent it, often with just a hand upon the item and moving the men as well. Annie regularly resisted the efforts of burly men to lift her hundred-pound frame." I was in the center of the stage, and I swept my hands out. "Who better to dedicate the bullet catch to than these women magicians who demonstrated control over metal? Lulu and Annie, if you have any aid you can offer me tonight, I'll take it."

I winked, and the crowd laughed. "And now, let's get under way. I'll need a volunteer from the audience to examine and mark the bullet that my lovely assistant will load into his gun."

I searched across the hands being raised for whom to pick, and then a man shifted to one side about midway back in the tent. As he did, I caught a glimpse of the woman who stood behind him.

My mother.

I swallowed. *Why was she here again?* I wondered. I needed to find out.

"You"—I pointed—"the beautiful woman with the red hair right there. You seem like a perfect choice, and you're already standing. Can you all help her get up here to us?"

I waited to see what she'd do. I wanted to talk to her, even briefly.

She could turn and run—or magically sweep the whole tent away, for all I knew—but it would make too much of a spectacle. Fighting her way out through the crowd wouldn't be easy. She started in the stage's direction.

Dez stood at my shoulder. He whispered, "Are you sure this is a good idea?"

Right. She'd be marking the bullet. She had blocked my magic last time, with nearly tragic results.

Too bad I didn't think of that before I invited her onstage. "No. But it's too late now."

I didn't *think* she wanted to hurt me.

She made her way slowly to the fore, waiting for people to move, rather than shifting to walk around them. And people did. There was a command to how she parted the crowd along the aisle to get to us.

She reached the side of the stage and climbed up the three steps we'd placed there earlier. She wore jeans and a tank top, as before.

My mother *was* beautiful. There was no hint of the pallor or weakness she'd shown outside the Airstream that night. Her green eyes weren't so different than my own, except I didn't have a tattoo that matched them. I could only see the side of it, but the snake was curled around something.

She did not have a welcoming or worried look. Instead, I was presented with a mocking half-smile that told me exactly nothing about why she was here or what to expect. She seemed . . . different than she had either of the other times. Could it be that we had a serious audience? She'd been so paranoid that first night. Perhaps the mysterious *he* was nearby.

"Hello . . ." I paused, leaving space for her name.

Dez looked like he was in pain behind her.

"Regina," she said.

"Well, Regina, thank you for being here and being a willing volunteer."

Her eyebrows lifted.

"Are you a fan of magic?" I asked.

"Devoted."

The queen of the one-word answer.

The audience was starting to get restless. No matter how much I wanted to try to pry more out of her, to see if this was the worst idea I'd ever had, the show had to go on.

"Regina, we'd like you to confirm this is a real bullet."

Dez, grave-faced, took the wax round from the box and handed it to her.

She squinted at it. "Looks real to me." She stage-whispered to the audience, "I'd have to kill someone with it to be sure, but . . ."

Her voice had gone just teasing enough that the crowd would assume she was joking. I wasn't convinced.

"Let's hope not," I said, and the audience rewarded us with laughter. I was surprised at how blind they were to what was happening in front of their very eyes, but I shouldn't have been. That was how magic worked. The audience only ever saw a sliver of truth.

Dez met my eyes, a plea in his to stop this somehow.

Sorry, no way out now, I tried to tell him.

I pulled a marker from my pocket. "Regina, I'd like you to mark the bullet with something unique to you, a symbol that we can use to identify it. I know there's not much space, but do your best."

Our fingers brushed when she took the marker, and I felt like Lulu Hurst, like I'd been hit by lightning. My magic stirred awake, my palms heating.

She reacted not at all, except to simply take the bullet from Dez. "Thank you," she said.

He said nothing, which was unusual for him. He gave me another pleading look while she was occupied scribbling on the bullet.

She held it up for us and the audience to see when she'd finished, settling into her role more.

I struggled to memorize what she'd drawn during my brief look— if I survived the next few minutes, I'd have to reproduce it. But the way my magic continued a low burn, I worried I'd do something by accident first.

After all, the last time I'd seen her, she insisted I stop performing. And stop using my magic.

She'd made a shape, oblong, with spiky points at the top and a flat bottom. I could see it when I briefly closed my eyes, but I had zero clue what it meant.

She was here again, though. That wasn't meaningless. What happened next wouldn't be either.

"Please stand to the side of the stage," I said. "And remain there so you can confirm that I catch the same bullet."

"Oh," she said with a full smile, "I wouldn't miss it for the world."

She nodded to Dez and sidled over to the steps and down them. "We're doing this," he murmured.

"Just like we rehearsed."

Then I spoke louder, to the audience once more. My voice was slightly unsteady, but that only made them drink the words in more readily. "Can we have absolute silence in the tent? And please stay in your seats, for your own safety."

Dez and I went to our opposite sides of the stage, separated by the glass and the distance. My hands heated the safety goggles as I donned them, and the bullet was already hot against my fingers. I managed to load it in my cheek, placing the mouth guard in for appearances. I didn't wait, pouring magic into the metal casing, into making that odd symbol appear on it as quickly as I could, before my mother could interrupt.

The bullet burned against my jaw. My magic eased a little of its burn, satisfied.

I found her, my mother, watching from just beside the stage, seemingly at ease. Wouldn't it be funny, I thought, if she'd turned the wax one into a real bullet and they found an identical one in my jaw?

Ha freaking ha. At least I'd make the history books.

Dez took aim, and I forced myself to stand still. Not to move or flinch or duck.

He fired.

twenty-nine

The shot rang out with a *crack!* that filled the entire tent.

I braced for impact. The glass shattered as the bullet passed through, and I wanted to take it all back, the whole summer, in those terrifying seconds.

But nothing happened.

Then I remembered I was still onstage and this was still a performance. I rocked back, as if I'd been hit, clapped my hand up to my mouth guard to remove it, and spat the bullet into my palm at the same time. I turned to reveal it to the audience and waved for my mother to come back onstage.

Dez was placing the gun back in its case, his hands visibly shaking.

It's okay, Dez, I thought. *We made it. She didn't decide to take me out to teach me a lesson.*

Some light applause had already started—people desperate for a cathartic release from the drama they'd watched play out. Maybe sometimes the audience does sense the machinations beneath the surface, and appreciates what they see all the more for it.

"Are these your markings?" I asked her. Asking people if it was their bullet was a tricky business, inviting closer scrutiny that would take too much time. The question was precise for that reason.

"Looks right," she said. "Yes."

I offered the bullet to her, nervous about our hands touching again and expecting her to decline. But she said, "What a souvenir to remember you by."

There was no zap of electricity when our skin brushed.

"I need you to tell me how to get the coin to you if I can find it," I said quickly, low enough for only her hearing.

"I don't think so," she said, just as low. "Don't try to follow me, and stop taking these risks. We can never be seen together again. He will find out."

She held the bullet in the air and gave the smile of someone who'd played a game and won. Which made me, taking my bow at last, the loser.

The crowd didn't hold it against me. They were on their feet, giving me a rousing standing ovation.

My mother began to slip away into the crowd. I hesitated, torn between taking her order and attempting to catch up with her.

She was already halfway to the exit, her flaming hair beating a steady if not hasty retreat. The lingerers in the audience were approaching the stage, their programs or posters in hand, and there was Thurston at the back of the theater. He'd either slipped in late or I missed him earlier. He offered me a salute. I was a headliner now.

There was no point in chasing after my mother, not tonight. Not unless I wanted to end up fired like Raleigh.

Dez still hadn't said a word. "You okay?" I asked.

He had a funny expression on his face. "Shouldn't I be asking you that? What if she'd . . ."

Made him into my killer? "She didn't. She wouldn't. I better start signing."

More confused than ever, I channeled my mother's ability to behave out of tune with what would be expected of a normal person in a given situation. In this case, that meant donning a fake mask over my real one, and pretending everything was okay.

What an exhilarating evening. What a brush with death. What a life.

Everyone bought it. But why wouldn't they? Like all magic, there was a kind of truth in it, wrapped within the layers of deception.

"She's got to be somewhere around here, doesn't she?" I asked Dez, in his tiny, hot compartment the next day.

His response was to keep putting his shoes on. "She seems to always be around."

Dez had been weird for the rest of the night, and so had I. But his weirdness was persisting into the next day. I wanted to talk this out, and he was the only person I had to talk it out with.

When he'd skipped out on lunch, I'd come to find him here. He was not as thrilled as he usually was to see me. By all appearances, he was about to take off somewhere—not that he'd said as much.

"I'm sorry I put you in that position," I said. That had to be it, right? He was freaked out and mad that he'd had to shoot a gun at me after what I'd told him about my mother and magic. That made sense. "I shouldn't have. Forgive me?"

"Please, don't tell me you're sorry. You don't have to do that."

"In your place, I'd be mad too."

He turned a shadowed grin to me. "Good thing I have no plans to hand you a gun and ask you to shoot. With my luck, you'd hit me right through here."

He reached out and took my hand and placed it over his heart.

I had the penny he'd given me, which I now thought of as the lucky penny, in my pocket. He'd told me to keep it.

Dez kissed me, but it was a too-brief kiss. "I have to go," he said.

"Where?"

"With me, that's where," Brandon said, appearing outside the opening. "No *girlfriends* allowed."

I bristled. I couldn't help it. "What, you going to a strip club? Classy."

"We are not going to a strip club," Dez said. "At least, I hope not. We have to go out for supplies. Totally boring. You don't want to come with us. Swear."

"Because you're not invited," Brandon said.

"Because he'll be there," Dez said, giving me another quick kiss.

"Now that's a convincing argument. I guess I'll see you later."

He pulled my hand back up to his heart. "I'll be heartbroken if I don't."

"Sweet talker," I said.

But I liked it. I got up and out so he could slide the door closed and lock it. He and Brandon set off toward the edge of camp, and I turned back toward it.

I didn't go far. Dez was still being weird. And this was the second time he'd disappeared with annoying Brandon since we got to El Paso. I knew he owed that creep Rex something and that Brandon considered him a brother. Plus, the way Dez hadn't outright said I couldn't come was a technique I recognized from some of the magic books I'd read. It was a con artist's technique. A way to get people to agree with what you want them to do, by thinking you have their best interest at heart.

I'd been managed into staying behind. His declaration that he'd be heartbroken if he didn't see me again had also been carefully worded. He had *not* said he'd be back or he'd see me later. It left open the possibility that he might not.

So I followed him.

The lack of a convenient fairgrounds in town meant we were set up at the University of Texas campus (Thurston was apparently a regular donor) in an older stadium called Kidd Field. Our campers and supplies were located in a big parking lot behind it, a little hike away. El Paso was all beautiful blue skies and a lively mix of bursts of green with desert browns. An impressive mountain sprawled right into the city.

The boys were heading in the mountain's general direction, out on a street with its grand name stamped on it in white: "Glory Road." I kept my distance. There were only a few students on the sidewalks, and if Dez or Brandon so much as glanced back, they'd spot me.

I breathed a bit easier when they turned onto a busier street, where I'd have more options for hiding. They passed restaurants and shops and, still, they kept walking, up into a more residential area.

Not only did they not look back, they didn't seem to speak a word to each other. Occasionally Brandon consulted the phone in his hand—looking at directions, maybe. I wondered where they were going.

I hadn't really envisioned a strip club, but . . . unless they were planning to climb the mountain, which I doubted, there was nothing out here but more houses.

They stopped at a quiet intersection, with homes a mix of very nice and downright stately on all sides, and then approached a big gray house with a cactus garden in front and a tall stucco fence around the backyard. Brandon led the way to the porch and then didn't even bother knocking. He opened the door, and they disappeared inside.

What on earth?

I moved carefully closer, noting the street sign: Coffin.

It's just a street name, I told myself. *No chills necessary.*

There must have been people in there, because the sound of music with a lot of bass reached me out on the sidewalk. I heard some sounds of chatter in the backyard.

"A party?" I shook my head. "Seriously?"

Something still didn't feel . . . right. If they were cutting out, if Dez was blowing me off for some random townie bash, I wanted to know. But I also wanted to see if he was in trouble or in danger from that family friend again. The guy had shown up in more than one city. He could be here too.

Knowing that maybe it was unwise (okay, it was stupid, I'll admit), I walked up to the door. I knocked, but either the occupants ignored it or the music was too loud for anyone to hear. The thump and thud of the bass resonated—or reverberated—through my head. So I did what the boys had done.

I twisted the knob and opened the door, and then I went inside.

part three

now you see her

thirty

No one noticed my entrance at first. The room was filled with people, lounging on couches and gathered around a TV that wasn't even on. It didn't have the feel of a party. Or it was the feel of a party three days in, when everyone's exhausted and wishes it was over.

Beer bottles covered a living room table and the kitchen counter, but the house was otherwise tidy.

A handful of small children raced around. One of them stopped and peered up at me. A girl of about eight with a tangle of black hair. There was a break between songs, and she spoke into it. "Hail," she said.

"Um, hi," I said.

Her eyes narrowed. "I don't think you're supposed to be here."

I didn't see Dez or Brandon anywhere. "I'm looking for a friend. His name is Dez—do you know him?"

A woman migrated over then and placed a protective hand on the black-haired girl's shoulder. "Dez is here. But who're you?"

"She's not supposed to be here, Mama," the little traitor said.

"I'm a friend of his," I cut in. "Just point me in his direction."

The woman gave a low whistle. She was dressed in a business suit, bright blue, a bizarre sight among everyone else dressed so casually. "Oh, he's in the shit now."

She pointed to the sliding doors that opened out into the big back-yard. "That way."

The music resumed its thump and thud, not quite loud enough to drown out a few hoots and calls and barks of laughter, as the woman relayed why I was here to the rest of the people hanging out in the room. I hurried to get to those sliding doors.

And then to get through them and out into the yard.

The smart move would have been to turn tail and leave. But I wanted to know what Dez was doing here too much for that.

I slid the door shut behind me, dampening the noise of the music. The fresh air of the yard was better. Pots of colorful succulents dotted the edges, next to the high fence. The yard also contained people, but there was a far more serious mood here than inside the house. A small cluster of men and women gathered around something or someone in a shady corner, and I made my way over. I still hadn't spotted Dez.

But I thought I saw Brandon up ahead. "Brandon?" I called softly from the back of the pack. "Dez with you?"

"Who, pray tell, interrupts?" a man boomed out.

Crap. I recognized that voice.

The crowd turned toward me as one before parting. Two people sat in high-backed wicker chairs, an arch of what looked like scrap metal leaned deliberately against the fence behind them.

It was Rex who had asked the question, and he grinned now in a feral way that made my blood run colder in my veins. He still had that beard that made him look like a devil and a fancy suit on, but today he also sported a pointy crown that looked like it was made of old metal.

And in the chair beside him was my mother, in a sleeveless green dress and a crown of her own.

Dez stood to one side of them, beside Brandon. His eyes were wide with panic; he shook his head at me.

"What is this?" I asked.

But I was figuring it out.

The crown my mother wore was brighter than Rex's, silver but still tarnished. I realized what her tattoo was, finally—snakes coiled around a crown. The one on her head had rude snake shapes carved into it too.

"You must kneel before the Rex and Regina," someone nearby said.

The Rex and Regina. My Latin wasn't the best, but magic books were full of it. I knew enough to recognize the terms for king and queen. Regina wasn't her name. And Rex wasn't his. These were *titles*.

My mother, one of the Praestigae, a secret society. Apparently with rulers. She'd been so afraid that some man would find out about me. That I existed.

This man.

The man who'd made my skin crawl talking about curling toenails and clawing out eyes. The man who'd given Dez a nasty black eye. The man Dez owed loyalty to.

Dez had clearly been lying to me this whole time. He'd known my mother was queen of the Praestigae. He'd *known my mother*.

Had he been watching me for her? Had he been *with* me for her?

"Moira," Dez said, his voice tight and afraid. "You have to kneel."

I leaned forward, hands over my stomach like I was absorbing a blow. I swallowed the urge to throw up.

This pain was worse than any my magic had put me through.

"Kneel, not bend," someone else said. It was Brandon. He encouraged me like it was the best idea in the world.

I managed to stand up straight, though I still felt sick. "I . . . don't think I'll be doing that."

"Desmond, you shouldn't have allowed your little girl to follow you here," the Rex said. "You were already in line for punishment, but this . . ." He made a dismissive, wet noise. The *tsk* of a devil.

I wanted to say to my mother *What are you doing? Stop this.*

She sat there, quiet, hands folded one over the other in her lap. Then she demanded, "Who is this girl?"

So that's how we're doing this?

The Rex answered, "She's from the circus. I met her one night. She ruined my poker game. And now she's ruining our accounting."

The Regina, my mother, lifted one beautiful shoulder in a shrug. She was as flawless in appearance here as she had been onstage for the bullet catch. "We could have her thrown out. I could make her believe she's seen nothing . . . or something else."

"No," the Rex said, voice coiled like one of the snakes on my mother's crown. "You will not expend a drop of precious energy on her. I'll decide what to do to her . . . or with her . . . later."

I trembled. Would my mother let something bad happen to me? I didn't know the rules of this place. She was playing it like we were strangers.

Which we were.

Dez looked like he was trembling too, shaky, like a leaf in the wind. "You shouldn't be here," he said.

I went nearer to him, choosing to stare at his shoes rather than look into his face. He had on beat-up sneakers, navy and what used to be white. A breeze stirred my hair into my eyes, partially blocking my view of his feet.

"I'm getting that."

One shoe moved closer to mine.

"Don't." I took a step back.

If he touched me . . . I didn't know what I'd do. Magically hurt him by accident probably.

How long had he known? When he pretended surprise at the revelation that I had magic, that the woman in front of us was my mother . . . he must have known by then. He might have known who I was the entire time.

During every kiss. Every touch. Our first date.

You lied to him too, I remembered.

Yes, but then I told him the truth.

The Rex laughed. "This waltz you two are doing is touching, and also dull as the grave. Not that I know how boring it is down there in the dirt . . . Desmond, you could find out. Have you discovered our coin's location yet? I assume the answer is still no."

My mother was difficult to read. I didn't know her well enough. But I knew from the tightening of her lips that the Rex mentioning this in front of me probably wasn't good news.

"The girl," she said.

He continued to look at Dez, awaiting a response. "I told you to forget her. She's no one."

Dez was trembling. "I already told you. We know the other person who was after it is gone, so now we're in better shape. I'll find it. I swear." He looked at me. "I'll make this right."

There's no way.

"You"—the Rex stood—"are in no shape at all until it is back in our possession. I have no choice but to remind you of your duty. Your father was a careless king. He lost us our luck. Now we need it back." He paused, and addressed the crowd. "Bring the table I set earlier."

There was movement at the back, and the crowd parted again. Two boys, maybe ten years old, carried forward a narrow table. Like something that might sit beside the front door in a nice house like this one.

On the table there was a large hammer with a wood handle, the end of the hammer a gleaming threat.

"Liege, may I speak?" Brandon said, like he had to fight the words free. He never talked like that.

"Of course. I would love to hear your report. You are there to watch him, to make sure he doesn't run."

"Dez would never leave us," Brandon said, sounding surprised.

I wanted to see if Dez's expression had changed, but I couldn't bear to look at him. I had to get out of here.

"It's hard to say what people will and will never do. Desmond, what would you say if I asked whether you'd rather me punish Brandon or you for your failures?"

"Me," Dez said, no hesitation.

"Then you'd just feel noble. Not nearly enough suffering for you to drive home my point." The Rex reached out and grabbed the hammer. He swung it through the air lazily. "Which is that I am sick of waiting."

There was no way that table and that hammer were being used for anything good. I prayed this was just a scare tactic.

"We do have your girl here," the Rex said.

"No," Dez said.

I curled my hands. It wouldn't take much to call my magic. My heart pounded, ready to fight.

"But she's just a girl. Brandon, put your hands on the table, please," the Rex said. "Flat. And close your eyes."

"Please do it to me instead," Dez said with a desperate edge.

"Silence," the Rex said.

Brandon took a shuddering breath and let it out, his thin chest rising and falling. Then he stepped over to the table, leaving it between the Rex and him. He held out his arms and lowered his hands deliberately to the table. After one last glance at Dez, who was shaking his head in horror, he closed his eyes. The crowd was completely silent.

This couldn't happen. The Rex would intentionally miss at the last second, right?

"Watch this, all of you. Desmond, no averting your eyes." The Rex lifted the hammer high overhead.

I couldn't let him do this. I started to step forward, calling on my magic, the heat flooding me—

And then I felt that press, my mother's magic sending mine away.

"No," I said. "No, don't!"

She shook her head at me, the slightest no.

I might be able to overpower her. She claimed to be almost out of magic, and I had a nearly full cup, as far as I knew. Brandon wasn't my favorite person in the world, but he didn't deserve this.

The Rex swung the hammer down, and I shouted, "Mom, stop this!"

The metal smashed into Brandon's hand. His scream was a horror.

thirty-one

Dez was there to catch him when he collapsed. Brandon had never looked so thin and fragile. Tears streaked both their faces.

They streaked mine too. My eyes burned with hot tears of shock.

I inhaled deeply, searching for a calm that was impossible to find. The crowd stayed quiet, but they didn't seem surprised. No one else was weeping. No one else had protested.

The Rex stood there staring at the hammer, barely having broken a sweat. "Did I say I was finished?" he asked.

Dez was shaking his head no, even as Brandon, sickly, ghostly pale, tried to fight his grip to get back to the table. His right hand was already misshapen, swelling, the skin an awful, angry red.

"I am done for now. But next time, it'll be you, Desmond. Those precious knives will not be flying any longer . . . Or maybe that pretty face needs a makeover."

Then the Rex stopped, turned to me, and winked. "So, girl, who here is your mom?" Then louder, "Who here has been lying to me, keeping a secret child?"

No one responded. My mother's hands gripped each other tighter in her lap.

Keep it together, I told myself. *This man just smashed Brandon's hand with a hammer, and now his attention is on you.* I wasn't sure I had enough control of my magic to use it here. And I wasn't sure what to do with it.

The Rex continued. "Nothing is more valuable than our family, than maintaining the numbers of the Praestigae. So why would one of you keep this healthy girl a secret?"

The people gathered craned their necks, looking around at each other.

The Rex took a step toward me, and another. Brandon moaned. Dez held his friend up and said to me, "Run. Try to run."

"Shh," the Rex said. "You're no prince here, boy. You're just the one who keeps disappointing me."

"Get a-away from me," I forced out, backing up a step.

He kept coming instead. He reached out, and I flinched away, but he clapped a hand on my shoulder and lifted the hammer. The two pointed ends raked against my cheek, pressing into, but not breaking, the skin.

My magic rose in me like fire, and my mother did nothing to send it away. I lifted my face.

Concentrate. Don't lose control now.

I let the heat flood up through my skin into the hammer he held. He dropped the wooden handle, smoke billowing from it.

"Fuck!" He whirled, his hand at his mouth. He sucked at his burned fingers. Then he pointed at my mother. "Why did you do that?"

The people around us buzzed with shock.

I saw her open her mouth to tell some lie.

No, I thought. I wanted him to know it was me.

"It wasn't her," I said.

He turned back, frowning. "Pretty sure I know magic when I feel it."

Why hadn't I made him pass out or something?

"Don't," my mother said.

That was all he needed. He gave me a closer look. He *saw* me for the first time. "Chin up, darling," he said. Then, "The eyes."

He faced my mother again. "I've looked into a twin pair so many nights in bed."

"Moira, get out of here," Dez said. "Now."

"Like you care," I said.

Okay, maybe that was unfair. It wasn't like I'd never lied. Or like I thought he wanted the Rex to have his way with me.

But as far as I could tell, everything about me and Dez had been a lie.

"Shh," the Rex said. "Explain. Why didn't I know about my child?"

My mother hesitated. She was frightened. "She's not yours."

The crowd around us erupted in shocked conversation, and the Rex's face grew steadily redder. I did not want to be near him when he exploded.

The moment ended anyway, the crowd hushing as he raised a hand. His eyes raked over me, obscene and considering. "Nineteen years ago. When you were working the job in Vegas so long . . ." He barked a laugh. "You were on that magician, trying to find out if he had our lucky coin. I guess you got lucky instead. Well, hell, we all did. She's one of us *and* she has magic."

"I am *not* one of you," I said, and I took a step back.

The Rex watched me.

I took another step away from him.

The people nearest me rustled, and I knew they'd grab me the moment he said to. The yard had grown more crowded, the people from inside drawn out by the action.

"Did you know that Desmond here is at the rich man's circus because his family owes a debt?" the Rex asked, examining me like he was looking at a prize mare. "I didn't think so."

I still wanted answers about Dez. I stayed where I was, and he went on. "His father, with his silver tongue, lost our luck to Roman Garcia in a poker game." He gestured to the arched scrap behind their wicker thrones. "This is a piece of the Gate of Luck recovered from this very city many years ago. Your mother, my queen, sensed its presence, and so we have a place to rest our heads while we are here. But we will not need trinkets like this with our birthright back. It is the coin that belonged to the first Rex and Regina of the Praestigae. Part of the prize for escaping the Circus Maximus, infused with all the lucky magic of our first Regina."

If what he said was true, the Garcia coin wasn't the Garcia coin at all.

"I can see this has all been a bit much for a welcome," the Rex said. "I'm no savage. You need time to get used to the idea of all this splendor. It's part yours now, princess. So you can help get the boys back to the circus and use your gift to find the coin. Don't think to run. Moira, was it?"

"Why didn't you listen?" My mother's voice was accusing.

When she'd told me to stop taking chances. When she'd told me that I was in danger. When she'd told me to leave.

"I'm sorry," I said.

"Go," the Rex said, "I need to talk with my wife."

He waved a hand in the air. "Never forget."

The crowd around us responded by rote: "Only the Praestigae are free."

Even Brandon, who looked like he was about to pass out, clinging to Dez, tried to join in the chant.

"Let's go," I said to Dez.

No way I was hanging around until this Rex psycho changed his mind.

Dez gingerly lifted Brandon into his arms. "Easy, okay, buddy?" he said.

Brandon grimaced against him and held his hand to the side. It drooped. His eyelids fluttered.

We moved fast to get out of there. I opened the front door, and as soon as we were outside, I said, "We have to get him to a doctor."

"No ambulance," Dez said. "No cops."

I heaved out a breath. "We have to get away from here. He might decide to come after us."

Dez nodded, and I summoned a car to the next corner using an app on my phone. We stood, tense and quiet, Brandon no longer conscious, waiting.

Come on, come on, come on, I thought, willing the car to come faster. *I don't want him to say anything. I don't want to hear it.*

"Moira?" Dez said, soft as a caress.

"Please don't." I kept my eyes on the street, watching for our car. "I'm sorry . . . about Brandon. There was nothing you could have done."

"It's my fault."

The plain maroon sedan I'd called came around the corner, and I waved it over. I was afraid the car would leave when the college-student driver saw Brandon, so I grabbed the back passenger door before she could and motioned for Dez to get him inside.

I circled around and climbed in the front seat.

"Does that guy need a hospital?" she asked.

Brandon moaned.

"Take us to Kidd Stadium. To the Cirque."

"Oh, you're with the circus!" she said, like that explained everything. Maybe it did.

I nodded tightly and thumbed out a text to Thurston's assistant: Brandon got in a bar fight, won't let me call 911. Can you get the doctor ready? Broken hand.

Understatement of the year—I wondered if it was even possible to treat the kind of injury Brandon must have like this, with a road doctor. The Rex's swing had been so hard, the hammer so high when it came down.

Dez spoke, "Moira, you have to call your dad. You need help."

Tears pricked at my eyes. "I know. And . . . I will want to talk. Just not right now."

Right now I was trying to get Brandon's scream out of my head. Trying to get how my mother hadn't attempted to fight out of it.

Trying to scrub the Rex's existence from it.

And failing utterly.

thirty-two

Thurston's assistant met us at the edge of the property. "Doc's waiting," she said. "I don't think Thurston would like this, not reporting it to the police."

Dez smiled at her, and I was surprised he had the energy to. "I know it's not the best," he said, "but Brandon had some trouble as a kid. Doesn't need more of a record. Okay?"

"We'll make it work." She frowned at Brandon's condition. "He looks shocky."

Waving us forward, she rushed us across the artificial turf—not that far, thankfully—to the medical bus parked behind the big top. She opened the door and left us to it. The interior was state-of-the-art, with gurneys, lab stuff, machines, all the things you'd expect in a clinic—just in this case, a clinic on wheels. But would it be enough to fix up Brandon?

The doctor raised his eyebrows, gently assessing Brandon's hand. "Morphine," he said to the nurse, who turned away and rushed to unlock a cabinet. "What happened? This isn't from punching someone."

"It got mashed. A guy threw a keg on top of it," Dez said. "Hard."

I blinked.

Pretty good story. He must have come up with that one in the car.

"You two get out of here and let us work," he said. "Does he have any family?"

"Just me," Dez said.

Outside, the sun beat down on us. A few other performers hurried past to rehearsals or on other business, acting as if it was a perfectly normal day. For them, it probably was. Normal felt lost to me.

I'd been wondering something on the ride, once I started to get past the immediate horror of what had happened. I assumed the answer would be no, but I had to ask. "My mom . . . have you ever seen her fix an injury like that?"

Dez looked at me. "With magic? No, I don't think healing is a thing, not for bodies."

"I figured." I remembered blacking out when I tried to change the penny back. Maybe repairing a person was sort of the same thing.

It broke some rule.

Though it was hard to believe in rules, that the universe made any kind of sense at all, after seeing the Rex's cruelty in action.

Dez sank down to the outdoor steps that led into the medical bus. "I'm going to wait," he said.

"Me too."

"You should call your dad."

"You don't get to tell me what to do." I closed my eyes and took a deep breath. When I opened them, he was watching me with what seemed to be intense longing.

Remember that charming smile he turned on Thurston's assistant. You just want the comfort.

"I need answers." I carefully moved to sit on the next step down, leaving a foot between us. "No one's around to overhear anything. I don't want to wait."

He raised his hands. "I have no more secrets to keep. I never . . . I never wanted to."

"To be with me, you mean?"

"No! To lie. To keep things from you."

I didn't want to talk about the us part yet. The rest was bigger, more important. Even if my heart wanted those answers first, these were the ones my brain demanded.

And my brain was officially back in charge.

"What did he mean, use my power to find the coin?" I asked.

"You still want to help her. After she let him find out about you?"

"That was my fault," I countered. "Not hers."

Dez shrugged. "I assume it means you can. Magic calls to magic? You just try?"

Frustrating. "So you don't really know anything about magic?"

"Not really, not much. Stories. What I've seen."

I kicked the step. "Tell me about the Praestigae. The word's Latin, right?"

He settled back against the door. "Started that way at least. It means something about the ones in the shadows, tricksters, jugglers. The reason you haven't heard of us is because no one talks much about us. No one needs to. No one ever leaves."

"Great," I said. The Rex clearly expected me to stay with them, become one of them.

"The Praestigae *are* a family."

"A megadysfunctional one."

"No argument there," he agreed. "It wasn't always as bad as it is now. Sometimes when the Rex isn't around, people talk. They liked Dad and the Rexes and Reginas before. Your mother can be kind. My dad was disgraced after losing the coin, the Praestigae's greatest prize. He died last year—he was older when he had me—and not long after, there were rumors that the coin was back. Somewhere at the Cirque. Roman always refused to play for it again, and others said Nancy Maroni had it, but there was no evidence. We knew she had magic of her own. Anyway, now I have to make up for what Dad did. The Rex decided, and when the Rex decides—"

"I can tell." I wanted to reach out and touch him, but I stopped myself. "It wasn't your fault back there."

He stared out in front of us at nothing. "Brandon is like my brother. Always has been. But he was wrong. I would leave in a heartbeat if I thought I could get away."

Brain in charge, not heart. "Keep talking," I said. "I want to know everything. How far back do the Praestigae go?"

"There's a whole legend how the people started, back in Rome. A beautiful daughter whose merchant father sold her into the gladiator pits. She had magic, like yours. She could transform things. She part-nered up with this other prisoner, a criminal who was a former gladia-tor. She could make a handful of dust into a deadly mace for him. They won their freedom and never looked back. Her magic passed down from Regina to Regina. The Praestigae vowed never to follow anyone else's rules again, besides their own rulers'."

How was it possible to escape people who didn't have to play by anybody else's rules? "What about that chant?" I said. "What did it mean?"

"'The Praestigae are freedom,'" he said. "'Anything else is death. We must always remember.' That's what we—they—believe."

"I don't think I'll like that kind of freedom."

Dez grew even more serious and looked straight at me. "Moira, he knows you exist now. I don't know how you can get away, but maybe your dad can help. I believe the Regina was trying to protect you. Keep you out of this."

"Those maternal instincts really kicked in today," I said. My mother had barely moved.

"I didn't know at first why she wanted me to get close to you and keep it quiet from him. When one of them asks for something, though, you do it. I thought it was because I told her Nancy Maroni was inter-ested in you. But then . . . it made sense. When you told me the truth."

"When did she ask you?" My heart waited for the answer. "Before that first date?"

He nodded. "Right before."

"Was any of it real?" I asked. Or was I a magician fooled by a regular old liar?

He raised his hands in front of him, looking frustrated. But he answered. "What was between us was real. You lied to me too, but it didn't make everything a lie. I know it's over. I was never good enough for you." His lips twisted into a smile with no humor in it. "We're from two different worlds."

"Stop." He was giving up. I wouldn't let him. "You could have told."

I hadn't seen it before, but now I couldn't see anything else. This was about punishing himself. He didn't deserve it.

"What?" he asked.

"You could have told the Rex about me. After I told you about my magic. You could have done it days ago. You could have done it today, and . . . you didn't."

"Don't make me more 'noble' than I am. Remember, Brandon's in there. And I *thought* about telling the Rex . . ."

"You thought about it, and you *didn't* do it. None of this would have happened if you'd sold me out. You'd be back on top. You would have gotten credit for bringing in another girl with magic, the next Regina-to-be. But you didn't say a word."

"I couldn't. Okay? I should have. But I couldn't." He sounded angry at himself.

"Look at me." I stood up and moved in front of him. I reached down for his hands, and he let me take them, though he looked skeptical. Like this was all a trick.

I pulled him to his feet. "I trust you. Mostly."

"Don't say that."

"I'm not running. We are going to do this together."

"You have to go."

"Dez," I said, "I think I love you."

He had nothing to say to that. His eyes went watery, like pennies at the bottom of a fountain. "I think I love you too, Moira Mitchell. You do know I'm the worst idea you've ever had, though?"

"Back at you," I whispered.

"We are so screwed."

His lips met mine, and he wrapped me in his arms, and I held on to him as tightly as I knew how. We sealed our truce, our partnership, our honest agreement, with a kiss. It was bittersweet. I had no idea how either of us would get out of this, if we even could. Maybe we would fail miserably. But we would do it together.

For once, I was in a situation that seemed truly inescapable.

thirty-three

We sat, side by side, exhausted and nervous when the doctor finally came to the door an hour later.

"I need you to talk to him," he said, obviously speaking to Dez.

"All right," Dez said.

"You want me to come with you?" I asked.

"I'd better see him alone."

Dez disappeared into the bus, and I went back to waiting. There were more people showing up at the field, performers and customers. It was time for the afternoon midway opening. I heard music in the distance.

I had a show to do. Two shows. We both did, the last in El Paso. We could cancel, but I didn't know how Thurston would feel about that. I had a feeling he was a big believer in the show going on.

Such a small concern, in the midst of so many huge ones. But it was an immediate problem, one I could solve right now. I turned it over in my head, making a plan B about what I could do for the audience on short notice, assistantless, in case Dez wouldn't leave. I wasn't going to make him.

I could back up Brandon as the assistant for Dez's sets, if he wanted to do them. For all I knew, the Rex might have some other spy who'd report that he skipped them, which would make things even worse.

Ten minutes later, Dez came back out. I got up to greet him.

"He isn't even mad," he said. "At him *or* me."

His hand balled into a fist, like he wanted to punch something.

"Because there was nothing you could do. He knows you'd rather be in his place. And the Rex is his leader, so he can't let himself be mad at him. How bad is it?"

"The doctor wanted me to talk him into surgery. It's the only way he'll ever get full control of his hand back. A long shot even then."

"If money's an issue—"

"It's not. Thurston would pay. The doctor called him. Brandon doesn't want to abandon his post. Or me."

"He could change his mind."

Dez relaxed his fingers, shook them out, and considered his own hand. Like he was thinking about what it would be to not have it work anymore. "They have to do it right away, if they're going to do it with a shot at success. Brandon told him to do the best he could and put a cast on. They have to put him under, even for that. He'll be here overnight. At least."

"I'm sorry. And I know this seems like nothing, but—"

"We have shows to do. I know." He held out his hand to me, and I took it. "I'm not going to make you do yours solo. We'll come back later."

"And we'll make a plan," I said as we started walking. "We will not let the Rex win."

I wished there was as much hope in my heart as in my words.

We packed up and left for Albuquerque the next day. I drove behind Remy and Dita; Dez rode in the medical bus with a still mostly sleeping Brandon.

There'd been no sign or word from the Rex or Regina, not even to check on Brandon.

That shouldn't have surprised me, but somehow it did.

Dez and I had made a plan in stolen moments when we weren't attending to Brandon or performing or driving, and I put it into play on our first rehearsal day in Albuquerque.

I waited for Remy and Dita to head off to lunch together, then I texted Dez. He must have already been lingering outside, because he knocked a moment later. He'd probably come from the medical bus, which Brandon would be released from in a couple of days, due to continued improvement. Albeit with strong pain meds and daily checkups. The doctor wasn't thrilled about skipping surgery and just resetting and immobilizing the bones as best he could, but he seemed tentatively hopeful the results might be better than he'd feared at first.

Until the next time the Rex felt like punishing Dez, anyway.

"Hurry," I said, waving Dez inside.

I had managed to convince Dez that I'd call Dad soon. Just not yet. The first step of the plan was for me to attempt to do exactly what the Rex had ordered—use my magic to find the coin. Once we had it, we would have a little leverage. My mom needed it. And it was a sacred item to the Praestigae.

But would the Rex protect her or think I could be a replacement instead?

We had no crystal ball, not even the benefit of Nan Maroni's tarot cards. This was our best shot at the moment.

"Did you figure out how you're going to do this?" Dez asked.

"Trial and error, I guess."

I closed my eyes and pictured the scene at that house in El Paso, the Rex picking up the hammer. The cool feel of the metal points against my cheek. My heart pounding, like I was back in those terrible moments.

I called on my magic, and it responded, my palms warming.

"This is going to look silly," I murmured, and opened my eyes. I lifted my hands and held them out.

And I began to walk through the Airstream like some kind of diviner or a kook with a dousing rod in search of water. Charlatan stuff.

"If this works," I said, "I can put it in my act. And start doing the worst magic tricks."

"I don't think zombie arms is a magic trick," Dez countered, following close behind me.

"Shh," I said, attempting to concentrate.

I felt exactly nada besides warm palms as we made our way into Remy's remarkably clean room, the bed made, even. There were stacks of mystery novels, the same kind Dita was always reading, lined up at the top of his bed. Some of that chalk they put on their hands and feet to prevent slipperiness sat there too. I waved my hands all around.

"Nothing?" Dez asked.

"Nothing," I confirmed. "And I can't tell if it's because there really is nothing, or because I'm not *doing* anything."

My phone rang, shrill, and I jumped and bashed my knee against the table. "Ow."

"Who is it?" Dez asked. "If it's your dad, you should answer."

It usually *was* Dad. I fished the phone out of my pocket and checked the screen, prepared to ignore the call.

"It's not him." I slid to answer. "Amber? Hi, what's up?"

There was a moment of silence, and then my father spoke. "Where are you?"

Oh no.

"I can explain," I started.

Dez's eyebrows shot up. "What is it?" he whispered.

I held up a hand for quiet. "Dad?"

"Yes. Where are you?"

I scrambled through my brain for what to do. We had four short weeks left after this, and we'd be creeping closer to Vegas the entire time. We were in trouble he might be able to help with.

My show was tight. There was a line after every performance waiting for autographs.

He might as well come now.

"Moira Mitchell, answer me. This is over."

If we could find the coin, we would have a bargaining chip with him too. He'd had Raleigh looking for it, after all. I only needed to buy us a little more time. Enough to locate it.

"I'm performing magic," I said. "With the Cirque American. Why don't you come and see us next week in Phoenix?"

"You're where? No, I will not. You will come home now."

"I won't."

"This is not a negotiation. You lied to me. You can't be there. It's dangerous."

"Because of the magic coin you sent Raleigh here to find? Yeah, I know about that."

"Why—"

"I'm an adult, and this is a job. You will come when I invite you, and watch me perform, and I will talk to you after. We have important things to discuss. Deal?"

I had much worse fears these days than worrying about my dad disapproving of my career choices.

Anger seeped out of the phone. "This is why you were asking about your mother. About my warehouse. The coin."

"Yep."

We were both steaming into the phone. Now it was a matter of who was most stubborn. Finally, he said, "Send me the time and place. I'll call in a favor for someone to cover the Menagerie."

I hit ended the call. "Well, that's great," I said to Dez.

"He's coming?" Dez asked.

"He's coming," I said. Which made the heat of my magic surge, accompanied by a bucket of nervous energy. "Let's check the rest of the place before they get back."

We found no trace of the coin anywhere in the Airstream or on the grounds or backstage. We conducted the entire search with me trying to be as discreet as possible about my lifted radar hands. By the end of the day, I had to admit the problem was more than likely me. The coin was here. I just wasn't finding it. "I don't think I'm doing it right."

"Maybe your mom can explain how." Dez frowned. "Though why *hasn't* she found it, if magic can?"

"Low on magic, remember. Maybe it's more complicated than it seems, takes too much?"

"What if it's not even here?" he asked.

"It is, and Remy and Jules know where. If this doesn't work, we'll have to ask them straight out."

Disappointing the Maronis and Garcias wasn't something I wanted to do, but I might not have any other option. It was all too easy to picture Dita's face when she found out her partner in crime, her roomie, was just the latest person keeping her in the dark.

Dez was on Brandon night-shift duty, so I went back to the Airstream and lay on my bed in the dark, staring at the ceiling. Dita and Remy hadn't made it home yet. I was alone. I called my magic to me and played with transforming whatever was handy without even looking. I was getting better. My fingers and then body filled with the heat that meant I was using magic. I no longer felt like it would burn me up from the inside out. Not when I had it under control and successfully guided it, anyway.

I made a coin into a paper heart, and then another. And another.

I pictured myself as a cup, the fiery red sea inside lessening a fraction with everything I transformed.

Maybe if I did this enough, I'd use my magic all up and things would get simple again. Except I *couldn't* use it all.

Or I'd shatter.

thirty-four

When our first day of Albuquerque shows arrived, Dez and I stood in silence behind the curtain, moments before we'd take the stage. I was doing the coffin escape for the early show, and the bullet catch for the late one. My tent was always full, but people seemed to appreciate the drama of the bullet catch more.

Which would be better for Dad to see? The coffin escape, maybe. I didn't use actual magic in a way he'd spot. But what if he wanted to watch both? He'd see in a second there was no way for Dez to get me the marked bullet, no other assistant to pass it to me when I donned my safety gear. Of course, I was going to have to tell him I knew all about my magic anyway. A demonstration might be in order.

"Ready?" Dez asked.

"Let's go."

Our spirits were flagging. The lack of progress in finding the coin and Brandon's doctor's troubled face whenever we saw him didn't help matters.

I was a little off during my performance. But I made it through, presto chango, abracadabra, free from straitjacket and coffin. I took my bows, and the audience applauded as loud as always.

This was what being a professional meant, I guessed. Even your not-best was at a level people would appreciate. I still didn't like phoning it in.

I signed autographs quickly, smiling as I posed with audience members for selfies and counting the seconds until I'd be done. I had a pressing question for Dez.

As soon as we were alone in the tent, I asked, "Can we get a message to my mother or go see her?"

"The Rex and Regina summon you or pay a visit. It's the only way."

"But they're trailing us, right? Around? We'll probably see them soon?"

"I wouldn't sound so eager," he said. "But yes. I'm surprised they've taken so long to show."

He wore a troubled expression.

"What is it? What did you just think?" I said, prodding. "Honesty, please."

He messed with the curtain in front of him. "That he's probably keeping her from coming to see you to be an asshole. Because he can."

"Ah. I can see that." But I wanted my mother to come. Then she could tell me what I was doing wrong.

I hadn't realized what an idyllic existence I'd had at the Cirque before. Now everything from my friendships to my job felt like a false front, an illusion I'd conjured. An illusion that would leave a terrible reality in its wake.

Dez pulled the curtain aside. "Shit," he said.

The devil was waiting for us backstage with a toothy grin in an overly fancy gray suit. "Language, my loyal subject," he said to Dez. "And in the presence of our princess."

I swallowed saying I wasn't his anything.

My mother was with him, polished in that way she'd described as an illusion. She had on orangey-red lipstick that clashed with her hair, and another long sleeveless dress. Black this time. I'd only ever seen her look thin, pale, sickly that once. It made me wonder.

I had no reason to distrust her completely, though. Not yet. She'd been right about how bad it'd be if the Rex discovered I existed.

So I could play nice for a few minutes to get a conversation alone with her. "I wish we'd known you were coming," I said, as pleasantly as I could manage, as much a performance as anything I'd ever done on the stage. "We'd have rolled out the red carpet."

"Do you have one?" the Rex asked, his voice so mild that you might believe he was a charmer, if you'd just met him.

"Afraid not," Dez said, careful. "What can we do for you?"

"We didn't want to risk another *scene*. But we wanted an update on your progress."

I pulled out the chair in front of the nearest makeup table and gestured to it.

"My queen," the Rex said.

"Thank you," my mother murmured.

I was still trying to be nice, but I caught a movement in Dez's jaw. He'd clenched it tight, probably without even knowing.

So I asked, "Did you also want to know how Brandon is? After the—"

"Punishment?" he said. "A fair one. He's alive, isn't he? That's all I need to know."

"He's alive," Dez said.

"So"—the Rex clapped his hands together under another grin— "where's the coin? I feel you are going to be lucky for us, Moira."

I fidgeted.

"Speak up," he said, harshness creeping in. "I can't read minds. Alas."

"Um," I said. "I think I need some help from my mother."

"You haven't found it yet?" The Rex's smile vanished, his expression serious as the grave he'd threatened to put Dez in that day.

"We've been trying. But I don't think I know how to use my magic like that."

He circled Dez and then me, looking at us both. "I don't see any under-eye shadows, any signs of frantic despair. I don't think you've been trying hard enough. How best to motivate you?" He made a ticking sound, his tongue hitting his teeth.

In my mind, I heard Brandon's scream. My own breathing grew shallow. I also didn't know how to use my magic *against* the Rex. Not with nothing in my hands. Could I try to transform a stray coin in my pocket into something of his to hurt him, like I had accidentally done with the penny and Dez? Incapacitate him that way?

"Rex," my mother said, "you're scaring Moira."

"It's time to scare Moira. She's one of my subjects now." He lifted his hand and slapped me.

My cheek stung, and my hand went to it. I couldn't believe it.

"Interesting," he said. "You don't know how to fight back. Good. Your little trick with the hammer made me wonder."

"I do," Dez said.

"I do think you are a good motivation for her," the Rex said. "Old Silver-Tongue's son has clearly inherited his charm with the ladies." His eyes migrated to my silent mother for a moment. "Here's your new motivation. If you don't find that damn coin before this foolish season ends, then Dez gets the dirt. The worms. The rot. The endless silence. You get what I'm saying?" He clapped his hands together. "Now do you still need Mommy's help?"

I nodded, my hand on my stinging cheek. "I wasn't lying."

"We'll leave you two to it, then." He clapped a hand on Dez's shoulder. "It's time for your performance, isn't it? I'll help you. I'm beginning to feel like maybe bigger things are in store for you after all. You're important now." The Rex turned and met my eyes with his. They seemed to be all pupil. Black and filled with endless meanness. "She's made you that way."

Dez stiffly left with him. I prayed he'd return unharmed.

Neither my mother nor I spoke until after I went to the tent flap and checked outside. "They're gone."

"You're lucky it was just a slap," my mother said. "Now you understand. Why I didn't want him to know about you."

"Yeah, well, too late." I considered her. "Do you really not fight because you're low on magic?"

She looked down. "If you fight and you lose enough times, you decide not to go into battle anymore. Dez's father . . . I could have been something like happy with him. But this Rex started out bad and got worse. That's why I didn't want you there. Why I went to your father."

"Why have me at all?"

"The Regina must pass on her power. Otherwise we're cursed. The Rex doesn't know that. The important thing is I saved you."

I couldn't read how she felt about any of this. She wasn't giving me much in the way of emotion.

"Thanks for trying, but I'm not feeling all that saved. If only you and Dad would have told me the truth."

Was that fair? Would I have let it go, or would I have investigated and tried to find her? It was impossible to know.

She stood up. "Give me your hands."

She took them in hers and held them lightly. "The magic in the coin is akin to your magic. To find it is a sort of call-and-response. Think of opening a door, and your magic is right at the threshold, all of it. You have to call it up. Or imagine the magic being right at the rim of your cup, if you'd rather think of it that way. And then call out for more of that same magic to answer you. You should be able to go right to it."

"I don't get it. You haven't done this already because you don't have enough magic left. How do you reach out and push mine away, then?"

She hesitated. "That's different. My magic isn't close enough to the top to call out for more. There may be less magic in the world now, but it's still here for a reason. It has its own fail-safes built in. If *every* person running low could just gas up with more or steal from others, then it would all burn out in no time."

"You mean the way you plan to use the coin?"

She shrugged one beautiful shoulder. "Its magic is our birthright, and our magic is special."

I tilted my head, considering. "Would you use that magic for battle?"

My mother was still. "My battle days are behind me."

"I'll find it." I pulled my hands out of hers.

But would I hand it over? Not without some way to avoid the Praestigae, becoming a shadow instead of a magician at center stage. And not without a way to keep Dez from the dirt.

"Don't wait too long," she said.

I thought about telling her Dad was coming next week. Even if I'd found it, I wouldn't want to hand it over before then.

"He said Dez has until the end of the season."

"I'll try to remind him of that, but in case you missed it, he's not the most patient."

"Whatever you can do." The heart-shaped penny was in my pocket. "One more question," I said, taking it out to show it to her. "I made this, back at the beginning of the season, and Dez felt it. He collapsed with heart pain. If *you* won't do battle, maybe I can. Is this how'd I use my magic to . . . hurt someone?"

She motioned for me to drop it in her palm, and I reluctantly did. "Dez wasn't hurt after you made this, though, not permanently?"

"The doctor said no."

She weighed it in her palm and passed it back to me. "Sometimes our magic knows more than we do. There is a magic behind things that it can touch, but we can't, not directly. You transformed something that was real but insubstantial into something with form. You hold Dez's life in your hands. You have since you made this."

Her words stole my breath. Dez's life was mine to protect?

She gave me a tentative smile. "Probably since you met each other. I didn't have to try hard to recruit him as my spy."

"Are we having a girls' moment?" I asked, incredulous. Not wanting to show her how much Dez's life meant to me.

"Is that so hard to believe?" she asked. "I'm your ally. Not your enemy."

The tent flap rustled, and the Rex came in first. I closed my fingers around the penny and put it in my pocket.

"Now this is a sight I like to see," he said. "My beautiful, dangerous girls together."

Dez behind him had a thin cut slashed on one arm, seeping blood. I went to his side. "What happened?"

The Rex answered. "Just a little nick. I helped with his act, like I said." He grinned. "We're just one big happy family, my girl. As long as you do exactly as I ask."

"You'll have your coin by the end of the season."

He walked over and offered his arm to my mother. "What if we want it sooner? The Praestigae have struggled for too long."

"You made a deal with me," Dez said, "and, by extension, with her. By the end of the season. We don't break deals with our own."

"She didn't know that," the Rex whispered. "Fine," he said, raising his voice. "Just find it."

"I'll do my best," I said.

"Do better than that," he said. "Show her something real, my queen."

Between one moment and the next, my mother went from beautiful with tacky lipstick to a wan woman with a swollen lip, a bruise on each of her cheeks suspiciously like thumbprints. Her appearance *had* been an illusion. She *was* using her magic.

"Enough," he said.

And she was back to beautiful and perfect again.

After they left, Dez pulled me into a hug, both of us shaking. I held on to him hard.

"I've never seen her end up hit before," he said. "Or so quiet."

I had no reason to doubt that my mother cared, that her concern for me was genuine. How far that went versus her loyalty to the Rex, I couldn't say. She'd been using her magic, but how much it cost her to was an open question.

"There's no way to know what's real," I said. "But we do know what's valuable to them."

I had to find the coin, fast.

thirty-five

I picked at my waffle the next morning at the breakfast mess.

Dita had her practice clothes on. The Garcias were rehearsing a new bit this morning. And I was going to summon all my magic to find this coin.

Dez and I had been too rattled to do much more than report back on our conversations the night before. He'd been spooked by what a good mood the Rex was in. I had told Dez everything except the part about holding his life in my hands.

"Hey, I've been wondering," Dita said, "is something wrong?"

You could say that. "No, why?"

"You're barely eating, and you've been really quiet lately. Is it something to do with Brandon?"

He'd gotten released from the medical bus, and he was now on strong painkillers and staying in a much better spot, which he called "a pity upgrade." He called it that to Dez, at least. He more or less ignored me.

"Or Dez?" she asked.

"It's a lot of things," I said. "Nothing I can really talk about. What about you?"

Dita glanced around us, as if we were in danger of being overheard. We weren't.

"I've been seeing someone."

GWENDA BOND

I hadn't expected that. "Who?"

She gave a wry smile and tapped her fingers nervously on the tabletop. "Not like that—a therapist. For a few weeks now. Thurston set it up. Over Skype." She was quiet, then she said, "It's helping, with the Sam stuff and the rest. He gave me something, and it's really been good, I think. Although I felt a little fuzzy for the first week. Now I . . . I only imagine screwing up in the air every few days."

"That's great," I said, and meant it. "I'm glad you felt like you could tell me."

I also felt like dirt, because she shouldn't trust me.

Remy and the blonde twin flyers who were also in their act were approaching, so I gave a warning. "Your rehearsal partners are here."

"Thanks," she said. "You can tell me, whatever is bothering you. I just want you to know that."

Oh, but I can't.

"Thanks back. Now go spin around really fast in the air."

She laughed and got up. I did the same, dumping my barely touched waffle on the way out.

I made my way to Dez's compartment, which was where we'd set to meet this morning. He was waiting, sitting on the edge of his bed, watching for me. "Hi there," he said, and gave me a lingering kiss. "Are you sure about doing this?"

"Once we have the coin, we have something they want."

"You are something he wants."

"Well, he can't have me." I hesitated. "Do you think my mother's telling the truth about her magic being almost gone?"

What he'd said about her acting differently and not usually being a victim of the Rex's violence had stuck with me. I had a feeling there was more to her story than what she'd confessed to me so far. But I also felt guilty for doubting her, and for wondering how much she was capable of manipulating me.

274

"I don't know. They would never admit she's running low to anyone. You were the first I'd heard it from. They said they wanted the coin back because it was ours, would make us powerful and lucky again."

"Maybe he doesn't know. If she runs out, she dies." Yet she'd been using magic to change her appearance the other night. She said casting illusions used less magic than transformations did, but based on the times I'd seen her at shows and at that house in El Paso, she did it constantly.

"There's no way you would run out," Dez said, "is there?"

"I don't think so. Not soon," I said, though I had no idea. According to my mother, what I was about to do took a lot of magic, more than she had left. But better for him not to worry about that. I waved him aside. "Move over."

After he did, I sat down cross-legged on his bed.

"Do you need anything?" he asked.

"Just magic." I closed my eyes and did as my mother had said.

I called to my magic, and when it came, the feeling of being in a fixed place in the universe faded. The bed I sat on might as well have vanished. I pictured the magic filling me up, almost running over the edges of the cup, and when it felt like it was bigger than me, like I was a speck in its ocean and it would protect me from everything, taking me anywhere I needed to go along its currents, I sent out my request . . .

And the other magic answered, like a distant voice responding to my question. Like it was pulling me in toward it, so I could hear it better.

The thing is, I recognized it. It wasn't mine, but I'd felt it before.

That first day in the tent, that sensation of something pulling me up toward the top of the tent.

This had the same . . . texture. A taste, almost.

I stood up. "This way."

I led us across the grounds, floating on the fullness of my magic, toward that answering call.

When we turned away from the big top, I frowned. But the call was strong, and I followed it into the maze of performers' homes. We wound through trailers until we were at the familiar silver Airstream, the mural of Remy and Dita on the side.

"Seriously?" Dez asked. "It's been here the whole time?"

I didn't bother to shush him. The call from inside was too forceful. I unlocked the door and went straight back to . . . the room Dita and I shared. The call reverberated through me so loud that it took a moment to pinpoint the location.

I went to the closet and brushed my hands across Dita's suits. Then I knelt and reached toward the very back. There was a rough carpet on the floor, and I tugged up the edge and felt for the point that was calling to me.

My hand closed around a small piece of metal, and the jolt of power nearly made me black out. I scrambled back and closed my eyes, curling my fingers around the coin tight. I wanted to hold on forever. My magic didn't want to let it go.

"Moira, are you okay?"

The fear in Dez's voice reached me.

With effort, I forced my fingers open and dropped the coin onto the floor. Then I pushed my magic back down inside me, silencing the call. It didn't want to go, and for a moment, I thought I wouldn't be able to make it. That this time it would consume me.

Finally, it ebbed.

I opened my eyes.

Dez was obviously freaking out, hovering over me.

"I think I'm all right." My voice sounded strange to my ears.

"That was insanely scary," he said.

He pointed at the coin on the bare space of floor between the closet and Dita's bed where I'd dropped it. "So that's it. It was right next to you all along."

"I don't think it was here all along," I said. "Dita hates it."

I remembered Jules and Remy's whispered conversations, and then Jules showing up with that gift for Dita. Those slippers. The coin seemed to whisper yes to me.

"They planted it on Dita. She must have figured it out."

"Do you think she'll notice it's gone?"

I considered. My fingers itched to grab the coin again. "I doubt she's even looked at it since she put it there. We should just be glad she didn't know how to destroy it."

Dez leaned over to get a better look at it. I did too, though it felt dangerous, like tempting fate.

Closer, I could make out the shape of a head engraved on it, and Roman numerals. An ancient Roman coin from the Circus Maximus—valuable even without a drop of magic in it.

The front door opened, and Dez and I both jolted.

"Moira?" Dita called out. "You here?"

Using my T-shirt to keep my skin from making contact with the metal, I grabbed the coin and jammed it in my pocket. I didn't want to touch it again *because* of how badly I wanted to.

Dez jerked me over onto my bed, mussed my hair and put his arms around me.

Dita appeared in the doorway and immediately looked up at the ceiling and turned around. "Oh God, guys, I'm sorry. I—"

"No," I said, sitting up. "We shouldn't . . . We didn't mean to . . ."

I still felt strange. The presence of the coin in my pocket was impossible to ignore.

Dez jumped in. "What I think Moira's trying to say is we accidentally got carried away. Sorry."

"It's your place too," Dita said weakly, disappearing in the direction of the kitchen.

When she was gone, I looked at Dez. "I don't want this near me any longer than it has to be."

The dry, dramatic desert landscape we drove through from Albuquerque to Phoenix was a perfect mirror for my internal state, particularly the way it was punctuated by giant mountains and deep canyons. My nerves over what would happen when Dad arrived—and everything else—made me feel just as jagged around the edges.

I hadn't kept the coin on me. I'd put it back where it was, under the carpet.

And I checked daily to make sure it was still there.

It was.

Tonight I did have it with me as I paced through the backstage of my tent. I'd stashed it in a carrying case with a few other coins in my pocket. It felt less dangerous without my magic actively calling to it, but not by a lot.

Dad would be here any minute now.

Dez pulled aside the tent flaps and entered. He'd dressed up in his suit for my dad.

"You're giving me a weird look," he said. "But it's okay, because I still dig the mask."

"I'm too nervous for flirting," I said.

He grinned, and it was almost like our old normal. But not quite. We were both tense. This was a big night.

For me in more ways than one.

"Your dad can't deny what's in front of his eyes," he said. "You're going to kill it."

So he'd sensed I was as nervous about finally performing in front of Dad as I was about the things my rational side knew should be much more important. It was probably ridiculous, but a fact was a fact.

"Let's hope. You still feel good about the plan?" I asked.

"Yeah, I do. It gives us leverage, like you said."

"As long as he'll take it."

I rested my forehead against Dez's, and we stood there, taking comfort in each other's presence.

I didn't want to keep the coin, but we weren't quite ready to hand it over to the Rex and Regina yet either. And although I thought my mother's life was in danger, there was a chance she was lying.

If the Rex had given Dez and me through the end of the season, he—and Mom, since she hadn't protested—must have believed she could make it until then. So we'd agreed that I would try to convince Dad to take the magic coin with him tonight when he left, and stash it with the rest of his treasures in one of his fortresslike warehouses. We could retrieve it when we got to Vegas.

Buying us time, a precious commodity, so we could try, try, try to come up with a way out of this life-wrecking mess.

Raleigh alerted us to his presence with a cough as he breezed in through the tent flap. "Love what you've done with the place, Pixie."

My mouth dropped open. "I didn't know you were coming."

So things had been fractured between us when he left. I still bounded over and hugged him. I couldn't help it. "It's good to see you."

"Likewise. And I mean that." Raleigh was dressed in navy pants and a gray shirt open at the collar, casual for him when I was so used to seeing him in a tux and tails.

"I get it. And Thurston shouldn't have fired you," I told him. "Dad's with you?"

"Front and center."

I gave Raleigh a little push on the shoulder. "I guess I deserved that."

"Why's that bad?" Dez asked. He seemed slightly awkward about my collegial friendship with Raleigh—which I realized, yes, was definitely a thing. Working together this summer had made us into equals.

"Because Dad will be close enough to spot even the tiniest flub or mistake."

"Oh," Raleigh said, shrugging and playing innocent. "Just don't make any flubs, then."

"I'll do my best." An echo of what I'd told the Rex.

"See you out there," he said, ducking back out the tent flap.

I checked my reflection to make sure I was good—red lipstick, mask, costume arranged as it should be.

"Hey," Dez said, "stop fidgeting. You look like what you are: an amazing magician. You'll knock your dad dead." He held up his hand. "Not literally."

"Ha ha." Our eyes met. "I guess we should get out there."

"I guess we should."

I took a step closer to him, because the curtain was a few feet behind him. He took one toward me . . . and I almost let us collide. But at the last second I reached out and touched his arm and turned him around.

"My lipstick," I murmured when we were at the curtain.

"Until later," he said.

I straightened my shoulders. At least he'd taken my mind off my father. Somewhat.

Here goes everything.

thirty-six

Walking out onstage should have been familiar at this point, as natural as palming a card or a coin. Instead, this could have been the first time I'd ever stood in front of so many people. All those eyes landed on me like a blow.

No mystery why. Dad's eyes were among them.

I looked down into the crowd, my vision swimming slightly, and saw Dad next to Raleigh in the front row. Thurston, beaming up at me, was on his other side. And beside Thurston . . . Brandon. His arm in a cast all the way to the elbow to help immobilize his hand more.

It was the first time I'd seen him out and about since the punishment.

My attention went back to Dad, the audience I'd wanted for so long. Dad's aesthetics and mine were different, but I hugely admired his skill. He was one of my heroes.

I'd always imagined him being impressed the first time he saw me onstage. The expression he actually wore was familiar from the few times I'd seen it, including that last night at the theater, and *impressed* wasn't the word for it. It was disapproval. The memory of standing on his stage, of him dismissing me, came back with a force I wasn't prepared for.

Followed by flashes of my disastrous audition for the Cirque, the way my magic had flooded through me—

"All good?" Dez whispered.

This was my chance. Here and now.

I took a deep breath and forced a bow. "Welcome to my show. I'm the Miraculous Moira."

I caught my hand gravitating to the pocket with the coin case in it. *No,* I told myself. *Forget you have that. It'll only make things worse.*

But wasn't the coin supposed to bring good luck?

The power in it had felt like too much the day we'd found it. I probably should have removed it before I went on.

Too late.

Dez continued across the stage, to the other side of the glass. We were doing the bullet catch first, to mix things up. "This is my lovely assistant, Desmond. Dez, for short," I continued, still feeling somehow disconnected from everything around me.

I gestured to Dez, and he propped one leg up in a show-off show-girl way, earning a laugh. It rang in my ears. Brandon, in the front row, smirked.

Get it together, Moira.

This was still the future I wanted, doing magic. "Tonight, there's a very special guest in the crowd. I'll bet some of you have recognized him."

There were whispers. Of course they had. Dad was the kind of famous that came with occasional TV specials, bit parts in movies, and his own packed houses in his permanent theater. "Yes, this is *the* Mysterious Mitchell, Master Magician." There was a round of applause. He put on a passive half-smile and nodded to accept it, holding up a hand to wave it off.

"Here's a secret: he's my dad. So I'm going to try to make this show tonight extra-special for him."

I strolled back and forth, wishing to feel less jumpy. More solid and in control. "I thought tonight we'd start with the bullet catch—I mean, what's the point of escaping a coffin first? If I can't survive being shot at, then I'll just have to do it later anyway." I winked.

The crowd laughed again. More ringing in my ears. Dad didn't even crack a smile.

"Dez, can you confirm that the glass is real and prepare the firearm?"

Dez tapped the glass plate at the center of the stage in several places and began to check the gun. I started my patter about Lulu Hurst and Annie Abbott, finally semi-hitting my stride. The crowd was with me, loving it all. I kept catching them craning their necks to get a look at Dad down front.

My dad remained absolutely unreadable throughout the lead-up. But Raleigh gave me an approving nod when I looked at him. Brandon continued to smirk, and Thurston to beam.

I thought about inviting Dad up to mark the bullet, but somehow inviting my mother had seemed less risky. I decided to go with a nice round-faced gentleman from the front row. Dez loaded the wax bullet, and I went over to my side of the stage.

"And now, can I have absolute silence in the crowd? And please stay in your seats, for your own safety."

I donned my goggles and mouth guard, and stood facing Dez, who leveled the gun at me. I called my magic and conjured the mark onto the bullet, feeling it heat inside my cheek as I transformed it. To try to calm my nerves, I envisioned the rest of the trick, the wax bullet leaving the gun and shattering the glass, the audience believing the bullet was traveling toward me, then their approving applause after I revealed the marked one in my mouth. Dad would have to be impressed.

Only then did I notice there was too much heat within me for what had become a simple trick.

The coin.

Heady power rushed through me, a roaring river of it. The flood of magic seemed to consume my own magic, threatening to consume me. It wanted something from me . . .

I staggered a step back, out of position.

The *crack!* of the gun sounded.

A hail of bullets might as well have been traveling toward me, like I was Addie Herrmann, holding out her hands for six at a time. I felt strong enough to catch them all.

Oh no. I shouldn't have thought that.

The glass exploded out, no longer glass but a score of metal shards, all flying fast toward me. The audience gasped. There were screams.

Please, please, stop.

I fought the flood of power and dove flat. My body still surged with the coin's fiery magic.

"What's happening?" I heard someone call, and I looked above me to see bullets hanging in the air across the stage, all around me.

I pictured them dropping. Harmless.

And they did, with a metallic clattering as they hit the stage.

One fell right beside my face, and I saw it was marked with the initials of the audience member, just like the one in my own mouth would be.

I spat out my mouth guard and the bullet in my cheek. The coin had made my passing desires into reality.

I felt powerful, dangerous, unstoppable. Like I should come with a warning: *Don't touch.*

"Moira?" My dad's voice from the crowd.

Echoed by Dez's. "Moira, that was . . ."

He was beside me.

You have to get up, I told myself. *You're performing.* The crowd couldn't know. They had to think it was an act.

I grabbed Dez's arm and used it to leap to my feet. I flourished at the bullets littering the stage.

I almost tripped over a handful as I made my way to the front.

Dad was standing, gaping at me, knowing that trick was impossible. That it could not have been a trick.

"Sir," I said to my volunteer, voice breathy, "can you confirm these bullets bear your marking?"

The trembling man came close enough to pick one up and nodded in amazement. "Yes. Yes, they do. How'd you do that?"

"A magician never reveals her secrets. I am the Miraculous Moira."

The crowd rose to its feet, applauding as loudly as I'd ever heard. They called, whooping and cheering. Thurston gave me a thumbs-up. Raleigh clapped, frowning. Brandon alone didn't bother to join in.

I wanted to leave the tent, but of course I had to stick around. My dad, on the other hand, did not. And how did he take the news that my magic had shown up? He strode over to the side aisle and out of the tent without a backward glance.

I took a bow and signed autographs, knowing I'd find him afterward. He would take this coin. He had to.

If the Rex and Regina got their hands on it, there would be no stopping them.

Dez had stayed longer than he usually did, not running off to do his own act. He was obviously rattled by what had happened out there, and when the last fan had cleared out, he steered me backstage and into one of the dressing room chairs.

I didn't have to go looking for Dad. He was waiting there, ready to pounce. We'd never been in a situation remotely like this, which made it far harder for me to predict what he'd do.

The first thing he did was scowl at Dez's hand on my arm. "I want to talk to you. Just you."

"Give us a second," I said to him.

"You all right?" Dez asked me, low. "You need me to stay? That was—"

"The coin," I whispered. "We can't keep it here. You go on, do your show."

"You're sure?" He brushed a strand of hair back from the side of my face, like he needed to touch me to reassure himself I was still there. "That was the scariest thing I've ever seen."

"Go. I'm fine." I still felt electric, the coin in my pocket. "I need to talk to my dad."

Dez pressed a kiss to my forehead. Then he turned and held out his hand for Dad to shake. "Excuse me, sir?"

I had to admit, his courage in saying boo to Dad right now floored me a little. No way I'd have steered into this familial squall by choice. Dad was in his full leather-panted, poofy-shirted casual-look (for him) glory. Plus, he was upset.

"I already said I'd like to have a private conversation with my daughter."

Dez didn't budge. "I just wanted to say that she's incredible. Fearless. You should be very proud of her. Listen to her. Help her."

Dad's scowl grew more troubled than mad, at least.

"Thanks, Dez," I said. "See you for the next show."

Dez slipped out the side of the tent.

My father blinked after him, then turned back to me once we were alone. He looked at me for a long moment, visibly searching for words.

"Yes, I know about my magic," I said. "That's what you saw out there. It started when I got here." I removed the coin case from my pocket and shook out the coin I wanted him to take. When my palm came into contact with it, I felt like I could do anything. That there were no limits to my magic.

So I set it carefully down on the edge of the dressing table.

I nodded toward it. "That brought it out. My mother said you guys figured I'd never come into contact with anyone or anything magic. You figured wrong."

He pulled over the other chair and sank into it across from me.

"Since you told me nothing about this, I was completely unprepared. I thought I was going crazy. The first time happened in Florida while I was auditioning. The coin was there, and so, boom, magic."

"You've met your mother," he said.

"Yes, and her husband, the Rex. I know all about the Praestigae, and they know all about me."

Dad bolted up from the chair, reaching for me. "We have to get you out of here. Right now."

"Dad, sit down. There's more."

He pulled at my arm. "You can't stay here, not if they know where you are. Your mother was very clear that they could never find out about you."

I gently lifted his hand away. "The Praestigae know I exist and that I have magic now. Nothing is going to be easy. Sit. Please? I want an explanation from you, and I have a favor to ask."

I didn't feel nearly as calm as I sounded. I was afraid he'd refuse my request. And, frankly, afraid I would never be able to trust him again.

His eyes swung around the small backstage area, as if we'd be attacked at any moment. They *could* show up again, the uninvited king and queen. I didn't think they would, though. Not so soon.

"Sit," I told him, more firmly.

Finally, he swung back into the chair, with clear reluctance. "You have to understand, sweetheart. I hoped the day your magic woke up would never come."

"*You* raised me to believe in science, in probability, to believe that the supernatural was bullshit that only fakers and con men would invoke. You had to expect I'd find out."

"I love you." His voice took on a pleading note. "I didn't want you to have to deal with it, to take the risk. Your mother told me there was so little magic left in the world that the probability was good you'd never have to know."

"It was inside me, waiting." My heart seemed to thump in time with my words. I forced myself not to look at the coin sitting on the dresser top between us. I longed to touch it again. To feel that rush. That power. "I *deserved* to know."

"You don't understand. It's not safe for anyone to know. At home, I can protect you."

I felt sorry for everything then, for telling him this way. We were so far past his being able to protect me. "It's not just me. Dez is in trouble too."

He shook his head dismissively. "That's not my problem."

"But it's mine. Dad, I . . . I love him. And I won't leave him to them. I'm going to see this through."

He went still. "See what through?"

I pointed at the coin on the edge of the dresser. "Raleigh told you about this—it's special to the Praestigae. The Rex gave Dez and me until the end of the season to recover it. They don't know we found it. It's too dangerous for me to keep here. You saw what happened tonight . . . That was the coin's magic at work."

Dad reached out and picked it up. He turned it over in his fingers. "If we give it to them—"

"We need time, to figure out how to get them to leave us alone. They want this, so it'll be like an insurance policy." I reached over and put my hand over his.

The coin called to me from within his hand, *I'm yours.*

"You have to take it with you. Put it in your secret warehouse and don't let *anyone* inside. Mom knew the minute I got a copy of my birth certificate. She has spies everywhere, I'm sure. I think she's on our side, but she won't stand up for us. She could have called you. But she didn't."

Dad looked surprised. "Your mother always wanted to protect you—that's why she stayed away all those years. I tried to tell her that I could help her, get her away, but she said no one could. Moira, if they know about you . . . Please, come home with me."

"You take that home and protect it, and I'll get over you putting me in this situation by lying to me for so long. Raleigh's your part-time treasure hunter, who somehow doesn't believe in magic? You're some kind of magical item collector who does? I get the impression that's how you met my mother."

"She was looking for this," he said, vaguely embarrassed, lifting his hand with the coin inside. His cheeks went pink, with no makeup to hide the flush. "I didn't have it. I had met someone on the road who convinced me that maybe magic was real, and that's why I decided to collect . . . I didn't have many magic treasures then. Just a couple. I'd just started at the Menagerie, only beginning to make enough money to collect them. Then Regina showed up and proved there *was* real magic in the world. And she left you with me. After that, I tried to collect *anything* anyone ever said had magic and keep it away from you."

"Dad . . . that's . . . ambitious of you." Then I put it all together. I'd known he thought he was protecting me by denying me my dream. But was it because of my actual magic? "Wait. This is why you didn't want me to do magic? Stage magic, escapes?"

"It's part of why—I know it doesn't make any sense. I just worried if you were doing the fake kind, it might happen by accident."

I laughed. I couldn't stop myself. "You do realize that I might never have found out, if you'd just let me perform for you. Given me a job on your show."

"I don't see what's funny about it."

"I take my laughs where I can get them these days." I grew serious. "Dad, hide that. Don't let anyone know you have it. I'll tell you when I need it back. *That's* how you can help keep me safe. Okay?"

He didn't outright agree. Still, he put it in his inner coat pocket.

I got up, remembering the stage littered with bullets. Someone had to get rid of those, and it might as well be me. "I have another show to do tonight. You don't have to hang around unless you want—I won't feel better until that thing is far away from me."

thirty-seven

When I stepped out onto the stage for my last performance of the day, Dad was in the same spot in the audience. Front row, center.

I hadn't been sure he wouldn't leave immediately. And I hadn't been lying before—I was eager for the coin to be away from here, buying Dez and me breathing room for the next couple of weeks.

No such luck. But, hey, I had another chance to impress my dad. And this time, I'd be doing the kind of magic Dad and I had in common.

Thurston was still beaming at me from one side of my dad. Raleigh sat on his other. Dad and Thurston seemed to be deep in chummy conversation. No Brandon.

Dez passed close behind me. "Everything aces?" he murmured.

"I think so. He took it."

He squeezed my hand, and then I launched into my patter. "Welcome. I'm the Miraculous Moira."

My dad and Thurston stopped talking and settled down to watch.

I was at my best for the entire act, every laugh line on point, the coffin escape executed just as intended. I beat my best straitjacket escape time by a full twenty seconds. My magic expressed like it usually did, and I controlled it easily.

I felt relieved that the coin was safely in Dad's pocket, unable to boost me into territory that made me feel like someone other than myself. Maybe I owed Dad. If he hadn't been so unreasonable, I might have gone my whole life and never known what I could do.

The Praestigae wouldn't have found out either, though.

When I finished my act, Dad applauded along with everyone else.

He, Thurston, and Raleigh stayed in their seats while I hopped down off the edge of the stage to meet people and sign autographs. Dez bent down and tapped my shoulder. "You need me to hang, just in case?"

"No, I'm good. Go throw pointy steel at random ladies and make them believe you love them."

"I will do the first part, but not the second." It was true, he'd taken the heart out of his act. I hadn't asked; he'd just stopped doing it.

I hurriedly vamped for photos and scribbled autographs, nervous that Dad was still around. We'd had our big conversation. He had the coin. He needed to get it away from here. He and Thurston were still conversing, and it only then occurred to me that I probably should be rushing to end that. Who knew what they were discussing? I hoped it wasn't Dad's collection of magical items. Real magic and the coin were the last things we needed Thurston to revive interest in.

The last audience member left, and I went over to face the real judging panel. I couldn't help it—I wanted Dad to recognize that I was talented. I wanted to hear him say he was proud.

He looked up at me and smiled, by all appearances a sincere smile. "Honey, you were great."

"Yes!" I fist-pumped the air, smiling so hard my teeth ached. I wasn't capable of playing it cool, not about this. I'd wanted him to say those words for so long.

He and Thurston laughed.

"She's fantastic," Thurston said. "The crowds love her." He took out his phone and glanced at it. "Your seats are secured. You guys will watch the main show from the best spot in the house, then come have a drink with me afterward?"

"Sounds perfect," Dad said. "Okay with you, Moy?"

Hmm. He was using his business meeting voice, the charm he laid on when he wanted something from someone. But how could I say no without raising Thurston's suspicions? "Of course—you shouldn't leave without seeing the Cirque."

"I can't believe you kept the fact that this guy's your father a secret," Thurston said.

"You would have looked at me differently."

"True enough," he agreed.

He led us all up the midway, narrating the journey. We passed Dez's stage as his crowd was clearing out. I waved to him and gave him a shrug that said I was going along for this ride.

Thurston's assistant was waiting for us in front of the big top. "Get these guys all settled," Thurston told her. "I'll see you at my trailer afterward." He put on his booming ringmaster's voice: "Enjoy the show!"

"I intend to," my dad said, silk-handkerchief smooth.

The assistant steered us inside and down to a section in the middle of the stands in front of the center ring, behind a flock of Jules's adorable fans, the Valentines, in red tutus and heart T-shirts.

I sat between Dad and Raleigh, then leaned toward Dad. I hadn't been able to say anything in front of Thurston, but now I could. "Dad, shouldn't you get going? Get that . . . gift . . . back home."

The lights went down and then came back up, settling into the level for Thurston's entrance and the acrobats who were up first.

"We'll leave tonight," Dad said. "I promise."

"I just . . . I want it out of here."

Raleigh butted in. "So, you guys are copacetic again? That was quicker than I expected."

"Getting there," I said before Dad could answer.

"I want to know how you did that bullet trick," Raleigh said.

There was no way that was happening. I pulled out a Mona Lisa smile. "Maybe someday," I said, thankful my voice didn't squeak.

"This has been good for you, being here this summer?" Dad said to me, keeping his voice low as the band started.

"All I wanted was to be a magician," I said, focusing on him. "Like you. Yeah, the performing part's been good. The rest . . . overwhelming sometimes. Scary." Concern crossed his face like a shadow, and I added, "But I wouldn't change it."

His head dipped, and then he turned to watch the show. He legitimately seemed to enjoy the first act, especially Jules's mom and her herd of giant milky-white horses. She flipped from one to the other and controlled them like it was her magical power.

After she finished, the lights brightened to signal intermission, and Dad got up. "Be right back," he said.

I stayed where I was. There was a lingering question I had for Raleigh, and this might be my only chance to ask it anytime soon. "Why *did* you take Dita's bow tie?" I asked.

He looked over each shoulder, then back at me. "We're going to talk about that now?"

"Just curious. Why?"

He shrugged. "I was about to get caught, and I had it in my hand, so I stuffed it in my pocket. Wearing it was dumb, but I never expected anyone to notice."

"Oops."

"Major oops." He shrugged, though, and said, "I'll be getting back out on the road soon. Thurston doesn't seem to be holding any ill will. Maybe I can steal *your* spot next summer."

I poked his shoulder. "Dream on."

"Oh, I will, Pixie. I'll have plenty of time to dream up some great new stuff."

We smiled at each other. And Dad returned, handing us both sodas.

The lights signaled the beginning of act two. Act two was where the showstoppers were. I pointed out Jules as a friend and the first breakout star, though the screaming joy of the girls in front of us had made her easy to identify. And when the Garcias raced out to take the trapeze, I pointed out Dita. "My roomie," I said.

Thurston's assistant appeared at the end of the show to tell us he'd meet us at his trailer.

"Dad," I said as Raleigh and I led him across the grounds, "you don't have to stay for this. I really think you should get going."

Raleigh coughed. "A little rude."

"He knows why," I said.

"A quick drink and we're out of here," Dad said, looping his arm around my shoulder. He was up to something.

I didn't like it.

When we got to the trailer, the lights were already on. Thurston popped the cork on a bottle of champagne as soon as we entered, and began filling flutes.

"What'd you think?" he asked. "Good enough company for your daughter?"

Dad accepted the champagne. He narrowed his eyes at me accepting a glass but didn't protest. "It's a great show. World-class. I can tell that Moira has learned a lot here."

I smiled.

"But I'm going to need you to release her from her contract," he went on. "I'm sure Raleigh would be happy to stay and take over."

My smile died. Betrayal burned in my chest, and my palms heated, but I forced the magic away. I set down my champagne flute and said, "Thurston, don't listen. Ignore him. I'm not leaving."

"Why would you?" Thurston asked. He set down the champagne bottle.

Dad didn't back off. "Mr. Meyer . . . Thurston . . . now that I've seen her, well . . . I was hardheaded. She wanted me to give her a job at the beginning of the year and I wouldn't even watch her. She needs to come back home and accept a job at the Menagerie, with me."

Thurston seemed to be considering.

Somehow I managed to keep my voice level. "I'm here through the end of the season," I said. "I appreciate it, but I decline your offer."

"Moira," Dad said, "that's enough."

"No, it's enough from you." He wasn't making the offer because he'd seen me. He was making it because he wanted me under his thumb. Which I could understand, but that didn't mean I'd go along with it.

"You told me to tell you if you were making things worse," Raleigh said. "You're making things worse."

He said it calmly. Dad scowled.

Thurston picked up his flute and took a sip. "I have the utmost respect for you, Mr. Mitchell, but my loyalty to my performers comes first. She doesn't want to leave. I'm not going to make her."

"She's just a girl," Dad said. "She should be at home with me."

"'Just a girl' is not a thing." I gritted my teeth. "And I'm eighteen. You can't order me around anymore."

"She's an adult. It's her call," Thurston said.

Relief poured through me. I wasn't ready to leave yet, to vacate my stage and leave Dez to the Praestigae's wolves. Besides, Dad couldn't save me from them. Only I could save myself.

And even that was a maybe.

I was done with this charade, though. "Dad, I told you what I needed from you earlier. Do that, and maybe I'll forget you tried to pull this stunt. See you when we get to Vegas."

Dad said, "Hang on now—"

"Thanks for everything, Thurston. See you tomorrow." I drained my flute and left.

I passed a handful of performers in the darkness lit only by RVs and security lights before I heard Dad calling after me. "Moira, wait!"

Against my better judgment, I did.

"Your mother and her associates . . . you really want me to leave you here, with them knowing where you are?"

I held out my arms. "Give me a hug, then go catch your red-eye back home. Put my gift in the safest location you have, and wait for me to contact you."

He hesitated. "I'll cut off your funds."

I sighed. "That's fine. I get paid. I have all the supplies I need until the end of the season."

I forced the issue on the hug, wrapping my arms around him. "It was good to see you," I told him, "even if you are being an incredible jackass."

"I just love you so much, sweetie." Dad's voice was strained. I didn't want to see or hear him cry.

Not when I was still mad at him over what he'd tried to pull with Thurston.

"Ditto."

"You can come home anytime, if you change your mind," he said. "And if there's any more trouble, call me. Please? You really were great."

"I'll be home in a couple more weeks—to perform. And I'll be in touch about this." I patted his jacket where he'd stashed the coin.

"I don't know . . ."

"Have a safe trip. Remember, keep everyone out of the place where you put it. Don't trust anyone near it."

I let go and left him there before we could fight anymore.

thirty-eight

After Phoenix came a trip up the coast to San Diego. I was currently curled up in my own bed in the Airstream because Dez had told me Brandon wanted him to drop by and hang out that night. Otherwise, we'd have been together, worrying over our lack of a viable plan.

Dez and I had both spent the days after my dad's visit looking over our shoulders a lot. I'd half expected the Rex and Regina to show to mess with Dad, but they probably hadn't heard he was coming until it was too late for them to make the kind of dramatic yet sneaky entrance they preferred. Something told me that neither one showing up to threaten us or request a coin update since then wasn't respect for our requested timeline.

Dita hadn't noticed the coin was missing yet, so far as I could tell. Dad had texted me an apology after he was home that said he was following my wishes.

A giant clock might as well have ticked in my ears all the time. I was caught in a straitjacket without any good method for getting out of it. Dez and I were running out of time, and other than stashing the coin, we had not come up with a grand plan to save our souls. Or our lives.

Still, San Diego was sunny and beautiful—even at the fairgrounds on the edge of the sprawling beachside paradise where we were set up. The ocean breeze and nearing the end of the season combined to create a sense of abandon among the Cirque troupe. Thurston had scheduled buses to take us down to the beach for a cookout the next night, before our first shows here.

I was finally closing in on drowsiness when my phone dinged with a new message. I fumbled to silence it, hoping the sound hadn't woken up Dita.

By all appearances, she was deep asleep.

It was from Dez: `Meet me out at the parking lot. Don't let anyone follow you. xxx, D`

I checked the time—*yikes, it was later than I'd thought*—2:45 in the morning. But I texted back: `Be out in five.`

Dita didn't stir as I pulled on pants and a jacket. I tiptoed up the hall, holding my breath as I crept past Remy's room and gingerly opened and shut the front door behind me.

The grounds were deserted. I had no clue what Dez would need at this hour, but it fit the pattern for the nonpattern of the Rex's and Regina's sporadic appearances. So I did my best to prepare for an interrogation, fabricating a cover story about having trouble using my magic to find the coin.

The wind wrapped around me, a constant presence as I walked through the darkened grounds. A border of swaying palm trees flanked the parking lot, and I approached them slowly, looking for Dez.

I didn't see him. Or anyone else.

Tucking my arms around myself, I continued on, heading toward the parking lot. A few overflow vehicles were parked out here, including my convertible.

I didn't see anyone out here either.

Until a motorcycle roared to life at the far end of the lot, its lights flicking on, brightness blinding me. I lifted a hand to shield my eyes as the bike hit a blistering speed in my direction.

"Dez?" I called, spots in my vision. I whirled to dash back into the safety of the grounds. I didn't care if anyone saw me and laughed. This entire thing was too creepy.

I blinked, my vision clearing.

And I stopped just short of barreling into a trio of guys, blocking my way.

I only recognized one of them. By his cast. Brandon.

Cold fingers of dread walked up my spine.

The phone Dez and Brandon still shared. Brandon had lured me out here. And nobody else knew where I was.

"Brandon, let me go back," I begged. "Think about Dez."

"I am," he said, and spat onto the ground. "He only thinks about you now."

The motorcycle's roar was far too close. I tried to feint around the boys, choosing Brandon's side. I collided with the cast on his hand.

He swore and shoved me back.

Wheels screeched on pavement as the driver of the motorcycle hit the brakes.

"You don't want to do this," I said, desperate. "Don't let him make you."

"Sure we do," one of the other guys countered. He was older than Dez and Brandon, with a sprawling tattoo that crept up his neck. A snake about to strike, fangs ready.

The roar of the motorcycle died. "Bring her over here!" the Rex called.

The boys came toward me as one. "Help! Somebody! Help me!" I shouted, and dodged to one side. I made it around them. If I could make it to camp, I could raise an alarm.

For that matter, where were the security guys now?

I grunted as one of the boys dove into my back, arms locking around mine to hold them down as he dragged me toward him. The sickly sweet smell of alcohol wafted off him as he hauled me in the direction of the parking lot. I tried to slip his hold like I would a strait-jacket, but he just moved his arms into a different position.

I called my magic. *Come, now.*

My magic answered, and I grabbed for the boy's shirt. But I froze up—I couldn't think of what to do. So I grappled with the boy instead, scratching at his hands. He marched me forward, and I stomped at his feet.

At last, he spun me around, and I faced the Rex.

He was helmetless, in one of his long suit coats. Like an undertaker.

"You can let her go, Jay," he said. "For now. Let's see what she has to say for herself."

What did that *mean?* I wondered. *Why was he here? Why did he want to see me without Dez?*

The guy holding my arms released me, shoving me toward the Rex. Brandon and the other guy approached, flanking me.

I came to a stop at the Rex's feet.

"I thought we had a deal," I managed to get out, backing as I stood. I collided with one of the boys and stopped moving.

"On second thought, maybe we should take you home for a full accounting." He gestured over his shoulder to the motorcycle. "Put her on the bike."

"No!" I said, shying toward him to get away from the grasping arms. "Just tell me what you want."

"You don't give orders to me," the Rex said.

He lifted a hand, and the boys stopped moving. It was a point well made. He had all the power here.

Or so he thought. I wouldn't go gently, not now that I'd had a moment to collect myself. I called my magic again, letting it flood my palms, ready. If I had to set that motorcycle on fire, I'd do it.

"Brandon here told us about your phantom-firing-squad trick. Sounds quite impressive—like the kind of thing you could do with the help of a certain coin. I take it you've found it, but for some reason thought you might just keep it? From me? From your *mother?*"

Brandon smiled proudly.

"You said we have until the end of the season." I fought to keep my voice steady but failed. "That's our deal."

"Do you deny you've found it?"

Think fast.

"I do. That . . . that was just an illusion." I seized on the explanation, borrowing from my mother. She could create illusions, so I probably could too. My voice shook even worse than before. "You know my mother does it. Br-Brandon, you should know the difference."

The Rex watched me. Maybe waiting for me to blurt a confession. To tell all.

I couldn't turn over the coin to him right now, not even if I wanted to. It was safe in Las Vegas.

"Liars are punished," the Rex said, stepping closer. He clapped a hand on Brandon's shoulder, well above the cast. Brandon almost hid his wince, but I saw it. "You know what punishment looks like. So I'd advise you not to ever get caught prevaricating to me."

"I swear," I said, voice still shaky. What if he didn't believe me? Could he tell I was lying?

Headlights appeared at the end of the lot again, and another motorcycle sped toward us. When it got closer, I saw the driver's red hair streaming behind her.

Mom. Whether she was willing to battle or not, the relief almost sent me to my knees.

The Rex loomed over me as she neared. "I want you to know, I could take you anytime. No one would help you. You're one of us now. Find the coin."

"I'm trying."

My mom pulled up beside us. "A party I wasn't invited to? Is there news?"

There was more fire in her tone than I expected. It added to my suspicions that her cowed demeanor before had been an act. I still couldn't figure out to what end, though.

"No news," the Rex said. "No party. We were just talking. She hasn't found the coin yet. See you soon, sweet girl. Next time we'll send a proper summons."

He waved his hand, and his henchguys disappeared back into the grounds, Brandon among them. The Rex got on his bike and left. But my mother stayed put.

"So sometimes you do stand up to him," I said.

"If he took you now . . . I'd never survive."

"You still have hope for me to get out of this too?"

"Yes," she said simply. "You grew up outside this. You see more possibilities than I ever could. I have hope that you'll get out of this, and save me too."

"Dad was here," I told her.

"So I heard. You're still here because of Dez. Right?"

"His life is in my hands."

I heard him then, shouting from the direction of camp. "Moira! Moira, are you out here?"

She nodded like she understood, and kicked the bike back to life.

I didn't watch her leave. I spun and ran toward the sound of Dez's voice.

I met him just beyond the palm trees and threw myself into his arms. I held on tight, breathing hard, fingers knotted in his shirt. I never wanted to let go. "Did he hurt you?" he asked.

"He was going to take me." I didn't want to tell him, but I had to. "Brandon . . ."

"Brandon left the phone. I woke up and he was gone, but I saw the messages and put it together. What happened?"

"The Rex . . . he was here. Brandon told him about the bullets. He thought we found the coin . . . I convinced him not to take me, or he left because my mom showed up. I don't know which." I was shaking like I'd never be warm again. "Some guy had me and I couldn't get away . . . couldn't think of what to do."

"You're all right. It's over," he said, tracing comforting circles on my back. "Brandon . . . he can't help it."

It took me a moment to comprehend what he'd said.

I pushed back from him. "Wait a minute. Brandon almost got me taken out. For good. There were three guys and the Rex against me. I've never felt so helpless in my life."

"I just . . . I'm sure he thought he was doing the right thing. He left the phone."

I couldn't believe this. After the panic I'd felt . . . "The right thing—helping to kidnap your girlfriend? To rat her out and get *her* punished? He said you weren't thinking of you anymore. Just me. But he was clearly wrong."

"He probably blames you." Dez scrubbed a hand down his cheek. "For his hand."

That didn't make this any variety of okay.

Dez went on. "*I* don't blame you, you know that. If anyone is to blame, it's me. But we've always been like brothers."

"Some brother."

The palm trees swayed, the wind kicking up around us.

"Moira, you didn't grow up like we did. The Rex tells you to do something, you do it. Same with the Regina. I told you I'd leave"—his voice lowered to a hush—"but I don't believe they'll ever really let it happen. Maybe you should have gotten out of here with your dad."

"Funny, my mom knew I'd still be here."

"Why?"

"She knows I'm staying here for you. To get you away." And, I was starting to believe, as long as it helped her get her magic refilled.

"Maybe you should listen to her."

After how scared I'd been earlier, I couldn't take him telling me this. "When we first met, you were always accusing me of running. Well, you always want to give up. I understand that we grew up different. But no one's going to hand you a solution. When Dad wouldn't watch me perform, I came here. I found another way to go after my dream. I won't let them take it away. And you can't just give in either. Don't give up because this is how your life has always been."

"That's easy for you to say. You could have left here and never looked back. You could call your dad in a second and be out of here. Sure, you'd have to be careful. But . . . I have no one except them."

"And me. You have me." I had to make him see. "Even scared out of my mind because that monster almost kidnapped me, I'd rather be here and fight. They *will* win if your heart isn't in this."

"It is."

I reached out and touched his arm, giving it a squeeze. I wanted to pull him into another hug, to kiss him, to shake him and make him believe he was worth fighting for. "It's not."

And I started back, suddenly exhausted. I motioned for him to play escort. I wasn't walking anywhere else alone tonight. "But you can change that anytime you want," I said. "Think about what I'm saying and get ready. Because they are not going to make this easy, not for either of us."

I shivered, thinking of how close that call had been. My mother still wouldn't go head-to-head with the Rex.

This was the most fight I could expect out of her. I understood that in a way I hadn't before.

I shivered with the knowledge, as it sank deep in my bones.

thirty-nine

"Don't move." I dragged the mascara brush slowly across Dita's eye-lashes. "Don't blink either."

"Sorry."

"You never do your own?"

"I have a thing about fingers around my eyeballs, especially my own. I always flinch. But I like how it looks," she said. "My mom, or the makeup lady, always does them."

"Perfecto." I finished it up. I had learned a lot about makeup hang-ing out backstage in Vegas.

"Hurry up," Jules called from the living room.

"Just keep making out. We're almost ready," I called back.

I heard Remy laugh. We were about to leave for the buses to the beach fete. I hadn't seen or heard from Dez all day, and I almost regret-ted what I'd said to him. His life was even more complicated than mine. He was in big trouble.

I couldn't get either of us out of this on my own. He was going to have to show up not just for me, but for himself.

My phone trilled with a call, and I expected it to be Dad. We hadn't talked since his visit.

Dez and Brandon's number popped up. My heart thumped as I answered. "Hello?"

"It's me," Dez said. "I knew you wouldn't trust a text."

"Good thinking."

Dita was watching me with curiosity, so I kept my tone light. I didn't think she had any idea I'd gone out last night. She'd given no sign of waking when I came in.

Dez went on. "I was thinking we could skip the bonfire. I heard what you said last night."

"You did?" I asked.

"Meet me at the Ferris wheel in half an hour. We'll start making a real plan—to save both of us."

"Come on!" Jules again, and this time she stomped back to get us.

"See you then," I said. And to Dita and Jules, "I'm staying here."

Dita blinked her freshly mascaraed lashes. She was dressed in a pair of knee-length shorts and a short-sleeved men's button-down for the beach. "What?"

Jules eyeballed the phone in my hand.

"Dez has got a lot going on," I said. "We're going to stay here and talk."

"You'd tell us if there was something you needed?" Dita asked.

"Of course."

Not.

They both looked at me; finally, Jules shrugged and said, "It's your call."

"You guys better get going, then. I don't want you to miss out."

Jules took Dita's arm and steered her out. I stayed in the bedroom, butterflies butterflying around in my stomach. To pass the time, I decided to practice some transformations. Never again would I freeze up like I had the night before.

I didn't have any wisdom to go on—only my gut. I tossed a coin into the air, calling my magic, feeling it heat me from the inside out and radiate from my palm, and watched a paper butterfly flutter down to the floor.

I checked the time on my phone.

I took a handful of prop coins from my case and tossed them in the air, then watched them float down on paper wings.

I imagined what I could do with my magic onstage, with more time and better control. Would it be so different than just doing regular magic? I'd thought of it as cheating, but I might have been hasty. Stage magic was all about the effect, what the people in the crowd saw. Giving them an experience they didn't know how to explain.

With another coin, I made a paper dragon and watched it sail past me and down. I imagined it breathing fire at the Rex. I checked my phone for the time.

It had only been fifteen minutes. I'd have just barely missed the bus out to the barbecue.

Maybe I should have wondered whether I was about to experience a repeat of the night before. It was possible I trusted Dez too much at this point. But while he'd defended Brandon, I still couldn't believe that he'd betray me outright. I picked up the paper representations of my nervous energy and stuffed them into the trash can.

I headed out the front door and through the darkened caravans and RVs. The midway was quiet and subdued with all of its lights killed, the last of the so-called magic hour right before sunset casting everything with a soft, slowly dying glow.

Apparently, I wasn't the only one of us who couldn't wait. Dez stood at the base of the Ferris wheel. He lifted his hand in greeting.

He moved to meet me halfway. There was no one else standing by to run it this time, and the wheel was as dark as everything else. In fact, we were probably the only two people around besides Thurston's security. Speaking of which . . .

"Are we going to get busted by the flashlight-and-Taser brigade?" I asked.

"I alerted Steven. He's a pal," Dez said.

"Steven?"

"Oh, he's on security tonight. He's, um, giving us some privacy."

"Where were the security guys last night?" I asked.

"Brandon's smart."

I must have made a face, because he said, "No, he is. He called in a trash-can fire on the other side of the grounds. They were probably checking it out."

I shivered again. Brandon had put more thought into what he'd done than I'd assumed.

Dez grew solemn. It was always a shock when it happened, his face showing what was beneath that rakish exterior. I felt like I had only the vaguest clue, even after all the time we'd spent together. But I also knew it was important that he let me see there was anything there at all.

"I'm sorry that I defended him," Dez said.

That was a good start.

"So, we're making a plan?" I asked.

"I have a confession to make first."

Don't tell me you were in on last night. I couldn't take it. "What's that?"

"This is where I come at night. Whenever we're not together, after everyone's asleep, I come here. Just lately."

"Here?" I glanced at the ground, relieved that the confession wasn't about Brandon's tip-off.

He raised his hand and pointed up. "No, there. I want to show you what I see from there, explain. Then, we plan."

"Let's go, then," I said.

"You don't mind climbing?" he asked, but he'd already reached into his back pocket and pulled out a flashlight.

"It's not like I haven't climbed it before. Just tell me when to stop."

Sunset had ceded to darkness. He flicked on the flashlight and shone it up the left-hand side of the big metal behemoth. A thrill raced through me. This was better than any beach barbecue.

I was glad I'd worn sneakers and jeans. I went to the first car and pulled myself up onto the arm, then again, finding a path and making steady progress. I jumped up and grabbed part of the arm above, climbed onto the next car, and did it again. Dez anticipated each move, the flashlight illuminating what I needed it to, and the security light taking over when I got too high for his beam to reach.

"There," he shouted up.

I swung down to sit in a car almost at the top, looking out over the quiet grounds. San Diego light pollution didn't hide all the stars, just most of them, and that ever-present breeze made the car sway slightly with a lullaby-rocking motion.

I looked down to see Dez making fast progress up the darkened wheel below, no light for him besides what came from the evening sky and the nearest security lamp. He clearly knew the way by heart, and my pulse kicked into high gear watching him. One hand in the wrong place and he would tumble down. He'd catch on metal on the way, or hit his head.

This is where I come at night . . .

If he fell out here by himself, how long until someone found him? Sure, I took risks, but I rehearsed. There were fail-safes. This was something else.

He finally reached me, pulling himself over the side of the red-white-and-blue-painted car and onto the leather seat beside me. I gave his shoulder a shove. There was nothing hot about the risk he'd just taken. The risk he'd been taking regularly, it seemed.

"You are reckless and stupid, Desmond—" I broke off. How could I yell at him without even knowing his full name? "What's your last name?"

"I think it's Robinson, but that could have just been a favorite alias of Dad's."

Two different worlds we came from, but his had a hold over us both.

"Anyway," I said, shoving him again, "this is dangerous. Stupidly dangerous. Not cool in any way. What if you fell?"

He settled back, resting his head against the metal lip that rose up behind us. He turned his head toward me. "When I sit up here, I've been thinking about just that."

His face was so much more familiar to me than it had been that first date night. *We*, the two of us together, were familiar. I reached over and touched his arm, and my pulse sped up again with the faintest skin-to-skin contact. Familiarity hadn't changed the chemistry between us.

"Just what?" Even though he wasn't in danger of falling anymore, my heart pounded. I had already fallen for him.

"About what would happen if I fell," he said. "How no one would care, really. It would make things simpler, for you."

"Hey," I said. "I would care. It would *not* make anything simpler."

He sighed. "But you shouldn't. And it would. You're wrong."

"Dez, I thought we were here to make a plan." This talk frightened me. I wanted him to see his life was more valuable than he considered it, not less.

"We are. I just wanted you to . . . understand." He closed his eyes and released a frustrated breath. "I'm messing this up."

"Let's start from a different place. What do you want, if you get free of them? What do you want to do with your life?" I could try to make him see that he was worth saving, that the future could be different than he'd imagined. "Any secret dreams? Like I want to be a magician, you want . . ."

"I don't know." He said it like it was ludicrous. "I never thought about anything except being Praestigae."

"You're making me want to push you off of here," I said, but the opposite was true. I wanted to make him see that he mattered. That they had no real claim on him. On either of us. "It doesn't matter if anyone cares if you fall. That is irrelevant. *You* should care. That's what I meant last night."

I was breathing hard, and so was he. We'd gone to a deep, dark place here, and he was resisting my attempts to shine sunlight on it. I wasn't sure if he'd push me away.

He was silent for a long moment. "I'm trying."

"Okay," I said, willing to take that for now. "Now, what makes you happy?"

"You."

"I should have banned that as an answer."

But when he held up his hand, I laced my fingers through his and rested my head on his shoulder. "What do you feel best at? Don't be funny. Be honest."

He was quiet for a long time, and I had almost given up on an answer. "This isn't what you mean, I don't think."

"Try me," I said, gazing up at him.

"So," he said, "the thing about running a con is that people are so easy to manipulate into what you want them to do."

"You're right, this wasn't what I expected. Go on, though."

"A lot of con artists talk about how dumb people are. How greedy. But I always felt like I could be a mark. The marks and me have a lot in common."

"How so?" I asked, genuinely curious.

"We want to believe the lies." He nudged his shoulder into me. "I think that's why I like watching you perform so much."

"You want to believe lies? That's not much of a goal."

"No. That's not it." He stopped and searched for words. "I want my life to be the kind where the stuff I always thought was lies is actually true."

"Where things *are* good," I said. "I love that. Now we both have something we're planning for—me to be a magician, and you to have a life where good things can be true. And no Praestigae for either of us."

He gave a wry smile.

"Don't start doubting it's possible already," I said. "Now we figure out how to con the con artists—including my mother, but mostly the Rex."

"Sounds easy enough," he joked. "Anything else?"

After last night I still couldn't necessarily count on my mother to stand up to her man. It had made me think I could count on her not actively contributing against us, though. She had something she wanted out of all this: power.

"There is something else. I know this is petty, probably stupid . . ."

"What is it?" Dez asked.

"I want to scare the Rex as bad as I was scared last night."

"I would like to see that," Dez said, but there was an undercurrent of fear in his voice. "I can't help with that part, but the other part, the conning part, I can. To get the Rex to a deal-making place, where he might let us go, he'll need to feel like it's possible for him to lose."

"To not get the coin, you mean?"

"The coin *or* you."

"Why?"

He grinned. "So he'll settle for the coin."

"Aha, okay," I said. "But he doesn't get you either in this scenario."

"Agreed."

We were both quiet, rolling over the problem. What had my mother said—that I could see more possibilities than she was able to? So I looked for solutions they wouldn't expect.

After a little while, an idea began to come together in my mind. First, we would set our terms to create Dez's possibility that the Rex would lose. Then, I would design an illusion that was so enormous I could barely begin to fathom how I'd do it. Dez had come here and fantasized about vanishing, so . . . why not make it happen? This could secure both our dreams: Dez's of a real future and mine of being a great magician.

For a disappearance on a mass scale to facilitate a trade (of the coin) and to mask a small-scale getaway (mine and Dez's), the Ferris wheel we were sitting on would be perfect. Making this massive metal monster seem to disappear and reappear would take a lot of preparation—and I'd need Dad's help—but if David Copperfield could make the Statue of Liberty appear to vanish, why not this? If we could convince the Rex and Regina that I truly *had* made it disappear, I could also probably convince them that most of my magic was gone. That I was too used up to be of use to the Praestigae, my cup all but emptied of magic.

For this plan, the gauntlet would have to be thrown to the Rex and Regina much sooner. We'd need as much space as we could get to focus on the illusion, without worrying about them showing up to monkey-wrench things again before we were ready.

"Last night the Rex said something about sending a summons next time," I said.

"That's how they usually do things."

"I think we should send one to them, and tell them we already found the coin and it's hidden away. That we'll let them know where they can retrieve it when we get to Vegas. It'll give them time to sweat. And they're so used to skulking around in the shadows, to secrecy . . . So we put together a public handoff of the coin during one of my performances in Vegas."

I'd explain to Dez later the size of what I was considering for the performance in question.

He was nodding. "If they want it, they'll have to be ready to make a deal. They can't do much with a bunch of people around. They might just take what they can get. It could work."

I smiled wide. "I know just the place we can invite them to, in LA, for the setup part. The kind of place even the Rex won't risk making a scene in."

Fingers crossed, at least.

"I want to know the part you're not telling me. There is that part?" he said. "But . . . we have the beginnings of a plan, don't we?"

"Right on both counts," I said. "Now kiss me, you fool."

Our grins at each other faded as our faces neared, and then our lips touched. This wasn't the overpowering heat, the matchstick striking we sometimes had, flames that would burn us both to the ground. It was gentle. It was solace. Care. Hope.

Now I just had to pray we could pull this off.

forty

Another perfect San Diego day sent its bright sun down onto us. Dez and I were already in the car, about to leave for Los Angeles.

Brandon was supposed to swing by and pick up our summons. Dez had asked him to deliver the invite I'd prepared to the Rex and Regina at whatever place the Praestigae were holed up in LA. So far, he had yet to show, and soon enough, everyone would roll out.

"He said he'd be here," Dez said, reading my mind.

"Then he will." Not that I had that much confidence in Brandon— or even wanted to look at his face again after the other night. But Dez had told him this had to do with his leaders, so I didn't think he'd chance flaking.

"Can I see it?" Dez asked.

I passed him the golden envelope. I hadn't bothered to seal it, in case Brandon was feeling snoopy. I'd just tucked the front flap of the envelope inside.

Dez pulled out a piece of the thick gold-edged stationery I'd grabbed in a fancy paper store. Production values mattered. Dad had taught me that. The Rex and Regina would like feeling feted, honored, by this golden missive.

At least until our revelation of its true nature.

I'd written on the page in thick black ink:

A dinner invitation for the Regina and the Rex. Fancy dress required. Come alone and discover how luck can be yours once again.

Below it was a date two days from now, *August 25, 7 p.m.*, and an address, *The Magic Castle, 7001 Franklin Avenue, Los Angeles.*

"How fancy's this place again?" Dez asked, refolding the sheet and stashing it back in the envelope. "*Castle* sounds fancy."

"I bought you a tie yesterday. You'll be good." I'd picked up a dress too. Dad hadn't cut off anything; my credit cards worked just fine.

I'd also used Dad's member number to make the dinner reservation. We'd be safe from any crashing royal henchmen at the Magic Castle, a private club that wasn't the easiest to gain an invite to.

Dez gave me one of those heart-stopping grins. "I hope you're paying for dinner. Otherwise, your mom will probably just hand the server a napkin and make him think he's seeing money."

"She does that kind of thing?"

"All the time," he said. "I doubt the Rex ever pays for anything."

"What about those houses?"

"People on vacation. She handles it if neighbors complain, but mostly they don't. She can make them see things as perfectly normal."

No wonder her magic was almost gone . . . if it was. Doing so many small illusions on top of whatever big ones had to take some kind of toll.

Brandon finally showed up, tapping on Dez's window with his cast.

I rolled down the window, and Dez held out the invitation. "This goes to the Rex and Regina," he said. "As soon as you can get it to them."

"You're welcome," Brandon said.

He ambled away with the envelope. He'd never apologized to me for the other night, and I didn't expect him to.

Minutes later, I navigated us out of the parking lot and into the long line of the caravan rolling out to our next-to-last city. The Vegas finale had been chosen because Jules was shooting a TV special at the Grand Canyon immediately after the season was over. There were always extra journalists around to stick a microphone in her face before the Cirque shows these days.

"I hope this plan works," I said.

"How can it not?" Dez asked, but I knew he had as many doubts as I did.

"And maybe next time I'm onstage I'll pull a real live rabbit out of my hat."

"Why couldn't you?"

There were all sorts of reasons I could have cited, not least the fact that when the trick was common, it was partly due to people not caring so much about the lives of the poor rabbits in question.

I settled for the following: "It's a lot harder than it seems."

"Oh," Dez said, "so it's just like everything else."

Two nights later, I turned my convertible off a street in Los Angeles with a squealing of tires and ripped up the hill to the chateau-style yellow-and-purple house atop it. We screeched again, to a stop. We were *almost* running late.

The valets were used to dramatic entrances, so they didn't even blink. "Welcome to the Magic Castle," one of them managed to get out before I thrust my keys at him.

The Fairplex, which the Cirque was using for its shows here, was farther than I'd expected from Hollywood, where the Magic Castle was. And I'd forgotten to account for the dystopian hell zone that was

LA traffic. Which meant we had gotten here barely in time to beat our guests—assuming we had. I wanted *them* off balance, not *us*.

Dez stepped out of the passenger side. "Relax. We made it."

He was as nervous as I was. His new tie was dove-silver-and-white striped, and with it and his suit he could've talked almost anyone into almost anything. I was in the required fancy attire too, a dress with a red sweetheart neckline that segued into a black circle skirt. With pockets for coins and cards, just in case.

The other attendant opened the Magic Castle's door for us. I presented one of Dad's membership cards to the hostess behind the front stand. I always had a few in my wallet. It was filled out with my name.

"Are we the first in our party to arrive?" I asked.

Her perfectly highlighted blonde head bobbed. "You are." She waved us toward a nearby wall covered by bookshelves, where a golden owl presided. The owl was the symbol of the organization that made its headquarters here.

"Whew," I said to Dez.

He was busy squinting at the owl and the bookshelf. "Where do we go?" he asked, quietly.

I couldn't help a smile at this. "Open sesame," I said.

And the wall slid open to admit us into the dark, wood-paneled, lush interior of the house, designed in deep shades meant to conjure an aura of gravitas and mystery. Despite some shabbiness around the edges, the overall effect was like being admitted into a secret magicians' fantasyland—which is exactly what it was.

The first-floor bar was packed with other dressed-up people. There was a smattering of older men who were likely entertainment attorneys, here on borrowed invites with their much-younger dates, something I'd always found an unsavory trend. The house that made up the Magic Castle was filled with secret rooms and passages, and galleries or stages where magicians of various kinds performed all evening long. The walls were emblazoned with portraits of magic legends and rare posters and playbills. Only members of the Academy of Magical Arts—and their guests—were allowed to visit, and no photography or recording was allowed.

Normally I'd have circulated, watching close-up magic in nooks and corners, finding out who was on the main stages, and spending some time with the rare books in the library downstairs. While I'd been practicing in secret all those years, I'd fantasized about being allowed to join and then blowing the minds of the members of the junior club. I still longed to come here and be one of the performers in the Close-Up Gallery, and to someday do an engagement on one of the bigger stages in the Parlour of Prestidigitation or the Palace of Mystery.

But it turned out my first visit as a magician myself had little to do with any of that. Tonight I steered Dez through the crowded bar and straight up the steps to the dining room. We were shown to a table for four in the corner, the one I'd requested. We sat against the wall, where we'd be able to see our companions arrive.

Dez was gazing around wide-eyed at everything, the way I imagined I had my first time here. "This is the kind of place you go to all the time?" he asked.

This was a fine-dining restaurant, with white tablecloths, overpriced food, and everyone up to the dress code. Still more paintings and posters that showcased the mystical arts hung on the walls up here.

"No," I said, though I knew what he meant. "This is the only place like this I've ever been. Well, except a private club in London once. But that one may be nicer."

"Nicer than this?"

"You should order one of the overpriced steaks."

He glanced down at the menu, eyes widening even more at the prices.

"It's all right. Dad hasn't cut off my credit card yet." And then I saw our companions coming up the stairs. "Showtime."

My mother entered first, ahead of the bearded devil. They turned heads, even here. She wore a slinky green evening gown, her red hair piled into a glamorous mass not unlike the snakes on her arm, and he was in what looked to be a very expensive navy suit, an ascot knotted at his throat, as if he'd been born to the aristocracy instead of seizing it in some sort of coup.

"Show no fear, remember," I murmured to Dez, touching his hand and pasting on an easy smile. "Like we're in control."

Dez took my hand under the table and gave it a squeeze. I wasn't sure if mine was the one trembling or his.

Please let us pull this off.

I wanted the Rex to pay for a whole lot of things, especially my almost-kidnapping.

The waiter pulled the chair out for my mother, and she oozed a smile at him. The Rex handled his own chair, waving away the waiter with a curt "Red wine, for the table."

The waiter frowned down at Dez and me, likely wondering if we were of age, but my mother added, "Please."

He hopped to, her order his pleasure.

Had she made him see us as the right age, another one of those small illusions taking a toll, like the way she'd disguised her busted lip from me? Or had she made that up? I still wasn't convinced the sick or injured versions of herself I'd been shown were real.

"We decided to forgive your presumption in summoning us," said the Rex. "Though Dez should know it's the height of impropriety." His eyes landed on Dez and stayed there for a long moment. "But I was concerned you might have the wrong idea about how much I welcome you to our family, Moira dear."

I didn't realize my grip had tightened around my silverware knife until Dez laid a calming hand over mine.

"Uh, yeah, I could see why you would be," I said, releasing the knife. "But don't worry about it. I found it a great help."

"Really," the Rex drew out the word. "How so?"

Here we go. "It made the nature of the relationship I want for us to have with you—both of you—very clear."

"What's that?" my mother asked, and the Rex gave her a sharp look. Like he'd told her to stay quiet.

"None," I said. Then, before they could respond to that, "I was able to locate the coin."

There was a brief silence.

The Rex broke it. "You can hand it over, then. No need to wait."

"And here I thought you'd want me to buy you dinner first," I said dryly.

Dez made a choking sound. It didn't escape me that he hadn't said a word yet.

"Well?" the Rex said, holding out his hand.

"We didn't bring it," I said. "But we have recovered it. And, just as you suspected, it is very powerful. I was using it when I turned glass fragments to bullets and then commanded them to fall to the stage harmlessly. Brandon was right."

The waiter returned with a bottle and presented it to us. "You can just pour," my mother said. She was watching me, and if I'd had to fill in the thought bubble over her head, it would have said: *be careful.*

Don't worry, I thought back. *I'm being careful with you both.*

The waiter poured us all glasses, then swiftly departed.

The Rex picked up his glass and swirled the red wine like he was a connoisseur, took a sip, and nodded.

I picked mine up, mostly to have something to do with my hands.

"My Regina, would you mind making their wine a little more demonstrative? Show them what kind of punishment disrespect often results in."

My mother nodded to him.

I gasped and set the glass back down. She'd made the wine in my glass and Dez's look like blood, thicker and brighter red than the wine.

The Rex laughed.

My mother picked up her glass, and I willed her to throw it in his face. She didn't.

"Nice," I said, hating they'd seen me react to the blood in the wineglass. "We're here to talk about a deal."

The Rex swirled his wine some more and took a drink. He set the glass down with an audible thump, the wine swishing up the sides. A few drops landed on the white tablecloth.

"I already described a deal to you," the Rex said. "Desmond returns the coin by the end of the season or no more Desmond."

"Hang on a minute," Dez said quickly. "We do have it. Just not with us. You can use it to do whatever you want."

"I, on the other hand, will never do what you want," I said. "We have the coin safely secured in a place where you'll never get to it. We'll give it to you in Vegas—but only in exchange for our freedom from you. For good."

"Why didn't you bring it?" my mother asked.

"Because I don't trust you. Either of you," I said. "We get to the end of the season, then we disappear for a while. Give you time to prove you're not looking for us. You do anything to either one of us in the meantime, you never get the coin." Dez gave my hand a supportive squeeze under the table. "Dez tells me if you make a deal with another of your own, then you honor it. The Praestigae code."

The Rex was doing that thing where he coiled like a snake. I'd banked on him not wanting to make a disturbance. But right now I wouldn't have been surprised by another kidnapping attempt, with him carrying me bodily from this dining room.

My mother put her hand on his arm. "So the deal is you give us the coin, then we leave you both in peace?" She looked at the Rex. "Maybe we should consider it."

Something passed between them, a look of communing that went on for a long time. Finally, he said, "You deliver us the coin in Vegas, we *might* leave you both in peace. You don't, and you'll never have peace again."

It couldn't be this easy. I wanted to jump up and down, victorious, even given the "might." But . . . it really couldn't be this easy. Could it?

"I am disappointed, however," the Rex said, "in both of you. Particularly you, Desmond. You have a responsibility to make up for what your father lost us. You accepted that task, and now you're planning to abandon your family."

"It's being returned," Dez said. "That's what you wanted."

My mother was remarkably quiet, which I didn't like or trust. We needed them afraid of what we might do, so that they'd be tempted to stick with the guaranteed outcome where they walked away with the coin.

The Rex went on like he was holding court. "Now that this nasty business is settled, we can enjoy dinner. Since we *might* have such precious little time together."

He lifted his glass, a signal for us to clink our glasses with his.

Dez and my mother did.

Tink. Tink.

He held his glass there, waiting for me to do the same.

I shook my head no.

I'd never tried anything like what I was about to, not exactly, but there was that time I turned air to water and back again. My mother's wine-blood illusion had given me an idea. I called my magic and waited for the Rex to lift the glass to his lips.

As soon as the glass touched them, I thought, *Burn.*

The wine in his glass burst into flame. "Shit!" he said, dropping the glass.

The flames flared and died, with nothing left to keep them burning.

I took a half bow, still seated, so the tables near ours would assume it was a magic trick. They applauded quietly and went back to their dinners, while the Rex pushed his chair back and stared bloody murder at me.

He reached out and picked up a knife on the table. "Rex," my mother said. Anger rolled off her in waves. At him or at me, I couldn't say.

I pushed my own glass back. I would not let him see fear. "I've lost my appetite. See you in Vegas."

The Rex was still for a moment. He frowned at me, but I saw what preceded the frown. Rage. He dropped the knife with a clatter and pushed back from the table. "Disloyalty and theatrics always have such a bitter taste. You've made a mistake here tonight."

My mother rose to leave with him, and they exited the dining room without a backward glance.

"That was amazing, with the fire-wine," Dez said, seemingly awe-struck. "And scary as hell."

The deal we'd come for was more or less in place, and maybe I'd given the Rex something to fear from us. That wasn't nothing.

So why was I back to fearing what would come next from him?

forty-one

Dez rummaged through his small collection of clothes for a clean T-shirt, and pulled it on over his head. The sun hadn't been up that long, which meant his tiny compartment wasn't yet broiling with the heat of the day.

"I'm nervous," I said.

"About your dad?" Dez asked, pulling me toward him.

I nodded against his freshly T-shirted chest. "He might say no."

"He'll probably say yes."

I had stayed with Dez the night we'd gone to the Magic Castle, and for the next few. After the evening performances were done, we curled into each other in his tiny bunk in the dark, sometimes desperate for each other, sometimes careful and quiet. Sometimes we talked until the smallest hours.

Neither of us wanted to talk about why. But we both knew it was because we couldn't relax until the deal was completed, the transfer made, and our disappearing act complete. I was also anxious about what came after. We had the few thousand dollars I'd made over the summer to fund our adventures, but that was all.

We'd be together until we came out of hiding, at least.

Our dinner reveal had bought us roughly a week, the first half of which we'd already spent performing. Now came the rest, traveling to and setting up in Vegas, where a last few days filled with endless show-stoppers were planned. In my spare moments not making out or talking with Dez, I'd been drawing notes and sketches for the magic grand finale that would assist our escape, making lists of necessary supplies. But I still needed Dad's input and the assistance of his crew to pull it off . . .

Thurston had been so excited by my request to close out the midway by making the Ferris wheel disappear and reappear that he not only said yes, but he was throwing a party for us tonight. A "welcome to Las Vegas" party. According to Jules, this summer had been relatively light on soirees compared to last year, so Thurston was making up for it. I wanted to celebrate, but I couldn't yet.

I still had to make my plea to Dad. I wanted to talk to him in person, when we got to Sin City. I planned to do it as soon as we drove onto the Strip that afternoon.

I'd thrown down a major gauntlet—a literal goblet of fire, with apologies to Harry Potter—and I had to pull this off. And I knew we could count on some sort of surprise from the Rex, so we had to be ready for anything.

Both my future and Dez's were on the line, whether we stayed together in the long run or not. So the bad guys had to end the season believing we had vanished into thin air.

In the car on the way to Vegas, I was too jumpy about seeing Dad to talk or to do anything other than mentally rehearse my arguments to him. The conversation played out a dozen ways: with us shouting at each other, with tearful hugs, with him saying yes, with him saying no.

There was only one thing to do—have the conversation and see what reality produced.

We drove into the side-by-side flashy, gorgeous, and tacky Vegas I knew so well. I broke off from the caravan and its destination of the relatively new festival grounds at the far end of the Strip and navigated to Dad's tall, ritzy building.

I stopped the car at the curb and gestured Dez to the driver's seat. "I'm getting out here. You take the car, and I'll see you later."

"You're sure?" he asked.

"Of course."

Dez leaned across the console for what he probably thought would be a brief peck, but I held on to the back of his neck and kissed him hard. When I pulled away, he murmured, "What was that for, so I can do it again?"

"For luck," I said. "See you soon."

The doorman, looking sharp in a black uniform with brass buttons, nodded at me and swung the glass door wide. "Home at last, Miss Mitchell. Your dad will be happy."

"He here?" I asked.

"No, he went out a little bit ago. I won't spoil your surprise when he comes back, though."

"Thanks, Daniel."

The lobby of our building was a faux art deco paradise. I knew the route to the condo as well as the feel of a coin in my palm, as well as sliding a card into my sleeve. But it was . . . strange walking in here. And I realized it was because I had changed.

Home was the same. I wasn't.

I waved my wallet in front of the pad to call the glass elevator. A special card admitted only those who lived here.

The doors opened, my floor already selected by the computerized system that read the card. The view on the way up was as magnificent as that from any hotel in town. The desert hovered like a mirage in the distance, and the tall, eccentric silhouettes of Vegas's famous hotels rose up beyond the glass wall. We lived in the penthouse.

Of course we did.

And Dad should have been home. I'd sent him a text and said I wanted to talk.

He'd written back: Name the time.

I was a few minutes early, though.

My key still fit the lock. The open, airy living space inside was just as it had been when I left to seek my fortune. Part of me wanted to go straight to my room and look at the drawings in my closet—to see if they were as ambitious in design as I remembered. Or to Dad's study, to see how I felt with all those great men of magic staring at me now, after this summer.

Instead, I took a seat on the leather couch to wait.

It wouldn't be long. With the way we'd left things, he wouldn't want to be late.

Or so I'd assumed. Thirty minutes later, I texted him: Dad, where are you? I'm at home, waiting.

He texted right back: On my way. I have great news.

I didn't want great news. I wanted to tell him my plan and hear him say that yes, he'd devote the guys at the theater to our cause and his expertise to me.

But for now, I was waiting, waiting, waiting . . .

I jumped up as soon as I heard the front door click open.

Dad came in, far more dressed up than I expected for a day off. He was in his schmoozing-investors suit, black like everything else he wore.

"There you are," he said, smiling, though I detected a nervousness in the awkward way he moved toward me. He extended his arms, and I gave him a hug. "It's nice to see you here, where you belong. Feel good to be home?"

I decided on honesty and trying not to be offended at the "where you belong" comment. "It's a little weird."

"Huh," he said.

"Where were you? Business meeting?"

"You could say that."

Okay, *he* was officially the thing that was weirdest in this house. A sense of uneasiness hit me. "Can't you just tell me where you were?"

He stood still for a second and then nodded. He crossed to the fridge and opened the gleaming steel to remove a beer.

"Drinking during the day?" I asked. Even late afternoon like this was unusual for Dad. "What, were you at a funeral? Broken wand ceremony?"

When magicians in certain organizations died, their fellows—usually all male—had a memorial where a wand was broken in symbolic recognition that they would never do magic again.

Dad took a long sip. Then he said, "Let's go into the study."

His sanctuary.

"I have a favor to ask," I said.

"You know I'd do anything for you."

I should've found that comforting, but my uneasiness grew.

I took the comfy leather chair opposite the giant desk he sank behind. The greats peered down from the heavy frames along the walls. Carter, Houdini, Herrmann.

"Why don't you start?" he said.

I slung my messenger bag off my shoulder onto the floor and pulled out my sketch pad. "Okay, that's good, because I'm nervous. But I think this will work." I paused. "Getting ahead of myself. Dad, I'm here because I need your help—Dez and I both do. You remember Dez?"

He nodded.

"Also, you have to let go of this 'You can't be a magician' thing. I *am* a magician."

"I've let go of that. You're good."

I smiled at him, a genuine smile. "I'm not sure I'm *this* good yet, but I think with your help I can pull it off."

I flipped open the oversized pad to show two full pages where'd I'd drawn the Ferris wheel from the angle I thought we needed to use. The audience was roughed in at a specific angle in front of the stage too, arrows indicating the perspective both would be to the Ferris wheel itself.

"I found your plans in the closet," he said. "I was impressed."

He meant the sketches of illusions hidden behind my clothes, on my closet walls. He half stood to get a better look at what I was showing him now.

"I want to do this on our last night in Vegas. I figure the audience is here." I tapped the paper. "But I'll need help with constructing a stage and one of those towered arches for the curtain that can conceal the Ferris wheel."

It wasn't like I could really make it disappear. David Copperfield's famous televised disappearance of the Statue of Liberty had relied on a slowly rotating platform to physically turn the audience, a tower to conceal the statue, and some showy lights. I could produce an illusion too, securing my future as a magician when I came back.

In the meantime Dez and I could run. I was going to ask for Raleigh's help to stage a presentation of the coin in such a way as to hopefully spook the evil king and my mother, getting them out of our lives for good.

"Well, what do you think?" I asked my dad.

"This could work," he said. "You know I always thought there was a way to improve on DC."

Dad and David Copperfield were rivals of a sort, often competing for the same treasures from magic history and for the same audiences. I'd never heard him say the man's actual name unless they were standing in front of each other, politely shaking hands.

"No time for a rotating platform," I said. "We'll have to spend most of it building that arch set. I'll need your guys."

"It's doable," he said.

"How do I account for not moving the audience?"

"The old-fashioned way," he said. "With smoke and mirrors. But . . . why do you need to do this so soon? There's more to this, isn't there?"

He hadn't said no.

"Yes, it's part of getting free of the Praestigae. Of my mother's husband. We made a deal with them, one they can't break under their own code. We agreed to give them the coin I had you stash, and in exchange we think they'll let Dez and me go for good. But just in case they feel like breaking it, we're going to disappear for a little while afterward. Watch to see if they're after us. I'm hoping I can convince them I actually made the wheel disappear—which would mean that I'm out of magic, or close to it."

Dad didn't say anything.

"It's a good plan, Dad. It'll work. *And* we get to one-up David Copperfield." I smiled at him.

A smile that wasn't returned.

"What's wrong?" I asked.

He eased back into his chair. "Moira, don't be mad at me. But we don't need to do this. I've taken care of everything."

Cold came over me. "What do you mean?"

"I didn't break my word," he said. "The coin is locked up safe and sound."

I stood. "What have you done?"

"Don't get upset. I was contacted by your mother a few days ago. I made a trade with them. Three magic items from my secret collection to never trouble you again."

"You did *what?*" My head was shaking. *I* was shaking. "Oh my God, what did you give them?"

My mind raced. Mom would have plenty of power again, assuming she could use any object to refill her cup. What would her husband make her do? How could I have any hope of besting her if she turned on me?

Dad rose too and came around the desk. He touched my arm. "Sweetie, you have nothing to worry about. I didn't give them the coin, because after what you said . . . I thought you might have need of it someday. And I didn't want to break my promise to you. But I couldn't stand by and do nothing. It's my job to look out for you."

"What about Dez?" I asked.

All our carefully laid plans, fragile though they might have been . . . He frowned. "What about him?"

"I love him. And they'll kill him if they don't get the coin back."

"He's not my concern. You're my daughter."

I gathered up my sketch pad and shoved it into my bag. Then I sat back down. "I can't believe you did this. I mean, I can, I get it. But . . . Dad, I really wish you hadn't."

He didn't keep telling me what a wonderful idea he'd had. He must have heard something in my voice that got through to him.

He lowered himself, crouching by my chair, and put his hand on my arm. "Did I screw up?" he asked.

Tears threatened. I sucked in a breath and tried to force them away.

"Don't cry," he said. "I can never stand it when you cry."

I nodded, finding a place of calm inside.

We can still do this, I told myself. *You can convince him.*

"All right," I said, "here's the problem. You're not one of them. You're not Praestigae."

His forehead wrinkled. "Neither are you."

"Ah, but the Rex thinks of me that way. And Dez *is* one of them. Since you aren't, it means they don't have to honor any deal they made with you. They only keep deals they make with their own."

He rocked back on his heels and sat on the floor. I didn't think I'd ever seen Dad look so small. He'd always seemed larger than life to me.

"Oh no," he said.

"Yeah. Oh no."

"I should have called you. Moira, I was just . . . I thought I was helping."

The pain in his eyes was real. "Shh," I said. "It's all right. You can make it up to me."

"How?" he asked.

"By telling me everything they have and what it does, and by helping us with this." I held up my bag with the sketch pad inside. "We still have a shot."

"You do?"

"You bet we do," I said. "No way I'm letting them win without a fight."

Even if that meant I had to risk pouring out every ounce of magic in my cup to prevent them from declaring victory.

forty-two

I got to the Cirque camp later than I'd intended. The party in the mess tent had already started, so I headed there to find Dez.

With my mixed news in tow.

The tables and chairs had been shoved to one side of the tent, and the lighting guys had rigged up some colorful lights for ambiance. Dance music cranked from speakers, something poppy and peppy I'd never heard before. Jules twirled in front of Remy in the middle of the makeshift dance floor. I spotted Dita dancing near them with a couple of the acrobats, a brother and sister.

The floor was crowded. End-of-season mania had officially arrived.

On the plus side, Dad was in. He'd taken my list and gotten his crew started on procuring all the items on it, and more. They'd be here bright and early tomorrow to start on the stage construction. On the bad side, we had new complications to consider, the ones created by Dad's ill-considered deal.

The only person I knew besides my mother who understood anything about real magic was Nan. I thought it was time to trust Dita's telling me that I could talk to her too, and Remy and Jules had knowledge of their own. I needed as many people we could trust as possible on our side. It was time to stop keeping secrets that put people in danger. If Dad had known all the things I had—or called to ask me first—he could have avoided making an already-impossible situation worse.

"Hey there," Dez said, behind me. I turned to see him smiling. "You're late—how'd it go?"

"Um."

He pulled me toward the dance floor. "We'll fix it. Let's dance first. Get you in a better mood."

The music switched from fast to slow. He drew me in close to him.

"So much for cheering you up," he said when I didn't smile. "Tell me."

"Dad had a surprise. He made a deal with them."

Dez stopped dancing. "What?"

"My reaction pretty much exactly, except with more 'WTF, Dad?' in it."

"What deal?"

"He still has the coin." I swallowed. Now was not the time to give up. I had to make sure that Dez didn't. "So we have that. And he's in on helping us—he didn't realize what an epically bad idea it was to try and outwit them."

"You mean like we are?" Dez asked, thick with irony.

"No, not like us. We have more info to go on."

"What was his deal?"

I decided I might as well just get it out there. "I go free in exchange for three magical items he traded them."

He started moving again, dancing. "That's not so bad. You don't have to save me. It's okay. I was born under a bad sign. We tried."

"Dez, you're not going back with them so he can do away with you. Not to mention, they're not going to honor a deal they made with my dad. Our plan's on. We still have a chance to pull this off." I paused. "I also want to tell a few other people tonight, see if they'll help."

We turned in an awkward half-circle, barely moving. Dez let out a long breath, and I felt it in my bones. I echoed his exhalation.

"Who?" he asked. "It's not that I don't want to. It's just I grew up being drilled on not talking to anybody about stuff like this."

"I get it. But I think it's safe to tell Dita and Jules and Remy. And Nancy Maroni."

"Oh, just four people? Not the whole Cirque? All right," he said with a wink. He kissed my cheek. "Let's divide and conquer. I'll talk to Remy."

We did just that, with Dez asking Remy for a word while I told Jules she should go home and get Nan. I fetched Dita, and she walked with Dez and me back to the Airstream. I hadn't explained what this was about yet, only that we needed to tell them something right away.

Half an hour later, Dita, Jules, and Nan sat on the couch in our little living room. Remy took a chair from the kitchen. I sat down cross-legged in front of them on the floor, Dez easing down beside me.

"This is not going to be a fun conversation," I said.

"Please tell me you two aren't getting married," Jules said. "Hang on. Do you *have* to get married?" She made a giant lump in the air over her stomach.

Jules could lighten any mood. "No, I'm not pregnant. And it's not the Middle Ages," I said, "so I don't think anyone *has* to get married anymore."

Although, come to think of it, the Praestigae did kind of hail from the Middle Ages. Their society was even older, in fact.

"I think the first part of this is going to go faster if I do a show instead of tell. Nan, I know you told me to keep this secret, but I trust everyone here with the truth."

She inclined her head. She understood that it was my choice.

"We trust you too," Dita said. But she sounded wary.

She'd put on her pajamas already, as soon as we got back. Remy seemed for all the world to have no idea why we were here having this meeting. I didn't know if Jules suspected anything, but I knew she was always trying to figure things out.

I took a handful of coins from my pocket. "These are ordinary coins. Inspect them for yourselves."

I thrust my hand in front of them. "A magic trick?" Jules said.

"Not a trick," I said.

They each plucked up a coin or two and nodded.

I had put on a sleeveless T-shirt. "I want you to watch my hands. I want you to be convinced that I did not do anything you didn't see. What you see is what happens, I swear. Got it?"

They glanced at each other. The room had taken on a nervous energy. Fitting. I'd decided to replicate the butterflies.

I closed my eyes and called my magic to me. It unfurled in my chest, the heat coming at my command and spreading fast throughout me, out to the centers of my palms. I opened my eyes and, slowly, so my audience could watch every move, I tossed my hands open, flinging the coins into the air. They transformed into paper butterflies, sailing high . . .

And then they drifted back to the ground on thin ghost-white wings.

"That was a trick," Jules said.

"I was watching her hands." Remy was frowning. "She didn't switch anything. But magicians have other ways, don't they?"

"She told us it wasn't a trick. You can do magic, can't you?" Dita asked. She was so calm about it. Then again, she'd suspected me on day one—at least, on some level. "Real magic. That's why Nan pulled you aside at the start. She can too."

When Dita looked to Nan, Nan gave a short nod.

Jules pursed her lips. "Why are you telling us this? And why is Dez here?"

"I'm getting there."

Dez laid his hand on my shoulder. I appreciated the move of solidarity.

"We found the magic coin, weeks ago," I said, watching Dita closely. She gave away nothing. "I actually believe it was what woke up my power, that first day. It must have been hidden in the tent then. Anyway, my mother is part of a secret group called the Praestigae, and so is Dez. He was sent here to look for the coin."

At that, they all sat up straighter. A sharpness came over Remy's face.

"I'll explain why, the reason is good. Your granddad, well, let's just say his story about it being a family heirloom was sort of true. Just, it wasn't your family's. He won it in a poker game."

"From my dad, who was a reckless bastard," Dez said.

"And royalty," I added. "The reigning Rex, or *king*, of the Praestigae. By the way, probably none of you should ever mention that word to anyone outside this room."

Nan was shaking her head. "How just like Roman to build a story about it having been his all along. It also explains why he was so angry about my taking it from him. He wouldn't have had access to its favor for long. I'm sorry, Remy and Dita."

"No need," Dita said.

Nan wasn't finished. She turned to me. "I take it your mother wants it back."

"It's a little more complicated than that," I said. "Dez was sent here to find it. We had a plan, but my dad screwed it up a little—I'll explain that next. Part of the reason I wanted you here is to ask you, is it safe to return it to them? They have other magic items now, but this one is special. This one goes all the way back to their beginning."

I'd felt it calling to me. Something inside me went all the way back there too. But it was that sense of a consuming amount of power inside it that worried me. Especially since my mother had other opportunities to refill her magic now.

I instinctively didn't want to hand it over anymore.

Nan considered. "You know more about them than I do. The Praestigae were only ever talked about in hushed whispers. That they are to be avoided by outsiders. That a brush with them inevitably leads to ill consequences. Roman had me use my magic on the coin—to make it more what it was. There was already power in it, but it should be more powerful than ever now."

"It is," I said, certain, remembering that feeling of being alive with power, of endless possibility.

"With a tool like this . . . I shudder to think what they could do." Her head angled in thought. "I suppose I also shudder to think what they must already have done with it, over the years. But now, with increased power . . ."

I had suspected as much. On that card of Nan's I'd transformed, there had been two shiny things in the air above the figures. I believed I now knew what they were. A real coin, and a fake. My mother and the indistinct figure of a man; it had to be the Rex. "Then they won't get it," I said. "I can create a dummy that looks just like it to fool them."

Dita raised her hand, so polite. "Are we going to talk about where you found it?"

"I thought she said it was in the tent," Nan said.

At last, guilt appeared on Jules's and Remy's faces as they saw where this was going.

"Can't we talk about this later?" Jules asked.

Dita laughed, a gentle chuckle, but genuine. We all looked at her.

"No, it's just that, Jules, did you honestly think I had no clue?" Dita sobered, pinning her brother and his girlfriend with a look that dared them to deny it. "I found it as soon as you gave me those 'lucky slippers.'"

"We can explain," Remy said.

"It was my idea," Jules said. "Be mad at me, not him. I put it there. And Moira was right—it was sewn into the very top of the big top before that. I decided we should move it . . . You were having such a hard time."

"Oh, Jules," Nan said. "Will you never learn?"

Dita looked at them. "It made me so mad when you gave me those slippers, that you felt sorry for me and thought I needed the coin to perform. I went out there in my new costume, the costume I loved, and smiled like nothing was wrong, and performed better than I ever had before."

"Oh," Jules said. "Oh, Dita. I'm so sorry."

"I never used it. I hid it in our room," Dita said, with a glance at me. "I kept waiting for you to confess, but then I figured . . . no one else could find it and get hurt by it. I wanted to get rid of it, but I didn't know how. Moira . . . if you'd asked me, I'd have given it to you."

"I wanted to tell you. I should have, before now. I hope we're still friends."

Dita waved an arm to encompass the entire room. "Everyone here has hurt everyone else at some point, more or less. We're family. The circus is a family. I told you that you could tell me the truth. I meant it."

"I believe you," I said to Dita. And to Jules and Remy and Nan. "I want you to know that. I trust you all. I do think of us as family. That's why I asked you here."

Jules reached across Remy to put her hand on Dita's arm. "It *was* my idea. I just didn't want you to be hurt. I didn't want you to lose trapeze, because I know you love it. And I thought . . . well, I told myself Sam would want me to help you any way I could."

"Sam would never have used it," Dita said. "We're the same that way."

Jules nodded. "You're right."

"Maybe someday you will learn," Nan said, seeming satisfied with this. "But what do you need from us, Moira? There must be something. You said you found the coin—where is it now?"

"Somewhere safe for the time being. And you're right. We're supposed to trade it to them at my last show. But there's been a complication."

"Just one?" Jules asked with a wry half-smile.

"A big one. My dad, it turns out, has a collection of magical stuff. Except most of it's apparently junk—at least according to my mother."

"Your mother saw this collection?" Nan said. "That definitely sounds like a complication."

"You're not kidding," I said. "My dad traded her three items from his collection. She walked through it and picked out the ones she felt power in—the others she said mostly weren't 'real.' So that means she and the Praestigae have access to a boxing glove that's supposed to increase anyone's strength tenfold. A magic lantern that's supposed to be able to create illusions so convincing that onlookers believe they are reality. And a clay cup from an archeological site in Mesopotamia fabled for its restorative powers, supposedly healing anyone who drinks from it."

Dez coughed, surprised. "I thought magic healing wasn't real."

"I think we know why she took that one. I'm going to guess if her magic was waning, then she's now back to full strength."

"Your mother—didn't she keep you away from her people all this time?" Nan asked. "What's her motivation for coming after you?"

"Honestly? I don't know the truth of what she's after. She's something of a wild card." I shook my head. "I made her husband angry. He's what you might call a monster. I think he's running the show."

Dita raised her hand again. "Do you think you could reform him?" she asked. "Like you did with Novio?"

The question was obviously for Nan, and one I would have to find out the entire story behind later.

"I suppose the only answer I can give is that Novio reformed himself," the older lady said. "I wasn't able to exert any positive influence on your grandfather. Redemption is not always possible. It requires . . ." She looked at Dita, then me. "Redemption requires a desire to be redeemed."

"He doesn't have that," Dez said.

"Agreed, and they're going to expect us to try to trick them," I added. "I can't promise this won't get dangerous. But I'd love your help, from all of you. I need it."

I took a deck of cards from my pocket, a regular deck, and flashed the backs of the cards toward the couch. I called my magic and fanned them again. This time they were edged in gold around a rainbow of colors, like that first day. "My cards are all on the table," I said.

"With special effects like that," said Jules, "of course we're in."

forty-three

The stage for the Ferris wheel disappearance was surrounded by billowing walls of cloth on all sides, hiding it from everyone except those with permission to work on the illusion. Dad must have been using a skeleton crew for his evening shows, because he'd sent every spare hand over here.

The result was that after a few days, two enormous wooden towers joined by a massive arch, thirty feet across, cleverly constructed and painted to look like the top half of the Ferris wheel itself, dominated the stage. My stage.

I admired them from close up, then leapt down onto the grass to go beyond the cloth to the midway proper.

The Ferris wheel would be framed in the arch until it wasn't. The arch itself was constructed to move, when it would hide the carefully positioned audience's view of the wheel a hundred feet in the distance.

I'd spent every daylight moment I wasn't performing supervising the set construction and rehearsing the plan with Dez and the friends who'd be assisting with his clean getaway, then mine after the dummy coin got presented.

Tomorrow the Cirque crew would bring out chairs and clear the crowd except for ticket-holders. We'd already worked with security to specify where people could and couldn't be without spoiling the effect.

After the amazing illusion, those lucky people would proceed into the big top for the last performance of the year.

Thurston had cut it down to one show tomorrow to make it even more exclusive. And if there was one thing Vegas loved, it was an exclusive engagement.

Dez was waiting for me beyond the curtain. Brandon was with him.

When Dez gave me a quick kiss, Brandon rolled his eyes. "Tickets?" he asked.

I reached in my pocket and removed the envelope with two tickets for my queen mother and the devil king.

I held out the envelope to Brandon. "Here they are. Make sure they get these and they know there's no coin unless they come."

He took it in his unbroken hand and nodded to Dez. "I'm doing this for him. Brother, I can't believe you fell this hard for a rich girl who's into bondage."

"I am not—"

He cackled as he left. Dez's imminent departure was a secret from Brandon, so I tried not to growl, because I knew Dez still cared for him.

Dez came close to my ear, speaking into it. "Sorry about that. Here come Raleigh and your Dad. Go talk to them, and then we're leaving."

The pleasurable tickle of his breath at my earlobe was enough to make me forgive and forget. "I should stick around to watch the last—"

"No. Leaving. Together."

My entire body heated in response. The same heat was there in his eyes. If things didn't go as planned, then this could be our last night together. Our worlds had collided, but now they could split back into two separate universes.

I was determined to prevent it. We were all banking on a lot of long shots, though—including one I was keeping a last secret from Dez. From everyone except Dad.

Dad was bringing the coin so I could copy it, but I also wanted it on me tomorrow. One last fail-safe.

"I'll make it quick," I said. "Meet you back at your place?"

"All right."

I walked up to Dad and Raleigh, and slung an arm around Dad. I'd worried we wouldn't get through this with our relationship intact, but I'd felt more hopeful with each passing hammer strike and every minute working side by side.

"You bring it?" I asked.

He slipped a small jewel box into my palm before I even saw his hand move. "You've still got the skills," I said, admiring his sleight of hand.

"This is the payload?" Raleigh asked.

"Just a sec," I said, holding up a finger. "I need to check one last thing."

I went back under the curtain. The workmen glanced over, but then went back to their jobs. Everything had to be done by showtime, after all.

Dad knew I was making a copy. Raleigh didn't.

The coin thrummed, even inside the box, like it was speaking to me. *You again,* it said. *What marvels we will do together.*

I took a close look at the coin and then picked it up. An electric jolt went through me as soon as I touched it, and I tried to make friends. *You and me,* I thought to it, *let's get along.*

Then I closed one fist around it, and another around a prop coin from my pocket. And I thought, *Make it look the same.*

When I unfolded my fingers, barely warm with the effort, I compared the two. Identical, as far as anyone who didn't know what the magic coin felt like was concerned.

After putting the real coin into its box, I hid it in my pocket. I ducked out to my dad and Raleigh with the fake in my hand.

"You're sure what I have in mind will work for your bird?" I asked Raleigh.

"We're all good. He'll come when I signal. You ready to give me that yet?"

"Here it is." The real coin was still a solid thrumming hum in my pocket. I handed him the dummy coin, and his ticket.

"Huh," he said, turning the coin over and over. "What a thing to lose a job over."

"No kidding," I said.

Dad pulled me off to the side. "Give me one sec too, Raleigh," he said.

"You two are getting way too similar," Raleigh said. He gave us a little space, though.

"You're keeping the real one on you?" Dad asked.

"I know it doesn't seem like a good idea, but—"

"I kept it for you." Dad kissed the top of my head, like I was still a little girl. "Good luck."

The coin buzzed and hummed with power I could practically hear, like it approved of our discussion. *What things we will do together,* it said.

Dez had turned on the little lamp when I got to the closet-sized space that had become so familiar. I breathed in the air, knowing it was silly to think of it as "Dez air," yet still trying to memorize it exactly. I took the box from my pocket and set it back beside the light, safe but not on me.

The sense of its presence dampened, now that I was no longer in contact with it.

Dez was lying back on the bed. I crawled in beside him and pressed my lips to his neck. He made a happy noise and tucked me into his arm. "Let's pretend," he said.

"Okay. What are we pretending?"

"That tomorrow isn't going to happen. I want to know everything that happens next, after the season ends, if none of this was happening and we got everything we wanted instead."

My heart was simultaneously growing and breaking. This summer had taught me so many things—that bad people could do good things, that people who thought they were bad could be good, that you could love someone even if they hurt you, that forgiveness was possible. And that I was strong enough to resist my father's will, to resist anyone's that got in the way of what I wanted.

My magic could save us, I hoped. No guarantee, though.

But in the meantime, we could pretend.

"Well," I said, "I ask if you want to stay in Vegas. My dad is scandalized. But he gets over it."

"You're probably getting your own place soon anyway. So I say yes. What do you do next? I want to know. Does your dad give you a job?"

This was something I had been thinking about.

"I used to think I wanted to open for him, be his apprentice, part of the show at the Menagerie."

He kissed the top of my head, and I angled my face to look up at him. "But now?" he asked.

"Now I think I ask him if he's willing to invest in a show of my own. Not as big as his, not so flashy, about the size of my show here. Well, maybe a little bigger. I want a theater, a home, a place where I can experiment. So I find this old theater that needs a little work in a less trendy part of town. I raise money and fix it up. I hire a crew, and a lovely assistant."

"Someone with experience, like me?"

"Someone with experience, like you. And then I launch, and within weeks every show is sold out."

Dez was serious. "You should do all that."

"Maybe I will. Someday." Even though we were pretending, I wasn't sure I wanted it to be that easy anymore. One thing my magic had given me was a new appreciation for what was earned. For what was real.

True.

"And what about you?" I asked.

"We've already established that in this pretend I am the lovely assistant."

I felt the pushback in it. He didn't want to spin out what his real future could be. He didn't know yet. I understood.

I just had to cross my fingers and wish on all the stars in the sky that I was as strong as I thought I was, strong enough to do what I planned tomorrow.

"Enough pretend," I said, crawling down to the end of the bed to close the sliding door.

All these nights we'd spent together, we were so comfortable with each other. But there was a line we hadn't crossed.

"I want to," I said. "Do you?"

"I do."

He wound his hand in my hair, and our lips collided. Our mouths were desperate, hot and open, and I moved my thighs to press against him. My Dez, so unsure anyone loved him. Our shirts went first, then the rest of our clothes. Hands followed mouths as we tried to get closer and closer.

So close no one could ever part us.

In those moments, I never wanted tomorrow to come.

forty-four

Tomorrow came anyway.

I went home to shower in the Airstream and put on my performing clothes. Dita was waiting when I came out, standing by her bed in a jacketless men's suit.

I had the little jewel box in my hand. I'd been afraid to leave it anywhere apart from me since Dad forked it over. I hadn't even bothered to open it again yet. The song it sang, like a Siren's, was impossible to mistake.

"I already made the fake," I said to her.

"You didn't tell us the whole plan, did you?" she asked. "What are you going to do? Use it?"

Of course Dita would guess. She'd gotten to know me as well as anyone ever had.

"What I have to do to make sure the people I love are safe. I mean, as much as any of us ever can. You'd do the same, wouldn't you?"

"I would," she said. "I envy you a little, for getting to. But it's dangerous, right?"

I nodded. I'd felt like the coin would consume me the one time I'd been onstage with it. Its crushing power convinced me I could do anything. And I was afraid that power would overtake mine and leave me with nothing. Leave me to break, to shatter into pieces, empty.

She hugged me. "Don't die."

"Fate has its plans, and it doesn't consult us," I said, quoting Dez quoting the Praestigae. "But death's not in my plans."

"I'll take it."

I peeked out from behind the curtain hung in the arch on my brand-new one-use-only stage. The people lucky enough to have seats for this outdoor illusion would be able to see the Ferris wheel *only* through the arch, which served as a pretty frame. The positioning was the key to the optical illusion of making the wheel seem to vanish and then the reverse, making it reappear.

Dad's helpful shadows and mirrors, and the position of the towers and arch itself would combine to hide it from the onlookers, then show it to them again. The stage was also positioned so I could make it to the Ferris wheel and be on it when it reappeared in their view.

And hope against hope for the best. I needed a show of power so dramatic that it would convince the Praestigae not to pursue us. If Mom took the fake coin and left, someday soon we'd be able to return.

I sensed Dez's approach and turned around to face him. "You ready?" I asked.

"Nowhere close," he said. "I feel like I should have more to do."

"You getting out of here—fast—is the key to everything." I gave him an envelope. It contained a mushy note about how I believed in his future, along with the few thousand dollars' cash I'd earned this summer.

He put the envelope in his pocket and reached out for my hands.

"Don't read the letter unless I don't show up," I said. "Okay?"

"You're going to show up."

"Just in case something goes wrong."

We looked at each other.

"I'll see you soon," I said.

"You are the best and the worst thing that ever happened to me, Moira Mitchell," Dez said. "And if you don't show up, I'll be a worthless, ruined soul. So nothing can go wrong."

I didn't want to lose my composure. I had to perform—both onstage in a few moments, and after, with the Rex and Regina. So I made a bad joke. I gestured at the enormity of the setup around us. "Not every girl would do all this for a guy, true."

Or risk her life. The coin would make me more powerful. But using it was a risk, and I knew it. I saw no other choice.

Dez's life was in my hands. My mom had said it, and the copper heart's existence made me believe it.

I saw Dad and Raleigh climbing up the back steps of the stage toward us. Raleigh had Caliban the crow perched on his arm.

"Don't screw this up," I said to Dez.

"Noted."

I leaned forward for one more kiss. I didn't care if Dad didn't like being forced to witness it. Not right now.

Our lips touched and lingered, soft as a breathless whisper, and it didn't seem possible this would never happen again. But it *was* possible. It felt like an ending.

I tried to erase the thought as soon as I'd had it, but it was too late.

The kiss ended, anyway. I couldn't know if my dad or Raleigh had noticed that I'd used it partly as a cover to sleight the heart-shaped penny from my pocket and slip it into Dez's.

His life was his own to live, no matter what happened today.

We looked at each other, but neither of us said good-bye. He walked away to get in position, with a gentlemanly nod to Raleigh and Dad. He said something I couldn't hear to them. To my surprise, Dad nodded back.

When he got to me, Dad reached out, straightening my mask, which I was certain was straight already. "You all set? Everything's in place."

"Let's see about that," I said. "And Dita's not here yet."

When I'd scanned the audience a few minutes before, the Rex and Regina weren't in their reserved seats. Raleigh had a seat set aside right behind them. The better to keep close so he could signal Caliban.

I shifted the curtain and saw my mother's face first thing. The Rex sat beside her, in an overly nice suit. They'd somehow gotten extra tickets. Brandon and two other guys sat in the seats next to them.

Hmm, I thought. But the only thing I said out loud was, "They're here."

Dad and Raleigh loomed over me, where they could see too. Mommy dearest shouldn't have been able to see us, but she sure seemed to be looking right at us.

"She looks ten years younger," Dad said.

"She looks fine," Raleigh said. He only knew that all this intrigue had to do with my mother and the so-called magic coin. He still didn't buy that magic was real.

Mommy dearest did, in fact, look the healthiest and most beautiful I'd ever seen her. It might have been an illusion, but I suspected it was the effects of the healing cup.

I wondered if she'd try to suppress my magic.

I didn't think the coin would let her, if it came to that.

Please don't let it come to that, I thought.

She had decades more experience than me, and I still wasn't sure what she felt about me. All I knew was that her actions this summer had gotten her something she badly wanted. Her power back.

Dita pounded up the back steps. "I'm here!" she said, extending her arm in Raleigh's direction. "Jules misplaced the keys, but we found them. She and Remy are in place, waiting for Dez and you."

Raleigh held up his bird arm, pointed the fingers of his other hand to Dita's outstretched arm, and gave Caliban a look. "Hop," he said. Caliban flapped his wings and landed on Dita's forearm. *"Craagh."*

"This'll be perfect. The Rex is superstitious," I said. "I appreciate you pitching in, Raleigh."

"A pleasure," he said. "You proved me wrong. You're a good magician, and this is going to put you on the map."

Oh yeah—my magic career. Funny how it had almost become an afterthought. I felt a thrill at the reminder.

Thurston finally strolled up the back stairs to join us, clipping on a wireless mic as he approached. He didn't seem at all surprised to see Dita holding a large crow or Raleigh heading down the stairs to rejoin the crowd. He nodded to Dad and me.

"Ready for the big time?" he asked.

I whirled and looked at the Ferris wheel in the distance, its lights blazing. Dez sat in a car near the top—his car, *our* car. He raised a hand and waved.

"Ready." I touched the coin in my pocket, and it sang back to me. *Yes, yes.*

"I reminded security no one's to leave their seats until the illusion is concluded," Thurston said. "But you may want to emphasize it too."

"Of course," I said. "For drama."

Dad was nervous, I could tell, that he'd been relegated to backup duty. I'd made him promise to stay behind the scenes and manage the towers and the curtain and the recordings. This was my night. The less obvious his participation was, the less chance the Rex would worry about me besting him.

"Then let's start the show," Thurston said. "This is so exciting."

You have no idea, I thought.

Dad stepped back out of view, behind one of the towers that bordered either side of the arch. Dita hovered behind him, stroking Caliban's feathers.

I pulled aside the curtain within the arch with a flourish. Thurston stepped out and walked onto center stage.

"And now, may I present the Miraculous Moira Mitchell. Moira will be performing the first-ever illusion of its kind done as part of the

Cirque American. A grand finale for our grandest season yet! Please welcome the astonishing, mysterious, miraculous . . . Moira!"

Every seat was packed.

I took a bow. Thurston walked to the side of the stage and hopped off so he could watch the show.

The sound guys switched my lapel mic on. We were on. There was no stopping now.

"Welcome to the final evening of the second season of the Cirque American." I strode around the stage, faltering only a little at the way the Rex watched hungrily when I met his eyes. He grinned. He must have assumed they'd outmaneuvered us.

My mother had the grace to look vaguely worried, if as regal as I'd ever seen her. I wished again that I could read her better.

The coin sang to me, *I am here when you need me. I am here waiting.*

I went on, trying to ignore it. "Typically I dedicate a new illusion to one of the women magicians who blazed the trail I am now on, women too often forgotten by history, despite their boldness and perseverance in a man's world. But tonight, I'll be doing the largest illusion of my career—and one of the largest illusions ever attempted in the world." I swept a hand to trace the arc of the Ferris wheel framed in the archway.

"This Ferris wheel is the largest transportable wheel in the world. Thurston Meyer had it constructed expressly for the Cirque American, designed to recall the world's first such wheel, created for the World's Fair in Chicago. It stretches some two hundred feet above the earth, and takes three days to assemble and a full day to disassemble. Rest assured, there is no way for it to vanish before your very eyes." I smiled at them. "And yet it will."

The crowd made an admiring coo, excited by the prospect. A few skeptics were shaking their heads.

Let them.

"I have been inspired by so many magicians. My father, for one. But tonight I dedicate this performance to all those women who ever stood on a stage or a street and produced coins from nowhere. To those who pulled cards from their sleeves. To those who were lovely assistants and box jumpers. To those who escaped from straitjackets and locked trunks. And to those who caught bullets. To all the women who dared to do magic."

I walked to the side of the curtain. "Let's begin. You'll see my assistant seated in a car on the Ferris wheel. He'll be disappearing too. All we need are a few simple magic words."

Someone in the crowd let out a whoop. The audience was waiting for me to show them a marvel. A miracle.

My heart started to pound, and the coin in my pocket seemed to pulse in time with it.

The Rex laughed, as if this were nothing but a small amusement. My mother gave a slight shake of her head and put a hand on his arm.

I hesitated. The seats where Brandon and one of the other men had been, beside the Rex and Regina, were empty.

A bead of sweat ran down the side of my face, and I was excruciatingly aware of it. And of the audience watching, waiting. Where was their miracle?

"Moira?" my father said, from the wings.

This was the moment. I had to keep going. Dez had to get out of here.

"And now I will make this Ferris wheel vanish. You are welcome to stand after the show is complete, but until it is concluded, please remain in your seats." I paused. "Or the kind security officers will show you back to them."

They were stationed around the edges of the audience. *Brandon couldn't get by them,* I told myself. *Could he?*

"Abracadabra!" I shouted as I pulled the curtain closed. Behind it, Dad's crew waited patiently in their places.

Smoke fired behind the arch and bathed the stage.

"You're good," Dad said, the smoke stinging my nostrils as I ran down the back steps.

"Alakazam!" I heard the recording of my voice begin to play, sounding like it came from the stage.

I took my predetermined path to the Ferris wheel, running in a fast crouch behind the tents and stages, to reach it before the crowd got restless. The audience should suspect I was behind the curtain.

"Hocus-pocus!" the recording cried.

I reached the Ferris wheel and looked up, searching for Dez. He was gone.

Whew.

There was no sign of Brandon or any of his guys. I tried to convince myself that they probably went for a cigarette break.

Dad and the crew were supposed to reopen the curtain to let the audience see the Ferris wheel was still in place only once I'd climbed into the front car, then boosted myself up to the second one, so I'd be more visible.

I switched the mic I wore back on. "Well, now, hmph," I said.

The curtain sailed open, letting me see the audience again—and hear their reaction too, a chorus of mystified gasps, as it was revealed that I was no longer onstage but on the Ferris wheel itself.

I waved and gave an exaggerated shrug. "Oops! I made my assistant disappear," I said. "But it seems I'm still here, and so is this Ferris wheel. Let's try this again and see what we can do about that."

The audience laughed and clapped as the curtain closed again, concealing me from view. I switched the mic off again and started climbing back down.

"Abracadabra!" the recording cried. It would play while I returned pell-mell to the main stage. When the curtain opened again, the audience would see no Ferris wheel at all.

The stage's arch was on sliders, and the crew would be moving them now, putting the large mirrors into their positions. This trick, which we'd borrowed from Raleigh's cabinet of wonders, would fool the audience into seeing nothing.

At the end, the plan was for Raleigh to signal Caliban to deposit the fake coin on my mother's lap. I would then show up in front of them and explain I'd used up nearly all my magic on the Ferris wheel trick. There was a chance I might not need to use the magic coin at all.

I finished climbing down off the wheel, prepared to beat a hasty retreat back to the stage. But I lingered, wanting to confirm nothing funny was going on with Brandon and the other missing guys. To make sure the Rex and Regina were still in place. I only needed a glance.

The decision would mean I'd have to run even faster back to the stage, but the peace of mind would be worth it.

Oh no. As the curtain began to pull back, I could see through the arch that the Rex and Regina weren't in their seats. I searched and found them. They were walking straight toward the Ferris wheel, getting closer with each passing second.

I didn't understand how they could have gotten past the security guards.

Not until I saw Brandon just behind them, a red glove where I'd grown accustomed to seeing his white cast. The boxing glove that supposedly increased strength.

He was carrying the magic lantern too, until he set it on the ground. His free arm went around in a cranking motion, and a spray of lights burst out of it, pointing back the way they'd come.

I could guess what it was. An illusion, a mirage, so that no one would come this way. No one from security would see what happened next. They probably wouldn't even hear it. For all I knew, the magic lantern my mother had chosen could fool the entire audience, should they get out of their seats and walk over.

They couldn't see it, though. In fact, I bet I was the only one they'd be able to see when the curtain finished reopening. They were expecting that the Ferris wheel would be gone. But the Rex and Regina were the ones who I needed to *see* and *believe* it.

Good thing I still had a trick up my sleeve to make sure they did.

"Stop, girl!" the Rex shouted. "Desmond is ours. Where is he?"

My mother strutted alongside him, but she stayed silent.

"Alakazam!" recording me said.

Starting to panic, I took the coin from my pocket and held it in one hand, placing the other back onto the Ferris wheel.

Dez should be off the grounds by now. This was up to me.

I almost swooned as I called my magic and the coin screamed to life, power reverberating inside me. It filled me up to the brim and kept on coming, pouring out over the top. Was I a cup? No, I was an ocean, a vast, angry sea.

I clutched the metal harder, feeling it grow hot against my burning hand, my heart pounding, my breath coming fast.

And I visualized the Ferris wheel vanishing.

As surely as Dez was leaving right now.

I pictured the metal spokes fading into invisibility, the empty air where it should be.

That seemingly endless magic roared through me.

"Moira, no!" my mother's voice yelled.

I poured and poured everything into the vision in my head of the Ferris wheel vanishing.

My whole body heated, flooded in panic and in anger and in fear that all of this was for nothing. I'd come so far to fail now. *Don't see it, don't see it,* I thought. *It's air.*

It's just air.

And I was oxygen and gasoline and fire mixed together, a searing pain. I was a flame, burning up from the inside out.

It's just air.

My hands might have held fireballs in them as the coin fed more and more heat back to me.

Disappear. It has to disappear.

My mother couldn't be allowed to get this coin.

More? the coin sang, asking me.

Use it all, I answered. *Let the cup break if it has to.*

I closed my eyes. Magic consumed me utterly.

And then I lost my grip on the Ferris wheel. I stumbled back and looked up at . . .

Nothing.

Where the Ferris wheel had been was empty air.

The same emptiness echoed within me. I'd made it disappear for real. My magic might be gone too.

The coin burned my palm. "Hocus-pocus!" I cried.

And then I fell into that emptiness, into that echo.

forty-five

The curtains must have been open, revealing the nothing that was left—the absence that was supposed to be created by smoke and mirrors and angles of light—because the crowd erupted into stunned applause. In theory, the Ferris wheel was going to be restored with another curtain close; the crew was expecting it.

I didn't think that was going to happen. I didn't even know if I could get up.

A boot slammed into my ribs, jolting me with pain. "He was ours! Where is he? Where's the coin?" the Rex demanded.

The coin's voice was smaller now. It whispered, *We're not done.*

It heated again in my hand. How much power could it have left? How much did I have?

Whatever you need to finish this, it seemed to say. It was a Praestigae coin, and this man had perverted what it meant to be Praestigae. Nan was right. He would never want redemption.

My mother appeared above me and pushed the Rex away. I saw Brandon approaching behind him, swinging his arm with the red boxing glove on it. The leather was battered and old.

I could get up. I had to. That enormous power started to build within me again, heat surging through my limbs. I took the opportunity to climb to my feet as I closed my fist tight around the coin. My ribs protested the movement, but then quieted.

"Moira, what did you do?" my mother asked, sounding faintly curious.

I staggered to the spot where the Ferris wheel had been. No one in the crowd could see me; the illusion was too well constructed. But they could hear me.

I pressed my clip mic on and shouted, "Look at that! Where once the largest transportable Ferris wheel stood, now there is nothing but air!"

"Hide us, Regina," the Rex barked, realizing what I was doing. Her hands on her hips, frowning at him, she didn't seem to take his meaning right away.

The crowd applauded more, but theirs wasn't the attention I wanted. "Friends, send me your help to get the wheel back," I shouted. "Come close! Come now!"

I prayed that Raleigh and Dita would understand my message. I saw Dita step into view at the back of the stage, Caliban on her arm.

She climbed off the back. Even if she couldn't see me, or wasn't sure what I'd called for, she was on her way down here. Whatever I was going to do, I had to hurry.

The curtain closed again.

"Just grab the girl," the Rex said. "We'll sort it all out later."

I turned to face him and my mother just in time to see Dez barrel past Brandon and knock the Rex down.

The Rex was on his feet again in a heartbeat.

But Dez knew what the glove Brandon wore was theoretically capable of. The fact the Rex and Regina were past security meant it almost certainly worked. And . . . wait. Why was he here anyway?

"You were supposed to go," I said. "To be long gone by now."

"Thought you might need me," Dez quipped, charming grin in full effect.

Then he took a hard right hook from Brandon to his shoulder, sending him to the ground. The Rex kicked Dez, keeping him down. Brandon bent over his friend, punching him again.

Dez made a terrible noise after Brandon hit him with the glove, but he stupidly continued to fight, kicking his feet at them both to try to prevent them from landing another blow. His teeth were coated in blood.

Brandon pleaded with him, "Stay down, please."

"Brother," Dez said, "let me up."

"Finish him off," the Rex said, like it was no big deal.

Brandon hesitated, then pulled his arm back. Dez lay on the ground, waiting to see what his friend would do. His "brother."

No way this was about to happen. We'd gone through all this for nothing? For Dez to lose his life?

I started to gather more heat, calling for magic—mine, the coin's, whatever was available—to flood me with power again.

"Moira," my mother said, "stop. Not that way. It'll be your end. You know I haven't been entirely honest with you. I've known how this would go since the day I laid eyes on you. Fate makes its plans, and it doesn't consult us."

I looked at her. She shone with a kind of ambition and confidence I'd never seen in her before.

"We can stop this," she said, eyes flicking toward the Rex.

I understood. She didn't need to answer to this petty tyrant any longer. She wanted real power. To be a true queen.

I held out my hand to her, the one that held the coin. She placed her hand over mine.

The moment our hands joined felt like a lightning strike. And then, after, it was as if all the centuries of women who'd held this coin had showed up for us at once. Like they were all here, ready to lend us whatever strength we lacked.

"Rex, my Rex," my mother said coolly, "come here, please."

Brandon was still hesitating over Dez while the Rex watched, grinning. All of them turned at the sound of her voice.

The crowd noise reached me again, sounding confused, strained. I hoped the curtain hid this inexplicable tableau.

"Come and take our coin from her, my darling," my mother said. "She's too weak to fight. It's in her hand there. It's so powerful I can feel it. All the luck we could ever need. I just need a little help to recover it."

She nodded toward my other, empty hand, which I balled into a tight fist.

The Rex knelt, face ugly and twisted as he pried at my fingers. I resisted only a moment.

"Nothing but air," I said, letting him succeed and grabbing his arm. "I looked, and there was nothing but air."

My mother's eyes met mine again, and she nodded. "Nothing but air."

The heat of a thousand fires boiled us within it, but my mother held on to my hand. *Nothing but air. Nothing but air.*

"You can't," he said. "You wouldn't! You can't!"

His voice shook with the rage always within him. The rage that defined him.

And then, where the Rex stood, there was nothing. One second I clutched his arm; the next, he was nowhere to be seen.

The coin vibrated in my palm, and the sense of it being there faded away. Its song vanished to nothing, just like the air in front of us.

Brandon had a stunned look on his face. Even more so when Dez tackled him and, even bloody, obviously hurting, wrenched the boxing glove from his broken hand. Dez tossed it to the side, breathing hard.

"I didn't want to," Brandon said. "There's this cup. They said I could fix my hand. But only after—"

Dez ignored him and stumbled toward my mother and me.

As did Dita and Raleigh, running into view from the back path I'd taken earlier. My dad wasn't with them—he'd kept his promise not to come anywhere near. He'd finally trusted me to handle my life, no matter how big and hard and weird it got.

My mother released my hand, and I curled my fingers, waving toward Dita and Raleigh. "We're okay," I said.

Dita and Raleigh stopped where they were, but Caliban kept coming. He flew over my mother's head and dropped the dummy coin behind her.

Before she could pick it up, I lunged for it. I didn't think she'd felt what had happened to the real one. I'd had the tighter grip on it.

"That's not the real one," she said with a laugh.

Dez dragged me up against him, and I could have kissed him, for so many reasons. But mostly for providing just the distraction I needed. The real coin was broken in my palm. It had shattered into pieces when the Rex disappeared. Its cup had broken, its magic spent, to rid the world of him and to save us. To destroy him, the coin had let us use all its magic.

But there was no reason my mother had to know that.

I slipped the fragments into my pocket as I hugged Dez and switched the fake into the hand my mother thought the real one was in.

"I'd like it," my mother said.

"Of course, but it's done," I said, passing her the dummy coin. "There's no power left here. You must've felt it go."

A cool smile took over my mother's red lips. "There's power in symbols, and now I have all of it I need. You did well, daughter."

So, she had gotten exactly what she wanted.

That was okay. So had I.

"What about you?" she asked, hesitating. "You could come with me."

I shook my head.

"Your deal is done," she said, encompassing me and Dez in her nod. "Come on, Brandon, get the lantern and let's go."

He scooped up the boxing glove, and they headed toward the magic lantern to retrieve it. Apparently, my mother wasn't one for sentimental good-byes.

But she just helped send her husband to nowhere, so yeah—you knew that.

I turned and shoved Dez's shoulder, even though he looked not-so-great after those punches. Brandon had left him weakened, but he grinned at me anyway.

"I decided this wasn't the right day to give up," he said. "But couldn't you have asked her to let us use that cup first, just in case? My ribs."

The second he said the word *ribs*, mine protested too, where the Rex had kicked them on the right side. "Tell me about it."

I looked around at the sun-soaked early evening midway. The big top in the distance. No Rex in sight. He was just gone. All that evil no longer in the world. There was no blood on my hands, but I had helped get rid of him. I didn't feel a shred of guilt.

My mother and I had that much in common.

The missing Ferris wheel, however, that would take some explanation.

"Um, guys?" Dita said. "Thurston . . . the crowd."

"Can you make it?" Dez asked.

"Can you?" I took a bow randomly, as if this was all part of the show.

And swooned a little.

Okay, so maybe the effects of the coin were wearing off a little bit. And my ribs really did hurt.

Raleigh said, "Someone's going to tell me what happened to the Ferris wheel and that guy with the beard, right?"

"Later," I said.

"Let's consider this a grand reappearance," Dez said, scooping me up in his arms. He carried me across the grass, even though I could tell it hurt him. The lunatic. It didn't feel that great on my bruised-feeling ribs either, but I appreciated not having to walk and I knew he wouldn't put me down.

I touched Dez's lip. There was a cut on it I hadn't noticed before.

There was no sign of my mother, Brandon, their guys, or their gear in our path. I doubted I'd ever see her again.

When Dez carried me into view of the stage and the crowd, I heard Thurston's booming voice saying, "Have you ever seen the likes of this?"

My dad ran out to meet us. "I should never have promised I'd stay over here," he said. "It was hard enough keeping everyone else over here."

He gave Dita and Raleigh dirty looks.

"I'm fine," I told him. "Mostly. I signaled them to come. What does the crowd think happened?"

Dad blinked. "They think you made the Ferris wheel disappear. And then did some kind of weird after-act."

"Okay, then. Open the curtain. It's still gone."

Jules and Remy now appeared beside the stage, applauding but looking worried. Nan stood beside them. Jules finally saw us and pointed. I waved.

"Moira, get up here and take a bow!" Thurston was calling for me to join him, and seemed oblivious to why I wasn't walking. Of course he was oblivious to why I wasn't walking.

We joined Thurston onstage. "How did you do it?" he asked me, quietly and not for the mic, before having Dez set me down to take an assisted bow for the ongoing standing ovation. The curtain opened again to show the . . . nothing.

"Magic," I said, done with lying. He deserved to know the truth. "Magic is real."

He gave a stunned laugh. "I knew it!" He paused. "Can you bring it back?"

"Um, I don't think so. It was a onetime deal. I'm sorry?"

"Are you kidding? I just saw the biggest feat of real magic that the world has probably ever seen. That's priceless. Who cares?"

His laughter was infectious. No one in the audience would really *believe* I'd made the Ferris wheel disappear. Already they'd be coming up with theories: that it was a 3-D projection, that the original had been taken apart overnight. But they'd also be saying that it was a wonder to see anyway.

No one would say it was accomplished with actual magic borrowed from a centuries-old coin.

"Moira Mitchell, everyone!" Thurston boomed, having turned the sound back on his mic.

The season was over. I stood on my own feet, and I took another wobbly bow, to the bright lights of Vegas and whatever the future held. Dez and I would get a chance. I might well get my dream.

Tonight, I was one of the world's greatest magicians, and we were both free.

Oh, and PS, Mom, I had all the magic I could ever want left inside me.

epilogue

Two Months Later

The theater I was playing in wasn't a dump, but it wasn't the Menagerie either.

I'd decided to strike a happy medium between Dad's level, where I was being courted, and Raleigh's, the bar circuit. The publicity I'd gotten from "the great Ferris wheel vanishing," written about in all the best magician specialty publications, and my time at the Cirque had given me enough cred for my new booking agent to set up a small sold-out tour of medium-sized theaters. Now that my bruised ribs—and Dez's cracked ones—were all healed up.

I was doing my illusions from the summer and introducing some new ones. No one was any the wiser about having seen real magic, but they started calling me the Queen of Miracles.

This particular theater was in a used-to-be-happening city. But no matter where it was, seeing my playbill in the window never failed to give me a moment of pride.

THE MIRACULOUS MOIRA MITCHELL
QUEEN OF MIRACLES

Thurston had let me borrow one of the images the Cirque's artist had done of me catching bullets in my hands.

"Milady," Dez said, opening the front door. We were early, bringing in our gear to set up.

"Tone it down, eye candy," I said.

He laughed and gave me a kiss. As much as he could while trying to juggle the bag with my gear in it.

So, it wasn't exactly the pretend dream we'd dreamed. Oh, sure, Dad had offered to set me up with a job on his show or whatever I wanted. But it turned out what I wanted was to make my own way. I believed that I could now, and no one would ever be able to accuse me of coasting to fame on Dad's name. That was the whole point of this.

When we went back to Vegas, maybe he'd even let me snoop in that secret warehouse full of goodies. I'd never gotten the chance.

Frankly, I'd become a little disenchanted with magical objects. But I kept the fragments of the coin in a locket around my neck; it seemed a fitting way to honor them. I didn't think they should be thrown away, not after the things they'd seen and done.

"Your dad sent you a present," Dez said, once we were inside the theater. He produced a manila envelope seemingly from thin air.

"You're getting better," I said.

I'd suggested if he was making this a career, he might give his sleight of hand some work.

"I wonder what this is." I took the envelope and pulled the open tab free as we made our way into the backstage dressing room.

There was a document inside in a plastic covering. I squinted at it, but as I started to remove it, a card fell down. Dez picked it up and read it aloud: "'Dear Moira, it took me a while to track this down. Consider it a congratulations present. I think she's one of your favorites. Love, Dad.'"

I stared at the page, realizing what I held. "This *is* a good present," I said, with a low whistle.

"I'm dying here," Dez said. "What is it?"

"A page from Addie Herrmann's diaries."

"Boring!" he said, but gently.

I rolled my eyes at him.

This was *my* fairy tale so far, with its unexpectedly happy ending:

There was a woman, the loveliest of the lovely assistants, and so talented she could have been a magician herself. No one knew she was a witch. But she was a leader too—sometimes a benevolent queen, sometimes an evil one. She left her daughter with a man she knew would make a kind father. The daughter was thus born lucky, and almost didn't realize it. The mother and daughter fought for a magic coin, and in the end, the coin saved them both. The daughter won, though.

Her daughter was not a witch.

She was a magician.

acknowledgments

I've been fascinated by stage magic as long as I can remember, and just as fascinated by the lack of (save a few exceptions) women magicians. I hope in the coming years we'll start to have more reference material about the amazing women who have contributed to magic history, past and present. Too often they've been left in the shadows. I'm also hopeful we'll see many more female magicians to come.

In the meantime, resources that helped me greatly were Taschen's *Magic: 1400s–1950s*; books by Ricky Jay; pretty much everything Penn & Teller have ever done; Jim Steinmeyer's *Hiding the Elephant*; way too many YouTube videos of amateur and professional magicians all over the world; the documentaries *Box Jumpers* and *Make Believe*; *Adelaide Herrmann, Queen of Magic: Memoirs, Published Writings, Collected Ephemera* (edited by an incredible magician, Margaret Steele); and the various magic message boards I spent too much time lurking on. I'd also like to thank the wonderful Timoney Korbar for scoring me an invite to visit the Magic Castle, and Kelly Link for being the best-ever companion for a friend writing a book to take to the Magic Castle.

The Praestigae are entirely my own invention and not based on any real group.

Some books come easy; some books are harder. I hope, like a good magic trick, this one looks easy now, but it was hard to master. As always, thanks go to my husband, Christopher Rowe, who listens to my despair and tells me the story will be there, and to my pets, who listen to my despair and then insist on walkies anyway. Immense gratitude to the amazing aerial daredevils at Bella Forza studio in Lexington, who've made me love the circus arts in a whole new way. A world of thanks to two different sets of writers at the Bat Cave workshop, who helped spitball this one early on, and to my magical agent Jennifer Laughran. And, of course, to the publisher and everyone who worked on the book: my wise and dedicated editors, Courtney Miller and Marianna Baer; my fabulous copyeditor, Elizabeth Johnson; cover designer extraordinaire M. S. Corley; and the whole team at Skyscape. You went above and beyond to make magic happen. I'm lucky to work with all of you.

Finally, the biggest thanks to my readers. I love hearing from you.

about the author

Photo © 2016 Sarah Jane Sanders

Gwenda Bond is the author of *Girl on a Wire* and *Girl in the Shadows*, whose daredevil young heroines discover danger and passion lurking beneath the big top. Her previous books include the young adult novels *The Woken Gods* and *Blackwood*. Her writing has also appeared in *Publishers Weekly* and the *Los Angeles Times*, among other publications. She has an MFA in writing from the Vermont College of Fine Arts and lives in a hundred-year-old house in Lexington, Kentucky, with her husband, author Christopher Rowe, and their menagerie. Visit her online at www.gwendabond.com or @gwenda on Twitter.